ANNIE'S THIRD WIND

A NOVEL BY

WALLY CARLSON

BOOK PUBLISHERS NETWORK
Changing the World One Book at a Time

Book Publishers Network
P.O. Box 2256
Bothell • WA • 98041
Ph • 425-483-3040
www.bookpublishersnetwork.com

10 9 8 7 6 5 4 3 2 1
Printed in the United States of America

LCCN 2014936337
ISBN 978-1-940598-32-1

Editor: Barbara Kindness
Cover designer: Laura Zugzda
Typographer: Marsha Slomowitz

ACKNOWLEDGEMENTS

I have many thanks for helping me along
with this continuing saga of Annie.

First, I have to acknowledge and be grateful
for my golden childhood in 1950's America,
and my parents Don and Colleen Carlson.

My wife, Vicki, and my children Skye,
Emily, Natalie, Katie and Taylor.

My devoted editor, Barbara Kindness,
helps me keep all my characters straight.

My enduring publisher, Sheryn Hara
of Book Publishers Network, keeps me aware
of deadlines, which I usually miss.

And a special shout out to Hugh O'Brian as,
unbeknownst to him, I was racing to get my book
to press before his. Dude, pull the trigger!

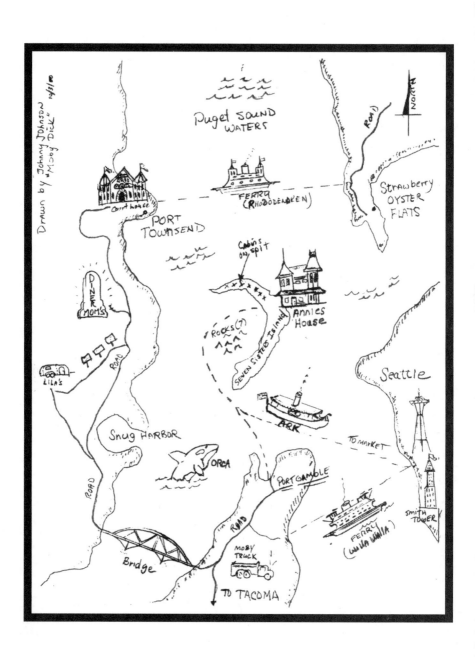

SEVEN SISTERS ISLAND

An island is a touchstone of the human heart.

Twelve thousand years ago the grinding crush of glaciers plowed the earth rough and sterile. In time, the icy tentacles retreated, leaving in their milky wake an island: the edges chiseled and raw, the uplands barren and rocky, and the shoreline protected by seven sentinel rocks. Only the healing rain and the power of the tidal moons could once again make the land fertile.

The land lured stouthearted men and wildcat women onto its protective shores. Their lives, patiently lacquered layer upon layer on the crust, changed the texture of the land forever.

To belong to an island is to grasp the satin edge of immortality.

CAST OF CHARACTERS

Annie Pippin Perkins... *76 years old, last of her generation of seven sisters, keeper of the island farm and raising orphaned twin toddlers*

Little Annie... *toddler, orphaned by the deaths of her mother, Sarah, and grandmother, Calypso, Annie's estranged daughter*

Zack ... *Little Annie's twin brother, first male in over twenty generations*

Moby Dick... *deceased porn star of the 1950s. Father to Christine*

South Carolina Storm... *part-time dementia sufferer, sister of North Carolina Storm. Every day is her birthday*

Sister Mary Catherine... *snarky, chain-smoking nun, karaoke champion*

Pickles... *eccentric Port Townsend store owner with feminine edge*

Owl/Al... *retired sewer savant, cheats at casket racing*

Pinky/Dorie... *tugboat friends of Annie*

Maxine... *30ish power lawyer from the East Coast*

Christine... *30ish piano virtuoso, Moby Dick's daughter. Running mate of Maxine*

G I Joe ... *military veteran, retired, with connections*

White Bear... *Native-American completing his vision quest*

Ziggy and Matty... *pot smoking, dead head gypsies*

John Colby... *oceanographer, protector of orcas*

Starbuck ... *the orca*

Professsor Spud ... *in the library with the candelabra, anthropology professor, retired*

Judge Strom... *progressive rogue judge who granted twin great-grandchildren to Annie*

PROLOGUE

T he telegram had chased Annie Perkins across four continents. It caught up with her high in the Peruvian Andes.

Aunt Amelia in coma, near death.
Come home as soon as possible.
Calypso.

Annie pursed her lips and gave a deep sigh. *Calypso*, the sea nymph, Jacques Cousteau's boat, Annie's self-named wayward daughter… her only child.

Annie went into her canvas tent to let the bad news settle. She knew Amelia, her closest sister, had been very sick. It wasn't surprising; after all, she was in her seventy-seventh year. The sixth of seven sisters was about to fulfill the legacy of death. A legacy some called a blessing and others a curse. It had started as mere coincidence and now it had taken on a life of its own. Nevertheless, Annie called it damned inconvenient. There was still work to be done.

The Red Cross point-woman for calamity, Annie was directing the rescue operation of a village that had been swept into the valley by an 8.1 earthquake. Shell-shocked villagers and burros wandered aimlessly as rocks the size of Volkswagen Beetles still tumbled through the village and down into the jungle below.

Annie hated to leave, but this was family.

Annie Perkins was going home.

She flew into Sea-Tac Airport and took a puddle-jumper to Port Townsend on the shores of Puget Sound. From there she phoned the three-lane bowling alley/laundry/pizzeria her daughter managed somewhere north of Seattle.

"Somewhere near Timbuktu," Annie grumbled as she dropped coins into the pay phone, trying to remember where the hell her daughter lived.

"Aloha Bowl," came the bored voice. "Can we help you make that spare?"

"It's me," said Annie, as though it had been four days, not four years, since she'd spoken to her daughter. "How is Aunt Amelia?"

"Glad you could make it, Mother," Calypso said sardonically. "She's still in a coma. She hasn't taken in any food or fluids for more than two weeks. They don't know how she's hanging in there. She's at Memorial Hospital, if you're interested."

Annie bit her tongue. Fifty-two years old and Calypso was still holding a grudge.

Well, Annie chastised herself for the ten millionth time, *you should never have abandoned her.* It was a mother's guilt she lived with every day.

"Thanks," Annie said. "I'm on my way."

Annie hadn't been to the hospital since she was a child. New wings had been added, creating a maze of halls that finally led her to the basement information desk where she asked in which room she might find her sister, Amelia Perkins.

The woman at the desk didn't look up. "Down the hall, turn left, Room 17."

Annie trailed her hand along the wainscoted wall as she slowly walked down the hall and turned the corner. Room 17 stood in front of her, the door closed. She involuntarily shivered as she turned the handle. Inside, a scrum of white-uniformed medical personnel surrounded what appeared to be an empty bed.

"She must be waiting for something," a nurse murmured. "It's a miracle she's still alive."

Annie peeked under the nurse's arm and saw the object of their attention: a frail, motionless, hospital-gowned skeleton. Abruptly the figure sat up and pointed a gnarled finger at the crowd. The doctors and nurses parted like the Red Sea, leaving Annie exposed.

Then she heard that distinctive gravelly voice.

"Annie," Amelia's eyes burned brightly, "you've finally come." She paused, as if gathering together the last vestiges of strength hiding in her shell of a body. "Get the farm back on its feet. It's your legacy now. I entrust the island to you."

Annie winced. So many witnesses. But she nodded.

The figure in the bed convulsed backward and stared slack-jawed at the ceiling. Amelia Perkins lay lifeless, her mission complete.

Annie sighed. Gone forever the retirement bungalow in the tropics, the ninety-degree days tempered by the gentle trade winds. Hello to sixty-degree summer days and the incessant rain clouds of the Pacific Northwest.

❦

It has been a long year and a lot has changed. Annie had dedicated herself to saving the farm, tangled in a web of taxes, rezoning, and unrelenting county officials wanting the island for development. There were only a few years left now before she would be the one turning the island over to someone else to carry on the legacy.

Her deceased sisters had given her seven extra years to raise her orphaned great-grandbabies, mindful of the old Jesuit saying, "give me the child for the first seven years and I will show you the man."

Annie yearned for a simpler time when her life as the front woman for Red Cross disasters had been merely filled with hurricanes and floods.

Chapter ONE

ickles sang a happy song of thanksgiving as he herded his '64 Volkswagen van down the winding road towards Red Apple Market. The rusting aqua-and-white flat-paneled body was festooned with vintage flourishes of paisley-inspired Hippie graphics. The intertwined vines, variegated green leaves, and platter-size fluorescent pink and gold daisies fairly joined him in song.

Pickles never bothered to learn all the lyrics to any of his favorite songs; just the melodies, thank you very much.

"Do do do doodle doodle do…and up came crude…and they moved to Beverly…Hills that is…swimming pools…movie stahs…"

He gave a sly smile as his latest victorious business coup deliciously sloshed around through his sometimes short-circuited brain waves.

He cackled aloud with delight. He had vacillated wildly between importing the camel cheese from Morocco or the possum meat from New Zealand. But now, he knew he had chosen wisely. With a maternal gentleness, he patted the frozen two-pound loaf of New Zealand possum loin that lay on the seat next to him. It was part of a shipment of twenty-five hundred pounds of grade AA Prime possum that Pickles had finessed through US customs and the FDA inspectors, courtesy of his new best friends.

Thanks to the internet, Pickles had connected with a support group of shoe fetish folks. Unlike support groups that acknowledged their weakness and wished to quit, no one online was really trying to kick the habit; it was a great resource for their endeavors as they gnawed, fawned over, and slobbered their way through life's difficult moments.

The bribe was considerable—and delectable. A veritable Old Woman in the Shoe cornucopia fruit cocktail, consisting of kiwi lime Manolo seven-inch pumps, raspberry Jimmy Choo slings fresh from the Academy Awards, and a pair of Ferragamo cantaloupe-colored mules that had iced the deal in a gray area of the meat import inspector's manual. Or, just maybe the shoes clouded the inspector's interpretation.

Pickles chuckled as he remembered the ecstasy of sucking on the toes of the virginal kiwi pumps and inadvertently putting a small tooth dent in the toe, which he skillfully massaged back to its original beauty before delivery.

"Sloppy seconds, my good fellow," he chirped, as he drummed out a Haiku rhythm on the steering wheel and jetted into a parking place near the entrance to the food store. Pickles scanned the parking lot and spotted another vintage VW van.

Not many of those babies left, he mused, as he looked over his presentation package while mulling over his sales pitch.

"Salvatore Ferragamo." Pickles said the words out loud and then again in an exaggerated Italian, "Salvatoreeeeeeeee. Faragaaaaaaaaaaaaaaamo!" Then in a gruff, unintelligible and garbled Brando interpretation, mumbled, "Salvatore Ferragamo."

In the back of his mind there was some seller's remorse, but business was business. Still, a fetish denied was…Pickles pursed his lips. No, better to think about the prospects of future possum fortunes and if not successful, there was always the fallback position with the camel cheese. *I wonder if they use a tall milking stool,* he pondered aloud.

Pickles wrung his hands, hoping he wouldn't have to dip into his shoe collection again anytime soon. He knew possum would be a hard sell at the market. Americans equated possum with road kill. It was a threshold challenge he relished.

He still remembered foundering the year before, getting in on the ground floor of emu and ostrich meat a bit too soon. He knew the market was all about timing and he felt that he had thoroughly covered the possibly dicey possum marketing—from its snaky tail to its twitchy snout.

This was definitely going to be different. Not only did he have the only FDA-blessed possum meat in these United States of America, he had packaged the meat with a small slick-paged cookbook bubbling over with colorful pictures: Steaming serving dishes heaped with piping hot possum. The old standby—possum and taters. Possum in couscous slathered with a fragrant fig gravy. And the pièce de resistance: a free CD of the first three episodes of the Beverly Hillbillies, with a glowing endorsement foreword in the cookbook by "Granny" herself.

Oh yes, he thought, as he slung the canvas bag that cradled his precious cargo over his shoulder and entered the store. *MUSTN'T FORGET THE PUNCHLINE: "Organic possum, the other white meat."*

Pickles nervously ran his fingers through his low maintenance, salt-and-pepper crew cut and nodded to the head checker, Rhoda Swartz. He hustled a little quicker and ducked into an aisle as he saw Rhoda raise her hand as if to initiate a conversation. *Oh no,* he thought. *I'm not going to get stuck debating the latest fad diet for her obese labradoodle.* Besides, Skip Campana, the store manager, had said eight o'clock sharp. Not only was Skip a religious stickler for promptness and compulsively on time himself—which was so unlike Pickles—but Pickles, in an intuitive way, always felt he and Skip just might be simpatico in life's closeted struggles.

No sooner had he skirted the pasta aisle when he heard a woman's scream, the quick scuffling of feet as if in the darkened alley of a Mickey Spillane murder mystery, and then the sound of frozen packages hitting the faux wood vinyl flooring in the frozen food section.

When he rounded the corner, his first thought was that a food terrorist had exploded a bomb in the frozen food bin. There were plastic pouches of vegetables everywhere. Farther down the aisle, he could see legs and arms waving like a frantic tarantula; it was a screaming woman in a pair of K-Mart black sandals. Her tie-dyed avocado and orange midi muumuu was hiked to her waist, exposing a black lace thong and tattooed love handles.

K-Mart sandals!, Pickles shuddered. *Could you ever make a worst choice in footwear? Even the Rain Man knew K-Mart sucks.*

Pickles peered into the huge frozen foods display case. There she was—a gray-haired woman with no makeup, half-naked, and covered with packages of frozen peas across her breasts and forehead and what looked like a baby wedged between her thighs.

Pickles grimaced. It was like a scene out of *Rosemary's Baby*. Mia Farrow in K-Mart sandals? I think not. Pickles wished he had paid more attention in the Red Cross training class when he noticed it was a Butterball turkey between the woman's legs. Ever the sucker for children and the upcoming Thanksgiving holiday, the maternal side of Pickles warmed to the woman's plight.

"Dammit," she suddenly yelled at him. "Cover me with more vegetables."

Pickles set down his bundle and piled on two three-pound bags of Ore-Ida hash browns. "Not potatoes, you fool," she barked at him. "I can't handle the carbos…just get me some green beans or cauliflower, for Christ's sake."

Pickles found a package of cauliflower florets and piled them on the woman's stomach, then rummaged and found a bonus-size family-style bag of mixed peas and carrots and gingerly fluffed them on her forehead.

"I want my hubby," the woman wailed.

"Where are you, Matty?" A man's voice wafted between the jars of Prego sauce at the top of the pasta aisle.

"I'm burning up and I'm stuck in the frozen food bin," she blubbered. There was a long silence.

"Again?" the man said.

Just as Pickles' Red Cross training was starting to kick in and he was ready to deliver the sixteen-pound Butterball and slap it on the rump, a stubby man with a flowing Santa Claus beard, green Carhartt jacket, and baseball cap skittered around the corner. He stooped to pick up the trail of the woman's clothing as he approached the display case and peered down into the open freezer.

"How we doing, mother?" he asked, casually.

"How does it look like we're doin'?" she snapped. "Hot flash, duh."

"I thought you were taking those herbs and stuff." The man pursed his lips.

"Apparently they're not working," she sneered, sarcastically. "This was a mega-blast."

Skip Campana hurried over to the freezer and looked in. A tall, thin, balding man with a long hula skirt of hair running behind his head from ear to ear, he shifted his glasses up over a sharp nose with tufts of too-long nose hair peeking out.

"Good gravy," he swore openly, as he wiped his hands on the bib of his green Red Apple apron. "What are we going to do here?" he asked, rhetorically, as he noticed that the contents of a bottle of spilled olive oil had spread out onto the floor in the map-like shape of the Italian boot.

Easily distracted and religiously cowed, Skip was always looking for a religious direction. Might this be a message from God? What did it mean? Should he become a vegetarian?

Feeling guilty, he thought it might be a sign that he had better make good on his promise to take his aged devout Catholic mother to the Vatican; or maybe it meant he should make the Red Apple girls' soccer team practice more free kicks; or maybe, hopefully on another level, his wife was going to wear her red stilettos to bed again. *So many questions, so few answers,* he thought.

"*Mamma mia,* God help me!" he beseeched the ceiling. Then Skip quickly snapped back to the matter at hand.

"Can I help you find something?" he ventured, even as the heat from Matty's body was defrosting the Butterball at an alarming rate and the plastic thermometer was just beginning to protrude from the breast meat.

"Might I suggest a side dish of julienne green beans with mushroom soup and crispy noodles," he warbled, remembering his mother's favorite side dish.

Matty lay back exhausted. "Just give me a few minutes and let me gather myself. That flash was like a far-out blast out of the Sixties, man. Like the mushroom cloud over Nagasaki. Like the ash cloud after Mount St. Helens erupted. Like…"

Pickles attempted to remind Skip of their meeting, but Skip waved him off.

"Another time, Pickles. This requires my attention now."

Matty looked like a vegetarian Mother Earth as the hot flash now seemed to be over. She looked almost serene as she closed her eyes and lay her head on a restaurant-size portion of lima beans, her long, stringy gray hair decorated with stray kernels of corn and loose balls of green Brussels sprouts frozen to the strands of hair like Jamaican dreadlocks.

"Ziggy," Matty instructed her husband, "fetch a towel and a blanket from our van."

Modestly, she adjusted the two Green Giant petite pea pouches on her breasts and wheezed toward Skip's direction, "That was a trip, man. I swear these hot flashes are going to be the death of me."

"If you would be so kind as to get me a cart," Matty said to Skip. "It seems I have a lot of vegetables to eat. This isn't my first trip into the frozen food section."

Helped out of the freezer by Pickles and Skip, Matty began to shiver as she slipped into a retro ribbed pink chenille bathrobe brought by Ziggy, and began to gather the slushy vegetables' containers and three Butterball turkeys into a grocery cart and lurch toward the checkout line.

Pickles did his public service as he gingerly picked up the discarded sandals with a broomstick and deposited the shoes in a nearby dumpster. Outside, Pickles offered to help them push the cart while Ziggy helped his barefoot wife to the van. As they passed by Pickles' van, the two looked at each other and simultaneously let out a war whoop.

"My God, it's Jerry," Ziggy shouted.

"It *is* Jerry," Matty screeched as she reached out to caress the chrome brow over the headlight on the Volkswagen bus.

"How did it…? Where has it…? I mean, it's our old van that was stolen five years ago."

Before Pickles could react, Ziggy dove under the van and wriggled toward the center framework.

"It's here," he shouted. "Ziggy and Matty—First Anniversary, July 4, 1977. Just like I brazed on the frame."

"But, I've had that car for three years," Pickles protested. "How could this be your van?"

Matty scooted up closer to the van and began nuzzling the fender like a cat in heat as Ziggy explained.

"Five years ago, this van was stolen in L.A. out of our garage next to our bedroom. I customized her myself and she's a legend in L.A., or was till she disappeared."

Ziggy lowered his voice and moved closer to Pickles. "This van has special properties." He winked. Pickles was on guard. Something was fishy.

Ziggy lowered his voice again and spoke out of the side of his mouth. "Any woman sitting in the passenger seat can get a real intense, uh...whoopee moment, under the right conditions.

"Sounds such as you've never heard before. The women, I mean." Ziggy rolled his eyes.

Matty blushed, but continued to caress the bumper. Pickles looked incredulous. Ziggy bobbed his head in truth. "I kid you not."

"How?" quizzed Pickles.

"I customized that van so much even I don't remember what I've done. I've tried to duplicate the changes, but I could never achieve the same effect, but now that I have the prototype back, I think I can figure it out. The trick is that you put the gal in the passenger seat, rev the van up to fifty and drive over those rumble strips on the side of the road and the vibration starts and then it only takes eleven to thirty-two seconds to achieve full results.

"Matty hasn't had a good 'whoopee moment' for the last five years since that van's been stolen."

Pickles looked over to see Matty had positioned herself squarely on the spare tire in the front of the van and was fairly humping the hub cap.

"Well, maybe you better take it for a spin," Pickles offered.

"Righty-o," Ziggy countered enthusiastically. "Don't have to ask us twice. Hop in the rig, mother, we're going for a ride."

Matty vaulted into the seat and Ziggy floored the old bus, wheeled out into traffic, and quickly slid over to the edge of the road. Pickles could hear the metronic thump of the tires hitting the rumble strips and twelve seconds later heard the most piercing yowl he'd ever heard in his life as the bus disappeared into the traffic. Ziggy was true to his word.

Entrepreneurial Pickles gritted his teeth and looked both ways up and down the street. He hoped no one else heard the sound of a lucrative business possibility just pass his way. He gave a little smirk. *Just what was a powerful orgasm worth these days?*, he wondered.

Five minutes later, Pickles saw the van come back down through the intersection. Apparently, Matty had a little left in her, so Ziggy cut to the side of the road to hit the ridges again and Matty and the bus squealed to a simultaneous stop. By the time Pickles had made his way across the parking lot, both pleasure-seekers were sharing puffs on a cigarette.

The Brussels sprouts had begun to splat onto the pavement as Matty's head lolled out the open window.

"I think mother has had enough for a while," Ziggy prophesied.

Pickles whispered to Ziggy behind the bus. "Do you really think you can duplicate what you just did if we got another VW bus?"

"Oh yeah," Ziggy said confidently. "Now that old Jerry is back."

"Jerry?" Pickles' brow furrowed.

"Jerry—like Garcia," Ziggy pointed to his tie-dyed tee shirt. "We're dead heads."

"Oh." Pickles gleefully rubbed his hands together.

" Ziggy, this is gold. We're gonna be rich." Pickles shook Ziggy's hand as he pitched the possum loin into a nearby shopping cart.

A van trade was made straight across as the prospective business partners loaded the groceries into Jerry and they drove over to the Ziggy replacement van which, although heavily modified, never really could perform the magic.

"What should we do with all these groceries?" Matty asked. "We're just passing through. We can't eat all this stuff."

"Follow me," Pickles countered. "We're going to take a trip to Fantasy Island."

Chapter TWO

When Annie Perkins woke up in her bed, she knew by the aching of her joints that she was living in the body of a seventy-six-year-old woman.

She closed her eyes and raised her hands and felt the smooth, peeled branch of a cedar limb that had been woven by her great-grandfather into a free-form lattice headboard before there was money to buy a proper bed. The family story was that when her grandfather finally had the money to get a properly carved mahogany bed frame, his wife wouldn't allow it in the house.

"I've conceived and bore my seven girls in this bed. It's earned its keep and that's all there is to it," she stated. Which became the family mantra of stubbornness.

On the top rail at the foot of the bed were two deep grooves carved across the grain into the inch-and-a-half cedar pole. The grooves duplicated exactly the new front teeth of an eight-year-old, standing with one foot on the other on the cold floor waiting for her parents to wake up on a Christmas morning long ago. Annie could still smell the wet, fragrant wood and the splinters that filled her mouth as she waited, and waited, in the darkness. Those were her teethmarks then and now it was *her* bed.

Annie no longer bothered to ask herself if her body was ready for action. She had no choice. She was the mother of seven-month-old twins orphaned by the death of her granddaughter. The body would just have to hold together without sympathy.

She staggered as she swung her legs out of bed and the old fir flooring squeaked in concert with her ankles as she took the first few tentative steps, wobbling down the hall to the children's room. She looked in, but already knew they wouldn't be there. She tiptoed into the living room where she found the infants sound asleep, clinging to the chests of her eccentric neighbors. Like barnacles plastered on rocks, their chubby hands held on for dear life and followed the up-and-down rhythm and horsey snores of seven decades of living and breathing that had become as steady and dependable as the tides.

Annie knew that old people and babies are God's favorites and destined to provide solace to each other. It never hurt either that God's two favorites shared their love of activities centered around urping, burping, farting, and a really good bowel movement.

Annie set a fire in the wood-burning stove and, closing the screen door quietly, made eye contact with the two dogs that lay half-asleep nearby, sucking warmth from the old iron stove. The three-legged strawberry coon hound, Trooper, pleaded rheumatism of the hips with his doleful eyes. Twigs, the mongrel shepherd, quietly thumped his tail on the wooden floor wanting to please, but not enough to accompany his mistress out into the cold.

Annie shrugged and headed up the mossy path to the outhouse. She gave a courtesy knock to the outhouse door so the resident spiders could scramble to safe havens. She propped open the door, turned around, and closed her eyes—remembering her dad's favorite saying: *revenge is best served on a cold toilet seat.*

Didn't she know it. The cold updraft from the dark hold puckered her cheeks as she contemplated the seven oyster shacks that were carved into the sand dunes on the sweeping crescent spit that flared into the sea.

Annie shook her head in amazement. Her life had been a whirlwind since she returned to the island a year ago when her last remaining sister, on her deathbed, had coerced Annie into promising to bring the island farm back to its glory days.

And how could she imagine that a sudden tragedy would force her to become the sole caregiver and provider to her great-grandchildren. Or that she and her island comrades would have to kidnap them from the hospital, escaping in the fog on a tugboat. Or that she would have to fight the state's Child Protective Services in court, just to raise her own flesh and blood.

In order to make ends meet, she started to take in ancient men and women who wished to measure their remaining days on earth with the rhythm of the tides and the fate of the winds. Souls that would not be confined to cubicles and cafeterias. And with these dreamers and short-timers came a power drawn from having nothing to lose; a wealth of wisdom, passion and networking that could solve injustice and celebrate each day as if it were their last.

"Superheroes really," Annie mumbled out loud.

Annie took stock of the current residents, not knowing who would come on the next rising tide to fill the two remaining, unoccupied shacks.

Presently there was Sister Mary Catherine, the no-nonsense, knuckle-rapping, chain-smoking nun.

John Hunt, the food editor for *The Seattle Times*, with the nine-foot sailfish in the seven-foot-wide shack he lived in most of the time.

South Carolina Storm, the slightly addled remaining sister of the North and South Carolina Storms, who thought every day was her birthday.

Owl, or Al, a blue-collar sewer retiree with a photographic memory. And then, Max and Christine, two strikingly beautiful women who spent part time on the island. Maxine, an East Coast powerbroker lawyer for nonprofits, and Christine, a concert pianist, had adopted the island during its time of need last spring.

That left two shacks on the sand spit open. Annie figured that fate already had someone on their way.

"Oh, there are stories to tell," Annie chirped to herself as she tidied up the outhouse and steamed downhill to the house, opened the door, and stood back as the dogs lumbered onto the porch and cozied up to the nearest tree trunk.

Annie meandered through the house planning her day. With her tugboat flight and the courtroom battles, there had come a rush of celebrity that she intended to take full advantage of. This afternoon she had promised to take the available island folk to Chimacum to try and bring her star power to bear at a hundred-and-sixty-year-old Scarlet Red Oak that had been a landmark for the town forever, but was now threatened to become cord wood by the construction of a new mini mall. *A few photo ops from the local paper should do it*, she thought, *and then a hearty potluck back at the island would be a nice way to finish the day.*

Annie warmed her hands over the old stove and went in to check on the babies. Zack was planted face down on Owl, who was now wide awake. Owl's t-shirt was drooly, and the grimace on his face was unmistakable—the call of nature beckoned. But he knew the old adage of sleeping dogs and babies.

Zack's twin, Little Annie, serenely nuzzled koala-like into Sister Mary Catherine's starched collar as the old nun slept with a saintly grin on her wrinkled face. Sister's calloused and gnarled fingers were attached protectively to Little Annie's chubby legs.

Annie warmed the bottled formula in a pan of hot water and listened as the old wooden house creaked and groaned, awakening to a new day. It would be a pleasant fall day in the upper sixties and Annie reminded herself to bring bonnets for the babies who were beginning to stir.

Owl sat up and handed Zack to Annie. Favoring his left hip, he traded places with the dogs as he headed outside to the nearest bush. Zack took the bottle as Annie sat back in the oak rocker and listened as the prince gave a satisfied hmm-m with each suck.

Little Annie was roused by the feeding sounds and was deposited into the other arm as Grandma Annie propped the second bottle in position with her chin. Little Annie was all about eye contact and she would spit the nipple out if you didn't pay complete attention.

Well, I guess I know where that control freak stuff comes from, Annie smiled. Still she knew there was no way to predict the way of children. *It seems to me, they pretty much come mostly hard wired,* she mused.

Max and Christine burst through the door giggling like schoolgirls. Mid-thirties, unattached and accomplished, together they had ripped through the Seattle dating scene all summer long and had become legends. Not just because they drove Christine's dad's dump truck named Moby Dick everywhere they went, but my, those women could party.

There were drinks in bars all over the city named after these women and radio stations kept track of where they were likely to light. One local station had something called the Tugboat Grannies Fox Watch.

With no ceremony, Max and Christine sang out their greeting in unison, "Morning, Annie," and each snatched a baby and bottle from Annie's arms and plunked themselves down on the dusty red vintage mohair sofa, cooing at the twins. Zack and Little Annie showed no distress as they shifted gears easily at the abrupt change of life force. Grandma had smelled like the vanilla cedar kindling and old wool sweaters, and they could feel her endurance and her spirit; the new generation smelled like spring flowers and their arms were firm and strong.

Christine gave the vintage sofa arm a slap and the dust vaulted into the air through the morning sunlight. "I just love this old thing," she said, readjusting the doily.

Christine had scored the sofa at a garage sale in Port Gamble, loaded it into a rowboat with the help of two nearby panting males, and then straddled it as they rowed her across the bay to the island.

Annie smiled at the younger women's confident entitlement. She had decided it would be important for the children to know that love comes in all sizes, smells, and smiles. Annie also knew she could start raising the twins, but she would never live long enough to finish the job. She just hoped the old Jesuit adage "give me a child till the age of seven and I will show you the man" was true. Annie wondered if Max and Christine were the generation that could finally answer that Sixties inspirational lyric by Carole King: *You never know what a satisfied woman might do.*

After a breakfast of oatmeal, the inhabitants of the entire island boarded the wooden *Ark* and powered to the Port Gamble dock. Wiggins, the postmaster, was sweeping the porch.

"What's your mission today, Annie?" he shouted.

"Going to save that old Scarlet oak up at Chimacum," Annie tossed out as she climbed the pull-down stairway into the back of the dump truck, and settled into one of the two red leather sofas, which were accompanied by two celadon green wing back chairs, and a coffee table bolted to the truck bed.

Max sang out to Christine, "This is one sweet ride ever since you won first prize on that TV show 'Pimp out my Dump Truck.' I just love the penthouse styling in this old truck of your dad's."

The babies were buckled into their custom car seats as Christine hit the air horn and off they bounced down the road followed by Pickles and his new business associates in their VW vans. Sister Mary

Catherine and Owl sat up front where they could smoke cigars without listening to all the whining about the smell. The trip down the valley was fragrant with promise as the sweet smell of the third cutting of hay and the harvesting of brown tasseled corn filled the air.

"There's the oak tree," Sister Mary Catherine piped up as she spotted the tree a good two miles from the town. "It's a big mother trucker, isn't it?" she asked rhetorically. "Annie told me it came out as a seedling along with starts for her Gravenstein apple trees. That makes that baby about a hundred and sixty years old."

When they arrived at the tree, there was a carnival-like atmosphere. The high school band instructor greeted them, and townspeople helped each island resident down the ladder from the truck bed. The Chimacum Elementary sixth-graders recited for the tenth time from memory Joyce Kilmer's "Ode to a Tree," and a latte trailer was setting up shop. A good-size crowd milled around for the showdown between the developer and the event organizer, the Green Movement Division of the Muskrat Society.

Well over a hundred feet tall, the tree had dominated the property for generations. The ground had been plowed up around it and there was a smiley face gouge in the trunk where someone had tried to push the tree over with a bulldozer.

Annie's troops began gathering around the tree when a red VW Beetle painted like a lady bug with black spots and antennae on the front bumper whipped into the parking lot, pulling a small trailer. A tall man with jug ears and a ZZ Top beard unfolded himself from the tiny bug. He was wearing a "Save the Whales" t-shirt, camouflage pants, and a Jones Soda ball cap, and his pony tail bobbed up and down as he explained what he needed even before introducing himself.

"We've been trying to get this tree on the historical register for the last five years," he said…"and the county planners and environmental people don't want to get their Birkenstocks dirty out here. We need the tugboat grannies to get publicity. Where are they?"

"We're here," Annie shouted.

"One granny isn't going to cut it!" The man sounded exasperated.

"Hey, Muskrat Bob," Sister Mary Catherine said as she grabbed the man by his ear and dragged him to one side.

"Didn't I read that your muskrat group was trying to save a nesting pod of muskrats over on an I-5 clover leaf in Renton where your faithful pitched your tents next to the freeway and used generators to blast out 'Muskrat Love' on twelve-foot speakers all night, while your group had some kind of initiation orgy goin' on, on the median strip?"

"No, no, no," the man explained. "That was a militant splinter group that got out of control. We deposed that muskrat chapter."

"Really!" Sister Mary Catherine said, looking skeptical.

"It's the truth," swore the man. "Can I have my ear back?"

"All right." The Sister released his ear and gave him one of her third-rate nun glares. She pointed two fingers at her eyes and then one finger at him. "Just remember, I've got my stink eye on you," she threatened.

The high school band and the cheerleaders were just getting revved up as the VW Beetle man commanded volunteers from the crowd to get the chain and padlocks from the trailer to tie Annie and her people around the tree.

Mary Catherine was still grousing as the muskrat organizer cinched the chain tightly around her waist and snapped a hefty padlock onto the chain. "This chain weighs a ton," she complained, lighting a Camel by using her thumbnail to start the wooden matchstick. "Where'd you get this stuff?"

"Got it cheap at the Navy surplus store over in Bremerton," answered her captor. "It had been there forever. Came outta some railroad cars."

"It still seems kinky to me," Owl complained. He was the next to be chained up around the tree. "Are you sure you're not from the Muskrat Love chapter? This looks a whole lot like bondage."

"Well, I did date one of their women for a while," the man confessed. "And there *was* some chains involved, but nothing like this. Perfectly harmless," he assured them, snapping another padlock in place.

Just then, Pickles and his new business partners showed up and wanted in on the fray. "Fresh blood," Pickles jerked his thumb back over his shoulder.

"Matty and Ziggy, welcome aboard." Annie motioned them towards the tree.

Max was wandering through the crowd with the babies in tow, Little Annie in a backpack and Zack strapped in front. The crowd recognized Annie and her troupe and edged closer to touch the infants. Approaching the tree, they shouted encouragement as the last of the padlocks were slammed shut on South Carolina Storm. South shoved out her lip. "But, it's my birthday," she said in her small voice.

"We'll get you some ice cream right after we save this tree," John Hunt said, searching the Sunday paper for his restaurant review.

"Oh, shit," the muskrat organizer mumbled as he threw his hands up in the air. "I've run out of locks and I need one more to tie the two ends together."

One of the high school girls, dressed in a black vinyl Goth trench coat and large brass studs on her tongue and ears, threw him a padlock from around her neck the size of a small Frisbee.

"Whoa!" The organizer looked the girl up and down. "Do you date older men?" he asked.

He snapped the shackle on the two ends of the chain just as the photographer from the *Port Townsend Leader* pulled up in his mini-van accompanied by six ominous black pickups with mirrored windows and bold lettering adorning the sides: CHOATE CONSTRUCTION.

The lead truck's doors opened and a short, dumpy man with a pot belly and jeweled flip flops emerged from the driver's side while a well-groomed, Soprano's-looking man in an expensive suit slid out of the passenger's side. The other trucks emptied and a foreman directed the men to take up positions on the heavy equipment that surrounded the site.

"Start up your motors," he called out to the men, and the air was filled with the choking sound of diesel engines.

"He's got his lawyer with him," Annie surmised.

"Yeah, well, we got Max," Christine countered.

Then things got ugly. Literally. A rusted-out flatbed pickup with grimy windows and its radio blaring Rush Limbaugh skidded to a stop just inches from ramming Pickles. A rubber shrunken head dangled from the rearview mirror and a shaggy arm snaked out from a jagged hole in the window and gave John the finger. Quick as a cobra, Sister Mary Catherine grabbed the finger, wrenched it, and the digit retreated, rubbing across the broken window shards and leaving a trail of blood as the arm recoiled into the darkness of the truck's cab.

Aside from the heavy drone of diesel motors on the heavy equipment and the wail of a police siren in the distance, there was no other sound. The crowd was completely quiet. Slowly, the door creaked open and a thick paratrooper boot hit the dusty ground. The figure stood up and his head was far above the door. A leather helmet covered the top of his head and masked his eyes. His shoulders were padded with thick leather scales and from shoulders down there was a mass of rivets and leather. The Goth high schooler squealed and fainted. With a sneer from his thick lips, the man looked at the chains and then turned and grabbed a gigantic chainsaw from the seat of the truck.

"Dude," Sister Mary Catherine taunted, "you've been watching too many Road Warrior movies."

The man growled and strode over to the contractor and they considered their options by whispering and pointing.

Annie suggested maybe they should sing a song.

"Don't ask me to sing 'Kumbaya,' Sister replied. "Ain't gonna happen."

"Well, then, how about that chain gang song," Annie chirped. "You know, 'I've been working on a chain gang…all day long…ooh…ah…' remember that one?"

"Annie, you lead out and we'll follow," Max blurted.

"How about, 'Blowin' in the Wind,'" the band director piped up. "We know that one, don't we, kids?" They all nodded and they began.

"*How many roads must a man walk down before they call him a man? How many…*"

Halfway through the song, the chainsaw started up and the crowd drew back. The developer and the chainsaw warrior advanced toward the singers as a patrol car rolled up, siren blaring.

Officer Katie Carlson, Chimacum High class of 1992 and homecoming princess, president of the Future Farmers of America, and volleyball captain of the Chimacum Cowgirls, got out of the car, donned her wide-brimmed hat, adjusted her nightstick, and put on her mirrored sunglasses. A Navy brat, she acted older than her twenty-eight years and she always had an attitude.

As she covered the ground toward the ensuing drama, she took in the principals. She had never personally seen the grannies but she had heard they would be here. The developer was an unknown but the chainsaw warrior looked familiar.

Officer Katie considered sunglasses to be the most important part of her arsenal. She twitched her ears just slightly to slide the glasses down her nose to give her eye contact. She pulled the nightstick from its sheath and tapped the warrior on his leather helmet. "Lester, that you in there?" she asked.

The warrior remained stoic. Katie sidled up to the warrior, pulled on his helmet, and whispered into his ear. "Lester, I don't want to have to tell these good people about that bed-wetting incident last time we ran you in. So why don't you just clear out of here before we do the photo op and we'll forget all about this little problem. And I don't want you coming back, hear?"

Lester scowled and there was a nervous twitch that jumped continuously from the right side of his lip to the left. Katie stood back, wiggled her ears, and the glasses jumped back over her eyes.

Lester turned off his saw and stalked back to his truck, threw the saw into the cab, gunned the motor, and the wheels churned backward, spitting rocks against the truck frame. He slammed into first gear and left only a dusty calling card.

"Gentlemen," Katie began, as she started herding the principals together, including the developer and his lawyer. "Why don't we all make nice over here with the tree and the chains and the band and all. It will make a really good picture for the newspaper." She stood on the sidelines while the photographer lined up the players as if it was a Civil War photo. Afterwards, Officer Katie called the developer and his lawyer over to survey the scene.

"Let me lay this out for you fellas. This is *my* turf. These are the tugboat grannie people chained to the tree, and these are the high school band members that go to school just two hundred yards down the road from here. *They* don't want you to cut down the tree. *I* don't want you to cut down the tree. Now, I don't know what the legal system has to say about this but I personally would like to see this tree remain standing. Can we agree on that?" Katie looked at both men.

The developer nodded his head. His lawyer was just beginning to argue when the developer raised his hand for silence.

"OK...then, I think we have a deal here," Officer Katie said, smiling.

She turned to walk away and then turned back and tilted her head in an inquisitive sort of way, as if she was trying to recall something.

"Oh yeah, I just remembered," she taunted. "I think I saw an eagle's nest up in that tree this spring and, as you know, eagles—they're as thick as robins around here—are still federally protected. If you cut this tree, the feds will be on you like...let's say...stink on shit! I just mention this in passing. Good day, gentlemen."

Katie walked over to inspect the shackles binding the island prisoners.

"Turn 'em loose," she commanded the muskrat captain.

"No problemo," the captain chirped.

He just twisted the Goth padlock off with his hand, and then produced a ring of keys for the other padlocks. "I don't know which is which, but it won't take long," he promised as he began fitting the keys.

Fifteen minutes later he still had had no luck. "Let me see those," Officer Katie said, examining the back of Owl's padlock.

"Oh jeez, these padlocks are from the nuclear division. They use them to chain up the nuclear stuff that the trains haul in for the Navy subs. If you don't have the right keys, you're not bustin' these babies, and the chain has the same insignia…which means there is nerve gas encapsulated in the chain so you can't cut it, Mr. Muskrat. You're up shit creek," Katie understated.

"Let me make a few calls," Katie said, trying to salve their fears. "This has happened before; supposedly they dumped all this gear years ago. It's stable but you just can't cut it."

By the time Katie came back from the patrol car, the crowd was gone, the latte stand had folded its canopy and motored off. Only Annie and the island people were left.

"I sure hope your wife doesn't get another hot flash," Pickles said quietly out of the side of his mouth to Ziggy. "Or that other thing, either."

"You and me both," Ziggy grimaced. "Man, I could sure use a joint," he said quietly. "I'm stressing out."

"OK, here's the deal," the officer began. "I phoned naval intelligence down in Bremerton and they said the padlocks were supposed to be destroyed and there are no keys to open them." John lunged for the muskrat captain but, true to his name, the muskrat quickly pulled back.

"The last time this happened was about ten years ago they tell me, and they had to get a padlock savant to open the padlocks."

"You mean, the Rain Man?" said South Carolina…"you mean, Dustin Hoffman and Tom Cruise are coming to my birthday?" and she began to weep. "It's all so wonderful," she blubbered.

"So where is the savant these days?" Annie piped up above South blowing her nose into a tissue.

"There is only one." Officer Katie shook her head. "He lives in Las Vegas and he has an aversion to flying so you will probably have to go to Vegas."

Muskrat had inadvertently walked too close to Pickles who put a headlock on the man and was beginning to strangle him when Muskrat breathlessly squeaked out, "I think I can swing some airline tickets. Just let me get on my cell phone."

Officer Katie's glasses slid down her nose in disapproval and Pickles gave her a toothy grin, releasing the neck but holding onto the muskrat's arm. The babies had sensed the threat and Max was scrambling to get a bottle down between their screams but they would have none of it.

"Give one to me," Mary Catherine coaxed. She rocked Zack in her arms and began a Gregorian chant in Latin. Zack settled in and began gulping his meal with his usual contented humming sound.

"What was that?" John asked.

"Oh, just a little circumcision prayer. It usually settles the males right down." Mary Catherine gave a half-smile.

"You play hardball," John said, cringing.

"OK," the muskrat leader said. "We have a bus on the way and someone donated enough seats on a shuttle to Vegas so within an hour we will be at Sea-Tac airport."

"What about Tom Cruise?" South wailed.

"I'm sure Tom will be in Vegas," Annie said, soothingly. "Remember, the Rain Man was counting cards."

"Yeah!" South beamed. "K-Mart sucks."

"Are you sure these chains and padlock are safe?" John Hunt asked Katie.

"The nerve gas is encapsulated inside the metal itself," she replied. "There is really no danger unless you try and cut the padlock or the chains. It may be inert but we just can't take a chance."

The Cedars Casino bus roared in on time and they loaded the troops awkwardly but efficiently. Max stayed behind with the twins and would spend the night in Port Townsend at Pickles' apartment.

Officer Katie helped the last protester onto the bus and, with her nightstick, slapped the dusty sign that proclaimed "YOU ALWAYS HAVE A SNOWBALL'S CHANCE WHEN YOU GAMBLE AT SNOW FALLING ON CEDARS CASINO." The casino had sent a cooler of martinis so halfway to the airport no one was feeling any pain.

Lately, South Carolina's dementia had morphed from channeling her dead sister's potty mouth to a kind of repetitive autism that was stuck in Hollywood mode. She kept babbling The Rain Man's "'Very twinkly, very sparkly.' Anybody got any toothpicks?"

At the airport the protesters had to walk to an escalator and to the ticket counter. Wary mothers kept their children by their side as the chain gang moved through. Mercifully, they managed to stack themselves on an electric cart and were whisked to the gate, a loose chain dragging behind the cart.

The plane had boarded a half hour before, but when the captain explained that the Tugboat Grannies were coming aboard and told about their day's trials, the first-class passengers gave up their seats amid great applause. The captain beamed as he schmoozed while stepping over the chains looping across the aisle. After several airline pony bottles of champagne and consuming someone else's steak dinners, the entire cabin fell asleep. Except for the few times nature called.

The muskrat leader continued to feel intimidated as Pickles glared at him throughout most of the trip, although he had a vague feeling they had chatted on the Shoe Fetish hotline.

When they touched down at Vegas, the crowd was met by a red limousine and the obligatory Elvis impersonator. The driver's sidekick was a cross-dresser who looked like Phyllis Diller pre-surgery. "Very scary," John kept repeating. He/she kept cracking terrible jokes, punctuated with a maniacal laugh that even gave Pickles the willies.

"I thought this was going to be low-key," Annie grumbled as the car pulled into Diamond Trump Tower lit with what seemed like a million blinking bulbs.

John shook his head. "Crap, I think I'm going to have a seizure with this crazy lighting."

The shackled troupe was ushered through the casino where people swilled the last of their drinks, dropped their cigarettes, left their winnings, and followed Annie's crowd through the maze and into the theatre. Their chains dragged up the stairs behind a backstage curtain and the lights dimmed as the master of ceremonies, who looked eerily like a version of Wayne Newton, recounted Annie's recent escapades, the infamous trial, and their latest adventures.

Suddenly, the curtain was raised and the entire troupe was in the spotlight. The crowd clapped and whooped and roared. Most of them knew Annie's story and they threw jewelry, scarves, hats, underwear, and keys onto the stage.

Someone yelled out, "Where's Moby?"

It was Annie's crowd. Grandmothers risked their lives and climbed onto tables and swung their mink stoles in circles above their heads and clicked their Bics. This went on for about five minutes before the Wayne Newton look-alike told a few jokes and sang "Danke Schoen."

"Oh, gawd." Annie rolled her eyes. Is this ever gonna end? she thought, shaking her head.

Finally, another spotlight poised on a smallish man in a tuxedo standing at the other end of the stage. The savant, Annie thought, and the closer she looked, the more the man looked like—Bill Gates.

The man moved toward the shackles and South blurted out, "*That's not Tom Cruise!*"

The audience laughed and the man tilted his head sideways as he shuffled across the stage and picked up the padlock around Pickles' waist.

He ignored Pickles, but carefully turned the padlock over in his hands. Then he gave a sly smile and reached into his pocket and pulled out a bent finish nail about three inches long and a paper clip, which he bent into a dog-legged position. He spit into the keyhole and inserted both instruments into the padlock as he wagged a long, snaky tongue that sometimes touched the end of his nose. He closed his eyes, mumbled something, and gave a quick twist with both wrists, pulled out his tools, and tugged on the padlock.

Nothing.

He pulled harder. Nothing.

The little man began to sob and great crocodile tears fell on the stage. He looked inquiringly at the padlock, shook his head, and shuffled off the stage. Annie was beginning to puddle up herself when she heard South say, "Is that why we came down here, trying to get these damn padlocks off?"

South searched through her purse and pulled out a slim nail file and a metal crochet hook. She grabbed Pickles' padlock, inserted the nail file, and then, after bending the hook, wormed her way through the tumblers. It seemed like an eternity, but finally the padlock fell to the ground. Pickles was free.

The crowd held its collective breath as South worked through the line, opening each padlock...sometimes quickly and sometimes taking a few minutes, but finally everyone was free.

Look-alike Wayne Newton was so happy, Annie was afraid he was going to break into another song, so she rushed up and shook his hand as the crowd rushed the stage, pushing past Newton, his pencil mustache and *faux* toupee, and fawned over the *real* celebrities.

Newton rescued the microphone from the stand and called for order. The crowd noise dropped to a murmur, and just as he was about to speak, South blurted out, "1,934,523 jelly beans in the '69 Mustang convertible in the lobby; and the next number on the roulette wheel is going to be—"

Newton slapped his hand over South's mouth as a group of gamblers stampeded back out into the lobby for the chance to play the $100 tickets for the jelly bean-filled Mustang that had been on the floor for three years. *Faux* Newton had heard what he considered urban myths over the years about card counters and savants breaking casino banks. He didn't know about South's channeling, but he did know he wasn't taking any chances.

"Not in my hotel, you don't," he murmured so only South could hear.

South took a good chomp on Newton's hand, gathered up her purse, and walked off the stage.

FBI officials had begun to gather up the chain and padlocks into a metal chest marked highest security, while Annie signed autographs and countless times told how she had been shackled to a tree and explained where the famous grandbabies were as she passed around their pictures.

There was a huge cry from the lobby and bells began ringing as somehow someone had guessed right on the Mustang. Newton cried in self-defense as he ushered all of Annie's people up to the magnificent eye-in-the-sky suite usually held for high rollers.

Annie's people marveled at the luxury and after ordering room service they bunked up in the six bedrooms and circular rotating beds with the mirrored ceiling. It had been a long, hard day.

Meanwhile, Pickles had motored down to the staging area for the chorus girls and scored some unguarded pink eight-inch pumps with feathers and only slightly scuffed.

The plane trip back the next day was uneventful. The crowd piled out of the limousine at Port Gamble and the muskrat organizer thanked them with muskrat canvas shopping bags and CD's of "Muskrat Love" sung by the Captain and Tennille.

Annie growled a grouchy sigh and grabbed Muskrat by the arm, escorting him to the edge of the parking lot. "That's enough. Scuttle back to your swamp."

Annie stopped by the store to get the mail. Wig volunteered, "I think there is a letter from the State in your pile of mail. You also have a pink Valentine envelope from your favorite people, the County Assessor. Seems like property taxes are due again. Those perverse bastards, sending their greedy little statements in pink envelopes so close to Valentine's Day."

Annie took the envelope and ripped open the top and shook the contents onto the counter. She picked up the assessment card:

> Property: Seven Sisters Island
> Zoned: Amusement park/recreational
> Property value: $22,562,000.57
> House value: 0
> Outbuildings: 0
> Tax: 1st half due March 15…$105,000.54
> Tax: 2nd half due October 15…$105,000.53

"Damn those bureaucrats," Annie swore, slamming the paper on the counter. "They just never give up. I told them it was a subsistence farm. We're grandfathered in and still they insist on ripping us off. They want the island for their own private park. I'd like to kick their…"

As *The Ark* cut through the channel, its churning propeller left a magical trail of light where the phosphorus from the summer heat glowed in the dusky waters of Puget Sound.

Summer was still wafting on the salt air and the memory of child-hood summers flitted past Annie's mind as she approached the island where Seven Sisters rocks stood lapping in the boat's wake, silent sentinels standing guard over the island for the last ten thousand years. The salty stench of the seaweed assailed Annie's nostrils. To some it smelled like sewage, but to anyone from the Pacific Northwest, it was the smell of summer past and as natural as the autumn rains which would soon begin.

A lone baby orca nuzzled the bow of *The Ark* and then disappeared just before Annie pulled into the boatshed.

Chapter THREE

Sister Mary Catherine had covered the kitchen table and window sills at Annie's with her confections—classic moon pies, lemon tartlets, cutie pies—and her standard, keep-your-bowels-moving bran muffins.

Sister had hummed *Oh Gloria* for the umpteenth time by the time Annie creaked down the stairs and checked on the twins, who were already under watch by John and Max.

"Smells good down here," she called, as Sister swished by, her habit sprinkled with flour, making her look like the survivor of a Gold Medal cook-off explosion.

"Idle hands are the devil's workshop," she replied, rushing into the dining room with another trayful of bran muffins.

"What's with all the baking?" Annie asked.

"My boys," Sister sang out as she dashed back to the kitchen at the sound of the timer. "I told you," she said. "These are the goodies for the Navy boys over at the Bangor sub base. I stand outside and hand them out to the cars just before they go into the base. My little attempt to bring about world peace and keep our fighting men regular."

Annie crammed the last of a bran muffin into her mouth. "Marvelous," she warbled as a few crumbs escaped her mouth.

"How would you like to help?" Mary Catherine scrunched up her nose in challenge.

Annie bobbed her head. "I guess I could."

"Tomorrow then...gotta leave around six a.m." Sister slapped at the flour clouds that drifted around her face. "*Ay, caramba!*" she complained. She went into a crouching Tai Chi position waving her hands through the cloud. "Bruce Lee, eat your heart out," she laughed.

Now well-fed and lying on the floor on a quilted rug, the twins were very conversational and looked up at Annie as she dressed them. Eight months and they were both up on their knees and rocking back and forth, almost ready to crawl and clearly frustrated when they fell on their face. They would look around the room and demand that each person pay attention. Then with a 'gotcha' smile, they would move on to the next victim.

"Those kids know how to work a room," Max laughed as she reached into Little Annie's drooling mouth. "It almost feels like a tooth on the bottom. What do you think?" she said, looking up at Mary Catherine.

Sister got down on her knees and felt the gum. "There's a bump," she confirmed. "Hard to tell, but she's been grouchy lately."

John leaned out the living room window and yelled down the path to the beach. "We might have our first tooth up here," he bellowed.

Like poking a stick in an ant nest, the word was quickly passed between the houses on the spit, and instantly doors flew open and there was scrambling up the trail. Trailing toilet paper from the top of his pants like a tail on a kite, Ziggy threw open the outhouse door and came on a dead run.

"Hmm-m," each one said in turn, feeling the gum. And then they tried to poke their fingers into Zack's mouth, but he would have none of it and clamped down hard on Ziggy's finger. Ziggy laughed as Zack gave him a stern, *don't try that again* look.

"Well, we'll just have to wait and see," South proclaimed after a long period of discussion.

The visiting herd's attention turned toward the fresh pastries and as Mary Catherine fended off a small number with good-natured churning karate kicks, the rest broke for the kitchen to score the remaining undefended goodies and pour healthy cups of coffee for themselves.

"God will punish you heathens," Mary Catherine yelled at them to no avail.

"Scare's on, Sister," Owl mugged, stuffing the last of a four-inch-round moon pie into his mouth. Mary Catherine gave him her best nun scowl and soon she too had found her coffee cup and settled into the kitchen nook with a bran muffin.

"What the boys don't know won't hurt them." She shrugged in defeat with an enigmatic Madonna smirk.

"Annie, will you tell us how the island got its name?" Ziggy asked, stuffing three moon pies into the kangaroo pocket of his sweatshirt when he thought Mary Catherine wasn't looking.

"I thought it was because you had seven sisters," John offered.

"It's a long story, but I'll tell it." Annie smiled, scooping fresh-ground coffee into one of the old percolating coffee pots with the glass top. She settled into the rocking chair and pulled her late sister's sunflower quilt around her legs.

"The local Indians used the island for their summer camp. The island was surrounded by clam beds and wild blackberries that grew across the top of the island—and several nearby streams provided salmon runs. The Indians would cut the salmon into strips and dry them on long racks over fires for their winter stores.

"The tribe on the island had several magnificent cedar canoes somewhere between fifty to sixty feet long made out of a single log.

At the end of one summer, they were invited to a potlatch given by a neighboring tribe about thirty miles away, near the mouth of the Dosewallips River. I think the local legend is that Dosewallips might be named for a S'Klallam chief who had two wives and could never get any peace so he turned himself into a mountain, from which the headwaters of the river flow."

"Amen to that," Ziggy commented, at which point he got a dirty look from Matty.

"Anyway," Annie continued, "the tribe left a few old men at the summer camp and loaded up the rest in the three or four cedar canoes and off they went down Hood Canal."

"What's a potlatch?" interrupted Matty.

"A potlatch is a big social gathering to impress another tribe," Annie explained. "The host would give lavish gifts like copper pots and woven quilts, and serve a huge banquet that would last for days. The tribes would try to outdo each other and sometimes they would bankrupt the tribe just to maintain social standing.

"The island tribe had partied for days and finally loaded up their gifts and began to paddle back to the island, but halfway home they were surprised by a marauding band of Quackquitl warriors from the coast of British Columbia, who had swung in behind them. The Quackquitls were a fierce tribe that came down to pillage the local Indian villages, steal their winter food, and take women and children back as slaves. They were said to be the only cannibals in North America.

"The island Indians were surprised but had a hundred-yard lead as they paddled furiously home to the island where they would have a better chance of surviving an attack. They had left their dogs and most of their weapons on the island. As they neared the island, the Quackquitls began to gain on them because their canoes were lighter war canoes and the island canoes were filled with their gifts, women and children.

"It was high tide and as they neared where the boathouse sits, the tips of the seven rocks were barely visible above the rising tide. The island natives lured the Quackquitls closer and because *they* knew where the rocks were, they maneuvered between them. The Quackquitls were not so lucky. Their four war canoes were flipped or sunk, and when they waded to shore they were all tracked down and killed.

"It was one of the last great Indian battles in the area and the island grew more famous as the story was passed from potlatch to potlatch how the rocks had saved the tribe. The island was named after the seven sister rocks that protected the island."

"Wow, good story!" Ziggy said, standing up and quickly stuffing his hands into his front pouch to disguise the telltale bulge of at least a half dozen more bran muffins. "I think I need to go home now."

When the crowd had cleared to begin their day, Mary Catherine carefully piled her confections into baskets. "I thought I had more bran muffins," she mused as she helped Annie put the twins down for their first nap.

"Remember, we're going to be filmed for local television tomorrow," Sister said.

"Zat so?" Annie stopped her coffee cup mid-flight.

"Yep, that woman from the county TV public access channel is going to be there," Sister said, tailing off her conversation as she couldn't resist one last rub of Little Annie's gum. Zack gave her a look of defiance.

"Yep, there's a tooth coming in," she said with final authority.

"It ain't so till Mother Superior says so," Annie muttered under her breath.

Mary Catherine helped clean the kitchen and looked in on the babies in their cribs one last time before heading down the trail. Annie put her robe on over her sweater and pulled her Morris chair over to the stove and stuck her feet inside the oven.

"A spa day, I see," Mary Catherine commented as she rushed out the kitchen door.

Annie loved her catnaps and before the screen door slammed shut, she was already dozing. Twenty minutes later, she was wide awake and refreshed. The percolating coffee pot was furiously rattling on the stove and coffee was gushing against the bubble top. Annie pulled the pot onto a cooler part of the old majestic stove and went out on the covered porch. It was hot for fall, *maybe over sixty-five*, Annie thought as she leaned against the porch post.

September had always been Annie's favorite month. Maybe it was the long shadows; maybe it was the savoring of the last of the long summer evenings and the heat that would soon be gone.

It had always rankled Annie that the longest daylight day of the year was June 21, before summer even arrived. "It's just wrong," Annie complained aloud.

The grass was the color of gold and the ferns and summer leaves gave off an oven-baked aroma of sweet roasted hazelnuts, and if the wind was right, Annie could smell the acrid vine-ripened wild Himalayan and Cascade blackberries that made a fragrant jam filled with seeds that would stick between your teeth. Jam to be eaten when the weather was gray and it rained for two weeks straight and the summer sun was a distant memory. Annie breathed deeply. She knew there would not be many summers left for her, but she couldn't help smiling. It was a glorious afternoon.

She decided to work on the bobble head tugboat grannie dolls with the wrinkled apple heads. Moby Dick, the carpenter who had refurbished the oyster shacks, had carved wooden bodies on a small pedestal. Annie and South had made small sweatshirts and embroidered "Tugboat Grannies" on the bib overalls and had sewn pockets with a red bandana hanging out.

Annie had tried to carve a no-nonsense grandmotherly look on the apple faces, but the faces ran the gamut from angelic to downright sinister.

Well, grandmas come with all kinds of attitudes, she shrugged, as she glued the heads on the top of the bobble springs.

Annie sighed wistfully. "I miss Moby," she said out loud. "That man could make me laugh."

The next day, Christine came to the house early to watch over the twins while Annie and Sister Mary Catherine went to the sub base to pass out more muffins and cookies.

At seven in the morning, the fog that promised to burn off later was still holding the sub base captive as the two women, baskets laden with the pastries, positioned themselves between the car lanes where the impatient sailors entered the base, and the military police saluted them in.

"There have been a few confrontations in the past," Mary Catherine warned Annie. "Just don't go past the guard station."

Annie had given two muffins to a square, clean-shaven Marine in a pickup with a steaming cup of coffee and was dancing between the rows to an open window where a hairy-armed chief bosun waited. Suddenly, the Marine staggered out of his truck and grabbed for his neck.

"He's choking!" Mary Catherine yelled out as she dropped her basket and bolted past the guard station. Annie was right behind her as the nun tackled the Marine from behind and began the Heimlich maneuver. Annie looked into his bulging eyes and terror-stricken face.

"Punch him in the solar plexus," Mary Catherine barked.

Annie rolled up her coat sleeve and punched the man's stomach just below the ribs. A glob of muffin attached to a piece of gum flew over her head and hit the guard in the face just before he wrestled Annie to the ground. Mary Catherine held on to the man as he slumped and another guard wrenched her arms behind her back and slapped cuffs on her. Crushed by the two-hundred-pound guard, Annie struggled for air as her wrists were bent back, she was hoisted to her feet, and shackled.

"You know the rules." The guard spat out the syllables in Annie's face as he stepped over the Marine, who was gasping for air.

The two women were unceremoniously shoved into the back seat of a black Chevy Suburban with black tinted windows, and the tires spun as the driver turned on the overhead blinking lights and cut loose with a siren's wail. "Off to the clanger with you two," the driver snarled, and gave a deep chuckle.

Annie and Mary Catherine were dazed but unrepentant as they were ushered into a cell room with two metal bunks, no mattresses, no windows, and a stainless toilet with no seat. Mary Catherine strained for dignity as she straightened her habit.

"No good deed goes unpunished," she complained, sinking heavily onto the wire springs of the cot. Annie was still dazed and her wrist was killing her.

The county public television network stationary camera had captured the events on tape as Kerry, the queen bee of "Coffee Klatch with Kerry," scrambled back to the station to air her footage.

On air, Kerry breathlessly described the replay of the scene as the two women passed out their treats, the scuffle, and then the drama when they were taken down and led away cuffed. There was the close-up of the muffin glob with the gum still attached sitting on the asphalt as the camera caught the black Chevy as it disappeared into the bowels of the navy fortress.

This was high drama for Kerry, whose program continually pushed at the lower depths of mediocrity: "arranging" *ad nauseum* a silk flower bouquet of the same worn-out flowers show after show; a segment of "Are You Ready for Marriage?," inspired by her daughter's contentious divorce; cooking episodes of her famous, never-fail Arkansas Flaming Chili, in which she never remembered to drain the hamburger; and her spin-doctored favorite: the reënactment of the 1963 Kennedy assassination complete with conspiracy theories. Using a soundtrack of "Dark Side of the Moon," by Pink Floyd, Kerry brought out her compelling props to re-create the Dallas motorcade.

"Forget the Zapruder film," Kerry would say, positioning her props.

The presidential limousine was represented by a two-foot-long pink Barbie convertible, complete with Dominatrix Barbie as Jackie Kennedy; a Harley-Davidson Ken doll (Barbie's sometimes-estranged boyfriend) as JFK; Skipper, Barbie's little sister, as Nellie Connally in the forward seat; and maybe gay Steven as Governor Connally.

A Barbie dollhouse became the Texas Book Depository and a small green towel spread over a Happy Hippo game created the grassy knoll from which Allen, the Barbie doll with a dark, swarthy complexion and scruffy terrorist beard and called Fidel by Kerry, was the real assassin.

With the players in place, Kerry would carefully mete out the timeline, scoot the car between the knoll and the book depository and with absolute finality every time, topple off Ken's (JFK's) head, held on with Play-Doh, over the back of the trunk of the Barbie car, proving convincingly that the real kill shot had come from the grassy knoll.

It was this segment, reënacted live at least once a week, that provoked most of the county to call her "Conspiracy Kerry" behind her back.

The program director had admonished her many times, but the threat would have carried more weight if he would stop sleeping with Kerry as she wore her Adult Barbie Halloween flight attendant costume.

Kerry re-created Annie's arrest using the pink car and some of the same actors, with Sister Mary Catherine played by a Penguin Beenie baby.

The admiral's mother at the navy base had come online late that morning and had been confused by the reënactment with the penguin Beenie baby somewhere between her second and third cup of coffee. It was only when she saw the film clip that she got on the phone.

She was the widow Mrs. Matilda Slattery, or Bunny as her friends called her, or saber-toothed Bunny as she was called behind her back. A name she earned when she detected any abuse...animals or people. She was fourth-generation Annapolis. Her people didn't only *marry* officers; they *raised* them from birth and Bunny was furious as she punched the numbers on her phone to the Pentagon.

It took her several minutes to cow her son's attaché into connecting her, but that was hardly a challenge to Bunny. The exasperated voice of the admiral came on the line. "What is it, Mother?"

"Don't take that tone with me, young man," Bunny admonished. "Have you seen the television?"

"No, Mother." He safely rolled his eyes. "I was in a high-level meeting with the defense secretary. I need to get back. What is it?" he repeated.

"Gadzooks, where to begin," she sputtered. "Well, your Gestapo military thugs just arrested a nun and one of the tugboat grannies for trespassing on the base."

"That's what they're supposed to do, Mother," Admiral Slattery said summarily.

"Code red, code red ..." Bunny was just getting warmed up.

"Good night, nurse, Theodore John Paul Slattery the fifth. You do not take nuns and grandmothers into custody when they were giving one of your Marines the Heimlich. They saved the man's life, for God's sake!"

"All right, Mother. I'll handle it from here as soon as I get done and survey the situation."

"Don't bother, John Paul!" Bunny was exasperated. "I'll take it from here."

"Mother, you don't have any authority on the base."

"We'll see about that!" she crowed. "You just go back to your meeting."

A half-hour later, Bunny pulled onto the base with a limousine flying full Admiral's flags from the front fenders. The crisply turned Marine guard peered in through the driver's side window and was surprised to see Bunny sitting in the back seat.

"Ma'am, I must inform you that you are unauthorized personnel and cannot enter the base, even in this car," he said.

"Back up, sonny," Bunny called out from the cavernous interior. "I'm Admiral Slattery's mother and I'm coming through. Shoot me if you must but aim high. You're going to have to get me with the first shot. Floor it, Percy," she commanded the sweating Marine private.

No shots were fired as the limo squealed away from the guard station, across the promenade, and parked near the holding area of the brig. Bunny got out as if reviewing the troops, stalked down the hallway, and shooed away with a wave of her hand any form of resistance from the Marines who came out of their various doorway offices like cuckoo birds, only to rapidly retreat to their cages.

Bunny finally came to the holding room and threw open the door.

Annie and Mary Catherine were sitting on a poppy-colored couch.

"Judas Priest," Bunny exclaimed as she clasped her hands together. "This simply will not do. Ladies, follow me. Bunny Slattery is the name," she announced as she ushered them down the hall.

The cuckoo birds smartly sequestered themselves as the three women whooshed down a small flight of stairs, down the hallway, and into the limo.

"Well, I declare," Bunny began. "At least you weren't shackled."

"Oh no, it was an honest mistake," Annie declared, as Mary Catherine lit up a Camel and rummaged through the velvet liquor cabinet between the front and back seat.

"No rocks," she mumbled as she poured three fingers of Crown Royal into a glass and settled back.

While Mary Catherine reflected into her snifter, Bunny and Annie grew quite chatty as they blew past the Marine guard post and careened north on the highway back to the island.

"Is there anything the Navy can do for you ladies to make up for this blunder?" Bunny warbled.

Mary Catherine pondered as she tilted her head to blow the smoke through the limousine sun roof. "I could use some duty-free cigarettes."

"Done," said Bunny. She gave an order and the car spun back through the guard post as the men cowered in the shelter. Three minutes later, she emerged from the commissary with a filled shopping bag. On the road again, Bunny soon decided it was time for lunch. "Do you ladies know a good place for lunch?"

"It's not much to look at," Annie began, "but Mom's Diner on the way to Port Townsend has good chowder and great pies."

"Sounds good to me," said Bunny grandly.

The parking lot was a moonscape of puddles as they tiptoed their path to the diner door. "Ladies!" they were greeted by a stout, bald-headed woman. "Come on in. I own the joint."

The warm welcome was volunteered by Garnet, former Vegas call girl, who had just recently traded years of hot flashes for ovarian cancer and radiation. "Have a seat." She gestured to a small white formica table, centered between two red vinyl benches.

Mary Catherine hesitated as she looked at the table's vista: a chorus line of men's butt cracks layered on the small vinyl stools lining the counter.

Garnet noticed and gave the first two men wedgies as she passed by and the rest she slapped on the cheeks, quickly solving the problem. "There." Garnet looked as pleased as a Cheshire cat. "That's a better view."

Susan, Mom's daughter-in-law, married to the laziest man in the world as voted on by Susan and Mom herself, pulled an order tablet from her red-and-white checked apron pocket.

"What'll it be, ladies?"

Annie pivoted her neck to peruse the day's specials, written in chalk on a blackboard behind her. "Hmm-m. Eggs Benedict. Is that still available?"

Garnet had trundled back into her kitchen. She poked her head out the pass-through. "Damn straight," she sang out, looking more like a brewmaster than a short-order cook.

The women conferred. "Three Bennies!" Susan called through the window. She shuttled down the stool line and pulled the tail end of several T-shirts down even further.

"Wha'd' I do?" the men all grunted innocently.

The women had just settled in over their coffee when a deep male voice thundered, "Damn it to hell, where the blazes is the gravy for my biscuits?" A jet black-haired man with Elvis sideburns and a curled lip crowed to the ceiling. He was wearing the signature black denim pants, a black-and-white narrow-striped shirt with the large red suspenders of a Pacific Northwest logger—underemployed in these environmentally sensitive times.

"I ordered biscuits and gravy, biscuits and gravy!—and now I've run out of gravy. Damn it, Garnet, I've run out of gravy."

"Smitty" was known to everyone in this small-town America and had feasted at Mom's nearly every morning for the last forty years while plundering the local hills for timber. He had been "retrained" several times over the years as a computer operator, despite missing three fingers from a sawmill accident; was set up with his own latte stand where, as a barista, he grew so lonely he would give away mochas until he bankrupted his state grant; and, as a last resort, was trained as an "environmental engineer," counting spotted owls in the rainforest near the Pacific Ocean.

Smitty had failed at any attempt to be retrained The last straw for the State was when he went "entrepreneur." A self-taught taxidermist, he made a small fortune stuffing the endangered spotted owl bookends for Republicans in the state legislature. He was on permanent dole as "unemployable."

And now, to add insult to injury, Smitty had been shorted gravy.

"I need gravy!" he continued to bellow. "I need gra-aaaavy," he wailed even louder.

Garnet swore a cook's oath and trundled out with a stainless steel pot of gravy and ladled mystery gravy onto his plate till it overflowed onto the table and then put a half ladle on the bill of his baseball cap till it dripped onto the plate. "There, that oughta hold you, varmint,"she hurled, walking stiff-legged back to the kitchen.

"Well, that's more like it," Smitty said, looking non-plussed and trying to save face. No one ever bested Garnet on her home turf.

The three women snickered, picked through their Eggs Benedict, and bonded over lemon pie and coffee. Mary Catherine brushed errant meringue from her black habit and told how she had ridden in the Pope-mobile in Buenos Aires. Annie countered with a story of how, while she lived in South America, she was so lonely for the sound of rushing water that she poured water from one bowl to the other as she staged an evacuation on the arid steppes of Bolivia. Bunny launched right into her abused animal shelter stories and regaled her new friends with a story she read of overfeeding geese to get enlarged livers for paté. "It's very painful to the geese," Bunny relayed.

"I may be able to help you there," Mary Catherine replied cryptically.

Chapter FOUR

The limousine had pulled into a parking space outside the Port Gamble store and post office next to a Jaguar, painted with a leopard design and a fan-shaped stencil of black letters on the door that read: "Trish l'Dish …all leopard all the time."

"There's a rig after my own heart," purred Mary Catherine, as she caressed the front fender. "Is the cat black with gold spots or gold with black spots?" I can never remember," she mused.

Wiggins, the postmaster/storekeeper, slipped his two-a-day flask of green absinthe into the rear pocket of his Dockers and met the women on the porch. "Annie, I have someone you need to meet." He motioned her inside.

The store was poorly lit, with the usual number of three burnt-out bulbs that created the mood lighting the heavy-lidded Wiggins referred to as "Philip Marlowe noir." Wiggins was an avid fan of whodunits.

As they got accustomed to the lack of light, they could see Wiggins motioning them to the back room. He handed a card to Annie.

She held the card up over her head to capture the faint hall light so they could all read the print, framed with a leopard border. "TRISH L'DISH, PhD, Exotic Dancer...Sociology Professor, University of Washington."

The door swung open into darkness, stabbed only by the water-reflected half-light that entered from the panes of a dusty, wood-paned window. The trio gave a collective gasp as their eyes caught the image of a statuesque black woman—dressed in a leopard suit, stacked heels, and a cascading leopard cape that reached to the floor. She was standing in front of the window overlooking the harbor, and as she gave a quarter turn, it was her eyes that captured them. Almond-shaped, huge and feline, they were made for the midnight hours. She was theatre.

The woman glided assuredly across the room and extended her hand.

"I'm Trish," she announced. "Carol Ann from Hospice referred me to you. Can we talk?"

She gestured toward a sturdy trestle table and heavy wood chairs that stood near the center of the room. Trish dusted each chair with her scarf as Annie and her troops sat down in turn. Sitting at the end of the table, Trish leaned forward as if at a boardroom meeting.

"I'll get to the point," she stated flatly. "I'm Trish l'Dish. That's not my stage name; that's my real name. Carol Ann sent me to you because I have just been diagnosed with stage four breast cancer and I need a place to disappear while I work out the details about my husband, who I just discovered has been molesting my children." She motioned to the darkest part of the room where two sets of almond eyes stared out into the light.

"Come here, girls," Trish beckoned her daughters out of the shadows. Annie guessed the eldest, Talisha, to be about eleven, and her sister, Alisha, about eight. With their mother's luminous eyes, the girls had a brown crème brûlée complexion and the bone structure of Parisienne models. They were going to be stunners. They gave each woman a strong handshake. Bunny bit her lip as her eyes began to water.

"The girls understand this is not their fault; it is their father's," said Trish. "They are in the gifted program at Madison Park School. And I will continue their education by homeschooling." The girls smiled at Annie as Trish hovered over them protectively and then ushered them through the door. "You girls stay in the store while I talk to these ladies for a few more minutes."

Trish returned to the table. "I'll cut to the chase. I have maybe six months to live. Maybe not good months, but I have some time to try and protect my girls and find a stable home. Their father was a good man when I married him fifteen years ago. He owned several car dealerships, but then he got into meth, heroin and crack and now he runs with several thugs. I can't even begin to understand this molestation. If he finds us, he will come after us.

"Carol Ann said it would be your call, Annie. It's a risk. Do you want to take us in?" Trish leaned closer over the table and looked into Annie's eyes, her wrinkled forehead betraying worry.

"I'll kill the son-of-a-bitch myself," Bunny sputtered, pushing back her chair.

Annie closed her eyes and shook her head. It was a lot of responsibility. She looked out the window toward Seven Sisters Island. She thought of the rocks that had always protected the island from harm and smiled as she remembered how her six sisters had gang-sheared one of her classmates who had dared cut off Annie's pigtail in second grade. The island had always taken care of its own.

"I'll talk it over with the island's residents and if they are on board then we'll do it," Annie declared. "Come on out to the island. They can meet the girls and we can have a meeting."

Bunny told the limousine driver to go have dinner and meet her back at the store after dark. Three hours later, the networking had done its job and everyone associated with the island was at Annie's with potluck in hand. No matter that there were twice as many desserts as main dishes. It had never been about the food itself.

Trish introduced herself and the two girls. Talisha, slim and graceful, wore glasses and a serious look. Alisha, her younger sister, was a little chunkier with a spitfire look. Annie excused them to another room and began the meeting. She explained Trish's cancer and her daughters' molestation and then asked for questions.

"What are we doing here?" Owl asked, sidling up a little closer to the kettle of stew Max had cooked. "We're gonna take 'em in, aren't we? Who else is gonna do it?"

"Domestic violence can get nasty, you know," Annie reminded him.

"It's getting kinda hot in here! And it's my birthday today, and I say we take the girls in," South said in a loud voice.

"What South says goes," John agreed, confirming what he knew everyone there felt.

Every head nodded and Annie gave a tearful smile and hugged everyone, including a surprised Ziggy who nearly swallowed his joint.

The vote taken, John Hunt opened the door and Trish and her girls came into a sweltering room of welcoming friends and a lot of chocolate desserts. And, of course, South, whose recent dementia included thinking every day was her birthday, opened her usual present of crystal candle holders…again. And was overjoyed and kissed everyone in the room…again.

Bunny was ecstatic as John took her back to Port Gamble and Trish drove the Jaguar back to the base to hide it in Bunny's garage. Bunny had insisted on being a part of the girls' homeschooling. Several of the cabins needed to be remodeled on the spit, so the new immigrants would stay with Annie and the twins until arrangements could be finalized.

Late that night, Annie sat in her chair with her feet inside the oven and listened to the creaks and groans of the old house. As she drifted off to sleep, she just then realized the house was not complaining;

it was just going through growing pains and was making sounds of contentment and happiness.

The next morning, after the twins were fed, Annie wrapped South's birthday candle holders again and gave them to her at her cabin. South always had a wide grin as she opened her present and proudly placed the two crystal pieces on the table and admired how the light passed through them and made a rainbow on the wall. Then she proceeded to tell Annie about the wonderful time she had at the Governor's Ball the night before.

"It was wonderful, Annie," she reminisced. "The music was by a string quartet and the ballroom was decorated in an Italian theme with statues and lattice with grape leaves. The ice sculpture was of David. You know, he wasn't as well-endowed as you would think, and they even brought the Pietà over from Europe just for the event."

South swooned. "It was just wonderful. And the food, the wines. I wish you could have been there, Annie."

Annie smiled and shook her head. She almost envied the fantasy life of South, who constantly recounted the dreams of the night before. They were so vivid that they carried South through the whole day talking about the event and the icing was that every day was her birthday. It was a joy just to think South was having that much fun. It didn't matter that none of it was true. Annie often thought that South's dementia was almost the gift of having lived an uneventful life.

Annie spent the afternoon working on the last of her apple-faced bobble head dolls. She had help from Owl putting the oysters and boxes of apples in the wooden *Ark* ready for an early morning sail to Seattle with Twigs.

The waters were still and the reflection of sky and clouds on the water erased the horizon line. It was as though Annie was sailing in a glass ball of timeless infinity. As the boat motored through the waves, the dozens of bobble head dolls all nodded in positive unison and Annie had to laugh when she turned the boat ever so slowly and all the bobble heads dutifully followed with negative movements. The heads were still trying to make up their mind as Annie pulled into the commercial dock by the ferry where John waited to help her transport her wares up to his car.

Pike Place Market was slowly coming to life as they drove down the cobblestone street. The flower vendors were already displaying the brilliant reds and yellows of tall-stemmed dahlias, and the sweet yeast aroma of the French bakery mingled with the acrid diesel smells of the transit buses moving through town. The truck farmers created uniform stacks of produce—endless rows of the greens, yellows and reds of cabbage, zucchini and peppers that made home gardeners awestruck at their flawless beauty.

The fish mongers had shoveled ice chips onto their slanted, stainless steel display bins that held artfully arranged rows of freshly caught king salmon, red snapper and cod, all staring wide-eyed at the now-burgeoning crowd. With an eight-foot arm spread, a Puget Sound octopus was perched atop the ice mountain above the fish, its tentacles splayed protectively around the schools of fish.

A balding monger, sporting a greasy sweat band that said Slick Watts, rigged up a hidden rope onto the tail of a monk fish that hung down at waist level with its enormous mouthful of teeth, poised and patiently waiting until small children—too curious to resist—invariably stuck their fingers in its mouth. Then, stealthily, the monger would sneak behind the stacks of translucent scaled king salmon, pull on the monk fish tail, and startle the children and their parents alike. The same trick had been pulled on unsuspecting tourists for a hundred years and it still brought smiles.

Ivan, the piroshki man and Annie's ally, who constantly used Hollywood to embrace American culture, spotted John's car, ran out and jumped on the hood, closed his eyes, and stuck his tongue out the side of his mouth. Then he slithered off and leaned inside Annie's window.

"Annie. I play like dead stag in *Deer Hunter* with Marilyn Streak. I am also liking Gordon Gekko…Greed is good. I work fingers to elbows. I have website now. Also am writing book and am a part-time film critic for newspaper in Vladivostok. America is good, no? Watch this…"

Ivan backed up, took a running start, and gatored himself across the hood of John's Volvo, He then somersaulted, jumped up, and ran to the driver's side window.

"I make like Keiko, the killer whale. How you like them grapefruits? Next time I do rapture impersonator from …*Jurassic Park*. Must go now," Ivan announced.

As John pulled ahead, Ivan slapped his hands on the trunk and left two floured handprints of success.

"You gotta like the enthusiasm of immigrants like Ivan," John said, as he helped Annie stage her wares on the wooden shelves. Thousands of Seattle shoppers and gawkers would soon flood into the old market. At thirty dollars, Annie wondered if the bobble head tugboat grannies were overpriced but, she mumbled to herself, *these are a lot of work.*

She rubbed her apples with a flannel cloth and stacked the sacks of oysters under the bench. With their grayish-black tiered, misshapen shells, the oysters reminded Annie of the terraced gardens that clung to the steep hillsides of the Philippines and Borneo.

"All that work," Annie said, as she took her oyster knife, pried open the shell from the hinge end, loosened the meat, tilted her head back, and tipped the gray-white delicacy into her mouth. Errant juices escaped the corners of her mouth as she savored the salty, metallic taste and felt the chewy textural crunch of outer muscles, then the smooth side as the oyster lingered between her teeth and then tobogganed down her throat. She pried open two more oysters that caused the sparse crowd of onlookers to alternatively cringe or salivate, depending on their palate.

John took a picture of Annie with her eyes closed and savoring the taste of the last oyster, the shell poised over her mouth as if choreographed by the Pacific Northwest Ballet. Annie opened her eyes and wiped the side of her mouth with her sweater sleeve. "Whoo!" She shook her head and shuddered. "That hit the spot," she said in a Pacific salute, as she tossed the shell in a slow arc toward the dumpster.

John excused himself. "I'll be back later," he reminded her. "Remember, we are going over to visit Whiplash Oil Exchange after the market."

Annie nodded and turned to make her first sale of the day. The bobble heads were a hit. It seemed everyone had a grandmother with the kind of "take no prisoners" attitude that the grannies had made famous.

During lunch, Piroshki Ivan explained the stock market to Annie and his latest reading of De Tocqueville. "He said that America is great because America is good, and that the common man has dignity. This I believe is true," said Ivan. "I work hard, I play hard, and I make good living here in America. Is a good country." Ivan emphatically pounded his fist against his hand. Annie agreed. She was surprised that Ivan had ventured away from Hollywood into history.

By the time the late afternoon sun had slid behind the old Seattle Public Market sign and the crowds had dwindled, Annie had sold out of everything. The Japanese flower gardeners were gathering up the unsold stately dinner plate-size red, orange and gold dahlias. The fish mongers packed away their wares into the refrigerated rooms and began hosing down the concrete floors as scavenging seagulls inched forward to snag the odd tidbit. The jewelry vendors closed their cases and the vegetable sellers re-boxed their produce from the tiered displays and threw the culls into the alley dumpsters. The day's selling was over and everyone's thoughts turned to home.

Ivan and Annie stood on the corner with Annie clutching her "to go" bag of piroshkis. John pulled up in his green Volvo station wagon with the Betsy 1 license plates. They loaded Annie's now-empty baskets and stopped as a gaggle of caffeine-crazed Japanese tourists exited the original Starbuck's coffee shop. Their necks were ringed with cameras and their hands filled with bags of coffee and boxes of souvenir mugs for their unfortunate friends back home who had never been to the Number One coffee shop Mecca.

John's car chattered down the cobblestone roads past the one-time sleepy fishing village of Ballard, and swung east to Fremont, the eclectic home of a gigantic Lenin statue by way of the old Soviet empire; by a garage-size concrete troll eating a Volkswagen that lived under the freeway; and farther down the street next to the locks that joined Seattle's Lake Union and Lake Washington with the Puget Sound, to their destination—site of the Whiplash Oil Exchange.

With Tugboat Grannies celebrity came fame and with fame came venture capital and endorsements. Annie and Pickles had sorted through the adult diapers, wines, and nonprofits to come up with "appropriate marketing opportunities," as Pickles had put it.

Annie had little time to research the offers, but Pickles independently had joined up with some of the more offbeat considerations that might not "meet the smell test," another one of Pickles' business expressions. One such offering was the possum meat futures for stores and restaurants, and another was a collaboration between Pickles and Madeline, Annie's old next-door stall seller at the public market.

Madeline, ever-voluptuous with her giant Angelina Jolie crimson lips, had started out in business with essential erotic oils and rubs that she created at home in her kitchen. Made primarily from olive oil and suitable for sexual enhancement and home cooking, the elixir came first in small jars and much later in pump varieties in barrels for "commercial" use.

Madeline and Pickles had started their enterprise with a unique business model that so far had taken the Seattle automotive industry by storm. Oil changes, mufflers and brake jobs done by women dressed in black-and-red leather dominatrix gear and half-naked men in

dirt-brown leather "man skirts." Pickles had set up a ten-week training class in Kansas City to ensure quality control of the mechanical
end of the operation and Madeline was in charge of costume design,
day-to-day operations, and keeping the investors "happy."

John pulled up to what was formerly an abandoned gas station,
now done up in red neon and stainless. Annie and John entered
through a ten-foot–tall, self-opening, glossy, black metal door with a
matrixed surface of brass nippled cones. On the left side of this glass
and metal building was a curved stainless steel bar studded with a
numbing array of wooden and metal-handled controls of over fifty
draft beers on tap monitored by beer tenders with spiked hair and
body art.

The rotating red leather-topped bar stools were occupied by a collection of males—from longshoremen in Carhartt garb to Microsoft
types in Dockers and penny loafers. There were tall tables with chairs
filled with women sporting short haircuts and sprayed-on pants,
and behind the tables was a full-mirrored wall of body oil offerings.
Sample pumps and partial statues with porcelain body parts invited
customers to experiment with the various fragrances and viscosi-
ties. All of this overlooked the bays below where the real work of car
maintenance was being orchestrated.

Seattle's favorite songster daughters, Heart, and their signature
song "Love is a Battlefield" blared over the racks of cars as leather-
dressed "cat women" with masks of leather and feathers and teetering
on five-inch heels drove in the cars, changed the oil, and lubricated
the cars with essential oils, while "foremen" stalked the runways with
whips strapped to their hips.

The occasional male slave would take the cars through a mirrored
garage door into an unseen room where brake work was done. The
sounds of whips snapping and snarling through the air provided
a stereophonic backbeat as a steady stream of cars—ranging from
rusted pickups to BMW's—all enjoyed the personalized service and

the performance art. "This must be a gold mine," Annie gasped as Madeline came from behind a door in the one-way mirrored glass behind the bar. Dressed in caliente red toreador pants, sandals, and a simple see-through silk peasant blouse, the usually flamboyant Madeline seemed over-dressed for the surroundings.

Madeline gave Annie a hug. "So glad to see you," she said, stepping back. She gestured with a sweep of her hand. "What do you think of this place?"

Without waiting for Annie's reply, she went on. "I can afford to send my kids to private school these days. And we are selling franchises from Portland down to L.A. and we are bringing in a tattoo parlor, health food store, massage and physical therapy. Pickles calls it one-stop shopping for your car and your body."

Annie and John were dumbfounded as Madeline led them to a table and ordered a pitcher of beer and Nachos. "Well," Annie began, raising her voice to be heard, "you and Pickles have tapped into the Seattle libido with this place."

"I know," Madeline confessed. "Who would have thunk it? Changing oil is not brain surgery. We have an extensive training program and we charge thirty percent more for changing oil than anyone else. We can pay way over minimum wage and we even offer health and dental for the employees—plus I get to smell leather every day. What could be better?" The three nibbled on the Nachos and beer, mesmerized by the action down on the garage floor. John rolled his eyes. "This place is too noisy for an old geezer like me."

Annie and John excused themselves, and as the front door shut like a bank vault, the strains of Nirvana's "Teenage Angst" escaped into the night air.

As Annie's boat churned through the Sound, the end-of-summer sky turned crimson. *Red sky at night, sailor's delight. Red sky in the*

morning, sailor take warning, Annie mused to herself as she adjusted the tiller. The venerable wooden boat settled into a watery trough and bolted for home.

Nearing the island, Annie heard the heavy splash from the front of the bow and watched as a ten-foot baby orca rubbed up against the side of the boat. Annie quickly choked the engine off as the juvenile orca gave a pleading look up at Annie standing behind the stern.

"What's up, little guy?" Annie gave a primal smile, one mammal to another. "Have you got a name?" Annie asked. "Where is your family?"

Annie shielded her eyes from the setting sun and looked up and down the channel. There were no other orcas in sight. Annie knew all the Puget Sound orcas were tracked from Whidbey Island as if celebrities. She couldn't remember if there were forty-five or thirty-five in the three families that cruised the waters looking for their prime food, king salmon. The boat tilted sideways as the little orca rubbed against the bow once again and then disappeared.

Annie waited a few minutes to be sure the orca was gone and then started the two-cylinder diesel and threw the wooden handled lever that engaged the propeller. The boat skimmed through the water and left a quiet wake shaped like an ever-growing v.

The waters darkened from crimson to black as the sun went down between the cleft of the two Olympic Mountains known as the Brothers. Annie remembered that the twin peaks were named by George Vancouver to try and impress his future father-in-law by honoring his two sons. It worked, and George married their sister Elinor in 1858 and named Mt. Elinor, a Paul Bunyan's stone's throw from her brothers.

"Some of us get mountains and some of us get islands," Annie mumbled as she took a deep breath of salt air.

Annie wearily struggled up the path to home and quietly feathered the screen door shut, noticing Owl was sleeping fully cradled in repose in the shabby La-Z-Boy chair, a swaddled twin on either side.

Annie had worried about the twins' safety at first, but the benefits to all involved were too important. The babies seemed to rejuvenate the old flesh as much as they enjoyed the bonding. Annie felt the twins needed to build trust with the people who loved them. One day, she wouldn't be here for them.

"A replacement, that's something I need to work on," Annie chided herself. *It does take a village to raise a child,* she sometimes forced herself to remember when she felt a motherly jealousy.

Annie crept up to the sleeping brood and noticed that they were all drooling. She gently swiped at each mouth with a clean cloth diaper. She suspected that both the twins might be cutting teeth and Owl, well he was sixty-five plus. Annie sat on the celadon green sofa and watched the trio slumber. Occasionally, any one or all of them might burp and fart as needed for comfort. It was a little like watching soup come to a boil, Annie decided.

As she reflected on these two stages of life before her—how alike and how innocent they really were—she smiled through her tears.

Chapter FIVE

The next morning when Annie awoke, the summer fog was thick on the island. The foghorns were mooing like lost cows and the tidal swells of a full tide made the bell on the buoy clang like a cow bell on the neck of the lead bossy heading to the barn for the morning milking.

Annie found the twins together in their crib where Owl had deposited them during the night, plus two empty baby bottles, rolled-up diapers, and a half-empty bottle of Wild Turkey nearby were further evidence that this surrogate daddy had taken care of everyone's needs and left. Annie quietly made her coffee, then sat with her steaming mug and looked out into the fog.

"Fog as thick as pea soup," Annie mumbled aloud. She felt her way with her toes along the grassy edge of the well-worn trail down to the boathouse. The tide was gently lapping against the pea gravel shoreline when suddenly Annie stopped. She thought she heard a splash. Maybe a chum salmon heading up to spawn. As she stopped to listen, the only sound was the creaking of the ancient cedar tree at the end of the apple orchard. "Singing in the wind," her father used to say. Then Annie heard the sound of a boat's bow gliding onto the gravel and the dull thud of a paddle hitting the side; then footsteps passing just out of her sight, disappearing down the beach toward the cedar snag.

Annie would have called out, but the fog was eerie and there was a complete white-out. Besides, she was bordering on vertigo. She followed the shoreline until she found a fifteen-foot hollowed-out cedar canoe in the Northwest Indian tradition; it had been hauled out above the tide line. The slab insides were scored with the uneven, layered cuts of a chainsaw.

"Hmm-m. Not exactly Old School," Annie murmured. The sides were painted black and the Salish symbol of two white bear claws was painted on the side.

Annie felt her way back to the boatshed and brushed away an errant trumpet vine that had fallen over the doorway. She gazed at the cedar shingles, upswept by the summer heat, that looked like curled eyelashes. The mist had covered her face and Annie squinted and blinked as she looked up again and counted the missing shingles on the roof that had been taken by the winter storms.

I'm going to have to find a carpenter before winter sets in, she promised herself, as she eased into *The Ark* and dedicated herself to sweeping away the barnacles that had fallen off the oyster shells and lay nestled near the wood keel at the bottom of the boat. As she leaned over, she spotted what she thought was a rag sitting in the bow, but it was a bobble head doll that had escaped capture.

Someone ran by the boatshed and pounded on the shingled wall. "Annie, come on out," the voice called. "Moby's pumpkin is going to be unveiled. They're taking off the cloth sunscreen."

By the time Annie arrived four cabins down, Christine was just turning off the battery-powered CD player that had been playing

"*In da godda de vida*" for the last three weeks. It was just one of the instructions left by her father, the old porno movie star, Moby Dick. The single rogue pumpkin plant was all that had survived an over-fertilization steroid experiment mishap in the Spring. Kept under a sunscreen, the plant lived on a daily dose of fertilizer tea and rock music.

Christine carefully lifted off the black filter cloth that protected the pumpkin from the direct sun and rain. The giant pumpkin, obscured almost entirely by the huge green leaves, only shone golden orange with peek-a-boo views. "I haven't seen the little fellow since Spring," Christine explained as she pulled back the leaves.

"Oh, my god," she squealed. "It's Dad!"

The codpiece of leaves removed, the pumpkin was a studly, six-foot-long, parallel-ribbed masterpiece shaped like a drooping, circumcised penis.

"I've never seen the like," Annie ventured. The rest of the island inhabitants stood in awe.

"It's like Moby came back from the dead," John added.

"More like that pumpkin has been on Viagra," countered South Carolina. "I think I'll light a candle next to that bad boy tonight."

"What are we gonna do?" John wondered as South jumped into the patch and pulled away more leaves.

"What else?" Christine shrugged. "We enter it in the contest. I'm sure it will win some award at the weigh-in."

"Maybe we should display it at the adult fantasy shop in Port Townsend," said Ziggy. "It's a one-of-a-kind piece, I'd say."

"Well, let's cover it up before we're all arrested," laughed Max.

Trish pulled off her leopard scarf and nestled it around the base. "Maybe it will grow some more tonight." She gave the pumpkin a maternal caress and stood up. "Annie, we could use one of your famous potluck suppers."

As the crowd moved away to organize the dinner, Max admonished the pumpkin. "Dad, enjoy yourself." She reached into the vinyl CD holder on the side of the cabin and put in a fresh soundtrack.

Christine turned away and explained to Max, "I guess I shouldn't have put any of dad's ashes on the plant. Maybe, in a weird way, that's what happened. Reaching out from the grave." Her glance seemed furtive, "and it's definitely Woo Woo" …she began to hum the theme from "Outer Limits" ..*do do do do …...do do do do.* The CD kicked in and the jazz strains of Ray Charles singing "Making Whoopee" wafted over the garden.

The fog had lifted. Walking past the boatshed, Annie could see only a slight furrow in the sand, now filled with the incoming tide, where the bow of the canoe had rested earlier that morning.

That night, the potluck was consumed amidst a pleasant temperature, the wind was still, and summer seemed like it would go on forever…but that was about to change.

A Pineapple Express, fresh from the flame-broiled Hawaiian Islands, was about to skewer the Pacific Northwest. Steaming over the Olympic Mountains, the rains left a ten-inch crust of white on the peaks and slathered a snowy sauce upon the great slabs of basalt and granite ribs that had been carved into steep mountainsides.

The wind whipped and tossed the Puget Sound waterways into a meringue of white caps. The rain peppered the brown earth into a chocolate ganache and formed puddles that were bittersweet to a summer too long without moisture. The Indian summer was put on notice—CLOSED UNTIL FURTHER NOTICE.

"Good Gravy!" Annie remarked as she pried off her rubber boots and looked out the tower window in the old farmhouse.

Next came the rain in a kamikaze diagonal that exploded onto the roofs and twisted the rusty galvanized gutters into water art. For twenty-four hours, the Pineapple Express Part Two pounded Puget

Sound and filled the rivers with churning waters that would coax the Chinook salmon up the swollen creeks to spawn in the pebbled side pools freshly washed by the storm. Overnight the sweet smell of summer was gone and the pungent smells of fall were everywhere.

Skipping over the puddles, Max had finally made it up to Annie's. She poured a cup of stiff coffee from the stove. She opened the conversation, curling her hands around the cup to warm her fingers. "That orca is still out there."

"That little guy is still out there?" Annie asked. "That's not good. The pod moved through here about two weeks ago. He must be lost."

Max's hand went instinctively to the orca talisman made of onyx she wore around her neck. She still remembered bonding under a full moon, going eyeball to eyeball—no more than ten feet away—with the spy-hopping matriarch of L pod. The magnificent tuxedoed mammal seemed to be suspended in air, and then Max was hit with the splash of baptismal salt water as the animal crashed back to her watery kingdom. Max had suddenly felt a cross-mammalian connection, as though she had been welcomed, accepted; as if she was coming home after being away for a long time. A feeling she had never felt before.

The next morning, Annie had fed the twins and had agonized over using disposable diapers for the thousandth time. The island had always used cloth and there were still some frayed survivors from her own childhood in the attic.

These were the times, when the house was quiet and the twins sleeping, that she would slip into the edge of grief over the tragic deaths of her daughter and granddaughter, but as she began to stray over the line, she would always pull herself back into the present. She had shed single tears many times, but she had never allowed herself to wallow in the injustice or place any blame. *Someday I'll take the time*, she promised herself. *I think that's Scarlett O'Hara's line*, she laughed to herself. *Mercy me!* The screen door banged, the twins woke up, and Annie was glad for the intrusion.

Max had been distracted by watching Trooper pad down on the spit toward Trish's cabin. "That dog has certainly perked up since those girls arrived," she said to no one in particular.

Moby Dick's three-legged hound dog had taken a protective shine to the two pigtailed girls. Trooper had allowed a leopard-colored collar to be placed around his neck and his relationship with the girls had grown in just a short time. His furry, mahogany-colored body could no longer get up without help. The pain of his arthritic hip was so great that he gave a silent howl of protest every time the two girls would boost his rump into the air. Once launched, however, he did a credible job of thumping his tail in gratitude and prowling the perimeter of the compound. It was the first time the hound had been the alpha male and, in spite of his discomfort, he was enjoying every minute.

Max kept prattling into Annie's ear, recounting her first orca encounter. "You remember when Pickles was making the freedom run on the good ship *Cucumber* to spirit the twins back to the island? And there had been a chance midnight meeting between me and that spy-hopping old matriarch orca, Big Mamma? When I went eyeball-to-eyeball with the ten-ton matriarch of the seas? It was a kind of Star Trek Vulcan mind-melt between species," Max philosophized.

"What dear?" Annie was distracted even as the twins burped and gurgled their way through their bottles. She stared out into the apple orchard, entranced by the yellow-brown maple leaves that had fallen to the ground. Whipped by a capricious south wind and the arrogant north wind, the leaves tumbled helplessly in a frothy tsunami that pushed the leaves back and forth from one end of the orchard to the other. By the time Annie put the twins down for a nap, the leaves had congregated like a snowdrift, head high and as long as *The Ark* against the wooden fence surrounding the graveyard.

"I remember you telling me about the orca adventure before," Annie answered absentmindedly.

"Can you watch the babies? I need a bit of fresh air," Annie said, reaching for her sweater.

Something was calling her outside. She went to the orchard, closed her eyes, and her mind flew back to the years of her childhood. She contemplated the pile of leaves and then burrowed into the center of the pile as she had done a hundred times as a small girl. The leaves were leathery and smelled of an earthy nutmeg. As Annie swam deeper into the pile, she did a dead man float and brushed the leaves from her face and stared up into the autumn sky. She watched as her breath condensed in a fog. She wondered what it would feel like to be dead and buried in the orchard. After all, the granite headstone with her name etched in an arc across the top was already sitting in a box full of sawdust in the back of the boatshed, waiting for her to come home forever. *But,* Annie argued, *I'm already home.*

Annie lay very still and quiet. She began to drift into a dream of the future but gave a bleat of defiance, rolled over and pressed her face into the wet leaves once more and did her best impression of a humpback whale, arching her back and wiggling forward into the pile.

Suddenly, Christine roared up the channel in *The Ark*, slid into the boatshed, and vaulted onto the dock. "All right," she announced to the pile of leaves. "We've got some bigwig from the orca watch on Whidbey Island coming in as soon as they can get their biologist rolling. Annie, what are you doing in that pile of leaves?"

"Well," Annie began but suddenly Ziggy and John breached from the middle of the pile and then burrowed once more into the yellow and brown waves of leaves.

The island met with two surprises the next day. The fog had tenaciously wrapped its octopus-like tentacles around the rocky crags of the island, clinging to its prey long into the morning until the afternoon sun vaporized the wispy spirals, revealing a round, domelike bunker at the very end of the spit. The structure had emerged like an adolescent pimple in the middle of the night.

The island folk walked around the twelve-foot diameter igloo of sandbags. Probing with sticks for openings, they found none. They looked in vain for marks of a shovel or tool, but the beach rocks had been swept clean by the high tide. They thumped on the rounded side with a shovel but the sides were as stiff as concrete. Puzzled, everyone grumbled and adjourned for breakfast at Annie's where they could watch the dome from the house. Annie ladled out stiff coffee and her Gravenstein apple strudel wrapped in time-saving phyllo dough that she had picked up at the Port Gamble general store.

"I like the raisins," John savored the dessert as the crumbs fell out of his mouth. "Did you get this recipe from that Peruvian Easter Island fusion restaurant article I put in the paper last fall? It had a dessert that tasted a little like this. Except there aren't any ghost peppers in this, are there? Scoville units, you know. A million units. The habañero pepper has only 300,000 to 400,000 units by comparison." Then, he added. "It's a little like adding chili peppers to chocolate truffles. Any strudel left?" No one was really listening as they all slowly sipped their coffee from mugs with their two hands and stared out the window as if a spacecraft had landed on the island.

"What the double toothpick are you talking about?" Sister admonished John, waving her cigarette about to clear the air. "Just like it says in the Good Book," Mary Catherine offered, stubbing out her cigarette in her cold coffee.

"Revelations. That's what it is. Armageddon. The alpha and omega. If anyone can pry out the critters or aliens or whatever is in that rounded pill box, it will be me. Bran muffins—that's the key," she mumbled. "Bran muffins will bring them to their knees. Mark my words."

Mary Catherine lit up a cigar, stomped out the door, and marched off to her cabin; the crew watched as if a runaway coal-powered steam engine was puffing its way down the island spit, trailing tufts of blue-gray smoke.

Max put the dessert dishes into the pan of water on the wood stove and went to fire up the wooden *Ark*. As they steamed out of the cove, Christine and Max could see the familiar silhouettes of the matriarchs that protected Seven Sisters Island and the Moby Pumpkin Christine had nursed all summer long.

With their long hair tangling in the wind, the two women set course for Port Gamble where they picked up Max's off-again, on-again boyfriend, Travis, his son Tate, and Pickles. They were coming out to help transport the great pumpkin down to the competition in Portland, Oregon. Sitting in the back of the boat, Max and Christine quietly reminisced and chuckled to themselves, reliving the long, torrid summer as tandem heartbreakers.

"Do you remember that Spanish place," Christine reminded Max, "where you did that solo tango routine wearing your three-thousand-dollar scarlet alligator five-inch stilettos while I pounded out tunes?"

"The top of that piano will never be the same," Max said under her breath.

"We left a cord wood of wilted, stumbling, wanna-be suitors in the parking lots this summer," Christine agreed.

"Whoop de doo!" Max ended the conversation.

Annie spotted South Carolina Storm heading in the direction of Ziggy's as *The Ark* scooted into the dock to load the pumpkin. South was slowly dipping in dementia, but she was having the time of her life as she cornered Pickles and John right off the boat with the stories of the magnificent balls, Hollywood dinner parties, and celebrities she conjured up in her fantasy world. "And the best part, it always seems to be my birthday," she wheezed as she hung onto John's shoulder and laughed.

John told her, "You're having more fun in your fantasy life than I'm having in the real world. I want *your* life, South." John remembered that he did get a recipe for his food column from South for Cajun Alligator Gumbo that she had written down from memory from her imaginary foray down to Mardi Gras that spring, and it was the most downloaded recipe on the West Coast until Memorial Day.

Annie tapped on Ziggy and Matty's door to see if they wanted to help with the pumpkin. Matty cracked open the door and peered out.

"Hi, Annie, Come on in. I don't think we've had a chance to sit down and really talk yet." Still wheezy from her maple leaf diving, Annie entered the cabin and sat down on a stool near the door. She noticed the walls were covered floor to ceiling with shelves filled with brass urns, canvas sacks, Chinese take-out boxes, bronze Elvis heads, cantaloupe-size golf balls, and a container the size of a quart of milk sporting a red tongue that looked like the jacket cover from the Rolling Stones' *Forty Licks.*

"What's this urn thing about?" she asked.

"Oh, just some people I picked up at garage sales, estate sales, or by word-of-mouth. Just poor souls looking for a good home."

Annie looked puzzled. "How many urns do you have?"

"Oh, about six or seven hundred here and a few thousand I keep in a mini-warehouse in Fresno. I try to rotate them so everyone gets out for a visit for a few months every year. Sometimes if I think they are lonely, I co-mingle the ashes. Usually boy-girl stuff and there has been a little gay action lately."

From outside there was a sound. The door opened and South stepped in. "Oh, Annie, I see you are meeting my new friends here at Matty's. I hear their voices. You know, I can hear them all talking, plain as day, isn't it so, Matty?" South beamed. "I find it very comforting," South continued.

Annie excused herself to see if she could help in the transport of the great pumpkin. "It's a damn vegetable memorial to the man himself," Annie groused to herself as Mary Catherine held her rosary beads, crossed herself, and said a silent prayer. "Or is it a fruit? I forget."

Pickles simply gave a great sigh and shook his head as Travis heaved the pumpkin up from the gravel with a two by six and Tate scooted a tarp under the giant appendage.

"It looks like the private part of a T-Rex," fourteen-year-old Tate noted, having intently studied the age of dinosaurs and, with the beginning of his puberty, was transfixed by the male anatomy. "I sure wish Mr. Moby was around; he told some interesting stories."

"Tate, remind me after we get the pumpkin aboard. I have a gift for you from Moby," Christine said.

Travis hooked up a rope to the tarp, winched the pumpkin over to his boat, and swung the davit arm over the side of the boat. The wooden scow moaned in protest as he plunked the five-hundred-pound pumpkin in next to the keel. "We're finished here," Travis announced. "Now what is that mound at the end of the spit?"

"We don't know," Annie shrugged. "It just showed up last night with no warning."

Pickles followed Travis and Tate down the beach. He was always looking for another way to market the island. Just last week, he had Annie sign a lucrative contract to be the spokeswoman for Skookum apples, and he was hard at work pursuing a line of bamboo cloth baby clothes. He was still a little miffed that Annie refused to endorse his possum steaks.

The men poked around the edges of the circular bunker while Tate climbed on top and found a small hole to stick his finger into.

"It's ace of spades dark in there," Tate proclaimed, pulling his finger out and pressing his eye to the hole.

"It's a mystery," decided Pickles.

"Tate, come on over here," Christine beckoned. She handed Tate an eight by ten glossy of Hollywood Moby Dick in his prime. Moby had written in a barely legible scrawl: *Tate...Success is not the moby dick in your life...it is the love in your heart...Moby.*

She then handed Tate a tiny canvas sack with a draw string. Tate opened it and out fell Moby's blue glass eye into his hand. Tate turned and mumbled a small thank you to Christine. Fourteen-year-olds don't do tears.

It was nearing dusk when the boat pulled into the dock where the photographer for the *Port Townsend Leader* took a picture of the pumpkin, while Christine added the Moby background. Pickles took control as he shepherded the pumpkin into the back of his VW van for the trip south. Moby had never won an award at the festival, but optimistically, Pickles knew this might finally be Moby's year. There were a lot of discretionary decisions made by newspapers around the country when the AP wire ran the photo.

After the pumpkin left the island, Sister Mary Catherine felt a sense of loss and mystery that could only be filled by baking. She fired up the wood stove in her cabin and took down the large yellow bowl from the warming oven and pulled out her dog-eared Sistine Chapel commemorative cookbook. From the corner of Mary Catherine's pursed lips dangled a droopy-ashed Camel. When the ash dropped into the bowl, she simply muttered, "more fiber," and continued on with her double batch of Saint Gabriel's Bran Muffins. She dolloped the batter into the greased muffin tins and, as the muffins baked in the wood fired oven, she began to hatch her plan until she dozed off.

Minutes went by when she woke with a start and rushed to the oven. The muffins were moist and perfect. "God is great," she muttered gratefully as she pulled the pan from the oven using the front of her habit as a pot holder. When they cooled, she took a pan down to Trish and her two daughters. Trooper met Sister at the door and ushered her into the tiny cabin where Trish lay on a single bed in the corner on leopard sheets and pillow cases. Trish propped herself up and slowly broke off small bits of muffin, savoring each bite. They each had one and then Mary Catherine excused herself to work her plan, which required a nap and three more Camels while she contemplated her target.

A little later, she stacked three bran muffins on a driftwood slab and set it in front of the rounded bunker, then went back to her shed to wash the dishes. Slightly after midnight, Sister Mary Catherine had to make a run for the outhouse, and on the way back she heard some scuffling and noticed the muffins were gone. She placed four more muffins on the slab and went back to bed.

Chapter SIX

The next morning, Annie was awakened by a distant conversation. She knew that most of the island had gone down to the pumpkin weigh-in. She peeked into the twins' room where South, sitting in a rocking chair, was feeding Zack a bottle while sharing with him her previous night's escapades on an African safari.

"The lions were just like you would imagine, only smellier," she said. Zack looked up from his bottle with earnest brown eyes taking in every word.

Annie quietly closed the door and made a mad dash to the outhouse with her alder stick to knock down the spider webs. She tapped on the door three times as was her custom to alert any spiders to seek refuge. Once inside, as she looked out the door she could see a man dressed in cowboy boots, blue denim wrangler pants and jacket, sitting up against the old cedar tree down at the end of the pasture and singing some kind of nonsensical song.

"The kooks are out today," she said to herself. When she was done, she quietly closed the outhouse door, then walked down the pasture toward the old tree. The hundred and fifty-foot tree had been there long before Annie's childhood. Only three craggy branches halfway up the trunk signaled that the tree was still alive. The top had been struck by lightning so often that a charred split spiraled down a good forty feet toward the base.

As Annie approached, the man stood up. She guessed he was at least eighty years old, but with Northwest Indians it was sometimes hard to tell. His face held kindly brown eyes and his skin was deeply lined and tanned as if he had spent his whole life on the sea. He took off his embroidered baseball cap that had White Bear Plumbing and a bear track on each side. His long gray hair fell to his shoulders.

Annie hoped he hadn't had cataract surgery; that he hadn't seen her sitting in the outhouse.

"Good morning, ma'am," he said, reaching out to shake Annie's hand. "Billy White Bear is my name. I grew up here in the area. You probably wonder what I'm doing here."

"Singing, I would guess," Annie offered.

"Actually chanting," Billy said, smiling. "You see, I'm looking for a special cedar tree to build a canoe to finish my vision quest. My power symbol is an albino black bear that I saw during my vision quest when I was fifteen. I had been living on clams and berries for two weeks when this white bear wandered down into the river to fish for spawning salmon, and that vision of power and resourcefulness has guided my entire life. I run a successful plumbing business in Seattle, but now my time is short and I need to find another white bear to lead me out of this life and into the next. I was paddling down Hood Canal in my canoe in a deep fog awhile back when I heard the tree singing to me."

"You mean that squeaking sound when the wind blows is singing?" Annie questioned.

"To my ears it is an ancient sound from long ago when my people lived here on the canal and summered on this very island. You know, when the mountains like Rainier, Baker and St. Helens send out seismic rumbles, my people say the mountains are sisters whispering to each other."

Annie laughed. "I guess when sister Mt. St. Helens roared a few years back, her sisters listened up!"

White Bear gave Annie an inquisitive look. "I feel like you know what I am talking about. You seem to know how sisters communicate."

"Do I ever," Annie laughed. "So, what makes you think this cedar tree would be any good for a canoe? It looks barely alive and it has that big split in the top. It must be two hundred years old, I would guess."

"A western red cedar, close to twelve hundred years," White Bear replied.

"How did you figure that out?" Annie said skeptically. "Did the tree tell you that?"

White Bear gave a sly grin. He pulled a long, rounded, stainless steel auger from behind the tree. "No," he said, showing the stick to Annie. "I took a core sample."

Annie laughed again. "You swing between mysticism and science, Mr. White Bear. Make up your mind."

"Call me Billy, please. Mysticism, science, religion—it's all the same. The reason I have come here to chant is so the tree can know my song, and I can come to know the heart of this great tree. If it is the tree that will carry me on my journey, I hope you can come up with a fair price so this tree can fulfill my journey."

Annie shook the man's hand. "I have to go finish feeding my babies," she said. "Let me know how it's going." By afternoon, White Bear was gone.

Meanwhile, Talisha and Alisha had trooped over to Mary Catherine's to see how the bran muffin experiment was working. Sister was working on another batch of bran muffins and invited the girls in to sit close to the stove.

"Remember, girls, always have a plan, a backup plan, and a plan C. The Lord helps those who have a plan. Look it up; it's in the Bible." She continued. "Last night, whoever is in that bunker came out and ate seven bran muffins and tonight we should get the results we are looking for. Just in case, we are putting out four more muffins just after dark."

As the girls munched on another bran muffin, Mary Catherine drummed on the side of a tea kettle with her wooden spatula to emphasize her words. "And then, then wham! bang! We have that sucker right on his knees, right where we want 'em."

It was in the early morning that Mary Catherine woke from a light sleep to hear a small scratching sound on her door and then a low moan. She lit a candle and slowly opened the door. On the porch was a small, jug-eared man dressed completely in a green and gray camouflage suit. The shoes were Marine Corps issue. Beneath a white-haired crewcut, there were black stripes under his eyes.

"Ya gotta help me," he gasped. "I think the Rooskies poisoned me." He grabbed his stomach and fell over to the ground. Mary Catherine's plan was coming to fruition. She handed the man a flashlight.

"Go get me four black rocks the size of golf balls, and I think I can help you," she said, and closed the door. Sister Mary Catherine stoked the fire in the stove and set out her harmonic tuning forks on the table.

Soon she heard scratching again and the man belly-crawled into the cabin. "Ya gotta help me, Sister," the man moaned. He handed her the four rocks. "Here ya go. Just help me live."

Sister Mary Catherine helped the man onto the bed. She opened the door and threw the four rocks out onto the beach. The man looked horrified. "I thought you needed those rocks," he panted with pain.

"Naw, I decided we don't need no stinking rocks. I'm going another way on this." The man gave a loud groan.

"What's your name, soldier?" Mary Catherine asked.

"Name, rank and serial number is all you're gonna get out of me." The man tried to look defiant between spasms of pain.

"I think we can do some work here," Mary Catherine said, unbuttoning the man's shirt. She peeled up his faded green issue T-shirt to reveal a stomach with a mass of scars and deeply trenched wounds that had healed long ago.

"Been in battle, I see," Mary Catherine observed.

"My lips are sealed," the man grimaced.

"When you get to feeling better, you come back and we'll talk."

"Doubt it," the man winced.

Mary Catherine took a chamois cloth and cleaned her largest tuning fork. "Ever hear of harmonic healing?" she asked, looking down at the exposed belly.

"Name, rank and serial number," the man repeated as he gritted his teeth.

"Have it your way, bucko." Mary Catherine shook her head and whacked the tuning fork on the wooden table. "Look out, sphincters, here she comes," she shouted.

She traced a serpentine track with the tuning forks on the man's belly till he grew quiet. She continued the therapy for several minutes more and then put the fork away in a red velvet case with the other forks, all graduated in different sizes, and rolled up the cloth until there were two strings exposed, which she expertly tied in a knot. She opened the door and sat down in a chair next to the fire, then leaned down and whispered into the man's ear. "In another minute, you're going to want to run out that door and take the biggest dump of your life. Remember, it wasn't the Ruskies, Greedy Gut; it was the bran muffins that got you all bound up."

The man looked stricken. He gave a low moan, hitched up his pants that had fallen around his ankles, and disappeared into the night. Moments later, there was a loud scream that startled even the seagulls sleeping on the farthest point of the spit where they had taken sanctuary from raccoons and other predators. Then the night was silent.

Several days later, South was regaling Annie for the third time with a blow-by-blow description of how she had been on the sound stage playing the harmonica for the famous public television cut featuring Roy Orbison, Bruce Springfield and Bonnie Raitt as the do-wop chick backup, when Annie heard the sound of bull horns out in the bay. She looked out and saw the triumphant *Ark*, laden with banners and people hanging onto the canopy. She carried the babies like sacks of groceries as their eyes opened wide on hearing the ruckus.

John leapt from the boat and dangled a plate-size best-of-show blue ribbon in front of Annie's nose just before doing a do-si-do in the gravel with Pickles. Christine followed, slinging a hefty black bag over her shoulder. "We brought back the old man's seed, Annie, and I can't wait till next year. Those two guys behind me are from *Playgirl*. They want to finish up their photo shoot featuring the pumpkin and dad, and a guy from *Porno Vegetable* magazine offered us forty thousand bucks for the pumpkin. We turned the bastard down. Dad is coming home with his dignity intact!" Christine grunted as she slogged up the beach toward her sometimes cabin.

Max was the last to leave the boat. "Did the orca guy show up yet, Annie?" she wondered. "I hoped he would have been here by now. We saw Starbuck come up to the boat again. The little guy is looking really lonely. I wish his pod would come back for him."

"Starbuck?" Sister looked perplexed.

"Starbuck, yeah, that's what I named him," Max called back as she trudged after Christine.

Ziggy came out of his cabin and put on his sunglasses. "Did anyone hear a god-awful screech a couple nights ago? It sounded like a cougar in heat!"

Mary Catherine had heard nothing further from the soldier so she went down to the beach and finally found the evidence she was looking for on the sand spit past the rounded bunker. The deposit reminded her of the years she had worked with the Sisters of Charity in a Calcutta orphanage, and the elephant droppings sometimes left behind after a wedding when the newlyweds rode the beast to the bridal suite.

Back at her cabin, she took a long drag on her Camel straight and snapped the still-smoldering butt onto the sand with her index finger. She tied a blindfold over her eyes, put a sword on a pile of driftwood, and did an elaborate ritualistic *kota* dance in the sand, leaving only the smallest trace of her passing in the sand. Then, she took up her sword with a flourish and knelt on the ground facing away from the melon. She prayed, then jumped up from her knees and spun, facing the melon in a single movement. As she advanced in a low crouch, she probed with the sword and, sensing when she was within striking distance, she stopped and rapidly twirled four times, each revolution punctuated with a loud "*hai*," and left four cuts in the melon.

After making a series of elaborate movements in the air with the sword, she knelt once more, facing away from the watermelon. She then placed the sword on the ground, turned, walked blindfolded toward the melon, and gave the stick platform a rapid sidekick—splintering the wood. The melon fell in clean slices as if they were cut on an infomercial by a slice-and-dice machine for only four easy payments of $9.95—which, of course, included the four ginseng knives and a Mayan pocket calendar to 2012 when the world would end.

Removing her blindfold, Sister Mary Catherine placed the sword against a driftwood log, picked up the still-lit cigarette, and took a long, contemplative drag—gazing across the water to the glaciers that crept down the slopes of Mount Rainier.

This entire performance had been noted from a small hole in the half-dome, but not by Max, who was being smitten with the twins she had commandeered from Annie back at the farmhouse. "You wouldn't know these two were related," Max remarked. "Zack gurgles and smiles so easily and he has a great belly laugh if you do trumpet lips on his stomach. But Little Annie plays it close to the vest. She withholds her smiles until she is sure of your intentions."

Little Annie rolled over and looked intently into Max's eyes. She gave a half-grin just to test Max who then leaned over and tried trumpet lips on Little Annie too, whereupon Annie gave Max a violated look of disapproval. Her brother, reacting to the sound alone, started to laugh until he began to hiccup.

"I think they might be developmentally delayed, but they'll come around," Annie announced to no one in particular. "They were preemies. They all catch up eventually and Lord knows we're not in any rush around here."

"Amen to that," agreed Max, pouring a mug of coffee from the pot on the stove and rummaging for any extra strudel that might have been left in the pan. All she found was an apple dribble skid mark, which she swiped up with her finger and sucked noisily to make up for the lack of bulk.

"Anyone up for a trip into Port Gamble for groceries and checking the mail?" Christine announced. "I could use some chocolate and some Fuzzy Navel wine coolers."

"I'm in," Max volunteered as she pulled Zack's T-shirt down over his ample belly and jumped up from her knees. "Let's go. Have we got time to drop in a few crab traps? We can get some bait from the store."

"Let's roll it out, girlfriend," Christine said, gathering up her hoodie. Annie watched the two city girls meander down the path to the boat and shook her head. She held her coffee cup to her chin and let the steam fog her glasses as she ruminated, *a few months ago those two city slickers didn't know a bow from a stern and were more worried about their nails than anything else, and now they are on their way to becoming as self-sufficient as the island itself.* "Those two won't last another year on their own," Annie continued prophesying out loud. "You know there are going to be men flocking all around those two goony birds."

"What'd ya say?" South mumbled. She was just settling in for a nap in the captain's chair that looked out onto the spit. "Did you say George Clooney?"

But Annie had gone out to get firewood.

Chapter SEVEN

It had been a slow morning at the general store. Wiggins, the confirmed bachelor, slightly lecherous, always hungry for attention and always dressed in blue jeans, deck shoes, a gray sweatshirt with the tag hanging out, topped off with a Seahawks stocking cap day in and day out, greeted the two women by removing his cap and, in a sweeping gesture, ogled Max and Christine.

"Morning, ladies. How are things on the island? I saw the article about Moby's pumpkin winning big down in Portland. I heard the seeds were going for ten bucks apiece. Is that right? The island has some mail when you're ready," he jabbered.

Christine and Max rustled around the store with baskets, gathering coffee, spaghetti makings, and were consulting over the chocolate selection when the store doorbell tinkled and a scruffy man came in. He was wearing a green and brown houndstooth jacket with leather elbows and a fedora. He shuffled up to the counter and set a small Styrofoam chest protectively between himself and Wiggins. Leaning over, he conversed in low tones when the store owner called out, "Girls, there is someone here asking directions to the island."

Max and Christine rolled their eyes and quickly decided on Cadbury bars with fruit and brought their basket to the counter. The man turned slowly around and offered his right hand while he cradled the white Styrofoam box with his left.

"Excuse me, but I'm Professor Nickolas V. Spudich from Idaho State. Just call me Professor Spud, or just Spud if you prefer," the man said, shrugging his shoulders.

From the misshapen wrinkled forehead to the sleepy blue hooded eyes, half-hidden behind wire-rimmed glasses perched on the end of his nose, the aptly named Professor Spud looked like a cross between a kindly distracted Einstein and a jowly Mr. Potato Head who knew his way to the tanning booth.

"I believe I'm expected. I've come a long distance and I hear I might be able to catch a ride out to the island with you."

"No problemo," Max said, plunking the basket on the counter and shaking the man's hand. "You said we had some mail, Wig?"

As the group began to leave the store, Wiggins called out, "Tell Annie I have a package from Seattle the Fed Ex guy dropped off. She has to pick it up herself, the ticket says."

"Okay," Christine answered as the store door slammed shut. She grabbed the professor's satchel as Max guided the plodding man down the boat ramp. "Be careful, professor," Christine warned. "You seem to have a metronomic cadence to your walk."

"Call me Spud," the man responded wearily. "It's by design, dear, a rhythm of the universe and to confuse the satellite tracking devices honed in on me."

"Okay with me, Spud." Max grimaced toward Christine and looked quizzically at Spud, but he gave no further explanation. The girls brought the boat into the island dock and Spud, still clinging to his Styrofoam ice chest while rifling through his suit-case, insisted on walking up to Annie's house by himself to make his own introduction.

"Okay," Max agreed. "Can I at least take your box up to the house for you?"

"Oh no, not the box. It's full of important, unauthorized specimens I need to personally take care of," Spud said guardedly.

Annie had read the mail from the week before and the introduction letter from Carol Ann, her sister's childhood friend and the head of the hospice group in Seattle that had first sent Moby Dick, the carpenter, to fix up the island's shacks for their patients. *Good ol' Carol Ann, she's still hanging in there*, Annie thought to herself. The letter read...

> *Annie, I am sending Professor Spud to you. He has an inoperable brain aneurysm that can let loose any time. He is a famous anthropologist and physicist and has spent many years in a Washington, D.C. think tank. He is very kind, absent-minded, and a conspiracy theory nut. Of course, I thought of you and your island immediately. If you need anything out there, let me know. I enjoy that Wenatchee apple jack whiskey you endorse— maybe a little more than I should. Hell, a lot more than I should. Shit, I could be dead by the time you get this. Pass me the bottle, Rochester. Apple Jack rocks.*
> *Carol Ann*

Spud had finally pulled himself onto the porch and leaned in the doorway. "Whew!" Spud pulled off his fedora and wiped his brow with the back of his hand. He mustered a cheery first class of the semester Anthro 101 smile for Annie. "Annie Perkins, I presume," Professor Spud chirped. "I have need of a respite and was told I could stay here on your island for a small donation I made to Carol Ann. Do I have the facts correct?" He bowed.

"We've been expecting you," Annie replied. She invited him in for coffee and some apple strudel she had hidden away in the pantry away from Max. Spud had a generous piece of strudel washed down with two cups of coffee.

"Thank you for your kindness. I am able to care for myself. I've brought some bedding and a small amount of food and I expect I shall learn to cope. I am privy to national, international, and inter-galactic secrets that must not fall into the wrong hands, and I must move at a specified gait so as to be undetectable by satellite. Because of that, I'm as slow as a three-toed sloth I'm afraid."

Annie directed him to the second shack and watched as Spud made his measured way down the path. That evening a potluck broke out when Christine and Max scored eight Dungeness crabs in their crab pots on the slack tide pull and White Bear brought an offering of twenty pounds of iced Chinook fillets caught by the Swinomish tribal nets that morning.

It turned out to be a reunion, as John, the restaurant reviewer from the *Seattle Times*, was back and Al, a.k.a. "Owl," had also returned to the island from using his thirty years of sanitation service to Bremerton and his photographic memory to catalog most of Bremerton's unmapped sewer system. The department presented him with a plaque engraved with the company's motto (which, incidentally, was also embroidered inside their official hats), "shit happens." Owl had pitched his plaque in a dumpster but put a headlock on his other parting gift—a com-memorative case of Wild Turkey Whiskey—and then headed back to the island to continue detailing his casket which had been under construction for the better part of a year.

As the sun set and the shadows grew long on the spit, White Bear skewered the fillets onto a willow branch snowshoe and plunged the skewer into the gravel facing the fire until the salmon nectar drizzled down the skewer and made sizzling sounds as the juices hit the coals. Christine and Max had wrestled a ten-gallon pot of saltwater on the other side of the fire to steam the crabs, and underneath the pit there were five gallons of littleneck clams, smoldering in seaweed, that were slowly being steamed to perfection.

John and Owl had put together a kettle of beans and fixin's. Baked beans, pineapple, sautéed onions, bacon, chili peppers and Ziggy's secret ingredient. A rickety, sway-backed, weather-beaten picnic table strained under the weight of the feast as the steaming clams, cracked crab, and salmon slabs were laid on fern leaves, and the steaming pot of baked beans held court on the end. The patrons sucked and slurped until the Northwest juices ran down their chins and dampened their clothes. There would be no cholesterol checks or caloric counts this day. "This is a feast to die for," Ziggy proclaimed.

As the fire died down, the oldest islanders refused to leave. They would not give into the night. As Annie trudged up the hill to spell Max with the twins, she heard Spud begin a soliloquy. *Oswald as the lone shooter just doesn't hold water...*

Back in her cabin, Mary Catherine had taken off her habit to air out the smoke. It was the crab juice and drawn butter that concerned her. *The Lord will provide,* she decided. *That and a little Spray 'N Wash.* She had no sooner popped into bed when she heard a familiar scratching on her door.

"Come on in," she cackled. "Don't break down the door."

The camouflaged man had come back. He took off his cap. "I want to thank you for the cure," he began. Then, apologetically, "I guess I should have tried to make contact sooner."

Sister could see the man was seventy plus but fit and trim, with transparent root beer-brown eyes that you could see behind and know that the wheels would always be turning. He moved with an easy grace, flipped the chair backwards, and sat hunched over the chair back, his head resting on his hands while he surveyed Sister.

"The name is Joseph O'Riley, but you can use my Special Forces code name—Spider."

"I'm Sister Mary Catherine of the Jesuit order and I will call you Joe," she said decidedly. I will not call a man of your age Spider. It's just not dignified."

"Joe it is then, Sister," the man smiled, showing perfect teeth.

"What brings you to the island, Joe?" she asked.

"I'm expecting special orders so I set up a forward command here on the island," Joe said reluctantly.

"Special orders from...?" Sister asked.

"I receive my orders in code over the radio. I've got to get back now."

"Wait a minute," Sister shouted as Joe tried to exit. "How come we don't see you during the day?"

"I've become kind of nocturnal over the years. I do my best work at night and my retinas just can't handle daylight anymore. Gotta go, see ya."

And he was gone.

Chapter EIGHT

Later in the week, Max coasted *The Ark* next to the dock on the island and before she could snub the lines, Lila, the perpetually flamboyant pet psychic from Chimacum, who had bummed a ride from the mainland, literally bounced off the boat and pranced down the dock. With blue and red Hermes scarves tied to her wrists, she flapped her arms as if she were a goony bird taking flight.

As she reached the end of the dock, she cupped her hands around the waiting muzzle of her old client, Trooper. "How are you doing, young fellow?" she cooed, as she bent down and went nose to nose.

"Ah, you are still getting over the death of your master, Moby. Well, it is the circle of life you know. And now I hear you have a new family. That's wonderful. What about that other problem? You know, the D word. Hmm-m, I still think you need more fiber. I'll talk to Annie."

Trooper thumped his hound dog tail on the dock in appreciation.

"Annie," Lila called, "I hear I have a new client."

Annie, Owl, and John came onto the dock and turned Lila in the other direction where she flapped her way back onto the boat and looked out into the whitecaps in the strait, where Starbuck appeared from nowhere. He nuzzled the bow and then popped his head up above the side of the boat as if he were counting noses. Max stroked his dorsal fin.

Lila smiled and said, "I need to get the vitals." As she reached out and put her hand on top of Starbuck's head, her head jerked convulsively three times and she was knocked backwards into the tiller. She sat up.

"Wow, you forget how powerful they are at the top of the food chain. I've been spending too much time with those wimpy meerkats. All right." She regained her position and felt the air from Starbuck's blowhole.

"I think we have a reading. He's a male all right. He got lost from the pod after he got into a tiff with one of his overbearing aunts and now he's worried that his mother is heartbroken. His cousin Springer, who was lost once, told him that sometimes he was fed herring filled with Flintstone vitamins and his family hates the Flintstones—apparently some prehistoric bad blood tens of thousands of years ago."

"You gotta be kidding me," Annie scoffed.

Lila shrugged. "I can only tell you what he tells me. And he worries that he might be gay. He shouldn't worry about that. He just has typical adolescent questions. No big deal. Some of my best friends are gay orcas," Lila confessed to Starbuck as he sank back under the waves and disappeared.

Nearing the dock, White Bear walked towards them. He carried a cooler filled with razor clams from the Makah tribe that lived on the Pacific Ocean.

"Won them at the casino," he boasted and suggested a potlatch to honor the great cedar tree. "When I came by canoe early this morning I could hear the tree singing in the winds and a Raven was sitting on the top branch. It was a sign that this was the tree destined to be my canoe for the vision quest."

Max and Christine's good luck continued as they pulled the crab traps they had set out that morning and found twelve Dungeness crabs that now scurried for safety under *The Ark* seats at the bottom of the boat. The women squealed and laughed as the defiant claws sometimes nipped at their ankles on the trip into shore. John and Owl dug steamer clams while White Bear built a large fire of driftwood logs.

Spud and Ziggy had formed a conspiracy theory alliance and were happy to bond by digging out a pit and carefully building a nest of seaweed for the clams and scooping coals over the seaweed, then placing a large kettle of salt water at the end to boil the crab.

South and Sister Mary left to put together a kelp and three-cheese macaroni casserole garnished with sea beans.

"My mother always said, 'When the tide goes out, the table is set,'" Annie called out to no one in particular. She labored up to the house to build the biscuits she had promised as the drumming of crab claws grew fainter against the metal pot full of boiling water over the fire.

After the feasting, when the embers began to glow and the evening sun was beginning to set, there was time for one more theatrical event.

The tugboat *Pissant* steamed into the cove. This was the flagship of the infamous Pinky, the pink urinal block king and self-obsessed amateur opera singer. His dutiful wife, Dorie, often accompanied his efforts on the giant pipe organ that had been laboriously crafted inside the hull of the boat. Dorie was at the helm and keyboard as Pinky, dressed in a Don Quixote outfit resplendent with an ostrich-plumed brimmed hat and sword, stood perched on the bowsprit. As they got closer, Pinky cut loose with his rendition of "The Impossible Dream." Trilling and with grand gesture, Pinky reluctantly came to the end of the song and—after promising Dorie he wouldn't—grabbed a rope that was tied to the top of the boat's reinforced radar mast, took a running start down the tug's deck, and launched himself over the rail. For the second straight year, the rope was too short, and he landed waist-deep, forty feet short of the shore.

Pinky shrugged and the bedraggled, yet still exuberant, famed windmill slayer waded ashore to much acclimation. Meanwhile, his long-suffering wife lowered the dingy with a fresh set of dry clothes and came ashore.

Annie gave Dorie a hug and Pinky a towel and invited them to the picnic table that perpetually strained under the weight of the feast: steamer clams with drawn butter, two-and-a-half inch-thick chinook salmon slabs three feet long, fried razor clams, the three-cheese macaroni casserole, and Annie's biscuits. The presentation wouldn't have made the cut at *Sunset magazine*, but no one noticed. They heaped their paper plates and sat cross-legged by the fire as night closed in and the fog began to roll in from the south.

As a delectable final act of the meal, John had made pans of Seven Sisters Floating Island, a triple chocolate confection topped with whipped cream he had kept on ice. Properly chocolate-d and coffee-d up, the party lasted long into the night, and there were the inevitable lies and tall tales.

South gave a detailed account of her latest dream where she was in Hollywood for the Academy Awards. She had walked the red carpet on the arm of a long-haired, blond—I can't believe it's not butter—hunky escort and, though she didn't win—again—South just knew she was the object of juicy gossip in Tinsel Town.

"It's going to be hard to top that," Lila conceded. "But I have a Hollywood story of my own. One of my clients is Rick the rhino, a classic square-lipped rhino with a five-foot horn, who lives up on the Olympic Game Farm that caters to retired Hollywood animals. Well, Rick is a puffy sort of fellow who likes to embellish, but he starred in the John Wayne movie *Hatari* and a Dr. Doolittle movie and has always been a little bitter about how his career ended. They said he 'just didn't have the right look anymore.' Rick tried cosmetic surgery and playing against type by changing his look to a hippo, who seem to always find work in African movies, but nothing worked. Like Norma Desmond, he began spending more time cloistered in his cage and refused to come out till his agent cornered a part in *Out of Africa* with Redford and Streep and he was on Cloud Nine.

"He began working out and lost a fair amount of weight, and there was a spring to his step. Suddenly that deal tanked and Rick was devastated. The residuals petered out, and the long-promised star on the sidewalk in front of Graumann's Chinese Theatre just never happened.

"Anyway, to make a long story longer," Lila continued, "Rick had been sleeping in his pen one night and when he woke up, he found he had been tied up to the fence and some guy in a ski mask had taken a chainsaw and snipped off his five-foot-long horn. Rick says he was scared 'shitless' and that he heard what sounded like Russian. He says that because he was cast in *Dr. Zhivago*, but I think he confused that with the *Dr. Doolittle* vehicle. Anyway, Rick is okay but he refuses to come out of his shelter and spends the entire day watching 'This Old House' and the Nature channel. Rhino horn is supposed to be an aphrodisiac to the Chinese and a horn that size would be worth a bundle, even though it's just made of twisted hair.

"I heard from two sources—a guinea hen that had a bad cough and a cow that had a bad case of mastitis—both up past Port Angeles, that they had it on good authority that the Russian mafia had a hideout in the middle of a cow pasture up near Forks. Rick won't let me go to the police because he is too embarrassed. I was thinking with the brain trust down here maybe we can think of a way to get the horn back and glue it back on."

"Absolutely," John said. "We need to come up with a plan. Let's plan a meeting for tomorrow morning and brainstorm."

Lila was pleased. "Thank you. I hope we can do something. A depressed rhino is not a pretty sight."

White Bear got up and looked around the campfire. In the flickering firelight, as the shadows played across the fine lines of his face, he looked every bit his ninety-plus years.

"On the morning tide, I came to the great cedar at the end of the pasture and saw the Raven sitting on the cedar tree branch. It was a sign that this was the chosen tree to be made into a canoe," he said.

"The Raven is a powerful symbol in native Pacific Northwest First Nations culture. It was the Raven who fooled the gods and stole the sun that had been kept captive in a box and brought it to our people. If I can work a deal with Annie, I will drop the tree into the water at high tide and float it over to Blake Island where the master canoe carver lives. Then I will hopefully find enough paddlers to help search for the white bear of my youth."

"I think we can make a deal," Annie piped up.

It was then that Spud tapped on the top of his Styrofoam box for attention. "Is anyone interested in discussing the moon landing hoax?"

With the exception of Owl, who didn't hear very well, and John, who was busy flossing the salmon between his teeth, everyone else called it a night.

Spud began, "The entire moon landing was filmed on a Hollywood set…."

🔥

Sister Mary Catherine had half-expected to hear a scratching on her door again sometime in the night and when she didn't, she fell asleep. When she awoke the next morning, she sat up in bed. With a start she noticed a large, hairy-textured rhino horn leaning against her dining table, the jagged end propped up against her door.

She stepped over the horn, got dressed, and wandered down the spit looking for coffee. She found it at John's who was sitting around the campfire.

Wise to the power of caffeine, after she had finished two cups of coffee and a cigarette, Sister gave a barely cheery grunt John's way and stared into the fire.

"That fellow Spud has an interesting take on a lot of things," John began.

Sister held up her hand. "I have the rhino horn in my cabin," she stated.

"What? How?" John sputtered.

"Don't ask me." Sister shook her head. "Can you get the thing and bring it down here so Lila can identify it? I don't imagine there are many rhino horns floating around, but just to be sure."

When Lila showed up at the campfire she was flabbergasted. She looked at the horn and the smooth, angled cut where the chainsaw had severed Rick's manhood. She clasped her hands, gave a piercing squeal, and did a Boot Scooting Boogie jig on the sandy beach. "This is so cool, this is so cool," she kept saying.

Max and South saw the coffee klatch from the window and joined in the revelry.

"I just wish whoever did this would light a fire under that guy from whale watch," Max complained loudly.

Sister Mary Catherine tugged on Max's sleeve. "Don't say that stuff too loud, dear. You never know who's listening."

Later that day, the entire island group loaded the horn into the dump truck and took a road trip up to Sequim. Hearing a rumbling, Rick left an episode of "House Hunters International" to look outside. When he saw the horn, he gave a snort of delight and jumped up in the air almost at least two inches. "Serious hang time for a rhino," Lila would claim later. She said there was no record of a rhino actually clearing air, so it was a big deal and she brought it up at the national pet psychic convention, as well as writing a report in the *Spring Pet Psychic Quarterly.*

Lila took some instant bonding epoxy glue she had flown in from Boeing engineering and repositioned the horn perfectly. Restricted from moving for half an hour of set time, afterwards Rick immediately shook his head and gave what looked like a big rhino grin. He almost skewered Lila as he began jousting with the horn. He moved the tip of his horn to delicately press the OFF button on the TV just as Norm was explaining the proper procedure for "Tiling a Shower Wall."

Rick danced out into the sunshine and celebrated by promptly burying the rejuvenated horn into the grill of a Ford F-150 truck, which was touring the farm where the animals were free ranging and the people were relegated to cars. Rick lifted up the front end and slammed it down as the radiator hissed steam; then he stood back and looked at his handiwork.

"I think he's pleased," said Lila.

Several days had passed when Trish l'Dish was body slammed by a second diagnosis. Her doctor had determined she also had ALS, which is extremely rare in women, her doctor cheerfully explained.

"Like that's some friggin' consolation," Trish fumed. "I wondered why I couldn't lift my arms any higher than my waist and my voice is shot, but I thought it was just fallout from the chemo. My girls are going to be devastated. First my boobs fail me and now," she tearfully confided to Max.

Max gave a scream of anguish and began to cry on Trish's shoulder in great sobs.

"Go ahead and cry. You have the luxury of not having to leave behind two girls," Trish said quietly. She closed her eyes as she stroked Max's blonde hair.

"But I'm not gone yet." She patted Max sympathetically on the back. "I have to stay strong for my girls."

"The girls!" Max wailed even as she wiped her face with her hands. "What's going to happen to the girls?" she blubbered.

"Well, they are not going to my mother or my sister either," Trish vowed. "Or to that son-of-a-bitch ex-husband. I'll think of something. I've got to think of something for the sake of my girls."

Later on, Max went to see Owl, who had made several caskets and was even now outfitting his with a sneaky concealed electric motor so he could be more competitive in the casket races. He had lost three in a row to Sister Mary Catherine. "She's been wiping my butt lately," he sniped. "Please excuse my French."

Max explained Trish's situation and asked if Owl could build a coffin with a leopard print inside and out. "It has to be a secret and I don't want to stifle your creativity; I want to make that clear up front," she sobbed as she put a strangle hug on Owl's neck. "What's going to happen to those little girls?"

Chapter NINE

Ziggy smoked the last of his morning joint, and contemplated starting to work on building a rock wall around the cemetery. He had broached the idea to his wife, suggesting that he could incorporate the hundred of urns full of ashes that she had collected over the years.

"I'll have none of that," she threatened, shaking the rubber spatula in his face.

Ziggy was still pouting while leaning against a tombstone in the orchard when he heard a motorboat approaching. He looked up to see a Zodiac with the words WHALE WATCH stenciled on the side. It skittered like a water bug onto the beach.

Still in a funk, Ziggy tried to ignore the intruder until the man bounded up the beach toward him with hand outstretched.

"John," the man said. "John Colby's my name. Call me Colby—like the cheese. I'm looking for a guy called Max who called in about an orphaned orca. Is this the right island?"

Ziggy pointed to Annie's. Colby followed the trail to the house, bounded onto the porch, and knocked on the door. "It must be company," Annie sang out from the back room where she was busy with the twins. "Nobody else bothers to knock."

Max opened the door, her eyes still red from the injustice of the morning. She gave a surly retort. "What!"

John was unfazed. "Colby. John Colby. I'm from whale watch. Just call me Colby—like the cheese."

"Oh." Max brightened as she wiped her face with the hem of her apron. "Come in," she mumbled, and went to the sink to splash water on her face. "Sorry, I had a bit of bad news," she explained. *Well, maybe we can save* one *orphan around here,* she thought to herself.

"I've come about the whale." John looked around the room. "I'm looking for a guy called Max."

"I'm Max, short for Maxine," she said, going to the stove. "Coffee?"

"Sure, sounds good." John took the opportunity to check out Max. *Nice body, but she's got Attitude,* he thought. He precisely ladled in three spoons of sugar, poured in a slurp of condensed milk, and concentrated on his stirring.

Max took her coffee black, which allowed her time to look over her cup and appraise John. *About my age, maybe thirty-five or forty, a little shorter than I like, impish green eyes and a shock of reddish-brown hair under that ball cap; strong, freckled forearms. Looks like he cut his hair with a machete, and do I smell fish?*

"Anyway, just call me Colby, like I said," John said absentmindedly as he flipped through his notebook.

"Okay, what do you know about this orca? I'm surprised we haven't had a sighting before this; usually the TV folks are all over orcas down here. The strangest thing though, I was on my way from Whidbey when a Whidbey Island helicopter with pontoons landed and said getting here was a matter of national security. I don't get it. Who does that?" He shrugged.

"That happens around here lately," Max said, and told him that the lone orca had been orphaned about a month or so. And then she told him what Lila had said. When she finished, John looked up from his page. "All right, we have a male orca who is homesick, hungry, angry at his aunt, doesn't like Fred Flintstone, and might be gay. Is that all the scientific data you have right now?" John looked smugly down at his page trying not to laugh.

"What kind of feelings do you think he might have for Barney?" John smirked as he looked up at Max.

"Are you going to help us or not?" Max challenged. "If you're not here to help, then just…"

"No, no, no, absolutely I am here to help," John said seriously, trying hard to avoid more sarcasm.

"The orca's name is Starbuck after the character in *Moby Dick*," Max said emphatically, her hands on her hips.

"Read you loud and clear." John looked amused. He followed Max down to *The Ark* because he said it would be better to approach Starbuck in a familiar craft. Trooper limped down looking for a ride. Max watched as John gently placed the heavy hound onto the bow seat. Max gunned the engine and Starbuck was right where Max thought he would be on the far side of the island. John took pictures as the orca rubbed against the boat and did a little spy hop to see who was with Max. He rubbed noses with Trooper and then swam out a little distance.

"Can you get him closer to the boat?" John asked

"Sure." Max stretched her hand out and the orca presented the top of his head. John took more pictures and then as Starbuck came parallel to the boat for another nose rub, he took a blood sample and a scraping.

"These are still wild animals," John said, shaking his head. "They can be dangerous."

"Just call me the Orca Whisperer then," Max retorted.

On the way back, John's ball cap flew back by the stern. Max took it and put it on her head even as John gestured with praying hands she would give it back. John gently lifted Trooper out of *The Ark* and onto the dock. The hound gave a doggy sneeze of mingled disgust and gratitude and then moseyed up the trail.

"We can debrief here on the beach," John suggested.

"I had you as a boxer man," Max replied, readjusting his cap.

"Ha, Ha," John said, starting back up to the house.

Sitting at the table, John started going over his notes. "This is what we know—scientifically. Officially he is 167 from J pod… Age: approx. 3 years…Approximate weight: 1000 to 1500 kilos… Mother: unknown…possibly Princess Angeline."

John looked up from his notebook. "This little fellow dropped out of sight three years ago. We thought he died. We have a picture of the patch near the dorsal fin which is his fingerprint, but he didn't get a name because they first have to live through the first winter. We don't know where he has been all this time."

Annie poured coffee into their old mugs and brought over dishes of apple cobbler. Between spoonfuls of cobbler, John, without any prompting, bolted into his life story. He'd picked up a Masters in biology and then a PhD in Oceanography and was working for peanuts for a nonprofit that scraped by on grants and donations. He worked insane hours trying to save a species that appeared doomed by pollution and civilization. He'd been on several sorties with the rogue ship *Sea Wolf* that continued to put itself between the Japanese whalers and the whale pods in the high seas off the coast of New Zealand. He was a wanted man in Japan for scuba diving into the port and, using a cutting torch, disabling the propeller of the largest processing whaler in the world. He was Don Quixote in a scuba suit.

Colby and Max strolled down to his Zodiac. He promised to come back in a few days with more information.

As she watched him speed away into the channel, Max realized she still had his hat. "No guts, no glory," she yelled out at him, pointing at the hat. John smiled and shrugged.

White Bear came into the cove late that evening. He had helped Pinky fix his toilet on the tugboat. A connection had come loose from a rubberized fitting, probably due to the boat's vibration, Pinky figured.

Repair work done, White Bear headed up to Annie's where he explained that he had come back ready to get a contract in place for the tree.

Annie gave him a quick *tut, tut,* offered him a cup of coffee, and proceeded to put together a dinner of pork chops, Yukon gold whipped potatoes, gravy, biscuits, and leftover apple cobbler. "My standard negotiation package," Annie chirped as they ate.

By the time White Bear was ready to negotiate, he was stuffed like a melon and could barely talk. In the end, Annie settled for two solar-powered, self-composting, state-of-the-art outhouses to replace the old ones, and two solar-powered tiled showers with wood boiler assist. The island would jump a full century in the plumbing department.

Colby was back near the end of the week with his Zodiac. Bareheaded, he landed on the beach and began searching for Max. He knocked at Ziggy's door where Matty was busy polishing the brass urns and sorting the others alphabetically, she explained.

John then stopped at John Hunt's and saw the giant marlin that dominated the tiny cabin. Then he made a stop at Owl's, where the sewer guru was trying to duplicate a leopard print on a casket.

This seemed odd to John, but he kept going, wanting to befriend the island folk, not make waves.

He made a near-fatal decision and was stuck at South's for over an hour when she began prattling to him about an Indian wedding she had attended, complete with elephants and Bollywood dancing, which she proceeded to demonstrate.

Spud answered the door holding his Styrofoam box and got into a discussion of Bigfoot versus Yeti evidence.

At Trish l'Dish's, she came to the door dressed in leopard, and at Sister Mary Catherine's, where she had just awakened from a nap, he was told to go away and she blew smoke in his face.

He was just about to flee when Max came up on the other side of the island in *The Ark*, after checking up on Starbuck. John waited to help dock the boat and gave a sigh of relief. *Finally, someone kind of normal,* he thought to himself.

"Here's your hat," Max said, sending it Frisbee-style over the open water. John caught it just as it was about to dive into the water. "NGNG."

"What does NGNG mean?" John asked as he snubbed the mooring line.

"Think about it." Max gave a wry smile. John readjusted the size of the hat as he talked. "Starbuck has lost a little weight and I've brought some herring over to feed him. I did some research. Herring and salmon are his preferred menu. Some of the pods specialize in seals. It is going to take a while before you can hand feed him. Orcas are fussy.

"His blood sample came back that he is basically healthy and has no overriding infections," John continued, "but here's the problem. Can you sit down a minute? He is slowly starving and, according to Washington State Fish and Wildlife and the feds, it's illegal to feed orcas or interfere in their habitat or well-being. They want nature to take its course, no matter what happens.

"As a scientist, that is also my official view, but as a conservationist I want to do everything I can to save every individual of the Puget Sound pods. There are about eighty-six members that navigate these waters and right now the number is dwindling. The only way to save this little fella is to supplement his nutrition, pump some vitamin and minerals into him, and feed him at night. The Native tribes, the State Fish and Wildlife, and the federal authorities are all going to be watching to make sure no one helps Starbuck. And forget trying to get him back to his pod; they'll just have to come back and pick him up on their way through."

Max looked stricken. "It's illegal? A federal offense? So how can he be saved?"

"I can provide the food and you are going to have to go out at night and feed him. They might have infrared cameras on him, but I doubt it. They don't have the funds," John confided.

"We have to feed him. I don't have a choice. I've bonded with Starbuck," Max said, crossing her first two fingers together in solidarity.

"I have the fish in a bucket. Let's try and feed him." John grabbed a white five-gallon bucket full of half-alive herring.

Max lured Starbuck inside the cove where the channel traffic couldn't see and John attempted to feed the orca. He slapped the fish on the side of the boat. He swished the fish in the water. He turned a half dozen cripples loose that could barely swim, but Starbuck ignored John's overtures. He preferred to play the clown this evening, rubbing on the side of The Ark, bobbing up and down, and occasionally jumping into the air and trying to splash the boat. Exasperated, John turned to Max. "I told you it would take time. Wanna try?"

Max slipped on blue vinyl gloves that reached her elbow and grabbed a fish by the tail. She spoke sternly to Starbuck. "You get over here right now, young man, or I will…I'll tell your mother."

Starbuck abruptly stopped clowning and swam over to the boat and poked his head out of the water. When Max offered him the fish, he took it delicately as if trained. He took four more fish and then the one that held the vitamins.

"No Pebbles, no Bam Bam, no Fred, Barney, Wilma or Betty," John confirmed, rolling his eyes.

Max looked down the gullet of the herring. "No little cave man vitamins in there?" She looked skeptical.

"Well," she said smugly, "it's not so hard to feed an orca after all. I just feed him the way I've seen them feed orcas at Marineland in Florida."

The two conspirators went into shore where John had pulled a two-place kayak onto the beach. "I'd like to get you acclimated to a kayak," he said. "It may be the only safe way not to be detected. Let me show you how to get into a kayak, but first put on a life preserver."

John showed her how to keep a low center of gravity as she slid into the cockpit, how to adjust the spray skirt to keep the water out, and how to paddle. "I'm going to have to teach you how to recover if the kayak tips over, but that we'll learn in a warm pool. It's going to take some time," he cautioned, as he eased himself into the back seat.

They paddled out to Starbuck and Max gave him a few more fish. The orca then cavorted close to the kayak, just barely brushing the mahogany sides. "It's almost like I'm swimming with him!" Max was excited. "But it's a little spooky, too."

"Don't worry," John advised. "He is a machine built for the water. He has perfect body control. If he wanted to tip us over, we'd be swimming by now." Starbuck bobbed up and looked Max square in the eye and they both knew there was a long struggle ahead.

Back on shore, John was about to shove off in his Zodiac when Annie came out on the porch and invited him in for dinner. She quietly and optimistically hummed "Matchmaker, matchmaker, make me a match" from *Fiddler on the Roof* as she shuffled around the kitchen clanging pots and pans and using a cup to dish out stew that had been slow cooking for three days.

She brought the steaming earthen bowls filled with onions, carrots, mushrooms, turnips, tri-tip beef, and lots of gravy. Gravy to dunk the fresh dill bread she had taken out of the oven that afternoon.

Meanwhile, Zack and Annie were on a blanket on the living room rug trying competitively to get up on their knees with encouragement from Ziggy and Sister Mary Catherine, who had just finished eating.

Zack did a face plant and began to cry. John scooped him up before anyone could move. Zack had never taken well to strangers. He took one look at John and howled. But not to be denied, John hung in strong and whooshed the baby into the air. In the end, Zack had a new best friend, but it took a good five minutes. Towards the end, John was singing Zack a lullaby and Zack closed his eyes as John carefully put him on the blanket, but then Zack began howling again.

"Looks like I have a dinner date," John said, sitting down at the table, and sliding the stew bowl away from Zack's reach as he bounced the twin on his knee.

"Do you want me to reheat your stew?" Annie offered.

"Naw, it was probably too hot anyway." John dipped a spoon into the bowl and tasted the stew. "Hmm-m, just right," he said, giving Zack a small piece of bread to gum.

"Looks like you know your way around babies, young man." Annie sat down at the table.

"I grew up with four younger brothers. One of my brothers didn't talk till he was two because I anticipated his every need, and the other three didn't walk till they were a year and a half. I was too busy packing 'em around. Babies are the ultimate chick magnets."

"So, you don't have any kids now?" she pried.

"Nope." John filled his mouth.

"Wife?"

"Double nope."

Max kept her eyes on her bowl of stew. When Zack started to drool, Annie promptly scooped up her boy and retreated to the living room, humming the familiar tune again.

"What is that song?" Max asked as she continued to concentrate on her stew. Annie just smiled and ignored her.

When they both finished, Annie said, "I can only offer you some over-the-hill apple pie. White Bear finished the last of the cobbler last night."

Max deferred but John accepted heartily. He declined coffee and a few minutes later pushed back his chair. "The days are short and it looks like rain. I've got to get back to the boat launch. Thanks for dinner," he said. Max walked him to the pontoon boat and John handed her a life vest.

"You're going to need this."

As Max shoved out the boat, she called out into the dark. "Hurry back. Starbuck is depending on you. NGNG," she added.

"What does that mean?" Colby yelled over the scream of the water.

"No Guts, No Glory," Max said in her normal voice, knowing he couldn't hear her over the roar of the outboard.

She went back up the path to Annie's to play with the babies, before turning in. Starbuck was a big commitment. PATH, a Seattle nonprofit focusing on world health, had offered her a job in their legal department, but Max's heart was with the big orphan. Her career would have to wait.

Absentmindedly, she opened the door to the kitchen and everyone was hanging around the table.

"So, how is it going?" Annie asked.

"So, how is *what* going?" Max tilted her head.

"We like John," Sister Mary Catherine blurted out.

"He's all right. A little geeky for my taste," Max answered slowly. "Hey, what's going on with you guys? You just about freaked him out when he went door to door down the spit looking for me, and now you're his best friend," Max said. "I think I'm going to bed. 'Night everyone," Max fairly shouted as she bolted out the door into the night and walked down the path.

"I think she likes the guy, but won't admit it," Sister weighed in.

"I think you're right, but like she said, she has a lot on her plate now," Annie agreed, still humming her subliminal song as she tucked the twins in for the night.

The next morning, Christine was awakened by a speedboat moving parallel to the island. It was a banana yellow ski boat that had a magnetic sign that read Jefferson County Health Department slapped on the low profile stainless steel bow. Christine trained her binoculars on the man piloting the boat. He was reed thin, sporting a blue watchcap. He had a twitchy nose duster mustache and his furtive, rat-like movements reminded her of someone her father had described to her when the Health Department tried to pass off some bogus dangerous nitrate level water analysis last spring, blaming the outhouses for polluting the bay. Then they went to court and tried to declare the island polluted and ripe for county takeover.

Snodgrass, she mumbled to herself. They're at it again.

Near the end of the island, the man bent over and scooped a water sample even as the boat moved at a good clip. Something clicked in Christine's brain and she went into automatic. She rummaged in the closet for her father's rifle. She rested the fore stock on the window sill and by the time Snodgrass had taken a third sample and was speeding away, Christine put a shot right into the heart of the one hundred and fifty horsepower outboard. Smoke curled up from the engine as the riptide carried the banana boat into the channel.

Annie heard the shot and peered out her window. She trained her binoculars on the boat and then panned over to Moby Dick's old cabin. Christine was still leaning out of the window with the rifle barrel still smoking. *Like father, like daughter. It must be a genetic thing,* Annie thought to herself.

Just before lunch, White Bear pulled up in a big yacht and ferried what Annie supposed was the master carver and someone with a chainsaw.

"Annie, it's high tide and a good time to take the tree," White Bear announced as he slipped into his green Helly Hansen rain gear. "I have the men and the boat to tow it away. We will warn everyone when it is ready to go down."

Annie looked out the window. The Raven was still in the same position as if he was stuffed. Annie had never seen the bird move. It was like he was guarding the tree.

The men had come ashore with a chainsaw, wedges and splitting mauls. They threw dry grass clippings in the air like they were golfers to detect the direction of the wind and by the nodding of their heads it seemed it would be a simple drop into the water.

One of White Bear's hires to cut the tree was the legendary Three-Fingered Jake. A fellow tribal member, Jake had won the falling contest twenty-five years straight at the Shelton Logging Festival. The festival was a revival of tree climbing, whipsaw contests, and log rolling, and Jake was the poster boy. Using only his chainsaw and no wedges, Jake would drop his eighty-foot pole at the fairgrounds directly onto a predetermined stake so far in the ground that for several years they never found the pulverized remains. He was the Buffalo Bill sharp-shooter of chainsaw artistry.

Jake had lost his pinkie and its neighbor on his right hand to a band saw at a shake mill after a healthy bender years before, but it never slowed him down. Married four times, he still played a mean guitar with the remaining three fingers and covered the tavern circuit up and down Hood Canal, from Belfair to Port Ludlow.

Jake looked up into the tree, "as crooked as a dog's hind leg with mange," he would say later as the ancient cedar barely had any branches to catch the breeze. He gave the tree a paternal pat to show who was boss. He then squinted and looked down the channel to see if there was any wind churning the water. Wind is the menace that drives logging fallers wild. It can turn a projected fall a hundred and eighty degrees. Jake knew there were a lot of dead fallers who confidently started cutting a tree only to have a capricious wind churn up at the last minute.

This time the weather was as calm as Jake had ever seen for a fall of a monster tree. Fully eight feet in diameter and a thousand winters old, the tree was no piece of cake, but Jake was not to be denied. He snapped the cord on his chainsaw and cut a big v-shaped notch on the water side to determine the direction of the fall.

Then he worked the back of the tree and began to cut toward the notch. The chainsaw ground its way to the center, throwing out aromatic curls of wood going backward in time. Two hundred years—back to the Declaration of Independence. Four hundred years—when settlers first came to America. The tree had been an easy two hundred feet tall. Six hundred years—explorers left Europe to find spices and found a New World.

Jake stopped. The wood chips were stacked up to his knees. Forty-five years of tree cutting told Jake something wasn't right. He grimaced as he felt the flank of the great tree. He looked skyward and was surprised the Raven was still sitting in the branches. Jake reached into his canvas bag and took out two metal wedges. He pushed them into the cut with the heel of his hand. The saw still dangled in the cut a good five feet into the tree. With each swing of the maul, the tree shuddered till the wedges disappeared into the cut. With the added tilt to the cut, Jake almost felt comfortable. He looked out into the channel again and the water was still as if holding its breath.

Jake began cutting again. Eight hundred years ago, the English monarchy signed the Magna Carta and peasants were well on their way to becoming free men. At a thousand years, the tree was in its infancy, back before the Industrial Revolution. The tree had held court over the island for many years and it had played its song on a million winds.

Jake let out his breath. The tree wobbled as he began to cut into the very heart of the old tree. The case of beer on ice in the boat was a sure bet, about to be realized. And then, in the last three inches of the core, the tree expressed a repressed memory of an event long ago.

White Bear's ancestors had long used Seven Sisters Island to dry fish from the surrounding salmon runs. A wild half wolf–half dog puppy had been tied to the cedar sapling and, as the day wore on, the animal kept winding his leather leash around the tree till finally the sapling trunk was twisted into a half circle. The giant cedar tree grew with the ancient twist embedded in the core.

The great red cedar began to turn with the final cut. The fibers were finally breaking free and releasing the energy—suppressed by twelve hundred years—in the core of its heart. The Raven, suddenly alive, squawked, jumping off the branch and sailing into another tree as the giant cedar twisted ninety degrees and began its descent. The film crew from the University of Washington, who were making a documentary of the canoe and the vision quest, bailed for the brush at the first sign of disaster.

The chainsaw began to twist and rotate, racing at full throttle as Jake tried to release his hand; but not before the saw, like it was spring-loaded, shot backwards as Jake put his hands up to protect his face. The saw snipped the remaining three fingers on his right hand.

The tree fell with a mighty thud that lifted everyone on the island off the ground. It lay parallel to the shore, mired a good foot and a half into the earth, and had driven the metal camera tripod into the ground as if it were a match stick.

When Jake looked at his bloodied hand, all he could think of was those wasted fifteen hundred posters he had printed the day before—**THREE-FINGERED JAKE, Musical Legend of the Pacific Northwest**. Those days were over.

Later that afternoon, the tugboat *Pissant*'s churning engines failed to budge the log. Standing with his bandaged hand in the air, Jake said it all, "This log ain't gonna move no how, boss."

And so the reality of an old adage came alive: If the mountain would not come to Mohammed, then Mohammed would have to go to the mountain. The canoe builder would be building the canoe on the island.

Sister Mary Catherine hadn't seen Joe since the rhino horn incident and when he scratched on the door about nine-thirty at night she was surprised. His face was completely blackened and he moved stealthily across the room to the table and sat down.

"Been on a mission?" Sister asked.

"Affirmative," Joe answered without divulging any more information.

"There's a plate of moon pies I made for you on the table under the dish towel," Sister offered. Joe scooted his chair back in subconscious retreat.

"Go ahead," Sister said. "They won't hurt you."

Joe ate two moon pies thoughtfully, declared them delicious, but refrained from eating more.

"Tell me about the rhino horn," Sister coaxed.

"Simple exercise." Joe was spare with his information. "Just a commando raid and recovery."

"Ever recovered a rhino horn before?" Sister teased.

"Elephant tusks in Kenya, live gorillas in Gabon, and a mummified alien in the Gobi."

"An alien. What did it look like?" Sister pried.

"Your standard alien type," Joe answered. "Had big eyes, withered body. Just got a quick glance. If I told you any more I'd have to kill ya," Joe smiled. "Really. Just stopped by to see if maybe you wanted to do some skydiving tonight? Ever done any skydiving?"

"Who hasn't?" Sister shrugged. "Night diving? I've got my certification, but diving at night is illegal, isn't it?" she added.

"I've got authorization." Joe stood up. "Are we on? Meet me on the beach at 2300."

"Sure," Sister agreed. She loved a challenge.

They paddled across the channel in a camouflaged raft and landed on the beach in Port Gamble where Joe covered the raft with seaweed. Joe looked around expectantly for a car. "There should be transportation," he said, frowning.

They waited for half an hour and no one came. Sister Mary smoked two Camels and then grew impatient. "I've got a car over in the garage I rent from Wiggins," Sister offered. She went over and slid open the door to an ancient leaning garage. "Besides, I have to get my chute. It's in there somewhere. Good night nurse!" Sister swore. "Half of my stuff fell onto the Mustang convertible. At least the chute was on top. I think there is some sort of motor bike on the side over there, but I don't even know if it will start. Wiggins said he would turn it over once a month for me.

"It's back here." Sister Mary moved aside three boxes marked wedding dresses.

"Is all this stuff yours?" Joe asked, helping her with the boxes.

"Negative," she answered. "I took a vow of poverty. This is crap handed down to me by my siblings—eleven of them to be exact. The only profession left to me as the youngest was prostitute or the nunnery. I chose when I was very young; otherwise, who knows…" She let the answer dangle. "It hasn't been an easy life."

"I can't believe you have a motorcycle!" Joe shook his head. "And you've actually ridden this motorcycle?"

"What do ya think?" Sister retorted. "Think I was going to ride around on a Vespa? Get a grip, shorty. I've got the endorsement. Ya want me to drive it? There it is back there," Sister pointed. "It might be our salvation yet. Praise the Lord and pass the biscuits."

Joe pulled the vintage motor bike into the light. "My God, it's a '47 knucklehead Harley. This baby is worth some serious coin." Joe stroked the tank and felt down the side pipes as if it were a thoroughbred.

"What's written on this fender? That's going to take away from the value." Joe took a towel and wiped the dust from the fender. "Looks like someone wrote in felt pen. What's it say?"

"I don't remember," Sister yawned. "We need to get a move on. I think it was from my brother who was an assistant producer in Hollywood in the early fifties. He retired and died two weeks later, in 1984 I think."

Joe moved the bike into a better light. "Marlon Brando is one name." Joe became excited. "And there's Elvis and I can't read the second part but it must be Presley. Steve McQueen, and what's this last scribble? Nicholson, Jack Nicholson, the guy from *Easy Rider*."

"I remember my brother saying to take good care of the bike cause it might be worth something, but not to me. Why don't you fire it up and we can get out of here."

Joe got on the seat and stomped on the jump start for ten minutes before the bike rumbled to life. Mary Catherine climbed on with her chute, "Away we go!" she yelled into Joe's ear.

A half hour later they pulled into Thunderbird field. The car that was supposed to be in Port Gamble was there with the motor running. Joe got his chute out of the truck and told one of the Marines standing by to take good care of the motorcycle.

An old-style aluminum riveted plane stood waiting with its side door open. Sister climbed up the ladder and sat down. Joe climbed up into the cockpit and gave some final instructions and they were off.

"We're going up about eight or nine thousand feet so you won't be flying long," Joe yelled into her ear. "We're going to be right over the top of the field so aim for the big floodlight they're going to turn on. Go on a short count and pull the chute."

Sister nodded and gave Joe the thumbs up. She hadn't heard a thing over the engine noise. She readied herself and tied the belt of her robe between her legs. When the plane motor slowed, Joe stood up and held out his hand. "Wait for my signal," he yelled.

But Sister ran by him screaming, "Last one down is a rotten egg," and was already out the door, looking like "Rocky the flying squirrel," Joe would say later. Bewildered, Joe followed her into the pitch dark night. Not until what seemed like an eternity did she open her chute, gliding toward the airstrip. By the time Joe hit the runway, there was a crowd around Sister Mary and the bike. He gathered his chute and began walking on the side of the runway when five warthog fighters flew into the tiny airport and taxied toward the crowd. The pilots climbed out of the cockpits and ran toward the hangar. When Joe approached the crowd, the airmen saluted.

"What's going on?" Joe asked.

"The word got out. sir. The lady, sir. I mean nun, sir, That is, Sister Mary Catherine said we could ride the bike if we were careful. Sir."

"Whatever the lady said, gentlemen." Joe smiled gently. *Gutsy broad*, he murmured under his breath.

"The lady could use a chair," Joe mentioned, and as two were requisitioned from inside the hangar, Joe caught Sister Mary Catherine's attention.

"What are you trying to do, kill yourself? You're crazy to jump out of a plane like that. We could have been still flying over a mountain when you jumped."

"Dude, get a grip. Let go, let God, I always say." Sister beamed. "When he is ready to take me, I'm ready."

Joe's rebuttal was lost as the airmen surrounded Sister with requests to ride the bike. The Marine pilots from Whidbey Island took turns roaring into the night down the runway, past the hangar lights, and then down to the opposite end—reluctantly returning slowly back to the hangar, savoring the experience.

All involved thought the historical motorcycle ride would be the highlight of the night, but they would be wrong. The throng retreated to the Spruce Goose Tavern and Karaoke Bar just above the hangar where there was free-flowing beer and loud music till the karaoke contest began. Usually the crowd would be mostly locals, but tonight was the Olympic Peninsula Karaoke Semifinals. The tables were packed and the walls lined with well-lubricated patrons to root for their favorites.

For hours the heat and music stifled the crowded room as the contestants sweated the outcome. Finally, the owners opened the doors to the outside deck overlooking the runway and they stampeded like cattle, their freezing breath dangling in the crisp air and circling their heads as if they were sitting in hot springs in the Olympic rain forest.

When Joe went inside to get a beer, one of the airmen leaned over to Mary Catherine. "How do you know Captain America?" he asked.

Sister looked surprised. "I didn't know he was a captain."

"Rank doesn't matter to a guy like that. He's the most combat-decorated military man in America. He's got like four or five purple hearts, a couple silver stars, bronze stars, the Distinguished Service Cross, and who knows what else. There are four-star generals who are afraid to be in the same room with him. He's a regular war hero and he has something on everybody." The pilot eased back into his seat when Joe came back.

"Do you do karaoke as well as you skydive?" Joe asked and smiled, handing Mary Catherine a beer.

"I can hold my own," she laughed. "If they have the right music."

"What's the right music?"

Sister whispered in his ear. Joe looked surprised, but he made his way up to the judges. He came back. "Better warm up those pipes, Sister."

After the next three acts the emcee grabbed the microphone, "We're in for a special treat tonight. We have the original flying nun who sings. Let's give a big round of applause for Sister Mary Catherine."

The crowd on the patio pushed into the room and all conversation stopped. Sister took the stage. "Well, folks, if you've never seen a flying nun before, this is your lucky day. I just dropped in here to the Spruce Goose after playing the Vatican for twenty-two years."

The crowd, most of whom knew she had been skydiving that night, laughed and soon everyone knew the joke. "I tried to get Sally Field, the original flying nun, to come but she chickened out." Sister held the microphone like a pro. "She claims she has these brittle bones and just the one life to live. Hell, I could have given her eternal life.

"I'd like to do a little tune for you from the early seventies that means a lot to me."

Sister sang the Roberta Flack hit "Killing Me Softly" a cappella with such passion, there were few dry eyes in the house when she finished. Joe couldn't tell if she was singing the song as a young girl in love or if it was a love song to God. He figured he knew, but he was rapidly learning that with Sister Mary Catherine, you could never be sure.

Sister called down to the judges for a stapler that sat on the table. She hiked up her robe to the knees and stapled the hem. She then grabbed the microphone.

"I know most of you have never seen a nun's legs. Some people don't think we have feet, that maybe we move around on wheels."

Someone called out, "Nice gams, Sister!" The crowd laughed.

Sister struck a pose and "Proud Mary" came alive. Sister pranced, shimmied and strutted across the stage till she owned the crowd. There were catcalls and whistles and hoots of appreciation that were not for an eighty-four-year-old woman but for capturing the song. Her dark whiskey/Camel voice was perfection. Everyone wondered was this a life that had not yet found a voice, but by the end of the evening, they knew she had lived every minute "my way."

When Sister and Joe left, the crowd followed them down to the hangar. There were men who actually cried when Joe hit the kick start and the roar echoed into the foggy meadow of the airport. A great shout followed them as they sped up the windy road to the highway.

How are we ever going to beat that?, the crowd thought to themselves.

There were no overhead lights on the Chimacum Valley road and the moon was behind clouds drifting in from the south. One of Sister Mary's favorite movies was *The Egg and I* with Claudette

Colbert she explained to Joe as they rode. "It was slightly before *I Love Lucy* and a comedy in its own right about a city couple trying to make a living on a chicken farm, surrounded by a bunch of eccentric locals. There it is," she pointed. The farm was on the road coming up and their headlight caught the sign, "Egg and I Road." She was still thinking about the movie when a young man stepped from the shadows and flagged them down.

"My wife is having a baby. She's in the back of the truck. Can you help us?"

Joe left the headlight trained on the truck that had a logo of vegetables and a sign that read Hoover Organic Farm. Joe put the kickstand down on the bike. Sister ran and peered over the edge of the pickup. A young woman grinned at her as she pulled up her peasant dress to reveal a baby's legs dangling out of her.

"Breech," Sister yelled, and climbed over the downed tailgate.

"How long?" Sister Mary Catherine asked.

"No more than a minute," replied the young man. "We phoned the hospital and the fire station is all volunteer and they don't have the training. We were going to meet the aid truck."

"Kid, get a new newspaper." Sister motioned toward the paper box near the side of the road.

"Joe, get in the back of the truck," she ordered. "Ease the legs out when we push and let the baby land on the clean newspaper. All right, young lady, I'm going to push on your stomach and Joe is going to pull on the baby's feet. On my count…"

Sister stationed herself on the side of the mother and counted "1…2…3… push with all you've got. Don't go soft on me, Joe," Sister warned as Joe reluctantly grabbed the baby's legs. "It's gonna get messy," she predicted.

Sister pushed down and gave a gentle twist and the baby slipped out onto the newspaper.

"Hallelujah, it's a girl!" Sister threw her head back and announced to the stars. "It's not over yet!" Sister said quietly as she examined the baby who was not breathing and noticeably gray and blue with the umbilical cord wrapped around the neck. She lifted up the infant's head and flipped the cord off her neck in one cowboy roping motion, bent low and gave a puff into the mouth, and began gently massaging the heart with her two index fingers.

"Come on, come on," Sister exhorted the child. At first there was a faint gurgling and then a wheeze and within seconds the color came back into the baby's body. When the aid car pulled up, the baby's name had been changed from Jesse to Mary and Sister had the promise of a weekly organic vegetable package starting next spring.

Before the aid car men had a chance to leave the truck, Joe and Sister took off like the Lone Ranger and Tonto into the night.

Exhausted, the two adventurers headed back to the garage, stowed the bike, paddled back to the island, and went their separate ways without a parting word.

The master carver and two assistants landed on the island the next morning. They put up a white army tent in the pasture with a stove pipe running through the middle. The carver, Jerry Sackman, who preferred the name Slick from the long mane of shiny black hair pulled back in a pony tail and tied with a greasy leather thong, spent hours pounding on the side of the downed cedar with a stick, then selected a fifty-foot section in the middle and had an apprentice pound while he used a megaphone made of alder bark to listen.

"I am listening to the heart of the great tree," he told Annie and Christine, "and when I find the heart I listen to see if the body of the tree is strong and noble. It must not be afraid of storms and the powerful winds. The Raven has led us to this tree and the spirit of the Ancient One runs strong beneath the bark.

"This tree has waited for twelve hundred years to be a canoe. It is anxious to come to life again, but I need to take the time to know its powers.

"Of course, I could just rent a portable machine from GeoTech that will tell me the density of the tree and give me a paper read-out and a video. It is much like a portable MRI or x-ray machine, which would tell me the same thing, or we could do this mumbo jumbo thing, but White Bear wants us to do it in the traditional manner without machines, chainsaws and power chisels—and he's paying the big bucks. It will be difficult and we must work quickly; he is an old man and his journey to the white bear may be lost and we won't get paid." The carver hoped to instill a feeling of haste in his associates.

He went to the boat and brought back a two-man whip saw with a twelve-foot-long blade. The work was strenuous, and the three men spelled each other as the cut bore slowly through. Although the blade was razor-sharp, it took better than two hours for each cut. They dug under one side of the tree and put in chocks to stop the fifty-foot section from rolling; then pulled the chocks and used a peeve to roll the separate canoe section free. They repeated the process till the log was a good twenty feet from the host.

Ziggy had left his cabin and was taking a toke on his marijuana joint as he watched the process unfold.

"Like man, if a tree falls in the forest and no one hears it—did it really fall?" Ziggy squeaked as he exhaled and then he giggled.

White Bear proceeded to explain. "After the tree was so stubborn and the tugboat could not move it, the shaman had second thoughts and said that the tree had made the decision to stay on the island and he wanted to honor the decision."

"The customer is always right," Ziggy shrugged.

Darkness was coming early and the carver worked quickly with a long hank of rope and chalk to rough out the shape of the canoe.

"Tomorrow the canoe will begin to reveal itself," the carver promised.

Chapter TEN

Sister Mary anticipated the scratching at her door the next night and when it came she didn't growl but got out of bed and answered the door.

Head to toe in camouflage, Joe looked carefully behind the door and then stood on a stool and cased the rafters. "Bugs," he whispered to Sister. "They're everywhere."

"Joe, it's a ten by ten shack. Get a grip." Sister sat down on the bed.

"Joe, do you have any connections to the Vatican? It wouldn't hurt my feelings if I became a saint."

"We have some minor people in place, but now if you want to have a government overthrown, I could do a small country like Tobago or Jamaica Mon, tonight. It's not too late to get something like that done and besides …what are you talking about? You're like some kind of Athena Warrior Princess already, with your bike riding, skydiving, and that karaoke."

"Dude," Sister Mary Catherine put up her hands in protest. "Just another night in the life of Supernun."

"Where did you learn skydiving?" Joe asked, refusing a Camel from Sister.

She lit up, inhaled, and looked contemplatively toward the ceiling. Exhaling, she began, "A bunch of us were on holiday in Belgium and we did the training. We have several chapters here in the states. The Flying Nuns. No, really."

Joe rubbed his chin. "So, I was thinking maybe we could go out and get some clams. I have some French bread and …"

"You have an oven in that bunker?" Sister Mary asked. "I wouldn't be surprised."

"Naw, I had it brought in from Paris."

Sister looked confused. "How did you do that?" she asked.

"You know the drill, Sister. If I told you, I'd have to kill ya."

"You and what army are going to take on Athena Warrior Princess!" Mary said, pleased to take on the challenge.

"Clams?" Joe asked. "I have the buckets and shovels out on the porch."

"You're on." Sister Mary started rummaging for her boots.

The two dug for an hour and then let the clams relax and spit themselves clean while Joe poured shots of Blue Nun and tequila. They each told war stories like the battle-tested warriors they were and finally they put a little vermouth in the steaming pot, covered the clams with water, and boiled the steamers till they opened their mouths in defeat. The two warriors tore off great hunks of bread and sopped up the clam nectar, dipped the clam meat in drawn butter and garlic, and soon were surrounded by shells and bad breath.

Daylight was just breaking when Joe realized he had to go. "Seems like you have a Dracula complex," Sister kidded him.

Joe turned and bared his teeth, hissed, and wove his way back to the bunker.

Ziggy had a terrible night. He grumbled as he slipped on his pants, pulled on his hooded sweatshirt, and stepped out into the raw November wind. He stretched and looked around while he urinated on the beach, coaxing out an unsteady stream. Glancing down the shoreline, he saw what looked like loaves of bread in yellow plastic bags stretching almost the full quarter mile of the spit bathed in moonlight.

He zippered up, tucked himself in, and wandered down the beach towards the bags. When he reached them, he pulled one open and with one whiff he knew he had hit the mother lode—BC bud—some of the most potent marijuana in the world from British Columbia. He'd had some a few times and it had hit him like a ton of bricks. He looked down the beach and roughly counted seventy—no eighty— bags brought in on the morning tide and left landlocked like jelly fish on an outgoing tide.

Ziggy was in rapture. It was as if all his limbs locked up at once and he couldn't move. He simply pitched forward onto his forehead on the beach, simultaneously drooling and twitching. His mind was whirling as he struggled to get up and ran to get the wheelbarrow from behind his cabin. He kept looking around to see if anyone was around and was soon out of breath trucking the loaves to his cabin.

What a way to die, he kept saying to himself as his lungs burned. He figured his wife, who suffered by on four hours of sleep and a leaky bladder, was up at Annie's so he stashed the booty under the firewood in back of the cabin under a blue tarp.

He took a paisley-ribbed turquoise chenille bedspread, smoothed it out carefully, and spread the contents of one loaf on the bed. Then he stripped down and rolled in it like a dog on a decaying carcass. He rubbed the leaves under his arms and on his stomach and on his privates as if it had curative powers. When his wife came back, they both rolled in the weed and had sex three times, reincarnated as if they were in back of the old VW bus forty years ago.

Ziggy began smoking his booty and didn't leave the cabin for three days except to eat fifteen bags of potato chips that made his mouth sore and still he didn't care. Life for Ziggy couldn't be better.

John Colby had come across the channel from Port Townsend long after dark in a Zodiac pontoon boat with coolers of live herring. He tried to roust Max from Annie's kitchen. "Don't you want to come out and feed your orca?" he called in through the half-open kitchen door.

"Get in here," Annie chided, "we're losing all the heat."

"Close the barn door," Max said in greeting.

Admonished, John came in and closed the door, holding his cap in his hand until Annie sent him out to get firewood on the porch.

"No work, no food," she said to John when he returned. She began concentrating on making crêpes in a big fourteen-inch cast iron skillet that she held with two hands. Pouring the batter in the middle and then working it around the edges by tipping the pan, she finally plunked it down on the wood stove. She flipped the crêpe over with a wooden spatula and slipped the steaming crêpe onto a plate in front of John. He buttered it, slathered on a thick layer of wild blackberry jam, and rolled it up.

"Eat up, young 'un," Annie instructed as if she was Granny on the "Beverly Hillbillies," and she kept them coming as Max kept pouring coffee till he put up his hands.

"No mas," he said. "No mas."

As Max cleared his plate, she asked, "Did you bring the fish?"

"Fish, vitamins, and a little something extra." John turned the handle of the coffee mug around and took a long sip while stealing an admiring glance at Max as she returned the coffee pot to the stove.

They sat in silence with only the sound of the crackling fire. Annie was still bustling at the stove with her back to the table. Suddenly, she said, "John, if you don't have some place to go for Thanksgiving…"

Max abruptly stood up. "We need to go feed Starbuck right now. I need to get to bed. I have to get an early start for Seattle tomorrow." They walked down to the beach where there were two single kayaks and the Zodiac. One kayak was John's and the other had been painted like an orca. On the side, it said ORCA WHISPERER.

"I kinda made a kayak for you." John pursed his lips. "It doesn't take long anymore, just a few days. I build them out of scraps from a big boat shop on Whidbey. I added a built-in container in the front so you can put the herring in there and get them out easily, and I laminated a paddle with a harder angle that you might find easier to use."

Max was stunned. She was used to gifts from men. It came with the territory. She had been given expensive diamond jewelry, paintings, clothing. Some idiot tried to give her a dog in a purse, and there was the Arab that delivered a thoroughbred racehorse in her elevator that became so expensive to keep she eventually gave it to Adopt a Pet—but not before they extorted over twenty-five hundred dollars for new horseshoes and three months' worth of room and board. But no one had ever given her a handmade kayak. It was as if she was being asked to re-evaluate her entire life, her values, her future.

John filled up the noticeable void between them. "You know, there is not a nail in her," he continued. "Everything was sewn and glued. You could drag it through the metal detector at the airport, no problem."

Max, the lawyer, who was never at a loss for words, knew it was well past her time to speak but it just kept getting worse. She couldn't speak at all and she was damned if she was going to cry, and there was no running away on an island where you only go in circles. John finally jumped in again. "Listen, no big deal. It may not even suit you. Let's go feed Starbuck and you can take it for a test run." Max managed to nod her head.

They loaded up the fish and Max adjusted her head lamp. She expertly eased herself into the orca kayak and pushed away from the shore by digging the paddles into the sand. Starbuck seemed overjoyed to see them and passed right between them with inches to spare.

"You know that there is no record of a wild orca eating a man, or a woman either," John said, trying to ease her fears. "I believe there is some universal bond between the species. Especially mammals." *This feels right,* Max thought to herself, as she fed the fish to Starbuck. *What else feels right?*

John suggested they go on an adventure to the lighthouse on Point No Point. "I know the name is a little confusing." He shrugged. "But the new kayak needs a little time to break in," he explained. "How is it tracking? I put in foot pedals for the rudder if you want to use them, or not."

"It's tracking very nicely," Max responded. And thinking, *but I'm not tracking very well.* As they pointed the kayaks toward the Point, Starbuck bounded on in front of them and, like a loyal dog, kept circling back to see if they were still coming.

The lagoon behind the Point was too shallow for Starbuck as the kayaks shot the bar and scooted into smoother water. It was hard work and Max was breathless as they rafted side by side at the mouth of a small frothy stream that tumbled down from the hillside, bathed in the murky light of sunrise.

Suddenly John said, "Don't move but there is a Water Ouzel coming our way." Max had no clue what a Water Ouzel was, but it sounded like it could be dangerous.

"Sometimes they call them American Dippers," John whispered, pointing at the waterfall.

American Dipper? Max thought it sounded like something coming from the Big Band era, swing dance, Big Dipper, Big Bopper, Big…

"There he is." John pointed to a brown sandpiper-size bird that was constantly in motion, bobbing at the knees to an unheard rhythm as it worked its way up the stream from stone to stone and sometimes disappearing into the swift-flowing water only to appear again a few feet farther upstream. "They fly underwater to forage and build their nests on the banks of the streams or behind waterfalls," he explained.

John struck a pose and began to recite: "'Ouzels seem so completely part and parcel of the streams that they inhabit, they scarcely suggest any other origin than the streams themselves; and one might be pardoned in fancying they come direct from the living waters, like flowers from the ground.' That's from John Muir," John confessed. "Water Ouzels are my favorite bird."

Max tilted her head and looked at John. "A romantic, you're a romantic scientist," Max said, enchanted by both the Ouzel and John as she strained to pinpoint the brown bird again, but it seemed to have disappeared.

"You know, I've never noticed these little birds before." Max continued watching for the bird.

"They're all over the US," said John, adjusting his paddle.

"I guess I'm not much of a nature girl," Max mumbled.

"What did you say?" John said, pushing off from the overhanging stream bank.

"Nothing," Max said, repositioning the hair band on her pony tail.

The trip back to the island was uneventful with a nice southerly tail wind pushing the kayaks that fairly flew home by themselves. When they reached the beach, John asked, "So do you think the kayak is going to work for you?"

"It's a keeper, definitely," said Max, feeling a little bit better about the gift. *Was this a road she wanted to travel?*

"It looks like somebody had a party here on the beach," John observed. A bottle of Blue Nun and tequila lay on their sides like spent spawning salmon.

"Well, I gotta go," Max excused herself. "Gotta get over to Seattle this morning. And me with no sleep. I hope I still have a job."

"Me too." John waved as Max slowly walked backwards up the beach. "Remember to tell Annie about the Water Ouzel," he sang out as he jumped into the Zodiac.

Before she left the island, Max was hailed by John Hunt who was coming down the trail from Annie's. "Just came over to firm up Thanksgivng plans," he explained as they stood around Ziggy's fire and talked about commuting together to Seattle. "Seen Ziggy around?"

"Not for a few days," Max answered, looking over at Ziggy and Matty's cabin. "They must be hunkered in for some reason."

"Well, I've got to get ahold of White Bear," John said, rubbing his hands together. "I found out something interesting about his vision quest."

"His canoe is here," Max said, pointing to the boathouse. "Isn't that him over by the fire?"

John, who had squatted down next to the fire, stood up and nodded, "Catch you later."

The canoe crew and White Bear were warming near the campfire when John approached. He grabbed a used mug and poured last night's remains on the ground and pulled the coffee pot from a rock near the fire. It was camp coffee. There were no apologies. Thick, black and too hot to drink, someone had thrown a handful of coffee grounds in the pot that morning and filled it with water. John grimaced as he strained the coffee between his teeth and spat the grounds into the fire, moving closer to the flames. The fire warmed one side but his backside was open to the November chill and would occasionally send shivers down his spine.

He waited for a lull in the conversation and, looking into the fire, spat out more grounds and his new-found information.

"White Bear, I think I've found a solution to your vision quest. Near Alaska on Grimbell Island there is a population of twelve hundred bears. A third of them have a recessive gene that makes the fur pure white. I got the information off the Internet. Here, I printed it out with a picture."

White Bear looked up from the fire and fished his glasses out of his pocket. He stared at the paper a long time. He handed the paper to the master carver and pointed to the picture of a white bear.

"This is what I have been searching for. I like those odds," White Bear said, looking into the fire. "The picture looks like the bear of my youth. I've been wondering what the chances are of finishing my vision quest and now you have brought me the answer. How far is it up there to this island?"

"By water, seven or eight hundred miles," John said, trying to remember the map.

White Bear bowed his head. "That is a long journey. Maybe forty, fifty days, depending on the tides. I have waited almost eighty years since I was a boy to complete the quest. You know the old story: a bear in the hand is worth two in the bush."

White Bear smiled, his face lined with the dry creek beds of a thousand streams, a road map where every highway signaled a dead end to a vibrant culture that had flourished in the Americas for fifteen thousand years. White Bear would be the last warrior to finish the quest of a lifeline.

He raised his head and looked at the clouds drifting in from the south. "They call them spirit bears or ghost bears. I like that." White Bear nodded as a tear ran down his cheek. "It has been a good life.

It must be finished properly with an honorable death. I thank you, my friend." White Bear put his hand on John's shoulder.

 Chapter ELEVEN

A few days later, Max had run out of herring for Starbuck and was becoming anxious. She thought she could see an improvement already. She needn't have worried. Like clockwork, the next morning John Colby was back at the island towing a cage full of herring in the rain behind a large working skiff.

After his first experience, he decided not to go door to door looking for Max. He headed straight to Annie's. Christine was introducing the two infants to applesauce mixed with rice cereal. John took over while she warmed bottles of milk.

Max bolted in the door and took off her raincoat. "Anybody want coffee?" she called, as she took the pot off the stove.

"I'm in," said John.

"Me too," said Christine.

Max set the steaming cups on the table. When John finished the feeding, he gave Little Annie her formula chaser while Annie put Zack on a blanket on the floor next to the table, with some plastic measuring cups to bat around. Zack was bound and determined to stay awake and chat but soon his thumb found his mouth and Little

Annie grew cross-eyed. Like puppies with full bellies, they cuddled together like spoons and fell asleep almost simultaneously.

John cleared his throat and stretched his legs under the table. "Max, we need to talk out this Starbuck deal."

"Should I leave?" Christine asked.

"No, I don't think so," John answered, setting his cup down. "The thing is, Max, the organization is getting suspicious about my travels. The fish I've been using is from donations from some orca groups friendly to Starbuck. But, there are other groups, including the federal Fish and Wildlife boys, that don't want any artificial intrusion into the orca. All these groups want to preserve orca whales; they just have their own way of doing it."

"Either you want to save the friggin' whales or you don't," Max bristled.

John put his hands up defensively. "I know, I know. You're preaching to the choir. I think the best way is to keep feeding him till he's healthy and then find a way to get him transferred north to his pod. I hate to say this, but maybe the pet psychic can settle this tiff between Starbuck and his aunt. The main thing is to keep him out of sight, out of the channel, and here in the cove. We don't want the media out here."

"I get it," Max shrugged. "I've already cut my lawyering days at PATH to halftime so I can get back and feed him at night."

Annie padded out in her patchwork of three overlapping shredded robes and mismatched fuzzy slippers in green and pink. She took a deep breath by the stove and hung her head. Grabbing her coffee, she sat at the table and put her head in her hands.

"You okay?" Max asked.

"My insides are killing me. Last night I never laughed so hard in my life. *Everything* was funny. And I just kept eating those brownies one after another over at Ziggy and Matty's."

"Oops," Max grimaced. "We need to talk later."

"I'm going to have to get back to Seattle," Christine announced. "I have some piano concert dates this spring and I have to get back to the studio, but I still want to stick around for Thanksgiving. John Hunt said it will be quite an event."

"I'll be doing a lot of sleepovers in the big city when you get settled in," Max promised.

"Let's go get the Starbuck food," she said as she punched John in the ribs and headed out the door.

Max had begun to mumble to herself and she knew it was a sign that she was getting stressed. On the trail she mumbled about her biological clock that had sped into triple daylight savings time. She mumbled about Travis, her erstwhile boyfriend, staying in Port Townsend for Thanksgiving with friends Max didn't particularly like, and the spark that seemed to fizzle when he said he'd had it as a single parent and didn't want any more kids. She mumbled, *Why not ask Colby for Thanksgiving? The guy had given her a kayak. Shit, she'd slept with guys just because they smelled good, but that was a long time ago. And it was Thanksgiving, for pity's sake. Get a grip, bitch!*

Max tried to get herself out of her funk by skipping down the rest of the trail and was surprised when she felt better.

Trish and Joe met later in the evening to discuss an electronic listening device Joe had installed in Trish's husband's rental house and he brought her a receiver so she could listen in.

"Isn't this illegal?" Trish asked.

"So," Joe shrugged. "Do you want to know what he is up to or not? I also left him a little gift."

Trish heard her ex-husband's voice swearing up a storm. They could hear him screaming and ranting for two straight hours as they heard a garage door opening and closing. Then there was nothing for awhile. The next thing they heard was his voice talking to a police detective.

"Somebody put concrete inside my Corvette convertible and I want you doughnut pushers to do something," he raved. "What am I paying you clowns for?"

A little later, Trish could hear him threatening her. "I know the bitch had this done. She's dead meat, dead meat." And then there was silence. Trish played the recording over and over and giggled every time.

Chapter TWELVE

I t was the day before Thanksgiving and most of the revelers had arrived that morning. Thanksgiving was a holiday not to be taken lightly on the island.

The year before, John Hunt had made turkey loco for Thanksgiving dinner. It required shots of tequila during the preparation of the turkey and there were some hours unaccounted for during this task. John's wife had attended the gathering, but had died on the island soon after from heart failure. John's spirit had flagged often during the past year, but there were children and grandchildren that still needed him and that would have to be enough.

This year, Ivan—the piroshki man from Pike Place Market—and Madeline, from the highly successful Whips and Boots oil franchise, had asked to cohost with John. Ivan was going to do something called the Moscow Turduckgoosen and Madeline had renamed it *turkey orgy*. It involved a forty-eight pound mammoth turkey, a goose, a duck, a chicken, a Cornish game hen, lots of bacon, shots of raspberry infused vodka, and an egg-shaped barbecue cooker.

What could go wrong? John thought as he dropped anchor next to the good ship *Pissant*. John loaded the birds into the wheelbarrow and trudged up the muddy path to Annie's. The porch reverberated as John slammed the huge ice chest down on the fir decking. Annie came outside, boiling hot. "John, we've got babies sleeping in here. Be a little quieter."

John grimaced and tiptoed down the trail for the remaining piles of foodstuffs. When he had staged the food on the porch, he sat on the porch swing and looked down over the sand spit and the cabin he had shared with his wife. His life had changed dramatically the last year with the loss of Betsy. She had spoiled him and he wasn't a very good bachelor. He didn't want to appear needy but he was lonely, even though he still worked full time as the food editor at the *Seattle Times*. He kept saying to himself, *John, you're a people person, you've got to open up*, but it was hard.

John got up from the swing and cautiously opened the screen door and turned the door knob ever so slowly. He opened the creaky door and felt like he had reached safety when the forgotten screen door slammed. He cringed as he heard a baby cry in response in the back room. Annie hustled in from the room and handed him Little Annie with the big brown eyes and a bottle.

"You break it, you buy it, Bub," Annie lectured.

John sat down in the rocker overlooking the spit, next to the roaring fireplace decorated with Thanksgiving pine cone turkeys and ponderosa pine garland.

"Annie," John called over his shoulder. "I've invited a guy that's still on the boat to the turkey day."

"I'll bite," Annie said flippantly. "Who's out there?"

"A rock 'n roll country crossover guy called Bobby 'Wildcat' Weston. You'll meet him later."

"Okay with me," replied Annie as she walked through the room and went up the stairs.

Ivan and Madeline were shuttled by *The Ark* across the cove and arrived just as John was starting to fret about his time line. A forty-eight pound turkey was going to take a long time. Fortunately, he was going to cook the turduckgoosen in a propane-heated ceramic egg to cut the cooking time to ten hours or less, he hoped.

Madeline strode into the kitchen in what she considered the conservative end of her wardrobe: four-inch snake skin boots and a mini-skirt of faux zebra, topped off with a rawhide bustier, and a half-dozen malachite and turquoise necklaces with stones the size of cherries. Plus the reddest collagen-plumped lips she could afford. Business at the oil change business she shared with Pickles was booming. In contrast, right behind her was her Bible-toting, eye-rolling daughter dressed in an ankle-length blue denim skirt and a white-as-the-driven-snow prairie blouse.

Ivan trailed Madeline and sucked the rest of the air out of the room as he rushed in and grabbed Annie by the waist, lifted her up over his head, shook her like a rag doll, then set her down on the floor, giving her a big hug.

"Annie," he croaked. "It is your little Russian pin-up boy come to fix Thanksgiving turkey Russian-style. You will like, no?"

Annie was used to Ivan's exuberance and usually tried to keep a table or chair between them during meet-and-greets.

"Ivan, it is an honor to have you cooking for us," Annie gasped as she tried to regain her breath. She moved behind the kitchen table before he could rush her again.

John had surgically lined up the birds in a row on the kitchen table along with three bottles of vodka and shot glasses. Ivan took Annie's pictures off the wall and tacked up a blue tarp that reached the floor, the excess providing a four-foot apron on the floor. Madeline furiously was main lining the birds with a giant syringe filled with a marinade of vodka, spices and Ivan's "secret ingredient."

It was at this moment that John's guest, Wildcat, swaggered through the door with his guitar strapped over his shoulder. Blessed with the nine lives of a cat, Wildcat had found a home in country music. He had a black cowboy hat stuffed with overlong stringy, greasy hair, a scraggly full beard, skinny jeans with no ass at all, and scruffy cowboy boots. It seemed that Wildcat had carried an entire generation on his back early in his career. He had generated folk songs for the peace movement in the early days, moved on to rock 'n roll, protest songs, love songs, songs about the wilderness, and then, just lately, he crossed over to country with the requisite pickup trucks and hound dogs.

Married five times with countless children in small town America, Wildcat had ridden on the wave of every drug that had been in vogue and, except for the swagger, he was a broken man. With a new liver, pacemaker, two knee replacements, sleep apnea, diabetes, prostate cancer—at sixty years old, all that was left was the song in his heart, a perpetual limp, and the swagger.

Wildcat surveyed the room, laid a lip lock on Madeline, and collapsed in a chair by the kitchen table. Madeline didn't miss a beat. She used her computer-generated degree in massage technique to ply the marinade into every fiber of those birds. Finally, she backed away and raised her hands in the air like a surgeon. Ivan stripped the gloves from her hands and poured a round of vodka for everyone around the table.

"What comes first? The turkey or the egg? Today, we are about finding out." Ivan took a World Series wind-up and pegged the game hen against the wall. *Splat*, the hen slowly slithered down the wall.

"Now you see how great Russian bear make American Thanksgiving. First, the vodka and then the breaking of the bones to release the inner juices. *Splat*, the hen hit the wall again and then took its original place on the table. Vodka shots all around.

Whack, the chicken bounced off the tarp and landed on the apron.

Something stirred Wildcat to action. He got up from the chair and began rambling about high school football and field goals. He instructed Madeline to hold the chicken in the field goal position and he lined up against the farthest wall and charged forward. As he neared the striking point, he noticed that the short zebra skirt had hiked to a point where it was obvious Madeline had gone commando and one sweat-soaked boob had wiggled itself out of the rawhide bra looking for air. Distracted, Wildcat whiffed and landed on his back.

Ivan rocked forward on his knees and laughed so hard he squeezed out a long and whistling fart. He fell over on the ground next to Wildcat and they both lay there stunned.

"We need more vodka," Ivan decided and it was thus so. The second time, Wildcat met success with a perfect contact of cowboy toe to carcass and the duck made a beautiful ark and hit the wall above the tarp. Wildcat grabbed his foot where he had fallen off a stage recently, but recovered and did a little dance and ran around the table with his arms outstretched in celebration, then collapsed in his chair with his head thrown back and mouth open. Ivan poured two shots down Wildcat's throat, launched the chicken against the tarp for the third time, and poured another round of vodka.

The duck launch was uneventful except Ivan had brought along a small box of duck calls to sound off during its flight to the tarp. Another round of vodka. The goose was so heavy Ivan had to shot put it against the wall. It took six throws and two shots of vodka before Ivan was satisfied the criteria had been met.

The fully dressed, forty-eight-pound turkey was a formidable creature. One could imagine toward the end the tom turkey would have needed a walker just to get around the yard, but Ivan would not be deterred. He grasped the two legs and twirled twice for launch, released, and the turkey sailed into the living room, bounded off the sofa, and out the open window. John Colby happened to be walking below with Max when the turkey fell from the heavens at his feet. He calmly picked up the big bird and pitched it back through the window where it hit the sofa and bounced into the kitchen, landing at Wildcat's feet where he made a feeble attempt to kick it. The crowd in the kitchen stood in amazement, but not Ivan.

"Instant replay," he shouted. "America, what a country!"

Wildcat came to life and began playing his guitar and singing one of his hit country songs about playing a record backwards and the guy's wife came back, his job came back, his pickup truck got fixed, and the dog came back to life from under the wheels of a Greyhound bus. Except that he translated the words in a speaking of tongues. Wildcat had re-invented himself again.

Ivan attempted three more throws—once where he was pinned to the floor with the turkey assuming the alpha position, and twice where the turkey hit the wall and bounced back against Ivan's feet, knocking him down. Turkey 4...Ivan 0.

At last it was time to assemble the Russian masterpiece. John Hunt watched carefully as a half pound of salted butter, a large wad of grassy herbs, and the secret ingredient—which looked a lot like the BC bud that John had been shown by Ziggy—were stuffed into each cavity. And then bird into bird until finally the mammoth turkey, like Jonah's Biblical whale, swallowed the entire package. Ivan carefully sewed the gaping orifice up and snubbed off the cotton thread with a flourish.

"Now, Russian turkey is ready to be cooked? But no, no, no, no."

Ivan busted out four or five pounds of stripped bacon and began to carefully cover the turkey with strips, poking in toothpicks as needed.

Ivan stood back. "We are done? But no. There is more." Ivan took eight stainless steel half-inch skewers that were a good two feet long and ran at the turkey like a matador finishing off a bull. "To conduct heat," he explained. "Juices from duck and goose flow to turkey, chicken and Cornish game hen to jucify the meat. You will see. Most succulent and delinquent. Now ready for cooking."

It had taken four men to install the egg-shaped, bright ceramic cooker on the porch. Ivan smacked the top of the cooker as if slapping a belligerent drunk.

"This is orange egg. You say, is it an orange? No. You say, is it an egg? No. Is orange egg. Period. No question mark. Most famous cooker in all of Russia."

Ivan turned on the propane, hit the instant starter, and cracked open the top half of the egg to reveal a yawning chasm full of preheated oil that looked like a black hole to the center of the universe. It swallowed the now sixty-two pound creature from the black lagoon in a single gulp and looked like it could handle more. Ivan closed the lid, spun around and slowly backed away, hands raised.

It had been a long and virtuoso performance and the crowd on the porch now numbered over forty. They gave Ivan a standing ovation. "Thank you, America," Ivan said, bowing.

The smell of cooking turkey wafted on a gently south wind that had the island population salivating. The day was filled with support food: Pumpkin pie, mince pie, banana cream pie, Seven Sisters chocolate floating island, fresh cranberry compote, sweet potatoes, yams with toasted marshmallows on top; surprisingly, a concoction of a green bean dish with mushroom soup and Chinese dried noodles; freshly baked crescent rolls; a black cherry Jell-O mold laced with sherry; mounds of whipped Yukon gold potatoes; gobs of vegetable trays; black and green olives; dressing (three kinds); mushrooms, with and without onions for the kids; and a suspicious noodle dish from Ziggy and Matty.

All afternoon, Ivan would wander out to the orange egg, lift up the jaw, look in and poke the bird with a well-worn spruce stick he brought from Russia. He would shake his head, sit in the rocking chair on the porch, and have more vodka. It was late afternoon and there was now an apprehension, almost fear filling the air. An expectation that Ivan might not deliver the bird this day or ever.

At last, Ivan the survivor—who had stolen aboard a freighter in Siberia and had worked his way up in America and now had his own web page, a blog about the mother country, and a book deal in the works—delivered in spades. The bell was rung on the porch and, just like in a Dr. Seuss book, the cabins spit out their people and their offerings and in a long line headed up the hill to Annie's house for Thanksgiving.

Annie looked down the loaded table at the line of hungry diners that began in the kitchen, went through the living room, took a dogleg to the left into a spare bedroom door, out another door, and emerged almost to the kitchen again.

The island had finally come alive last year after decades of decline, and Annie knew this year was more vibrant than ever. There were a great many people to thank. Annie made her dedication with tears running down her face.

"I say a prayer to the great Moby Dick. I stand in awe at the resurgence of Seven Sisters Island," she began. "This is the prayer that has sustained the island on this day for the last one hundred and fifty-six years.

"There is a time for everything under the heavens.

"There is a time to be born and a time to die...."

The turduckgoosen received rave reviews and the feast that seemed in jeopardy commenced amid a sound of clattering dishes, clinking utensils, and silent gratitude.

After the meal, there was an exodus to the cabin for naps, and the children put on their coats and went outside to play on the rope swing or to explore the tidelands. Wildcat and Madeline made a beeline for the attic and locked the stair door. For the others, the entertainment and dessert would come later.

Lila watched as Max walked down the trail with John. "That girl will be married with three children on her plate by spring," she predicted, digging her elbow into Annie's ribs as they both stood over the sink washing dishes.

Sister Mary put a heaping plateful in a Tupperware container and set it close to the bunker. She wondered how Joe would know who made the turkey, but when she came back, just before pie, the container was empty with a note thanking Ivan.

The sun had been down for a good two hours when the bell rang again and, with bloated stomachs but high expectations, the troop marched up the hill one more time.

Slices of pie had been set out, five coffee pots percolated their song on the wood stove, and the entertainment was about to begin.

Wildcat had recovered from his reverie with Madeline, and he had escaped a wildcat in her own right—with only two hickies on his neck. He played his early standards of "Ramblin' Man," "Intersection to Paradise," and a country ballad, "The Devil Don't Have No Home."

Christine played a duet piece with one of John Hunt's granddaughters and charmed the audience with a shopping list of Mozart, Chopin and Liszt.

Sister Mary Catherine, accompanied by Wildcat, sang "The Garden of Prayer" and a gentle English church hymn, "Morning Has Broken":

Morning has broken like the first morning
Catbird has spoken like the first bird...

Sister Mary Catherine finished the evening singing a cappella "Moon Shadow," by a mystic rock artist called Cat Stevens.

Not afraid to break tradition, it had been another one-of-a-kind Thanksgiving at Seven Sisters, full of memories that would last forever in the heart.

Chapter
THIRTEEN

A nnie woke up early that next Saturday morning. The storm from the day before had left calm seas and a silver frost, which made walking on the dock to the boat treacherous, especially with the rusted coffee can lids that had been nailed over the missing knotholes over the years. She pulled on a pair of gloves and zipped up her sea-green waxed canvas Filson jacket all the way to her chin, tucked her red gray-flecked braid under her watch cap, and warmed up the motor on *The Ark*.

It was to be the last run of the year to the Pike Place Market and Annie checked under the canvas roof to see if everything was in order. The last few boxes of Gravenstein apples sat in a corner and the eight or ten boxes of the giant king apples were well-marked.

Six bags of oysters in gunny sacks had been hoisted aboard by Owl and Ziggy the night before. Annie was anxious to see how Pickles' one-two punch of marketing the Seahawk Sea Grannies bobble heads would go, but Annie had to admit that while the odds were good, the goods were odd. But, Pickles was seldom wrong and Annie had a good ten thousand invested in this latest scheme.

The Ark swung out into the cove and Annie could see the v-shaped wake curl away from the boat and slowly meld back into the Puget Sound waters once again to make a large flat pond. The shifting clouds with their jagged and sometimes tufted corners were reflected in a mirror image as if the world was an Ansel Adams photograph. Annie felt like she was living in a world inside one of those glass balls that you tipped over to make a snow scene.

When Annie docked, there was Pickles in his trench coat slapping his gloved hands together to stay warm. He had two men load the produce into a small pickup truck. Annie was to ride on the horse-drawn carriage for a grand entrance, even though it was only eight in the morning. Pickles was all about theatre.

Annie opened Pickles' side door of the VW van to throw in her purse and paper bag, but the back was piled high with women's high heels, hundreds of them in every color and shape. Pickles rushed over and scooped up shoes that had fallen out of the van.

"Just some garage sale items I picked up," he laughed nervously. "Come over to the carriage and meet Dolly." Dolly was a solidly built chestnut Budweiser beer draft horse, who squinted at Annie's offering and finally took the apple that Annie had saved. She rubbed the velvety nose of the giant horse and then Pickles helped her up into the seat.

"I'll follow you in the van," Pickles croaked.

The carriage meandered up the old cobblestone streets to the produce alleyway that was filled with truck farmers unloading the last of the fall produce. They all knew Annie and waved, but Ivan came storming out as usual, plucked Annie out of the carriage and carried her on top of his broad shoulders even as she protested. They marched through the maze that was the market—past the fresh meat smell of the butcher shops, the garlic airs escaping the pasta bar, the yeasty smell of Three Sisters Bakery, the aroma of the first Starbucks coffee shop, and the salty smell of fresh seafood from the Bering Sea to Mexico. Ivan set Annie down at her booth, gave her a hug, and disappeared into the crowd. Annie knew she could count on at least one more Ivan sighting before the end of the day.

As promised, Pickles had piled the boxes up in the back of her stall and had set up a display in easy reach of her customers. Today's pick of the week was the Sea Grannies bobble head doll. The face looked identical to Annie except for Pickles' artistic license to slip glasses on the figure. "More grandmotherly," he had said. The bobble head doll wore a blue Seahawks jersey with the number 12 and a blue-and-green Seahawks ball cap on backwards, Griffey-style, and a braid down her back.

It was unnerving and a little embarrassing to Annie to have several hundred Annie bobble head dolls looking down at her from the pie rack Pickles had found second hand. Pickles had phoned Max and Christine to help sell, and sell they did. At twenty bucks a head, the dolls flew off the shelves. When lunchtime arrived, Ivan came over with piroshkis and apple juice. He was wearing a look-alike Annie bobble head costume with Seahawks jersey, glasses, ball cap, and a braid down his back. Annie pulled the braid off and began whipping the cowering Ivan while they both laughed.

Pickles had cut a deal with Macy's and Nordstrom to handle the dolls after this weekend. Ever the entrepreneur, Pickles knew there could be some money in the dolls with Christmas just around the corner.

At the end of the day, with the bobble head boxes flat and the produce gone, Max and Christine stood Annie to a Fat Bastard ale at Ivar's by the ferry dock and then shuttled her onto her boat for the voyage home. Max had to go back to feed Starbuck and took the helm, while Annie—exhausted from the long day—slept under the bow where she had slept as a child when her father piloted *The Ark* back to Seven Sisters Island. As she fell asleep, Annie smiled as the rush of water underneath and the slap of the waves against the bow made her dream of bobble head dolls and disco dancing.

Several mornings later, Annie woke to a helicopter taking off from in front of Spud's cabin. She checked on the babies and found Ziggy and his Matty tending to their needs. She threw on her coat and boots and went down to see if Spud was okay. She knocked on the door and heard scurrying sounds; then Spud came to the door.

"Hi, Annie," he greeted. "What can I do for you? Come on in."

Inside, Annie told him of her concern and Spud just waved it aside.

"No problem, really," he said, offering Annie a chair, some fresh coffee, and an English pork pie. "I just had an old Physics buddy stop by for a chat. He's not in too good of shape these days, but he's hanging in. Maybe you heard of him? Steve Hawking from England. He's got a bit of a reputation."

"Hawking? The physicist that has MS was here last night?"

"Oh, yeah," Spud said, casually. "He had a seminar in Tokyo and was passing through."

"What do you talk about?" Annie was intrigued.

"Mostly guy stuff. He has to talk through a simulator and it takes forever but he tells the raunchiest jokes of anybody I ever met. Absolutely filthy. We talk a little physics, anthropology, some universe stuff, the atom collider in Switzerland, and aliens, of course, always come up. We had a deuce of a time getting that wheelchair over the gravel, but the guy always has a smile on his face. The mind is still good but the body has just completely failed him."

"Does Hawking have anything to do with the Styrofoam box?" Annie asked, something she had wondered about since Spud hit the island.

"Naw, sometimes we look at the stuff, but he's got his own collection. Tell ya what. Come down to the campfire tonight and I'll show you guys some of the stuff."

By nightfall, the news of Hawking's visit had managed to granny-step the hundred-yard length of the spit, and everyone scooted together for warmth around the campfire, waiting for Spud's Show-and-Tell. There were two communal bottles of wine circulating while Spud, in slow, plodding, professorial tones, told his story of Hawking's visit and answered questions. Then he slipped the bungee cord off the Styrofoam box.

He prefaced opening the lid with, "Now, knowledge of these items cannot go any further than the island. You cannot tell anyone. There are groups out there that are looking for this stuff and me, but I know I can trust you guys."

He removed the lid, reached in, and with two hands pulled out what looked like a large pickle jar. The slash of grayish-white surgical tape had smudged letters—Parkland Hospital.

"This," Spud said, "is what's left of JFK's brain. It's been missing since just a few hours after the assassination. I've done DNA testing and it's his brain all right." He twisted the jar in the campfire light and pointed to a jagged hole in the pinkish-gray mass.

"Right there is the entry point of the shot from the grassy knoll. I've been involved in slicing sections of the brain, doing MRI scans, and there is no doubt about the entry and exit wound."

Spud opened an envelope and pulled out x-rays marked Parkland Hospital, Dallas, Texas. On the bottom was written J Kennedy. Spud held the pictures up against the light of the fire and pointed out the bullet trajectory into a skull. "These x-rays were confiscated by the CIA right after the assassination, but later I happened to have people in the right place at the right time," he explained.

"It probably doesn't make much difference to most people, but to some it's still a dangerous piece of information. The evidence could open up a whole new inquiry. The Warren Commission Report was a political hack job."

Spud set the x-rays down and rummaged through a pile of wrapped packages and assorted jars. Finally, he pulled out a large Tupperware container. "I'm going to tell you what you're seeing and that will help," he said, as he pried off the lid. "I came across this behind a stump at the edge of the blast zone at Mt. St. Helens.

"I believe it is the remains of an alien that was monitoring the mountain and died before it could get out of the way of the blast. Why the alien was there of course is mere speculation, but the physical evidence is quite conclusive. If you look at this section..." Spud placed a backbone and partial skull on a board. "You can see the curvature of an elongated cranial dome. And here is a complete eye socket and the top half of another socket. Large eyes—exceptional really—for a creature no more than two feet tall." Spud carefully maneuvered the remains to another vantage point.

"This is the spinal column of an organism that walked upright— maybe with a stoop, as we found areas of arthritis nodules, so we know the specimen was not young, but then we don't know what kind of longevity we're dealing with here."

Spud pulled a sketch from a yellowed manila folder on the side of the box. "Here is a sketch using anthropomorphic measurements. Of course, all alien pictures look alike after awhile, however this specimen is considerably smaller than any other remains. I've been in area 51 and what they have there doesn't hold a candle to what we have here.

"Now, one of the areas of concern that Professor Hawking and I were discussing last night was the discovery of a large asteroid—perhaps a tenth the size of our moon. It's hidden behind Jupiter right now and the Hubble telescope is having a terrible time tracking it, but Hawking's last vectors showed a high probability that it may hit the earth in..." Spud pulled out some scribbled paper from his shirt pocket. He frowned and put on his glasses. "Steve says roughly two hundred and four years, three months, two days, and some ten hours before a cataclysmic event that his projections show could result in a nuclear winter.

"Now, one of the projects in my think tank was how to set off enough nuclear devices to affect a change in the earth's orbit in order to escape the catastrophic path of something like this asteroid. Of course, that could be dicey and the after-effects would be 'absolutely mind boggling,' according to Steve. And he would probably be right. Steve thought that intercepting the asteroid in flight might be achievable, but the logistics are beyond us at this point. Of course, you can't let information like this get out to the general public. There would be chaos."

Spud then pulled out the spiraled shell of an abandoned sea snail.

"Hold it up against your ear," he encouraged John Hunt. "Do you hear it?" he asked John.

"It's a roaring sound," John said as he passed the shell to Annie. "I've heard it before."

"That sound you hear is the big bang," Spud nodded his head in affirmation. "It is the echoing sound of the universe being formed billions of years ago."

Sister Mary grunted and rolled her eyes. Annie looked in the box and spotted something sparkling. "What's that?" she asked, pointing at the cloth.

"Oh, that is the gown that Marilyn Monroe was wearing on JFK's birthday. You know, Happy Birthday, Mr. President. The dress they sewed on to her."

"So, do you know anything about how she died?" Ziggy asked, leaning forward over the box.

"I know everything." Spud's eyes darted around and he seemed suddenly guarded as he quickly filled the Styrofoam chest with his treasures and closed the lid. Everyone around the campfire could see he had a lot more trophies in the box. The island inhabitants were stunned to have access to this kind of information. But, it didn't deter South from taking her turn at Show-and-Tell. She began to tell about the Broadway opening she attended last night, but Annie patted her hand. "Not tonight, dear, the party is breaking up."

Sister Mary walked over to Spud. "We're going to throw down a few brewskis at the Whistling Oyster later tonight. Would you like to come along?"

"I think I'd like that," Spud decided.

"Be at my cabin at ten," Sister cackled. "I just may have a surprise for you."

When Spud showed up at Sister Mary's cabin, she introduced him to Joe. "Ah, the bunker man." Spud shook his hand.

"I enjoyed your recitation on JFK and the alien last night," Joe complimented Spud as they walked to the raft.

"Did I see you there?" Spud was puzzled.

"No. Electronic surveillance by drone," Joe explained as they hopped into the raft. "I think I can help shed a little more light on your theories."

"Really," Spud grunted, as they began to paddle.

Joe extricated the Mustang convertible from the garage and soon they were sailing down the road to the Whistling Oyster. The ceiling at the bar was hung with logging memorabilia, ancient hundred-pound chainsaws, long misery whip saws, huge block-and-tackle sets, and pictures on the wall of small men and giant trees, hundreds of feet long and twelve to fifteen feet in diameter. Trees that put the Pacific Northwest on the map.

The bar was built of rustic logs with a Douglas fir slab counter three feet wide and forty feet long without a single knot hole. Below the front of the bar was a foot-wide copper half-pipe that ran the length and drained into a hole in the floor.

"Still has the urinal intact," Spud pointed out. "So the loggers could just keep on drinking and never had to leave the bar for a piss. They'd just stand there and let 'er rip."

"How convenient," said Sister, wrinkling her nose.

They found a table in the corner where they could survey the poorly lit interior. The barmaid smiled behind a gold front tooth as she dealt out round coasters as if they were cards, threw a grimy wet rag on the table, and stood, hand on hip, snapping her gum. "Whaddaya have?"

"What's on tap?" Joe asked, as he picked up the rag and wiped the table.

"Alaskan amber, Mack and Jack, Bud, Bud light, Whistling Oyster amber," she rattled off.

"Three Oyster Ambers," Joe said, looking around the table. "Yeah, three of those."

"And six oyster shooters," Sister Mary added.

Three men leaning at the bar kept staring at the table until finally one of them came over and just stood looking down at Sister Mary. Finally, he slurred, "My mother made me go to Catholic school and the nuns treated me like shit, and the priest was buggering my brother."

"Sorry to hear that," Sister said sincerely.

"Yeah, well, sorry don't cut it." He weaved from side to side. "You and your kind are nothing but trouble. I think I need to even up the score."

Joe stood up. "Back away from the table, buddy, now!" he ordered. The man leaned over the table belligerently.

"Oh, yeah? You and what army are gonna throw me out of the bar?" The drunk looked over his shoulder and nodded to his buddies, who trotted over hoping for a little cheap entertainment.

Before the event spiraled out of control, Sister swept the man's feet out from under him and his chin slammed into the table top. He was out cold. The other men retreated to the bar.

"Wow!" Spud exclaimed. "That was impressive."

"Zena, warrior princess." Joe shook his head as he pushed back his chair and stepped over the inert body as they moved to another table.

They all sucked down the oyster shooters and had another beer. Joe leaned back in his chair.

"You know the twelve pictures the guy took of the book depository in Dallas just before and right after the assassination?"

"Yeah, I've seen those. They seemed a little fuzzy," Spud said, setting down his beer.

"I've got enhanced images that conclusively show Jack Ruby coming out of the building right after the assassination. And, I've got a guy in my old unit that was there and he has a piece of occipital bone that he found at least fifty feet to the rear of the limousine.

"You know what that means, right?" Joe leaned over the table. "There had to have been…"

"Uh, excuse me, I'm going outside for a smoke," interrupted Sister.

When she came back a half hour later, the two men were still deep in conversation. She threw two ropes and a couple of three-foot one-by-sixes on the table.

"Time to go to work, boys," she smirked.

"What are we going to do?" Joe asked, picking up the rope. "Lynch some red-necked loggers?"

"Is there another kind?" snarked Spud.

"Nope, we're going out to do some crop circles this evening. The frost is out there and it makes for easy trampling," Sister announced. "I'll even stand you guys one more beer before we go."

"Crop circles," Spud pondered. "I thought that was some kind of weather phenomenon or something and I always hoped it was aliens."

"You wish. I've done 'em all over," said Sister, who caught the barmaid's eye and nodded. "From Europe, South America, and here in the good old US of A. And I'm hatching another plan. You boys know anything about *foie gras*?"

"I've heard of it," Joe admitted. "Something to do with goose livers?"

"I've had it at a few retreats." Spud nodded his head. "But I think it was duck."

"Goose, duck, who's counting?" Sister sneered. "The point is, that it is inhumane to force feed the birds with funnels to enlarge their livers. So I'm thinkin' about rustling some of the feathered critters. You boys interested?"

"Is it illegal?" Spud asked.

"Illegal as hell," Sister smiled.

"Then I'm in," Spud declared as Joe nodded approval. When the three beers were set on the table, Spud leaned over in a low voice. "Some of those crop circles are pretty elaborate. What kind can you do?"

"It's a Catholic thing," Sister took a sip of beer and set it down. "I'm just a circle kind of gal. I missed the seminars in advanced design, but I'm good at what I know.

"You boys in or do I have to do them myself? The cornfield is just a few miles over toward Port Townsend and right over the flight path of the local airport so we will get plenty of exposure. It's gonna be fun."

"Okay," the men agreed again, but Joe bought a pint of whiskey at the bar. Just to keep warm, he said, slipping it into his camo coat pocket.

"Oh, don't worry, you'll stay plenty warm out there," Sister promised.

They parked on a small knoll that overlooked the cornfield just as the fog was beginning to drift among the tasseled stalks as if they were the fingers of an incoming tide. It was only a half moon, but in the frosty air you still could have read a newspaper.

"You know," Joe began, "this is about the size of the grassy knoll…"

"Enough already!" admonished Sister. "I have a little information I might share with you myself later, but you guys are on my clock now."

Sister Mary had scouted a trail to the side of the cornfield and she showed them how to slip between the stalks to leave no trace of passage.

When they reached the middle of the field, she pulled out a folded diagram of her design. It was four overlapping circles, "somewhat similar to the Olympics logo," she said, tracing the circles with her finger. Each circle was about forty feet in diameter with a bigger one free-standing off to the side. "Just to keep 'em guessing," she whispered. She folded up her paper and played out the rope to Joe.

"That's it," she called out quietly. "Keep the rope taut, rotate around me, and trample everything in a circle. I'll let the rope out a little more on each revolution. Move it out, soldier." Joe went around until Sister felt the knot she had put in the rope.

"Okay, that's it for the first one, Bud," she called out.

Joe stood back to survey his handiwork. As he bent over to catch his breath, Sister twittered, "Stand up straight, soldier."

Joe had left layers of clothes lying everywhere and he was still dripping wet as the steam rolled off his forehead as if he was on fire.

"We've got to pick up all the clothing. If we don't, the jig is up and I'll hear about it from the mother office," Sister threatened.

Spud did the next circle, but was so slow that he had extorted a few more rounds of beer from Sister by the time he finished. The last two circles Sister did herself after showing Joe how to hold the rope.

"It's not brain surgery, it's just damned hard work," she panted as she trampled the stalks.

They went back to the knoll to survey their work while sipping on the whiskey. Sister lit two cigarettes and gave one to Joe. When they finished, she buried the butts under a clump of moss. "Leave no butt behind," she squeaked, as she strained to pull herself up off the ground.

Sister gave one last look at the field. "I'm inspired," she announced to the weary men. "I think we will do a concentric circle for the last one, now that you boys are warmed up." She went to the far northwest corner and worked back to find the center and then they took turns doing the circles and leaving untouched rings of stalks. "Just like the rings of Saturn," Sister kept saying.

They picked up everything, as Sister kept obsessing, continually looking behind them as they walked out of the field. The last view from the knoll was gratifying. "Some of the best work I've ever done," Sister acknowledged. "Let's get back before last call."

The men groaned in approval.

"This will be one night I don't need my Tylenol PM®," Spud wheezed.

Chapter
FOURTEEN

W hite Bear had invited Annie to come to the Makah Indian reservation on the Pacific Coast to see what the finished canoe would look like.

"I'd have to bring the twins," she said. "They need to go to Port Townsend for their shots anyway," she whispered.

"Why are you whispering?" White Bear whispered back.

"Because they hate their shots," Annie whispered behind her hand.

"They don't know what shots are," White Bear continued to whisper self-consciously. "They're too young."

"I'm not taking any chances," Annie said out loud, "and that's all there is to it."

"Tomorrow, then," White Bear whispered.

Trish spent most of her time in the darkness of the cabin worrying about her girls. She had given up treatment for the breast cancer. The galloping ALS slurred her speech, and now one foot was dragging. She was trying to be brave for the girls, but the loss of facial muscle control only allowed a cruel half-smile. Fearing they would be discovered by her husband, Trish was reluctant even to let the girls out to play on the island, but she finally had become resigned to the fact that they couldn't spend every day inside. So when Annie and Max invited the girls to go to the ocean, she relented.

When they got out of the car at Cape Alava, the girls—who rarely left Seattle—had no idea that the world's biggest ocean was just on the other side of the mountains. Annie had brought two backpacks for the twins, and put knit bonnets on their little heads. A very compliant Zack was bundled into his carrier and strapped to Max's back, but it took all four of them to get Little Annie, who kept arching her back, strapped onto her great-grandmother.

"She's a little dickens," Annie said, shaking her head when Little Annie was finally trussed up.

"She's a handful," Alisha agreed, rubbing the top of Little Annie's hat.

White Bear and the others padded down the flat, well-worn, muddy path that led through the spindly alders. Soon the trail began traversing down across the hill, the canopy changing to thick-trunked spruce with stringy clumps of moss that hung like shrouds on the branches. As the trail turned steeper and the distant rumble of the ocean rattled the trees, moisture-laden fog pushed hard by the west wind stung their faces and made Annie squint and pull down her stocking cap.

Talisha and Alisha had never seen the ocean, and despite Annie's warning, Trish had dressed them in shiny patent leather shoes, Nordstrom three-hundred-dollar wool coats, slacks, and matching black French berets that made them well-dressed for their annual Santa pictures but hardly warm enough with their long hair blowing in the persistent ocean winds that forced the trees near the ocean edge to grow sideways.

The twins became round-eyed when they first heard the primal crashing of the ocean waves against the centuries-old cliffs of basalt, while the beads of moisture on their chubby cheeks pushed sideways into their mouths and for the first time they tasted the salt of the Pacific Ocean. Delighted, they giggled and kept drumming their fists on Annie and Max's heads.

The ocean beach was made of small pea-sized rocks that had been worn smooth by the pounding waves, and each time the waves receded, there was the soft fizzing sound of foam evaporating and the subtle clinking of a million tiny rocks tumbling over each other, pulled down the sloping beach toward the water's edge.

Farther down the beach, there was a rustic wooden workshop where the canoe carver had worked his magic to create a sleek black paddling canoe that could challenge the sea on its own terms. Annie and Max peered into the canoe and saw the thousands of overlapping adz marks—each slash smooth as if done by a machine. There were tribal symbols on the gunwales and a small mast in front. The seats were a single slab of cedar, notched into the hull. Holding onto the side of the canoe, White Bear looked out to the sea. "The boat is worthy," he grunted.

Beyond the workshop was the engineered log-framed longhouse that served as the community center of the Makah village and a museum that housed artifacts from a dig into a Native midden mound near Lake Ozette.

Max asked Mariana, one of the Tyee tribal council members, if it was difficult for the locals to belong to one culture and try to assimilate into another. "Especially out here on the coast, a hundred miles from Seattle, I certainly find myself falling further behind the computer generation," Mariana admitted. "I'm in my mid-thirties and I feel like I'm being replaced already. The culture is cell phones and online.

"Talking and the human touch will change a heart, but the computer connects us to the world, even out here." Mariana looked wistfully at her village of modular homes and broken cars. "The European way is not our way. The change has come too swiftly and our people who have succeeded must find a way to come back to us and show us the way forward. The other tribes have casinos, but we are working on a wrinkle to promote tourism that I picked up in Central America. Come with me to the longhouse," Mariana beckoned.

She took them to a video room and dimmed the lights. The Makah tribal logo of an eagle straddling an arching salmon flashed on the screen and then there was underwater footage of men swimming with whales.

"Gray whales," Mariana filled in the blanks. "We have a grant to try to tame the local gray whales and some of the humpbacks that come every summer to our waters to feed. They can become quite playful, but they are powerful. So far no one has been injured, but we are working to see if it can become a tourist industry to come and swim with our whales. Whales live for a very long time and have excellent memories and it is easy to distinguish one whale from another.

"There," Mariana pointed to the screen. "There's old Gertie and her calf. And there is the footage of one of the boys riding on the back of that old gray whale." The video was nearing the end.

"It's just a pilot program, but I think we can make whale riding as popular as swimming with dolphins and maybe better if we throw in some local folklore and a touch of mysticism. Whales can be very regal," she concluded, as the film ended with a scene of whales breeching in the surf. A lot more fun than a lumpy manatee.

"I understand, White Bear, that the University of Washington is filming the making of the canoe and the voyage. That sounds exciting." Mariana ushered them into the lobby while she talked.

"The film may be a lasting legacy that we can share with other cultures," said White Bear. "The American culture's dealing with death is dysfunctional. Maybe the video will make a difference. I don't know. I think the definition of a good death is to go out on your own terms and that's what I intend to do."

"Amen to that," Annie agreed.

While Annie was at the ocean, life was calm on the island. Trish was packing some of her clothes and Ziggy was taking a nap in his cabin while Matty had gone up to Annie's for baking soda, lemon juice, and a soft cotton towel to polish her bronze urns that were turning green.

Christine had never heard a boat motor rev that loud and she looked out in time to see a needle-pointed ski boat hit the beach and three men dressed in black hooded sweatshirts and baggy jeans jump onto the beach and pull handguns. They started to kick in doors and were just about to kick in the door of Ziggy's when Joe fired a rocket launcher. The explosion blew the boat apart and the smoke and flames curled into the air. The lead man turned to watch the flames.

When Trooper rounded the corner, the man fired twice, grazing the dog's shoulder, whereupon Trooper rolled over once and sprang back to the attack, clamping down on the lead man's gun arm. The man managed to fire two wild rounds before Trooper bit down and forced the gun from his hand.

After firing the rocket, Joe put on his sunglasses and had taken up a position behind Ziggy's cabin and rushed the second man. He kicked the gun away and spun around with a roundhouse kick that cold-cocked the intruder. A third man was running at Joe when Christine shot him in the thigh and he went down writhing in pain. Joe pried Trooper off his quarry, pulled the man's arms behind him, and slipped the plastic handcuffs on. After Joe had cuffed them all and treated the man's leg wound, he made them sit on the beach.

Christine had immediately gone to tend Trooper, but with all the blood on his fur she couldn't find the entrance wound. Joe patted Trooper on the head and took his knife and cut away the bloodied fur on the shoulder until he saw skin.

"Ah, just a flesh wound, soldier, you'll be all right in a few days." Trooper licked Joe's hand and struggled to get up. "Stay down, big fella," Joe ordered. "You've done enough for one day."

"Hey, dude," the lead gunman mouthed. "Dude, we just want what's coming to us. We're looking for the BC bud that we had to throw overboard. I heard it might be around here."

Joe hunched down in front of the three men. "You boys from around here?"

"Maybe," another one snarled.

"Familiar with that little incident in that pasture up past Port Angeles?"

"Yeah, so what." The third man was getting cocky.

"That was the Russian Mafia," Joe said as he put his knife back in his sheath. "If you think you're tougher than those boys, then you're not as smart as I thought. If you ever come back here, I will personally fill your ass with c-4 and blow you up. There's nothin' here that you boys want, trust me."

Joe frisked the three men and found a few knives and two metal throwing stars. He straightened and flipped one star underhand and stuck it in a lone pier pole in the water a hundred feet away. The remains of the fiberglass boat were still burning in the water when Joe marched them past and into his raft. He loosened one man's cuffs with his knife, gave him a paddle, loaded the other two men, and shoved the raft with his foot. When the boat was near the lone pier, Joe flipped the other star into the aft end of the raft. As the raft began to deflate, Joe called out to them. "There's two good chambers left, boys. If you paddle real fast, you might make it to land."

"How ya doing?" Joe shook Christine's hand. "I don't think we've ever met. I'm from over in the bunker."

Christine smiled. "I'm Christine, and you showed up just in the nick of time."

"Not really," Joe deferred the credit. "You and Trooper had 'em on the run."

Joe shaded his eyes with his hand. "I've got to get back to my bunker. The sun is killing me. Can you pour a little peroxide into Trooper's wound and then put on a little Neosporin. The bullet went just through the skin. And you tell him for me, he was a hero today."

Joe put his hand on Christine's shoulder. "Good shot, by the way." And he was gone.

When Christine told Annie of the day's events, Annie only had one thought. "It's time for a potluck and parlay," she declared.

Ziggy came out of his haze and apologized to everyone twice. So, by the time the meeting started after dinner, he was ready to take responsibility.

"I'm sorry," Ziggy repented. "I didn't know it was going to be such a big deal. I know I'm going to have to get rid of the stuff, but for awhile I was in heaven."

"No one blames you, Ziggy, but we do have to get rid of the pot and I think we need to get it to a medical marijuana distribution center," said Annie, opening the floor for discussion. "There are several in Tacoma. They'll be glad to get the stuff."

"I think we need to have some here for our own needs and especially Trish. It might take the edge off of her days a little. Just one bundle or so," Christine pitched in.

"Any ideas on how to move the merchandise?" Annie looked around the room.

"We could use the tugboat, but if we get caught they would confiscate the *Pissant* in a heartbeat." Pinky rubbed his chin.

Owl decided to pony up. "Pickles and I can do it in the VW van. We hauled a body down to Tacoma and back last year so I'm sure we can handle a little pot."

"We'll make our move in a few days," Pickles confirmed. Heartbroken, but resigned, Ziggy went home to his treasure to get in one last good roll.

To earn money for Christmas, Talisha and Alisha had taken over baby-watch pretty much full time, except during the homeschool classes taught by Max, and helping to feed Starbuck. They had gathered enough money and sweet-talked Ziggy—who seemed to have no resistance to their pleas—into taking them into Port Townsend for shopping. They stopped on the way at Mom's Diner for milkshakes.

Garnet was looking haggard as she waddled out from the back with her spatula and quizzed the girls about the island. They told Garnet about feeding Starbuck, the nun at the end of the spit, the crazy man in the sandbag bunker, and lastly about their mother and her sickness. "She's not going to get better," Alisha volunteered.

Mom looked at Ziggy for verification and he nodded. "Well, then, you will have to take a pie home for your mother. What kind does she like?"

"Shoo-fly pie, I think," Talisha guessed. "Mama used to make it for us before she got sick."

"I've heard of it," Garnet admitted, "but I don't know how to make it. But, you stop by on the way back and I will have one ready for you to take home."

The VW bus rolled through the soggy December fields of Chimacum Valley and they pulled into Pickles Emporium just after lunch. Pickles had been inspired by his business partner Madeline's "Twisted Sister" apparel at Thanksgiving, but in a Christmas-y sort of way. He had on black patent leather boots with a five-inch spike heel, accented with brass buckles stacked from ankle to knee. His red velvet jumpsuit was sloppily tucked into the boots and there was a coiled whip dangling on one side of his eight-inch black belt, topped off with a big brass buckle that read Harley Loves Bad Santa. On the other side was a misery whip with razor-spiked stars every six inches that hung past his knee.

Pickles had spent days fashioning a bustier with battery-operated, tiny, colored twinkling lights sewn onto the cups and around the back. The Santa hat, which hung down his back, was flaccid with six restrictor rings and three balls at the end.

"Wait, wait wait," Pickles cried as he ran to the light switch, turned off the lights, turned on the bustier, and began to dance through the aisles to Madonna's "Santa Baby," complete with shimmys. The girls watched in amazement and then clapped in appreciation. Pickles was tickled as he turned on the lights.

"My mama has an outfit sorta like that," Talisha said, looking at the jar full of half-eaten floating pickles.

"Exactly like this?" Pickles pouted.

"Not exactly, but kinda," Talisha answered, still transfixed by the pickles.

Pickles straightened up and felt vindicated. "What are we looking for today, ladies?"

"Something in leopard," Talisha said decidedly.

"Leopard, leopard, leopard." Pickles liked to say things in threes while he was thinking. He closed his eyes and tapped his teeth with his finger. *Shoes, shoes, shoes.*

"Ah ha, I have it." He went to the door of the store's walk-in safe, spun the dial, and twisted the large stainless steel handle. The door swung open and a light automatically lit up the interior. The girls peeked around the door. The sides were lined with racks of shoes. Thousands of shoes. Pickles was standing in the safe still tapping his teeth. "Imelda Marcos, no...Monroe...no...Garbo...no...Grace Kelly...no...Esther Williams...Esther Williams...Esther Williams... of course, I love it," he said, taking a pole, unhooking a pair of shoes above his head, and sliding them down to the grip.

Leaning against the safe door to close it, Pickles walked to the counter and plunked down the cutest pair of leopard pumps. "Size six. I know that is the size your mom wears because I-saw-her–at-Thanks-giving," Pickles chanted melodiously.

"They were worn by a famous fashion model that was also an Olympic diver. She wore these shoes in a photo shoot wearing a leopard swimming suit," Pickles said absentmindedly as he flipped through his cross-referenced filing cabinet.

"There it is. Here's the picture of her wearing the suit and the shoes."

"I like them," Alisha decided as she picked up a shoe and smelled it. "I like the smell of leather. Let's get them for mama." Wiser than her sister, Talisha asked, "How much are they?"

Pickles fingered the misery whip on his hip. He calculated. He lusted after the shoes, but had haggled with the seller for five days and finally paid five hundred plus shipping on eBay two years ago. On delivery he discovered the shoes were open toe and that didn't give him much to chew on. They weren't bad shoes. They just weren't something he could get his teeth into.

"We don't have a lot of money." Talisha opened her wallet and pulled out two tens and a five. She unsnapped the coin pocket and dumped out two quarters and a nickel. "There, that's all of it."

Pickles thought maybe the shoes could kind of be on a loan basis, given the situation, and he would have a shot at them later down the road.

"Okay," he capitulated. "Rock-bottom price is five and a quarter with tax, but if she doesn't like them I want to buy them back."

Pickles wondered aloud if their mother would like them.

"They're leopard, silly," Alisha admonished Pickles. "My mom is all about leopard."

"Do you have anything in a leopard thong?" Talisha asked. "I think Max might like something like that. She's hot." Pickles pulled one out of his Personals drawer and smelled the crotch. "Slightly used but in excellent shape," he declared. "It's on the house."

Pickles put the shoes and thong in a box. By the time they left it was dark and Pickles turned on his outfit and stood in the middle of the road, waving as they drove away.

Alisha turned around for one last look at Pickles. "He's weird," she announced firmly, "but in a good way."

Ziggy thought to himself, *Well, that would be a legacy anyone could live with.*

They stopped at the diner and picked up the shoo-fly pie, but Garnet hadn't been feeling well and went home early,

After dark, Annie, Ziggy, Spud and Joe took *The Ark* over to the mainland and sat at a table at Wiggins' grocery while they poured over the layout of a house of alleged abuse as well as some photographs that had been sent to Sister from her source in the local parish after Father O'Malley failed to have any effect on the parental abuse.

"We'll put the fear of God in 'em, by cracky," Sister predicted as they loaded into the VW. The house was a small rambler on isolated acreage near Port Hadlock. They parked Jerry, the VW bus, on a side road and waited while Joe planted some explosives, and they struggled into their costumes.

"You call this brown chicken Halloween costume a disguise?" Owl complained. "It looks like a potato sack with feathers, I can't find the eye holes anywhere, and this plastic yellow beak is heavy."

"Shut the H E double toothpick up," Sister snarled in return. "I got 'em on craigslist for five bucks apiece from some gone out of business chicken restaurant. The eye hole is just a slit in the neck. Here, I'll poke my finger through so you can find them," she added impatiently.

"Ow!" Ziggy bent over in pain. "You poked your finger in my eye."

"Oh, I thought you were Owl," Sister apologized as she put on her chicken head.

Joe returned. "Aw jeez, Sister. Chicken costumes? We look ridiculous."

Sister was in no mood for criticism and took her plastic chicken foot with the red nails and planted it in Joe's shin.

The four chickens stumbled and grumbled their way up the sidewalk to the door, losing crepe feathers along the way. Ziggy tripped and his disguise went askew. He repositioned the head on backwards, but by holding on to Spud's tail, he managed to keep up.

Sister rang the doorbell. She could see a man sitting in the living room watching television. "Get the door," the man called out to his wife. "I'm watching the game."

The wife gave a mumbled excuse and the man swore, threw down the paper, and opened the door. "What do you want?" he challenged. Then, "What the…" He began to laugh.

"Hey, Loretta, gotta see these butt ugly costumes. They are the worst I've ever seen. Where'd you get those losers? They're pathetic!"

Joe gave a loud, audible snicker. Sister sputtered, and before she could get her speech out, the wife showed up. She laughed, "You mud hens are two months late and a dollar short in the brains department. Hey, look at that dork over there. His beak isn't even facing the right way."

A bedroom door behind them opened and an old man poked his face out the door. He still had the remains of a black eye and his cheek was swollen.

"Get back in your room, you old bastard," the man threatened. His wife threw an empty beer can and the man ducked back behind the door.

Annie got her game back. "We're here because there are reports you have been abusing your father and stealing his retirement and social security checks."

"So what if we are? What are you chickens gonna do about it? Lay an egg?" he snickered. "And besides, dude, you're molting on my front lawn." The man laughed out loud as he began to close the door.

Joe wedged his chicken foot in the door and pressed the first button on his remote detonator. A fifty-foot maple tree in the front yard exploded and toppled over.

"Whaaaaaaaaaaat? You're crazy!" The man opened the door wider. "I'm phoning the police." Joe showed the man the buttons on the detonator. "Care to try for two?" No response. So he pressed the second button and the Costco lamp post at the end of the driveway launched like a rocket and landed across the road.

"I'm calling the…"

Joe showed the man the label on the third button, which read "car" and number four, "truck." "All right, all right, maybe I've been a little tough on the old man, but he's a lot of trouble," the man said in excuse.

Shaking her wing at the man, Sister continued. "We are an advocate for the elderly. If we get further reports your father is still being abused, we will contact the proper authorities and then we will be back to take care of business. We know where you work, we know where you live, we know the marina where you have your boat, we can access the IRS files, we can hack into your social security file, and take over your identity. We have the tools to hurt you. Think it over."

The man closed the door. "Shit, we're in trouble, Loretta. Those chickens mean business."

Ziggy stumbled again getting back to the bus. They threw off the disguises. "Well done, I'd say."

"I'm sweating like a Thanksgiving turkey," Joe complained.

"Well, I'm itching like crazy," Spud whined. "Sister, did you fumigate these suckers? Ever hear of head lice?"

"The guy was right about one thing," Owl said, jumping into the driver's seat. "Those are the ugliest costumes I've ever seen.

"We have the tools to hurt you," Owl mimicked. "Did you get that quote from a Dirty Harry movie?"

"Bite me." Sister Mary punched Owl in the ribs and they were off.

Chapter FIFTEEN

The week before Christmas the weather had threatened snow all week.

"It never snows at sea level," Annie assured everyone. "We haven't had snow on Christmas for years."

It was Thanksgiving *deja vu* all over again for Christmas. There were the people, there was the feast, and there were the presents. Even Joe had come out of his bunker at Sister's request and attended the party, protesting mightily, but attending nevertheless.

Talish and Alisha watched anxiously while their mother painstakingly opened their present, and when they told everyone the story of Pickles, they laughed and laughed, especially when they told everyone about the pickle jar.

The girls put the shoes on their mother who was in a wheelchair, and except for the curl in her lips and the droopy half of her face, she was still stunning, and inside, her mind and spirit were still strong. She had only one mantra these days—finding a home for her girls. Her body was crumbling. It was no longer a race. Breast cancer be damned, ALS was going to have its way first.

Ziggy told how Alisha had said, "Pickles was weird, in a good way." Everyone agreed and slapped Pickles on the back. Pickles cried a little to think his complex nature was understood and accepted by a child.

Owl had finished the leopard casket on time and it was a beauty. He had the outside professionally painted by a faux artist and the spots looked 3-D real. The inside was done in a leopard print by an upholsterer in Port Townsend, and Owl had painstakingly carved Trish's name on the lid. It had a pneumatic hinge that closed slowly so as not to pinch fingers. It was a bittersweet present, but Trish gave Owl a kiss on the cheek and he blushed.

The entertainment started when Annie turned down all the hurricane lamps and Max, sitting by the fire, read *The Night before Christmas*.

When the lights were turned up again, Pinky launched into a medley of show biz songs from *West Side Story, Jesus Christ Superstar,* and *Showboat*. Christine played "Jingle Bell Rock" while Talisha and Alisha did a tap dance routine, and John Colby ended with a harmonica solo of Gershwin tunes. Dessert was over the top as usual and everyone said it had been a lovely evening.

Max had been thinking lately about her life—a lot. Beautiful and accomplished, with a healthy trust fund, she had always had life on her terms. Many times she had deftly sidestepped the "messy" side of life and stood watching as the tide swept by without her. Now, she found herself swimming in a world of babies, an orca named Starbuck, two little black girls, John Colby, and the most courageous people she'd ever met. They weren't hiding on the island like she first thought; they were fighting windmills every day. Now, she knew for the first time in her life she wanted to fight windmills. Every day for the rest of her life.

She told John to meet her at her father's old cabin on the spit after the party. The wood stove had kept the cabin warm and the hurricane lantern was flickering low. Men had usually tried to kiss Max first. Max hadn't initiated a kiss since Bobby Hopkins at the sixth-grade dance. But now, she kissed John and he returned with a strong kiss of his own.

"Well," Max said, putting her arms around his neck. "I've decided I want to spend my life fighting windmills." John looked puzzled.

Max continued, "I'm thinking about adopting Alisha and Talisha, and I'm going to find a way to get Starbuck back to his mother, and I want to have a baby. And I want to spend the rest of my time fighting windmills—with you.

"What do you think about that?" Max asked, staring at him and waiting for his response. "Did you want to do some negotiating?"

John gave her a goofy look and said, "What's to negotiate?"

Max laughed and dropped her jeans. She knew Pickles had worn the thong first, but she wanted it all, Pickles to Starbucks and everything in between. "I was hoping, Santa, you could slide down my chimney and put a little something in my stocking," she pouted.

John slid the velvet box with the ring back into his pocket. "I think I have something for your stocking that is just the right size," he smiled.

Chapter
SIXTEEN

New Year's Eve on the island had always been a reflective time. The island's champions were all at a crossroads. They recalled the victories and losses of the past year and knew they would fight those battles along with new challenges that would continue to attack their old bones. They knew in their heart it was a losing battle, and they also knew they would meet the future in the same way they always had—loving and crying, accepting and denying, hoping and praying, devastated and elated, exhausted and relentless, but with courage, day after day after day.

Annie knew that the coming year would be an active year for her children. She also knew it was going to take a village. And she hoped her sisters would keep their promise.

Annie took stock: John Hunt was hoping to come up with a solution to the Mom's Diner situation, continue writing his food column, and greeting the grandkids.

Al, called Owl because he was hard of hearing and kept saying "who?," had recently got some new hearing aids and was forever working on improving his casket and wondering when his time would be up.

Ziggy and Matty had been fairly new arrivals on the island and they were more wanderers than anything else. Jerry Garcia, their '64 Volkswagen bus, was due for an oil change.

South Carolina Storm had deteriorated significantly since the death of her twin sister, but her social fantasy life of dinner parties and Academy Awards was the envy of the island.

Max was headed in a new direction and she was excited to make lasting commitments to John Colby, to orcas, and to children.

Christine, the concert pianist and daughter of the island legend Moby Dick, was still finding her feet, but she came from "good stock," had a great sense of humor, and had proved herself a dead shot.

Pickles had the full-time job of just being Pickles.

Professor Spud, occupant of the fourth cabin over from Annie, with his Styrofoam chest, would probably continue wielding his conspiracy theories.

And Joe and Sister? Who knew what they were up to.

Pinky had wedged himself into the crow's nest on the good ship *Pissant* with his bagpipes, They all listened with reverence as he played "Danny Boy," "Strawberry Fields Forever," and "Amazing Grace."

The island took a communal deep breath and would begin work on their new journeys in the morning, the beginning of a new year.

With the passage of the Solstice on December 21, the island had turned a corner. The crocus along the path to the house had ventured out and there were shoots on the willow and wild sumac, but the islanders knew that there was a lot of winter to plow through before spring.

Max put on her rubber boots and trekked to Trish's cabin. She knocked, and heard something that sounded like "come in." The door swung open and the heat from the room galloped from the room.

Trish shivered in the wheelchair and tried to look with her eyes but they no longer focused.

Max had been making overtures to Trish for weeks about her girls. Trish gave a garbled interpretation of a mother's worries. "I don't have anyone on my side of the family I trust and I sure as hell don't trust that dog of an ex-husband, but I don't know if my girls could adapt. I just don't know at this point. Blended families can be a problem. I've got Professor Singer in the sociology department digging up some information on the family tree, so we'll just have to wait and see, dear. We still have time. Not much, but some."

Owl and Joe had been designing a casket for Joe. They decided on a matte finish chamo exterior and an aromatic Tennessee cedar finish for the interior after Joe's old hometown, Buzzard Roost, Tennessee. "Smells like home," Joe said, sniffing the pungent cedar boards.

As he helped Owl cut out the planks of Douglas fir, he said, "it never hurts to be prepared. No one gets out of here alive so I reckon I'll be planting my roots in Arlington some day. If they'll take an old war horse like me."

Owl countered, "I just want them to put me in my casket and float me out to the middle of Puget Sound, wire on some weights, and sink me right down to the bottom. I've always loved the water. Sewage water, fishing water, fire water, it's all the same to me." Owl slapped the top of his casket.

The canoe builders stood knee-deep in cedar chips as they continued working day after day using only their short wooden handle adz and their trained eye to fashion a hull that would slice through the treacherous coastal waters surrounding the islands of British Columbia. When the outside of the hull was finished, they flipped the log over again and began to carve out the inside, again using only the adz and putting their hands on the outside and inside the hull to feel the thickness. This would take weeks of backbreaking work.

With the holidays over, Ziggy was in the doldrums. It was to be expected. He had been the owner of one of the largest stashes of BC bud that anyone had heard of on the west coast. "It was like winning the lottery," Ziggy explained to anyone who would listen, "and then they cut off the checks."

Smoking the last bit of the bud, Ziggy became inspired, or as Matty called it, "*Cannibis compulsive.*" Ziggy became like Richard Dreyfuss in *Close Encounters of the Third Kind* except by a factor of two. He began building two mounds everywhere he went. When the tide went out, he put on his rain gear and built two equal mounds all over the beach. He built them of sand, gravel, rocks, sand dollars, trash that floated up on the beach, and when he was tired he would sit and gaze at the mounds. Big mounds and small mounds, medium mounds and teensy tiny mounds out of the Chinese-capped sea snails. To him they were all a symbol of beauty, but he knew there had to be a higher power involved.

"More than likely a brain tumor," Matty snorted after the obsession had been going on for three weeks. Ziggy was not a religious man but he went to the library and spent weeks trying to interpret his vision. He talked to Professor Spud, who found research material from the Egyptians to the Incas of Peru. "It's like those sculptures on Easter Island," he explained. "No one knows why they built those."

Ziggy would eat only foods that could be made into a mound. He lived primarily on rice and mashed potatoes. Peas drove him crazy until he finally mashed them up and sculpted the mounds. He went to Costco and got huge cans of jellied cranberries and carved them into perfect tapered mounds and then studied his translucent creation from all angles, from the sun coming up in the morning, to the sunset and the moon at night.

"There has to be a message there," he kept mumbling. It was driving him and everyone on the island crazy. He built mounds of cedar chips down by the boat and sand mounds on Wiggins' porch in Port Gamble.

"He's gone completely bonkers," Matty wailed to Annie. "Do you think the bud got to him? He needs professional help."

Ziggy had never been the sharpest tool in the shed, but even he knew he needed professional help and when Lila came to do a reading with Starbuck, she threw in a session with Ziggy.

First, Lila went out with Max, Talisha and Alisha to get a read on Starbuck's mental health. He came charging up to the boat and lifted the bow of *The Ark* three feet and let it slam down. "He's feeling his oats today," Max said as she put vitamins in the dead herring and the two girls fed the orca.

"He seems very gentle, but even as an adolescent he's powerful," Lila warned as she reached over to touch his head. She closed her eyes and there was an audible electric hum coming from the connection between mammal and mammal. Lila opened her eyes and pulled her hand back. "I had a good reading," she said. "He is putting off positive energy and he says he has gained some of the weight back. He's still lonely for his mother and the pod except for the one 'crabby aunt,' he says. There must have been a real falling out. He's still a little worried about the Flintstone vitamins and he's worried about acne and if he is small for his age. I didn't even know orcas could get acne?

"Maybe John Colby can get back to me." Lila wiped her hand on a towel. "I'll be back in a few weeks. I'm still surprised no one has discovered him in this cove, but it is still winter."

They caught up with Ziggy making mounds of clam shells on the beach. Lila explained she was going to do a reading with Ziggy and how she had helped to find lost children as well as diagnosing animal psyches.

"It won't hurt a bit," she reassured Ziggy and she had him close his eyes and sit cross-legged on the sand.

Lila put her two hands on his head and closed her eyes. Her head rocked back once and then she was very quiet. Suddenly, he pulled back and looked puzzled. "Ziggy, this is a simple one," she announced. "Ziggy, the BC bud triggered a primal response from your childhood. You have an oral fixation problem that stems from being weaned too early. You are trying to compensate for this abrupt disruption of comfort when you were approximately three months old. That's why you are building these mounds to make up for that loss. You are equating mounds with breasts. I think one way to effect a cure would be to find or build two very large mounds that would satisfy your craving that you would never run out of your mother's milk. Or, you might want to spend the rest of your life sucking on a pacifier," Lila said not too kindly.

Lila walked towards Max's cabin. "That was spooky in there," she said, mostly to herself. "I hit that oral thing right away and then there was nothing, nada, mush. It was just a complete existential void. I was damn lucky just to get back out of there. I could have been lost forever. That only happened one time before when I was working with a fuzzy wombat. It was spooky, just plain spooky."

The next morning, Ziggy woke up and looked down the spit at Joe's rounded bunker and he imagined an effigy which translated as an epiphany. Smugly, Ziggy slept all day and talked Joe into building a bunker annex that night.

"Two mounds, two bunkers, two boobs," Ziggy announced. What could be simpler. Happily, Ziggy filled sand bags and he and Joe would build all night until they finished the second rounded bunker. Still, he was strangely dissatisfied until he figured out what was missing—nipples. "I need nipples," he shouted at the top of his lungs one morning.

Ziggy went into town and to The Everyday Grind latte and internet shop where he logged onto craigslist, bought vintage copies of *Playboy*, and spent hours pulling out the centerfold. Using a magnifying glass, he built a scrapbook of breasts and nipples and studied day and night until Matty thought his eyes would cross permanently.

"Miss April 1967," Ziggy shouted out one morning.

Then he began to fashion the huge erect tits on top of the mound using bags of concrete mix and rebar. It took several days, but finally, one morning, Ziggy felt happy when he looked down the beach and the compulsion to build mounds was over, although from time to time he would take his sleeping bag and sleep in the cleavage and occasionally wear a pacifier around his neck if he was feeling insecure.

Everything had been quiet for weeks when the Jefferson County sheriff enforcement boat stormed the beach and surrounded the two bunkers. Unfortunately, Ziggy had a relapse and had pitched a tent between the breasts.

Owl had taken the police action in and ran hurriedly over to Joe's bunker where he had spotted the nose of the rocket launcher slowly inch out of a hole in the side of the bunker. Owl, with his new hearing aids, had heard the safety switch on the rocket launcher click to ready as he dove and pushed the nose to one side just as the rocket launched. There was a trail of smoke and the top of an enormous fir tree at the top of the island exploded and hinged in half.

"What the...?" The officers looked to Owl.

"Navy exercises again," he said with a shrug.

The other officers had subdued Ziggy, cuffed him and read him his rights. They showed him the warrant for lewd and lascivious behavior. A protestor *par excellence* from his days at Berkeley, Ziggy had gone completely limp and they had to support him as they dragged him down the beach.

Ziggy began singing, "This land is your land, this land is my land, from the New York..."

Max had not left for work and she and John Colby stormed out
of her cabin. "I'm the lawyer of record for this man," she challenged
the officer. "What are the charges?"

"Lewd and lascivious behavior," the officer answered.

"What?" Max asked, puzzled.

"For creating these two giant breasts for public display."

"That's ludicrous," retorted Max. "He's done nothing wrong. It's
part of his therapy."

"Take it up with the judge, ma'am," the sheriff deputy threw back
as they put Ziggy in the patrol boat and shoved off.

Ziggy had changed his tune to "We shall overcome some day…"
His voice trailed off as the boat disappeared up the coast.

Matty came up the beach in her robe with a quilt wrapped around
her shoulders. She gave Ziggy a peace sign of solidarity as a southerly
gale force wind whipped her long gray hair around her face.

In the middle of the Pacific Ocean, the tropical winds of Hawaii
were sucked like a bowling ball toward the Pacific Coast as if under
the spell of a Dirt Devil. They did a shake-and-bake on the coast and
cartwheeled their way past the Olympic Mountains and shimmied
up Hood Canal until they met a nutcracker of an Arctic wind that
had sashayed south down the chair rails of the Cascade foothills. The
warm winds and the cold Arctic air did a vegematic slice-and-dice
over the Olympics, burying the mountains in mounds of feather
duster snow as white as the wings of a Las Vegas showgirl.

Chapter
SEVENTEEN

John Hunt had been worrying about helping Mom at the diner keep her business afloat and when she wrote him and asked him to cover the diner for two days, he jumped at the chance.

He had lined up the battling Maldano brothers, sporadic and volatile genius chefs of the Cajun Persuasion Bistro on Queen Anne Hill in Seattle. The brothers had battled their way up the grunge ranks of Seattle restaurant society and were now at liberty—banned from their bistro after clocking the maitre d' at the Purple Door with a saucepan and pouring a pitcher of mojitos on his head after some unfortunate wording about the crust on their sweet potato pie. Marvin and Melvin, when not battling each other, could rise to three-star status if the spirit moved and they were eager for a venue change.

The brothers, honed to a shiny ebony finish, were Southern-bred Sumo wrestlers with colored scarves around their neck, corn-rowed hair, tattoos of naked women up and down their massive forearms, and stained white chef shirts that advertised last night's menu.

Pickles also had his hand of fate in the selection with a Blue Light special on his ton of still unsold New Zealand possum. Saturday morning the brothers took over the diner and had whipped up mounds of hush puppies, Cajun quiche with chicken livers, Mardi Gras binets, omelets with shrimp sauce, and New Orleans French toast with persimmon jelly.

The locals were thunderstruck that Mom wasn't there that crisp January morning, but they cowboyed up and politely choked down the cuisine with a 2002 Arkansas Chianti.

Marvin and Melvin had gone for a smoke behind the diner and were instantly unnerved by the aromatic pile of dung behind the neighboring farmer's barn, the local dairy cows leaning over the fence within licking distance, and the giant draft horse that was trotting across the field toward them. Both lactose-intolerant and phobic about large mammals, they scrambled back to the safety of the kitchen.

"My gawd, it's like Jurassic Park out there," Marvin gasped, his back leaning against the rear door as he tried to catch his breath.

Lunch and dinner sidled into one another with Cajun chili, fried green tomatoes, Little Smokey's shrimp gumbo, and for dessert, Mardi Gras molasses cake with crème fraîche.

The local crowd had thinned out early and the small gas/mini mart next door was completely out of Pepcid when the battling brothers went at it. With a large wooden spoon the size of a canoe paddle, Marvin was standing on a stool stirring a second big vat of Sunday's alligator gumbo on top of the stove, and Melvin was rolling out the crust for possum pie with taters—the original recipe endorsed by Grannie on *The Beverly Hillbillies*—when Melvin began kibitzing about the amount of okra in gumbo. Harsh words were spoken.

"You just keep you black ass over by that table," Marvin threatened, as Melvin began to wander over to the black iron South Bend gas stove where the gumbo was simmering.

"Don't you touch my gumbo," Marvin yelled.

"You, and what army, is gonna mess with me?" Melvin took offense.

It wasn't like the brothers didn't know which button to push on each other, having grown up outside of Little Rock, Arkansas, dirt poor and both dyslexic. They had come to cooking honestly by memorizing their grandmother's recipes that always started with a double handful of this and a fistful of that.

Marvin took the oar from the kettle as his brother continued to advance; then without warning hit his brother square on top of the head with the gumbo oar, which only infuriated Melvin. He attacked by grabbing the tail end of a frozen possum loin, flailing away at his brother's shoulders. Melvin dropped his brother to his knees and finished him off with a possum uppercut to the chin, and Marvin was down.

The diner was late opening the next day and by midday the brothers had left town in their yellow '67 Buick Skylark convertible and scuttled back to the big city.

When Mom came in Monday morning early, still rummy from the chemo, she was startled by the two stone-cold skinned possum carcasses on the stainless steel preparation table. She whacked them with a broom until they died a second time and fell on the floor.

Mom turned the remaining gumbo and possum pie over to a homeless shelter in Port Townsend. The gumbo was slurped up appreciatively, but the four big pans of possum were shunned till the director phoned up his last resort: An inspector for the health department who prized his ability to never pay full price for a meal. Mr. Snodgrass savored the delicacy and smacked his lips as he put the other three pans in his freezer.

John came over later in the morning to apologize and help clean up the kitchen.

"I'm really sorry, Mom," he kept saying. "It won't happen again. I've got some more responsible chefs for the next round if you just give me another chance."

If Mom hadn't still been completely out on her feet by the chemo and the torn rotor cuff from thrashing the possums, she might have whacked John with the possum carcass herself.

Chapter
EIGHTEEN

Sister Mary had once again marshaled her troops fireside. "It's time to take down the *foie gras* operation down near the coal mines by Black Diamond, south of Tacoma," she said, pointing out the city on a road map.

"Just what is *foie gras*?" Owl frowned.

"It's mashed-up goose livers. It's a great delicacy in France. They have to force feed the geese every day with a hose or pipe down their throats. That's called *gavage* and that overloads the geese's stomachs. That causes the livers to become five to eight times larger than an ordinary liver and the geese are in constant pain. Didn't we already go over this, dude?" Sister explained. Owl shrugged, taking no real offense.

"Then they kill the geese. It's like veal where they cage the calves and overfeed them till slaughter," Sister continued.

"Are you sure we need to do this?" Owl looked hopefully over at Joe. "Couldn't we just blow up some mailboxes again and save some old guy from his children? You know, stuff closer to home," he said hopefully.

"Absolutely not." Sister looked agitated. "Besides, I commandeered a few bales of that BC bud myself. Just to sweeten the deal," Sister said.

"I'm in," Ziggy stepped forward expectantly.

"And, I think Max and John Colby are in too," Sister added.

The next morning they took the Mustang to Bremerton and rented four large cube vans and drove to Tacoma and had lunch at the Pick Quick hamburger stand on Puyallup Avenue across from the Bates Motel. "These are good hamburgers," John warbled, stuffing some fresh cut fries in his mouth.

"What's the plan from here?" Max asked.

"We meet the goose amnesty people a few miles down the road from here and they will give us last-minute instructions and a cashier's check to pay for the geese. Market rate. We are not paying for the livers. The amnesty folks sent the goose farmers a free dinner at the Space Needle and unlimited drinks at the Kingfish Café afterwards. I predict they'll be gone till late tonight.

"We load the geese into the vans and drive down to Centralia where the amnesty people will give us a ride back to Bremerton. They'll take the geese on down to Lake Havasu in Arizona. You know, the place where they took the London Bridge that turned out to be another bridge? The geese can winter there or move on down south if they want."

"How many geese we talking about?" Max asked.

"A thousand or so, give or take," Sister said offhandedly. "Let's all take a nap in the trucks and get going at dark." Sister yawned.

At five, Annie crawled into the cab of each truck and applied black to all their faces and gave them each a black watch cap. "We look like the Dirty Half-Dozen," Owl chirped.

"Close enough," Max replied. Looking in the mirror, she shuddered.

The amnesty folks met them at a highway rest stop and steered them onto a country lane till they came to a broken-down farm and a double-wide trailer held together by rust. It wasn't till they got out of

the trucks that they heard the cacophony of the honking geese wad-
dling everywhere in the faint floodlights that lit the free range field.

"Shee-et," Joe exclaimed as he looked out over the mass of necks
and black beaks. "They look like they have a lot of attitude."

"I'll show you attitude," Sister said factually. She struck a match
that briefly lit up her face and fired up her Camel straight. "Back the
truck up and we'll put a net to the fence and clip the wire pen with
wire cutters. And Joe you, John and Owl get in there and herd those
critters our way."

She gave each man a wooden staff to herd and protect themselves
and sent them in to fend for themselves. The geese were less confused
than defensive. Owl was heard howling as he roller-skated across
the field of dung chased by six aggressive ganders, as Joe and John
doubled over with laughter.

Engineering the net tunnel to the back of the truck, Max saw huge
piles of geese that had died from overfeeding stacked up just outside
the fence. "Yee haw." Joe challenged the geese as he ran toward them
and waved his stick menacingly and then took a pratfall in the goose
droppings that covered the entire field. The geese honked defiantly
and put up a good battle, but soon the four trucks were filled with
flighty geese.

Annie got on the handset. "Breaker, breaker, this is Mother Goose.
We are ready for lift-off."

"I read you loud and clear, Mother," the handset crackled. "Come
on home." They drove the trucks the hour and a half to Centralia and
rendezvoused with the amnesty team from Arizona. The spokesman
for the group wore a sweatshirt that said, Got *Foie Gras*/Shame on You!

Owl elbowed Max in the ribs. "Check out that car bumper," he
gestured with his chin. The bumper sticker read: Red Meat, it's what
is rotting in your colon. "Hard core," Max agreed out of the side of
her mouth.

They turned the silent geese over to the animal rights group and began the ride home. They cranked up the heat and the stench from the goose manure on their boots was overpowering. They stopped and left all the boots in a dumpster next to an unmanned State Patrol booth for weighing truck tonnage. "Do you think they can trace those boots back to us?" John worried.

"Trust me. Any dumpster diver worth his salt will never touch those shoes," laughed Max as she cuddled against John Colby.

By the time they got back to the island they walked barefoot back to their cabins and collapsed into bed. Max screamed when she looked in the mirror the next morning as she saw her face blackened and covered in goose down. "Tarred and feathered," she mumbled to herself. "Why didn't anyone tell me?"

Ziggy had spent a day in jail at Port Townsend when his case came up before Judge Strom Thurman, who was well-acquainted with the inhabitants of Seven Sisters Island. The bailiff read the charge and Strom rolled his eyes and looked over at Max with a look that said, "Think of something and get this off my bench."

It was Pickles, who just happened to be in the courthouse on another matter, that came up with a creative solution to the "two-breast problem."

As a kind of memorial to Trish, he explained.

"We simply fashion a bikini top out of something like a thin fiberglass paper—like Tyvek used by construction people underneath the siding of houses. It looks a little like wrapping paper. Well," he went on, "we paint a leopard print and sew the whole thing together and voilà, we solve the modesty problem *en toto*." He grinned.

Strom wrapped his mind around the twin peak solution. Problem solved. "You've got two weeks. But, keep those blue tarps over those girls till the bikini top is finished. The defendant is free to go," he said as he slammed down his gavel.

Pickles had come into town on a matter that he had been incubating in his brain for years, and now all the pieces were coming together beautifully.

During a summer fifty-mile hike, a Port Townsend Boy Scout troop had found a critically wounded Whistling Marmot in Seven Lakes Basin near the high divide in the Olympic Mountains. The animal had barely survived a cougar attack. The boys built a cage of alder branches and carefully packed it down the Soleduck River to the hot springs.

An animal shelter in Port Angeles nursed the rodent back to health. With the sex unknown, the boys had christened the marmot the non-gender-specific name of Patty. Patty was a very appreciative and trainable little creature who was taught to whistle on cue, but was too crippled to fend for itself in the wild.

Pickles had obtained the blessing of the Fish and Wildlife Service and had named the now-portly rodent Port Townsend Patty, and he hoped the rest would be history.

Inspired by the movie *Ground Hog Day*, in which Bill Murray lives the same February 2nd day over and over until he learns what love really means as he is surrounded by the raucous celebration of Ground Hog Day and the famous Puxatawney Phil, the famous Ground Hog Alpha Male Pickles had brought Patty to a Port Townsend Kiwanis meeting the previous fall and pointed out the possibilities of their own ground hog celebration. The city fathers, who kept the town coffers full with one festival after another—jazz, wooden boats, parades, movies and more—were charmed by Patty and the possibilities. The planning began that very night.

A small pink tutu and bonnet were made for Patty by the Daughters of the American Revolution and the wooden boat builders association had made the cutest cottage, and the Sweet Adelines had been working on a duet with Patty to perfect a song that sounded a lot like "Meet the Flintstones," if you knew what to listen for.

February 2nd had dawned gray and foggy, but no one in the town was worried. They knew the Pacific Northwest tourists would pour in to celebrate the demise of winter or bitch about another six weeks of winter.

"It's all good," Pickles had coined the motto for the day, which hung on a banner across First Street along the water where the day started with a pancake breakfast and eating contest and followed right into a parade that had culled the best bands from the surrounding high schools.

The crowd followed the band up to the top of the hill to the courthouse, where a bandstand held the town board dressed in tuxedos and top hats, all gathered around Patty's Victorian cottage.

For a full half hour, the bands battled back and forth and the lattes flowed till Patty was pulled from her cottage. Following the movie script, Patty whispered the decision about winter into the mayor's ear and then he took Patty to the microphone where she whistled the first eight bars of "Yankee Doodle Dandy" as clear as a bell. The crowd roared approval and Patty, who was well on her way to being a diva, threw her head back and let loose with an ear-shattering whistle. Patty saw her shadow. Six more weeks of winter. Everyone was happy. It was all good.

Down the coast in Portland, Oregon, they had caught wind of the Patty movement from the Port Townsend website, and attempted to compete, using a reluctant Australian, a Northern hairy-nosed wombat from the Portland Zoo. To make matters worse, when they pulled "Portland" out of his box, he promptly bit the mayor's thumb all the way down to the bone and dove back into the box. The crowd grew ugly and the inept mayor was ousted later that spring in a recall. The ceremony was dropped for the next year.

In some kind of West Coast hysteria, San Diego was also in hot pursuit of the Patty Phenomenon, but in their haste they used an endangered kangaroo rat only found on the lower Mexican Sonora desert. The illegal alien kangaroo rat with no documentation had to be deported back to the Mexican desert in keeping with the international Endangered Species Act.

Meanwhile, the city fathers of Puxatawny, Pennsylvania, wrote a scathing editorial in their local newspaper condemning the entire Patty shadow dance, and Phil—stressed by his handlers—came down with a stubborn rash on his genitals that didn't go away till late summer.

White Bear was down on the dock near *The Ark*, loading boxes onto a barge. "What's up, Billy?" Annie stooped to untie her boat.

"These are the solar composting toilets," he said, patting the boxes. "And over there on the boat ramp are the solar wood boiler showers. In a week or so I think everything should be operational.

"You know, the canoe is coming along fine. I just have to find paddlers. I put an ad in the paper, but I think I'll have to go to the colleges. I'd like to use kids from the tribes, but you know kids these days. I would have thought ten thousand dollars for a month's work would be plenty, but I'm not getting much interest, but it's early. I still have a month or two left before I have to leave. I think they're going to need some kind of conditioning. Seven hundred miles is a long way.

"It makes me think my vision quest guide should have been a pet poodle or something," he laughed. "It sure would have been a hell of a lot easier. I could have just taken a trip to Paris. Oh, well."

Annie laughed. "Walk a mile in my moccasins."

When Annie arrived at the house, Sister and Matty were pretending to chase the twins around the sofa. The twins would tease the women and then totter off as fast as they could on their chubby little legs with the two women in slow pursuit. Scooping up the babies in their arms and blowing rubber lips on their bellies, the women delighted in the twins' giggles that soon turned into hiccups. Babies, grandmothers—all laughing, hot and sweaty, and having the time of their lives. Annie smiled. Again, it was just another reminder that she would not be here for the twins forever.

Annie woke up close to midnight and looked out the window at the reflected moonlight glistening on the frosted leaves; the water mirrored the wispy clouds that stood frozen in the sky. She shuddered from the cold and wrapped her quilt around her as she stuffed her slippers on and looked in on the twins. They were illuminated in the moonlight like little gods with pouty lips. Their even breaths took in the crisp air as if living on an island, frozen in a bygone century; it was the most natural thing in the world. Annie tucked the blankets around their chins and went back to bed.

The sisters came that night as they had always come. In their own way, on their own terms, and in their own time. In Annie's dream she was an old woman wearing a robe and sitting in a rocking chair in front of a fire, and her six teenage sisters were sitting on an intricately woven Oriental rug of golden saffron and periwinkle blue. They were wearing juniper green jumpers and white frilly long-sleeve blouses. Their hair cascaded down their back and were shades of red from copper to flame, and they tossed their heads as they laughed and giggled while playing a new board game called Chinese checkers. Annie's oldest sister, Emma, looked up from the game and addressed Annie. "Well, Sister, I suppose you know why we are here. Some of the girls have changed their votes. They want you to come right now with us so we are a complete family again."

She got up and walked towards Annie and knelt down by the rocker. She smelled like mint as she whispered in Annie's ear. "Of course, those sillies think they all have a vote when it's really my call. Mother put me in charge.

"I'm not leaving anything to chance. I've put in safeguards and the people in place to help you make the transition. It's all predetermined. Whatever you do, it will be right for the family. I think the bobble heads were a nice touch, don't you?" She laughed at her own joke, then walked over to the board game, sat down, and smoothed out her dress over her legs.

Annie awoke with a start. She felt the reassurance of the smooth branches of the headboard with her hand. It had been another dream. She found her slippers where she had left them and was grateful to put on the three robes. "It's still freezing in here," she said to herself, cinching up the belt on the robe and clumping towards the stairs. She jammed her hands in the pockets to keep them warm and started down. Halfway, she felt something in the pocket and pulled out a blue marble.

Well, they didn't think of everything, she thought. *The twins could choke on something like this. There could be more marbles if they didn't pick up the marble game after themselves.* She checked the Oriental rug in the living room and found a red marble lying by the hearth. "Well, those smarty pants need to grow up." But, she didn't say it very loud.

Next to the Wiggins Emporium and Port Gamble post office was the derelict movie theatre, deactivated some time during the early talkies, where the symposium on Starbuck was just getting under way.

Anchoring the front table were the State Fish and Wildlife people, the Sierra Club, and the Orca Watch Society as Annie, Sister Mary, Max, Lila, and John Colby sidled into the second row, ready for a lively session of how to deal with what the local newspaper called the "Starbuck Stalemate." John was particularly interested in getting funds for food or transport to take the whale home.

The meeting began with Starbuck's vital statistics, pod number, family connection, and pod history; then each group made their pitch. Fish and Wildlife wanted the animal to follow a no-intrusive, hands-off approach that might include a reunion with Starbuck's pod which *might* pass by next fall—or not. The national group was most concerned with boaters keeping a five hundred-foot distance from the whale, and Orca Watch was concerned about Starbuck's health but recommended no heroic methods to make sure he survived.

There was a rowdy, vocally abusive group of orca watchers who kept cat-calling from the back of the theatre wanting to know why none of the agencies was being proactive to ensure the survival of Starbuck.

A young male, looking like a Tufted Puffin with disheveled straw hair poking over his ears from under his ball cap, called out, "Dude, stop calling him J 167. The dude has a name—Starbuck. Think about it!"

Unrattled, one bureaucrat after another pointed out the enduring policy of not interfering with nature and the international difficulties of transporting Starbuck to Canada.

One woman in a granny dress and blue bonnet ran down the aisle, grabbed the microphone, and insulted the symposium leaders by throwing a dead fish on the table, accusing the whole lot of them as "uncaring, blood sucking bureaucrats, that stink like three-day-old fish" and something else a lot stronger that no one heard because the microphone failed at that instant.

The meeting was winding to a close when the back door of the theatre swung open and representatives from three local tribes came in and sat down in the front row. Their spokesman got up. "One of our chiefs had a dream and believes the orca in the cove by Seven Sisters is the reincarnation of the spirit of Chief Seattle, a venerable chief during Seattle's pioneer days, namesake of the city. He died in 1866." With that, he unfurled a document and began to read Chief Seattle's words of long ago:

> "There was a time when our people covered the land as the waves of a wind-ruffled sea cover its shell-paved floor, but that time long since passed away with the greatness of tribes that are now but a mournful memory. I will not dwell on, nor mourn over, our untimely decay, nor reproach my paleface brothers with hastening it, as we too may have been somewhat to blame....
>
> "To us the ashes of our ancestors are sacred and their resting place is hallowed ground. You wander far from the graves of your ancestors and seemingly without regret....Your dead cease to love you and the land of their nativity as soon as they pass the portals of the tomb and wander away beyond the stars. They are soon forgotten and never return. Our dead never forget this beautiful world that gave them being. They still love its verdant valleys, its murmuring rivers, its magnificent mountains, sequestered vales and verdant lined lakes and bays, and ever yearn in tender fond affection over the lonely hearted living, and often return from the happy hunting ground to visit, guide, console, and comfort them.
>
> "Day and night cannot dwell together. The Red Man has ever fled the approach of the White Man, as the morning mist flees before the morning sun. However, your proposition seems fair and I think that my people will accept it and will retire to the reservation you offer them. Then we will dwell apart in peace, for the words of the Great White Chief seem to be the words of nature speaking to my people out of dense darkness.

"*A few more moons, a few more winters, and not one of the descendants of the mighty hosts that once moved over this broad land or lived in happy homes, protected by the Great Spirit, will remain to mourn over the graves of a people once more powerful and hopeful than yours. But why should I mourn at the untimely fate of my people? Tribe follows tribe, and nation follows nation, like the waves of the sea. It is the order of nature, and regret is useless. Your time of decay may be distant, but it will surely come, for even the White Man whose God walked and talked with him as friend to friend, cannot be exempt from the common destiny. We may be brothers after all. We will see.*

"*We will ponder your proposition and when we decide we will let you know. But should we accept it, I here and now make this condition that we will not be denied the privilege without molestation of visiting at any time the tombs of our ancestors, friends, and children. Every part of this soil is sacred in the estimation of my people. Every hillside, every valley, every plain and grove, has been hallowed by some sad or happy event in days long vanished. Even the rocks, which seem to be dumb and dead as the swelter in the sun along the silent shore, thrill with memories of stirring events connected with the lives of my people, and the very dust upon which you now stand responds more lovingly to their footsteps than yours, because it is rich with the blood of our ancestors, and our bare feet are conscious of the sympathetic touch. Our departed braves, fond mothers, glad, happy hearted maidens, and even the little children who lived here and rejoiced here for a brief season, will love these somber solitudes and at eventide they greet shadowy returning spirits. And when the last Red Man shall have perished, and the memory of my tribe shall have become a myth among the White Men, these shores will swarm with the invisible dead of my tribe, and when your children's children think themselves alone in the field, the store, the shop, upon the highway, or in the silence of the pathless woods, they will not be alone. In all the earth there is no place dedicated to solitude. At night when the streets of your cities and villages are silent and you think them deserted, they will throng with the returning hosts that once filled them and still love this beautiful land. The White Man will never be alone.*

"Let him be just and deal kindly with my people, for the dead are not powerless. Dead, did I say? There is no death, only a change of worlds."

The bureaucrats, always looking to avoid responsibility, realized a lifeline when they saw one and quickly huddled on the stage.

When they came back, the state representative was succinct.

"We believe Starbuck might be the reincarnation of Chief Seattle and, as such, we leave the entire matter in tribal hands. We only ask that you do not attempt to move the orca into Canada which might create an international incident."

Before anyone could comment or object, the bureaucrats had exited the stage, hopped into their respective cars on the outside street, and roared off into the night.

The crowd was stunned. They stood up and looked around and put their hands out in gestures of dismay. These were the experts. The people charged with saving Puget Sound. The habitat, the animals, the future. They had hoped for scientific answers and suggestions about reconnecting the orca with the family pod, but the "friends of Starbuck" were left with nothing.

Pickles picked that moment of indecision to make his entrance. Resplendent in a black turtleneck, chartreuse blazer topped with an orange fedora, paisley green and orange bell bottoms, and faux alligator cowboy boots with silver spurs, and slathered in Stetson cologne, Pickles had proved again he was more than capable of filling the leadership void.

"All right," he said, rubbing his hands together as he worked the crowd. The three chiefs stood in a circle drinking coffee when Pickles came up and gave each chief a hearty handshake, words of encouragement and an envelope.

"Annie." Pickles was ebullient. "How did you like them apples? We sure put those scalawags on the run, didn't we?

"You know, that supposed speech by Chief Seattle in 1854 is a powerful tool, damned eloquent, I think." Pickles waved at the chiefs and gave them the thumbs up and then sat down on a fold-up chair.

"You orchestrated the whole thing," Annie nodded approvingly.

"You expected less?" Pickles retorted, rubbing his freshly minted chin. "All right. We have the chiefs' blessing as long as we protect the orca and check in with them from time to time. You can thank White Bear and a handful of three-day, all-expenses-paid getaways to Vegas for rounding them up. So what do we want to do? I've jotted down a few off-the-cuff ideas in this twenty-page prospectus," Pickles explained, as he passed out the folders. "It's time we moved on."

"So what does that mean, move on?" Max asked. "Can we continue to feed Starbuck?"

"No problem, all we need to do is check with the tribal council and I think they trust you more than they do those bureaucrats," Pickles smiled and waved to the group representing the Sierra Club.

Pickles ushered the island group into the cool winter night, down the gangplank and onto *The Ark.* "We've all got to be on the island in the morning for the unveiling of the bikini top and, Annie, we need to talk…"

The next morning, an Arctic wind had scoured the skies of clouds and the temperature had dipped into the low teens. The unusual phenomenon of frozen fog—twisted white tendrils of mist as thick as young alder trees in a clear cut that rose from the warmer water and the frigid air—created an eerie illusion, as if Sherlock Holmes was cruising the Baskerville Moors.

From inside his bunker, Joe picked up his bugle and played the familiar refrain from the Kentucky Derby call to post while Pickles and Ziggy pulled a shroud from a large cloth bag simply marked...40,000 DDDDDDDDDDD.

It was a gigantic leopard bikini top, as instructed by Judge Strom's courthouse edict to enforce modesty that had been built in a cavernous sail loft in Port Townsend. The primarily male workers, having sucked it up and caught in the pure grandeur of the task, had worked late into the night for a good week to complete the Dolly Partonesque task.

The bikini top was a work of art as four men clambered up the twenty-foot-tall lofty bunkers to pull the bulky cups up onto the sandbag breasts. The nipples, well over four feet alone, were a strange study in wet t-shirt engineering. When the task was completed, the sun had chased the fog into hiding, and the leopard-topped peaks sparkled in full splendor.

"A thing of beauty is a joy forever," Owl beamed as he chomped on his cigar.

"Too much of a good thing," Trish slurred as she gave a muffled chuckle from beneath the leopard scarf that South had wrapped around her to protect her from the cold.

South gave a disapproving grunt. "I don't know what this generation is coming to," she grumbled, as she rolled Trish's wheelchair along the path back into the cabin.

Pickles took several digital photos of the leopard top as proof for Judge Strom. An overhead satellite focused on the island and by the next morning there were two million hits on the site depicting the giant bikini top. The State Department took note, sent a memo to Homeland Security, and the next day, Seven Sisters Island was under siege by air, land and sea.

Ziggy was ecstatic. It was as if *Playboy* magazine had mated with Victoria's Secret on steroids. That night he took his new leopard sleeping bag out between the breasts and curled up for the night.

"I doubt I'll ever see him back at the cabin," Matty sighed.

Just after nightfall, Snodgrass from the county health department had canoed close to the island and began scooping test bottles of water, hoping once again to prove the island was polluting the cove. Unfortunately for Snodgrass, Max had come home that evening and was trying out a new set of night vision binoculars that Joe had given to Sister Mary to scout if anyone was trying to sneak close to Starbuck.

It wasn't long before she spotted the shadowy figure and had taken out her father's long range thirty-aught-six with a night scope and rapidly punctured three holes below the waterline of the green, old town canoe. The last she had seen of Snodgrass, he was paddling the still-floating front half of the canoe for his life and swearing so loudly that he disturbed a flock of widgeons that had settled into the cove for the night.

Hunkered down at Annie's, Pickles was settling into his second bowl of apple cobbler. "Annie," he paused with his spoon mid-air as if the thought had just struck him, "I was thinking, how would you like to run for county commissioner? You could do a lot of good. Heaven knows those bureaucrats could use a stern lesson in civics. You know they have coveted the island for the last ten years for a park; that's why they keep raising your taxes hoping you will default."

"I think you would be a better candidate, Pickles," Annie countered. "You have all the ideas."

Pickles had no interest in going legit, thereby losing his ability as a puppeteer and taking a cut in his power base with an elected position.

"Well, I would if I had the celebrity." Pickles tapped his spoon on the table. "But you, Annie, would be the perfect candidate. You obviously aren't going to be a career politician and you have a strong following. You'd be doing it for the twins and the rest of the downtrodden property owners. And I, The Pickles, would be your right-hand man," Pickles mugged. "Just sayin'."

"I don't have much extra time with the twins and all." Annie shook her head as she motioned for Pickles to bring his bowl over to the wash water. Pickles slid the bowl into the sudsy water and picked up a dishtowel from the rack behind the stove.

"A two- or three-hour meeting every other week and everyone knows where you live if they have a real problem," Pickles said as he plucked a jelly glass from the rinse water and stowed it on the shelf next to the stove.

Pickles scrunched his nose as he looked disapprovingly over the eclectic jelly glasses that made up Annie's glassware.

"I think we need to get some decent glassware out here," he fussed, shaking his head.

"Every one of those jars is an antique," Annie snapped. "Look at 'em. They are green, blue, pink and yellow. It takes thirty or forty years for the glasses to get that patina from the trace chemicals in the glass. My sisters have used these glasses."

"Yeow," Pickles quickly tacked, "I guess I stand corrected. Anyway, consider running, Annie. All the candidates they have so far aren't very electable. There is a carpetbagger real estate guy from California that just moved up here and some community activist guy that doesn't play well with others. So I've heard. Scuttlebutt and all," he shrugged.

Annie took the dishtowel from Pickles, folded it once and neatly arranged it on the iron oven handle on the stove to dry. She put her hand on Pickles' shoulder and let out a deep sigh. "I don't know about this political thing. I don't know if I have the right stuff, if you know what I mean. I've got a lot of baggage."

Pickles silently counted up the political chits. The twins, SeaGrannies, Starbuck, the judicial surprise of the decade when Annie got custody of her twin great-grandbabies, a giant leopard bra, a nun, a nocturnal military man whose motto was, "The difficult we do immediately, the impossible takes a little longer."

Oh yeah, Pickles thought to himself. *We're running. We're running hard.*

Chapter
NINETEEN

The cedar shavings from the canoe had such a sweet fragrance that South was lured to make linen sachets to hang inside all the cabins, and because of her soft spot for dogs, she also made a dog bed for Trooper—who had taken up permanent residence with Trish and her girls—and another bed for the stationary Twigs, who insisted on sleeping under Annie's stove and never seemed to change position.

Looking like the back of a great gray whale, the canoe had been flipped over again after the inside had been painstakingly hollowed out. Next, the canoe master took a two-handled draw knife and began the final sculpting of the outside of the canoe. The iron blade, drawn with two hands toward the canoe builder, gave up long reddish curls of the ancient wood that reminded Annie of shiny ringlets of hair that she and her sisters had worn to elementary school.

The curls mounded hip-deep below the hull as the Native workmen straddled the rounded hull as if lovers. Caressing, teasing, and

coaxing the tree to give up its last secrets. Exposing the final destiny
of the venerable red cedar, by using instincts that had lain dormant
in their sinewy muscles and in the corners of their minds. And when
exhausted, the craftsmen sprawled on the freshly minted cedar shavings and rested till they could begin again.

The tight-grained spiraled layers were testimony of a thousand
years of too-short Puget Sound summers, cold, wet winters, and the
sounds of their forefathers whose spirits spilled out of the tree itself,
inspiring them to sing strange chants that they heard first in their
hearts and then when the sounds came to their lips, they were at first
embarrassed. And now, nothing else mattered. The carvers and the
tree had become as one.

White Bear was pleased and there was an urgency to his step bely-
ing his ninety-two years. He was ready to make good his promise.

The outhouses and showers were delivered by barge to the island
after the solstice began making inroads into the daylight, two minutes each day. Each shower and composting toilet was approximately
eight feet by six feet, and made of a gray driftwood-colored vinyl. The
workmen immediately began screwing on weathered barn boards so
the buildings looked as rustic as the originals, while the insides were
a damp, rag-easy clean plastic.

The solar collectors that were installed on the roofs had the look
of rusted steel and the wood-fired boilers and built-in cisterns for
the showers were hooked to roof gutters so there would be no more
dragging pails of hot water down the spit. White Bear also had hot
water lines run to the hot tub, which inspired Ziggy to throw on his
black speedo and sprint across the sand and dive into the tub.

"Come on in. The water's fine!" he chirped as he spat water out
on his lips like a walrus.

When the installations were complete and the workmen had left
the island, White Bear gave a tutorial on the use of the composting

toilet. "Simply twist these handles once a day and the cylinders will mix and dry the night soil," he instructed. "Every few months you open the trap door and a few brave souls can scoop the soil into wheelbarrows. The solar panels will sterilize the manure and you can use it for growing vegetables or plants. They've been using systems like this in Europe for decades," he concluded.

He moved over to the showers. He explained that the solar panels pre-heated the water and the boilers finished the job.

"You're still going to have to haul firewood." He shook his head. "This isn't Arizona where the sun can do all the work." He showed how the used shower water was filtered and put back into the system. "It's a contained system," he continued. "The cisterns are more for backup. You notice," White Bear continued, "that each of the four buildings has two toilets and two showers so you can use the buddy system out here." And he opened the toilet door. "The toilet seat is always warm. The first bit of solar goes directly into the toilet seat."

South put a finger on the seat and closed her eyes. "Praise the lord and pass the biscuits," she said reverently.

"And," White Bear paused, "if Annie agrees, I found grant money that will allow private contractors to come in and insulate every cabin with hypoallergenic fiberglass panels—walls, floors and ceilings—and then put on new wood walls. You can keep the oddball windows, but your places will heat a lot easier. But, only if you want to."

Everyone looked at Annie. "Works for me," she laughed and gave White Bear a hug and tugged his pony tail.

"So who goes first?" White Bear looked out expectantly to the crowd of islanders.

"That'd be me." Ziggy stepped forward in his speedo. "I won the lottery."

"What lottery?" Max asked, leaning against Colby with her hand in his pocket.

"The lottery where we guessed when you and Colby were going to consummate your relationship." Ziggy looked incredulous that Max hadn't heard.

"And, just how do you know when that happened?" Max sniped.

"Oh, we know. Don't worry about that." Ziggy looked smug. Max blushed and hid her face in Colby's jacket, while Colby had a good belly laugh.

"Go to it," White Bear said, opening the door. "Ziggy can make the first deposit and then we will go through the process of composting."

Ziggy swaggered through the door and there was a long pause and several loud grunts over the next few minutes. Finally, Ziggy opened the door looking sheepish. "No luck," he announced. "Too much pressure."

"I'm next." Owl bounced up to the door and quickly went to work. There were some long farts and escaping gases as Owl readjusted himself on the seat, but soon he reluctantly opened the door. "Can't work with an audience," he growled.

"Me next, I chose Christmas morning," South sang out confidently toward the other losers. She closed the door and quietly went about her work. Two minutes later the door opened and South smirked. "I think we have a winner here."

The crowd shuffled to the back of the toilet building where White Bear opened up the trap door and peered in. "Jesus H," he bleated. "Will you look at that?"

The crowd surged forward and peered in. There was a yellowish deposit reminiscent of a coil of Polish sausage, perfectly oval—the tail touching the head.

Ziggy looked in. "The golden turd," he mumbled in a biblical soccer miracle kind of way; said as though mesmerized by the enormity of the movement.

South looked pleased. She knew she had an edge on the competition with a dinner the night before of polenta and two cans of creamed corn.

"I win." She clapped her hands.

White Bear declared victory and threw in a handful of sawdust from the canoe, closed the hatch, and turned the load-assisted crank three times.

He opened the door and the golden turd had turned into finely chopped nuggets coated with sawdust.

"If all goes well," White Bear announced, "the compost will be ready in three or four weeks. That is, if you can produce a few deposits," he challenged Ziggy and Owl.

"Give me another chance," Owl meekly called out, but the islanders had turned back to their warm cabins with visions of insulated walls that would make driftwood collecting on the beach a much-easier task.

That night, while most of the talk centered indelicately about the golden turd, Spud was having one of his séance moments when he announced he was about to take some more of his treasures from the ice chest.

The flickering firelight illuminated the circle of islanders as they gathered around, reminiscent of a medieval sorcerer working alchemy.

Spud slowly opened the top of the chest and rummaged around, setting out a small package that was labeled Amelia Earhart. He then extracted a purple velvet cloth wrapped around a round object the size of a dinner plate. He carefully slid off the cloth, clicked on a foot stand, and put a round solid Ferris wheel kind of machine on the top of a stump. Everyone was silent, wondering.

"An almost-perpetual motion machine," Spud announced. He spun the outer wheel and the machine went into motion. "Tesela…

Tesela was an electronic inventor in the early twentieth century. He worked with Edison on electric current and radio waves. He was finally given credit for inventing the radio after research showed he was far ahead of Marconi's first radio. Anyway, this politically flawed genius rigged up this perpetual motion machine using magnetic attraction and drag that allows this miniature machine to run virtually forever while producing electrical energy. That was almost a hundred years ago."

"So why aren't we using the technology?" John Hunt looked up from the whirling machine.

"Rooskies," Joe muttered under his breath.

"No, not Rooskies. Tesela also rigged up a tall tower to transmit wireless electrical waves to illuminate electrical bulbs and we know that worked, but we haven't been able to duplicate his experiments," Spud explained.

"Tesala was working on a giant transmitter for the industrialist J. Pierpont Morgan when Morgan pulled his financing because Tesala was working on technology that would have used the earth as a huge dynamo. It could project electrical energy in unlimited amounts anywhere in the world. Morgan said, 'If anyone can draw on the power, where are we going to put the meter?'

"Pure capitalism," Spud shook his head. "And you wonder why I'm into conspiracy theories? He was on the cutting edge of discovering cheap energy, but not everyone wanted him to succeed."

"Rooskies," Joe muttered again. Annie yawned and began to fidget.

"Tesela was done in by corporations that didn't want cheap energy sources," Spud whispered in a conspiratorial tone, as if he didn't want the message to escape the edges of the firelight.

"Rooskies!" Joe yelled out again.

The copper-colored machine spun its circle while the island contemplated Spud's theory.

After a few minutes of silence, Spud grabbed the machine, folded the cloth carefully around the edges, and tucked it into his ice chest.

"That's not why I called the meeting tonight," Spud said as he shifted a few objects. "Minutes from the Dick Cheney meetings with big oil," he muttered, and then pulled out a twenty-inch-long plaster cast of a foot. He held the cast up to the light. "Bigfoot," Spud said reverently.

"Yeti, abominable snowman, Sasquatch—whatever you want to call them. The Lummi Indians over near Bellingham have legends of Bigfoot that go back hundreds of years. Adult Bigfoots should be six to ten feet tall and weigh about five hundred pounds.

"I know the evidence is sketchy, but there have been sightings up here in the Olympic Mountains, just across the water from here. I've found some droppings or scat in the hills above the Whistling Oyster that would indicate a family of Bigfoot in the area. I think with Joe's infrared binoculars and the infrared camera, we might run into something. Anyone willing to join me will get free all-you-can-eat-pizza and beer at the Oyster."

The crowd was silent and skeptical. "Does that include microbrews or just domestics?" Owl asked.

"It's gonna be colder than a witch's tit out there," offered Colby. "Does the offer include hot chocolate with schnapps or hot toddies?"

"How long would we be out there?" Max questioned.

"Yes, yes. Anything you want to drink and we would only go out at dusk and stay in your assigned positions for three hours."

"What kinda pizza?" Joe asked from the darkness of a nearby cabin.

"Pizza, all kinds." Spud was exasperated. "Are you guys in or not?"

There was murmuring and 'I will if you will' and then a consensus. The island was all in except Christine who was staying with the twins.

"I'm gonna get me a Bigfoot," Annie growled as she lumbered back into the warmth of the old Victorian farmhouse, Matty giggled, and South reminded them that it was her birthday tomorrow.

The caravan of Max's pink dump truck, Sister's Mustang, and the two Volkswagen buses headed out an hour before dusk, rambled past the Whistling Oyster, and continued up into the foothills of the Olympics on gravel roads made by the Forest Service to fight forest fires. They all stopped at the first gate for instructions and maps.

Joe was dressed in full camouflage with two eyes peering out from a blackened face as he handed out the maps, cameras and keys to the other roads that had lock boxes on cables stretched across the roadway. He pulled keys from a huge key chain with hundreds of labeled keys.

"Where did you get all those keys?" Ziggy wondered as he slipped his keys into his pocket.

"Oh, let's just say I did a little shopping at Ranger headquarters up in Port Angeles last night," Joe said, slipping off another key for Colby.

Standing in front of the headlights, Spud read from a sheet spread across the hood of the Mustang that paired everyone with a partner, how to use the cameras, the maps, and how to get back to the main road where everyone would be picked up. Last, he handed each party pictures and sketches of Bigfoot.

"Whoa!" John Hunt caught his breath. "I think I dated this one in high school."

"Very funny, very obligatory," Spud responded. "Okay, everyone, hit your spots and let's bag us a Bigfoot tonight."

Spud, Ziggy and Pickles had taken the post farthest away. They drove to a cable stretched across the road and Spud jumped out to open the lock. Pickles drove through and Spud locked the gate behind them and soon their headlights were piercing the total blackness of the forest. The long-trunked fir trees cast eerie, stick shadows from the headlights reflecting against the bare rock cliffs where the road ploughed up the side of steep canyons next to the Duckabush River— snarling and sloshing its icy flow to the salt water below.

The bus skidded to a stop. Trees circled an amphitheatre of a steep rock buttress with a toe of shale skree that melted into the grassy meadow.

"Perfect," Spud exclaimed as he opened the side door and got his camera with the huge telescoping infrared lens. The two men pulled on stocking caps, snapped on their flashlights, and headed into the center of the meadow. They found two rocks and the two men sat down and waited in the dark. An hour passed.

"Hey, I was thinking about putting out some bait," Pickles confided.

"What kinda stuff?" Spud whispered.

Pickles arched his brow. "I know a few things about the ladies. I brought some girly things you would have to get at a store. I brought a purple bra, a size 47 triple K. I figured that might fit a Sasquatch chick. A bottle of Chanel No. 5 perfume, and some thong underwear. You know, the basics."

"What the hell do you think Bigfoot is doing up here? Having some kind of orgy?" Spud was exasperated. Pickles didn't answer. "Chanel No. 5 is so Old School," Spud complained.

Ziggy interjected, "Even though it was created in 1921, Chanel No. 5 is still highly popular. The sultry ylang ylang note with its unique juxtaposition of wintergreen brightness and ripe mango sweetness unfolds first the honeyed rose and jasmine notes and continues as the fragrance moves into its dark base. Of course, the woody notes of sandalwood offset the decadent languor of the floral notes. Vanilla and coumarin envelop the base notes. The parfum has an alluring radiant quality and yet the overall sensation is soft, caressing and gentle."

"Where are you getting this shit?" Spud challenged.

"I get around," Ziggy smiled.

A few long minutes later, Spud relented. "Okay, put the stuff out there about fifty yards on sticks and we'll see what happens."

Pickles scuttled into the clearing and propped the clothing on sticks and took the ribbon off the perfume and hung it on an alpine fir. Spud trained his infrared heat-seeking camera on an opening in the clearing while Pickles resumed his spot near his rock and rolled onto his back, staring up into the night sky.

The winter sky was blue-black and the stars drew Pickles into another dimension of time and space. He concentrated so hard that his chin fell down on his down jacket and he began to snore softly. "Wake up," Spud jostled Pickles and Ziggy awake. "Time to go. We've been here for three hours."

Pickles rolled over slowly and used the rock to leverage himself erect.

"Wow, that went pretty fast." Pickles wiped the wet grass from his jacket. "Did you get anything?"

"No, not a thing," admitted Spud. "It just wasn't our night. Go out and get your stuff and we'll get out of here."

Pickles turned on his flashlight and tiptoed out into the meadow. He found the sticks, but his offerings were gone. He looked around the brush to no avail and made his way back to Spud. "See anything out there?" Spud called out.

"None of the stuff is out there," grunted Pickles as a dead branch poked him in the ribs.

"Probably some bear got it," Spud nodded. Ziggy grunted.

"Maybe," Pickles agreed. "Let's get back to the Oyster. I'm freezing my bucket off."

When they drove past the other drop-off points, all about a half mile apart, everyone seemed to be gone. So when they got to the Oyster, the party had been going for a long time. Sister Mary Catherine and Annie were doing a duet and dancing to "You're So Vain" at the jukebox and there were boxes of pizzas on the bar with the lids flipped open. Everyone else had a beer or drink in their hand and chattering away.

"Did anyone get anything worthwhile?" Spud sang out over the roar.

"Don't get your tail in a knot, Spud," said John, who sidled up to liberate a piece of pizza. "It's all under control, Dude. I'm having the pictures developed over at the drugstore. They said it would be an hour or so. Should be any time now."

"How long were you all out there?" Spud wondered aloud, sensing another pizza conspiracy. No one answered, but a clerk from the pharmacy next door dropped off a packet of pictures.

Spud began to sort through them. There were full face nasal photos, Sister squatting in the brush, giving John the finger, Annie bundled up in a blanket, Max hiding under a tarp, and Matty smoking a joint wearing mittens. There were dozens of dark photos of trees and stumps and one of purple dots in the middle of a field. Probably an overexposed photo, Spud figured.

Spud held the picture up. "Who took this photo?" he yelled. No one seemed to hear him and he turned back to sort through the pile again.

"What about it?" South queried behind his back. Spud dealt through the photos again, and pulled out the photo with the purple dots.

"Yeah, that's mine," South admitted. "I turned on the flashlight and there were two purple dots on something black or dark brown. The shape only stopped for a second. You must have seen it. We were just a quarter mile down from you guys."

"How did the picture happen?" Spud squinted at the photo.

"Well, I smelled something real stinky in the wind and then that went away and then something rancid like sweat and then I smelled something musty like fruit. It reminded me of Chanel No. 5, one of my all-time favorites," South explained. "And then I saw these purple kinda dots and I took a picture. End of story. I need another beer."

Spud shook his head and smiled. It was always something. He would blow up the picture tomorrow, but he knew the quality was poor and the shapes very indistinct. He bit into a pizza and quaffed a half mug of beer. "Well," he chuckled, "at least someone is going to have an interesting night."

The next morning, Owl was prowling the shallows in his hip boots and a rake looking for Dungeness crab. He was jousting with a red-shelled crustacean that was hiding underneath the shelf of a rock when he was startled by a voice.

"Mr. Allen Pocious Simpson?" A man dressed in olive Carhartt overalls and a baseball cap leaned over the side of a rowboat. Owl grimaced at his given name and clamped down on his Panatela.

"Who wants to know?" Owl challenged.

The city of Bremerton, sir, is having a problem with a sewer lateral location. We tried to find the manhole with a remote camera, but we're not having any luck. You're our last hope."

"Have you got the standard fee with you?" Owl pursed his lips in anticipation and then scowled as the crab scuttled sideways too deep to wade after.

"Yessir, a case of Wild Turkey."

"Float it in here, son." Owl opened up the gunny bag with the first crab in the bottom and corraled the six bottles.

"What'ya want to know?"

The young man came to shore and watched as Owl's photographic memory pinpointed the manhole on a map. "It's gonna be a good ten feet under the asphalt," Owl said, rolling up the map. He shared a swig of his Wild Turkey and went back to crabbing. An hour later he had four crab and had finished off one bottle of Turkey. He shared another one with Ziggy, gave another to the canoe builders, and stowed three under his bunk. It had been a most productive day.

The outer hull of the canoe had been preened smooth. The canoe master had rubbed the outside of the canoe with an elk antler to smooth the grain before Owl, Ziggy and both Johns had helped them flip over the canoe the week before. The builders had finished the final stages of hollowing the inside and were now beginning work on flaring the sides of the cedar canoe.

They took buckets of salt water and filled the inside of the canoe almost to the top. This swelled the wood grain so there were no leaks. The next morning before sunrise they began to heat stones in a fire and drop them into the boat till the water steamed, and a fog rolled off the sides. On the outside of the boat, a fire of coals using the tree bark cooked the canoe from the outside. At lunchtime, the men threw into the canoe a gunny sack of little neck clams for lunch that cooked in ten minutes and the men watched and waited for the hot water and fire to do its work.

At dusk, under a crimson sunset, the sweating craftsmen danced around the beds of coals and hammered in graduated lengths of wrist-thick, knot-free Douglas fir wedges against the two sides from inside to flare the now-supple upper sides of the canoe. The sides flared fourteen inches near the bow to six inches in the middle. By midnight the job was done and the waters would begin to cool. The canoe had finally found its shape and the workmen slept soundly till late morning under a canvas tarp.

Starbuck was taking in three hundred pounds of winter run herring a day that Colby constantly brought over from Friday Harbor, and with the extra vitamins and minerals supplement, the orca was downright spunky. Spy-hopping most of the day and crashing water into anyone who was careless enough to get close, except for Max and the girls.

Lila had come in for a late dinner with Annie and a consultation that evening with Starbuck about his behavior. She would have to ride that thin teenage edge of independence that Starbuck's aunt had crossed and created this predicament. There were indications that Starbuck could be a hothead, but then he was only four years old.

"And he's a teenage male," Lila shook her head. "Teenage angst. All mammals have some of the same growing pains."

Max and the two girls slipped on their rubber gloves and began stuffing the foot-long herring full of Sea tabs that were filled with water-soluble vitamins, especially vitamin B1, thiamine. Talisha stuck her tongue out as she used her finger to poke the pills into a herring's mouth. "This has a yuck factor of nine point five," she grimaced, as she dropped the herring into a rubber bucket. When they got out into the netted area, Starbuck rolled his nose over the transom to be stroked.

"How much does he weigh now that he's healthy?" Talisha asked.

"Colby says he weighs about seven to eight thousand pounds," Max said absentmindedly, as she turned off the outboard and looked across the net where several tourist boats had gathered. "You know, with Starbuck's need for human attention, boats and motors are a real danger to him."

"That's why we put the net up in the lagoon," Alisha answered firmly. "To keep him safe, right?"

Max grunted a worried, "Sure" and then she brightened. "Do you girls know how to tell a male from a female orca?"

"Do we really need to know?" Talisha blushed. "It might be totally gross."

"No, it's not hard at all," Max continued. "John Colby showed me how to tell the difference."

"Duh," Alisha smarted off. "Everyone knows the difference. Boys have, you know…"

"White patches where the genitals are and the girls don't," Max said smugly. "Watch when Starbuck spy-hops," she said, throwing a herring out away from the boat. After Starbuck had eaten the herring, he celebrated with a spy hop and the girls, now fascinated by the sex ed talk, watched intently.

"Yep, he's a boy all right," a relieved Alisha confirmed, with pre-teenage certainty.

"From the size of that patch, he must be well hung," Talisha said with equal authority.

"Well, now that we have established that," Lila said stifling a smile, "I need to do a psychic reading." She reached over the bow and put her hand on Starbuck's forehead and closed her eyes. Her head jerked convulsively as if receiving jolts of information for a full minute and then she sat down abruptly on the boat seat.

"Whew, that was a lot of information." Lila shook her head.

"What'd he say?" coaxed Max.

"He said he'd like to vary his diet with some salmon. Chum salmon, okay, but preferably King salmon. He thinks it's time to go home, but he doesn't want anyone to feel unappreciated and he'd like to go and greet boaters, but he knows that's dangerous and he wants me to know that he is extremely well hung. In his pod, his nickname is…"

"Whew." Alisha clapped her hands over her ears. "TMI, Too Much Information!"

Later that evening at a spontaneous canned goods potluck at Annie's, John Colby got down on one knee and proposed to Max all over again and pulled out the ring he had personally designed. It was a traditional braided gold band with a tiny black and white onyx orca swirled around a three-quarter carat marquise-cut diamond. "It's my grandmother's diamond," Colby confessed as he slipped the ring on Max's finger. "I could never afford a diamond that big."

From the salt water, Max's hands were dry and cracked and smelled of fish, even though she tried to soak her hands in milk that evening to kill the smell and the jagged nail on her ring finger had been ripped that morning from constantly wearing rubber gloves. Max's eyes filled with tears as she looked down at her hand. She knew her life was going to be beautiful. Not New York beautiful, not *Bride Magazine* beautiful, not a beauty that she ever knew existed or had read or heard about from her girlfriends. It was going to be a messy, dirty, smelly life of commitment, of joy and pain, and she couldn't wait to get started. Everyone was pleased.

South couldn't stop talking about the gala wedding she had been to the night before and how they must decorate the island for a wedding, while Trish, in her wheelchair and no longer able to lift her arms to embrace her daughters, cried great crocodile tears that fell on the leopard scarf around her neck. Her pact to try to leave her girls with Max was coming true.

White Bear sang a wedding chant that he taught the men as they partied separately on the outside porch with their good friend, Wild Turkey. The women planned an engagement party and the house was loud, warm, sweaty, and full of life.

That night, Colby and Max took the double kayak out to see Starbuck, and Max, who had been plotting for weeks a way to make love in the tiny open kayak, consummated the impossible under the watchful eye of Starbuck, who kept a keen eye on the proceedings and then nuzzled the kayak, all in the light of a rare blue moon.

Annie watched as the kayak disappeared into the moonlight bathing a golden glow of flickering firelight on the men working on the canoe, the tiny shacks on the spit, and through the window and onto the twin cribs of the new island royalty.

The island was bursting with life. Babies, children, orcas, weddings—and Annie wondered if she couldn't bargain to stay longer, to make sure that the success would continue. Seven years. It wasn't a very long time. After all, she'd already done seventy-six. What's a few more years? she reasoned. She decided she would talk to the sisters. *Maybe they will come to me tonight,* she thought, as she wiggled her legs under the covers to warm the bed. Surely if she called them, they could come…and then she fell asleep.

Someone did hear Annie's call and was there to answer—Snodgrass.

Thwarted in his last two attempts, and running out of boats and motors, Snodgrass surfed the internet and came up with what he thought was an ingenious way to get samples of what he hoped was polluted water surrounding the island. The health department hoped to quarantine the island and the county would have to take it over to clean up what Snodgrass had eloquently coined Seven Sisters toxic waste. He cursed the new state-of-the-art outhouses and knew this might be his last chance.

Snodgrass had siphoned off funds from a grant to re-plumb low-income housing, and had leased a small one-man submarine for an underwater approach and retreat from the island. The training alone was two weeks, ten thousand dollars, and a flight to Miami. Snodgrass had sacrificed as never before. Living and working on the white sand beaches of the Caribbean for two weeks at full pay, a *per diem*, and with an unlimited expense account and a bevy of escort services that exhausted him. All of this with the blessing of the county commissioners. They wanted Seven Sisters so badly they had made their bed with the slimy Snodgrass.

He had the tarped submarine delivered under cover of darkness to a county-protected sewer site the week before. The training sub had been black, but they had delivered one in screaming yellow. When Snodgrass had his colors done by his supposed fourth wife, he had tested winter. His colors: gray and black-grayish.

Interestingly enough, the Snodgrass marriages were annulled when he was found to have not bothered to divorce himself from the previous three marriages. The women had fled to the far corners of obscurity. One had emigrated to Tierra del Fuego; one worked in an orphanage in Botswanaland under an alias; and one had a sex change operation. The fourth still lived in Port Townsend and drank—heavily.

Yellow was not the Snodgrass color, but he was not to be denied. He donned a wet suit, climbed into the claustrophobic pilot seat, and began humming the Ringo Beatle tune "Yellow Submarine" as he disappeared under the water.

The periscope worked beautifully as Snodgrass barreled towards the island at full speed under the cover of an overcast night sky. He had surfaced several times along the perimeter of the island and scooped plastic bottles of the seawater. He now was ready to penetrate into the lagoon for his final sample. With the scope, he could see the shacks on the waterfront and the boatshed. The landscape looked deserted. Victory was in sight. Snodgrass wished the sub carried torpedoes.

He coasted into the lagoon when he felt the submarine lurch and then stop. It would not go forward. He hit the rear thrusters, but the sub held tight.

"Dammit, Jim," Snodgrass swore a Star Trek curse. He surfaced and carefully opened the hatch. It was pitch dark. He fumbled for a flashlight, finally found the switch, and panned the bow of the sub. He could see he was caught in some sort of a web, some kind of netting, and then he heard a splash and spotted a shark fin no more than a few feet from his elbow. Those were his last thoughts.

Joe had the island under radar alert 24/7. So when Snodgrass approached, Joe had several lines of defense open to him, but when Starbuck's pen netting captured the sub, the rest was easy.

Snodgrass woke up. His head hurt and he heard the crackling and ping of electronic equipment, but he was blindfolded, gagged, and his hands tied behind him. He struggled at the bonds but knew it was useless. He was in the care of a professional. He was summarily loaded into a large sack and dragged to the beach and loaded into a boat. It was a short trip across the water and Snodgrass reckoned he was in Port Gamble. He was then unloaded into a cart and wheeled up the dock. He could hear dogs barking and the sound of a car trunk opening and then it was quiet except for the drone of the car engine. Snodgrass determined he was in the trunk for at least two hours when the trunk opened. He heard aircraft landing and taking off, but with the blindfold he could see nothing. Still in a sack, he was loaded into a cargo bay and he felt the plane take off. There were two more airports and then the cargo hold got very cold. Snodgrass was exhausted and slept fitfully until he was dumped out of the sack in the back of a cargo plane in flight.

That's when he saw Joe. Dressed in full Camo, black face, bandoliers with knives, grenades and guns draped across his shoulders. Snodgrass' only thought was, Rambo. But no Rambo he had ever imagined.

Rambo in a C-170 cargo plane. Leaving the gag in place, Joe busily ushered Snodgrass into a fur-lined parka, insulated boots and down pants. He carefully laced Snodgrass into a parachute and stuffed a chocolate bar, nylon stockings, and a few rubles in the parka vest pocket. The back of the plane opened its yawning rear door that could accommodate an armored tank. Joe walked a struggling Snodgrass to the end of the rear door that looked out into an unknown blackness.

"I don't even know if they use rubles any more," Joe apologized. He untied the gag from Snodgrass' mouth. Snodgrass cut loose with a stream of obscenities and ended with, "I don't even have a wallet or a passport or..."

"Like I care," Joe smiled as he yanked the rip cord and pushed the sewer man off the ramp and into the night. Joe heard Snodgrass' trailing scream and then there was quiet. Joe buckled himself into a seat, lit a cigar, and pulled a silver flask of single malt from his coat pocket. An army of one, Joe smiled and settled in for the trip home.

Chapter
TWENTY

With the net torn, Starbuck began churning out into the channel to socialize with traveling boats. Federal law prohibited boats from approaching to within five hundred feet, but Starbuck—ever the teenage social butterfly—would charge out to greet the boats.

"He's going to get hurt from one of those boat props," Max fumed every night when Starbuck would come in for his feeding. "It's just too dangerous out there. We need to get him back to his pod."

With the latest attack by the health department and the county bureaucrats, it was obvious that Annie had to ramp up her campaign for county commissioner and Pickles was ready to hit the ground running. Annie did newspaper photo shoots feeding Starbuck, caring for the twins, boating over to the Pike Place Market. The newspapers were happy to give Annie and her eccentric lifestyle free press for her agenda in the damp, cold, gray overcast days of a Pacific Northwest winter.

Annie wanted the county government to promote affordable housing, be more accountable, less secretive; provide more free right-hand turn lanes, and lighted crosswalks for schoolchildren. Impossible, said her opponents. One afternoon, Pickles had come over to caucus with Annie and the island. "We just need to do more," Pickles quietly pounded the kitchen table with his fist.

"Shhh…be quiet," Annie scolded. "The twins are sleeping."

Pickles rolled his eyes and stared at Annie. "Oh, no. I know that look." Annie shook her finger at Pickles. "I'm not getting back into that Sea Grannies cheerleader outfit again. You can just forget about it."

Pickles kept staring. "What? What is it you want now?" Annie got up and poured herself some coffee and returned to the table.

"You're well-seasoned," Pickles began diplomatically. "And your opponents are in their forties."

"I'm just plain old," Annie countered. "Nearly seventy-seven. Remember, my sisters all died at seventy-seven."

Undeterred, Pickles plowed ahead. "I think we need something to show you are young-at-heart."

"Like what?" Annie asked tenuously.

"Just a few ideas I had," Pickles began as he pulled out a sheet of paper with a short list. "Let's see." Annie snatched the paper from his hand. "Skydiving…no!" Annie said. "Shot out of a cannon at the circus…Where do you get this crap? Waterskiing…no!"

Pickles remained undaunted.

"Snowboarding…no. Rumors I'm pregnant?…Unbelievable, Pickles!"

"I'm not suggesting anything crazy like that." Annie threatened Pickles with a metal whisk. Pickles put his hands up defensively.

"God, no. I would never think of putting you in danger," Pickles continued, still keeping his hands up. "I was thinking about you whale riding."

"Riding the back of a whale…Now that's reasonable," Annie said sarcastically. "Can't we just run on a good, solid platform?" She folded her arms.

Pickles laughed, shook his head, and poised his large blue coffee cup and held it defensively in front of his mouth. "Of course not!

"We have an appointment with the Makahs to ride a whale next Thursday. The whale is tame and I had a wet suit made for you and you simply *have* to do it," Pickles said rapidly, quickly hiding behind a long drink of coffee so he wouldn't have to look at Annie.

"What? Are you trying to kill me?" Annie fumed.

"I think you need this." Pickles peered out from the top of his cup. "I really do."

"How safe is it? Has anyone done this before? I can't even spread my legs out wide enough to get on the back of a whale; it's ridiculous," Annie spitfired.

"No, no, no, no. It's very safe." Pickles set down his cup and gained momentum. "Surfing. Remember when we went out to the Makahs' to look at that canoe and they were training the whales? Their favorite humpback came back a month ago and she has a calf and is very domesticated. They have been riding her for nearly a month. Besides, the tribe could use the publicity too. It's a Win-Win."

"I'd look ridiculous in a wet suit," Annie sputtered, waving Pickles off with her hand.

"*Everybody* looks ridiculous in a wet suit," Pickles agreed. "I have the suit in a nice navy blue with dark blue pinstripes with your name on the back. Here, take a look at the picture."

Pickles handed her a photo of the suit. "Hmm-m. It doesn't look bad." Annie shook her head. "I'd look like I was on an underwater bowling team. *Absolutely not.*"

Undeterred, Pickled pressed on. "The ride might be as long as a hundred yards, but remember this would help jumpstart the Makah economic base. You know they are too far out in the boonies for a casino and again, it would help the little Indian children on the reservation," Pickles whined.

"How is it going to help the children?"

"All the money from the whale rides would go to the schools and healthcare. They project hundreds of thousands of dollars in revenue based on what a swimming with the dolphins resort in the Bahamas brings in. And it would help acquaint people with whales. They are planning on a whale museum once they get the funds and the whale riding is under consideration by Whales International as promoting whale awareness, and you would look good in this suit." Pickles waved the photo from his safety perch across the table.

Annie went over into the living room and attempted to surf the green velvet foot stool. Pickles held her hand as she wavered. "Uwgh... I can't get up on a whale," Annie protested. "They're slippery."

"Actually, they're not that slippery and they have special boots. I think you need to lean more forward," Pickles coached, "and remember, I have the Costco bottle of extra strength Aleve, and I will surf with you," Pickles reluctantly sweetened the pot, knowing he was lying.

"I'll think about it," Annie promised, stepping down from the stool, "but not very hard."

White Bear was anxious. The canoe was nearing completion and he was still advertising for paddlers. After finishing the inside and placing a series of flat-planked seating from side to side, the canoe was flipped over, exposing the charred hull, which was rubbed with flat granite rocks. It was a dirty, gritty job, but soon the hull shone smooth and polished. It was painted with a mixture of burned cattail rushes and whale oil that the Makah had given Annie on her visit. The inside was finished with a mixture of red ochre and oil and glued to the top flattened edge; the carvers inlaid the half shells of butter clams for decoration.

White Bear had carved a bear clinging to a tree as a bowsprit out of the great cedar tree, and it was attached with wooden pegs to the bow and a single twenty-foot spruce pole was placed in a drilled hole in one of the front seats and seated deep into the canoe keel to support a sail.

The documentary film crew had been on site for months and they gladly helped White Bear and the carvers lever raise the canoe onto poles and roll it towards the sea on a rising high tide. They collectively held their breath as the canoe slipped into the water like a water ouzel and floated as lightly as seagull down.

White Bear had cajoled eight paddlers to join him—three from the University of Washington crew, two of the documentary filmmakers, two tribal casino workers, and a foreign exchange student from Zimbabwe. They all wanted the ten thousand dollars apiece, but no one had ever paddled a canoe.

The paddlers and White Bear waded into the freezing waters and clambered aboard. Using paddles shaped like pointed spoons, the paddlers churned the water in futility, the canoe turning in circles as they searched for a sense of harmony. White Bear sat in the bow, put his hand on the carved bear, turned his face to the wind, and began a chant of thanksgiving, thumping a thick cedar club against the bow in a metronomic cadence that gave the paddlers a rhythm. Soon the canoe was slashing forward into the waves.

"Well, enough of this nonsense," South chipped in, watching the paddlers, her breath rising in the cold air. "We have a potluck and an engagement party to get rolling."

Annie put her arm over South's shoulders and guided her up to the house. "That's true. Let's all go up to the house and get this celebration on the road."

When Annie went out into the kitchen, Pickles was staring in the back door window. Annie motioned for him to come in.

"Are you stalking me?" She turned and reached for the coffee pot.

"I'm your campaign manager, remember?" Pickles held out a mug.

"Oh yeah, I almost forgot." Annie stopped pouring. "I'm not getting on Starbuck. Don't even think about it. Don't you have a couple of tons of possum meat you can't sell? Another one of your good ideas?"

"Don't even go there, Annie," Pickles countered. "The market will bounce back on possum loins, trust me. No, No. Not Starbuck," Pickles implored with his hands extended.

"Kalakala."

"Kalakala. That's the name of the old aluminum ferry between Bremerton and Seattle." Annie set down her cup.

"No, not the ferry!" Pickles was getting exasperated. "Not the ferry. I told you before, it's a mother gray whale and her calf that live out on the Makah reservation. It's perfectly safe and you would be helping the Makahs. Remember, they want to start a tourist trade based on whale riding. Like I said, it's too far out on the coast for a casino. You know, ecotourist stuff. Man and nature stuff. We already went over this, remember?"

"Listen," Pickles prattled on. "You put on a dry suit, the whale comes alongside the boat and you ride on its back for a hundred yards or so, maybe less, and the whale dives and we pick you up. The media will cover it, you'll be a celebrity, and we'll put the clip on YouTube. We already went over this!"

"YouTube?" Annie shook her head. "What's that?"

"YouTube is this cutting-edge thing where you can use a computer to put short videos on the internet and people can Google you up. I thought Max put you on Facebook." Pickles looked confused.

"Google you up?" Annie took off her glasses. "What is Google it up? You know I don't know how to work a computer."

There was a polite knock on the door and Sister Mary Catherine came in, poured a cup of coffee from the pot on the stove, and took a seat at the kitchen table. "What's happening, Dude?" She looked from Annie's face to Pickles.

"Google," Pickles challenged Sister, thinking she wouldn't have a clue.

"Cool," Sister responded.

"YouTube." Pickles raised the ante.

"Groovy, what are we up to?" Sister spooned sugar into her coffee and stirred counterclockwise as she always did. "Corialis effect," Sister noted brightly as she caught Pickles watching her.

"Corialis what?" Pickles questioned.

"Corialis effect. The toilets flush counterclockwise on the other side of the equator. Down south."

"Really?" Pickles was surprised.

"Well, actually, it's not really true," Sister confessed. "Been there done that. So what's this jive about YouTube?"

"As part of the campaign, I want Annie to ride on the back of a whale," Pickles explained. "You interested?"

"I'm all in," Sister decided quickly. "When and where? Annie, you're going to do it? It's so right up your alley, gal."

Annie began to hedge. "I don't think it's safe."

"Gray whales don't eat people," Pickles spouted. "They are filter feeders. They eat tiny crustaceans that they scoop up from the bottom of the ocean and usually their right eye becomes blind because of all the abrasions and they don't seem too bright either."

"So they're as blind as a one-eyed pirate," Annie wailed. "How is that safe?"

"You like one-eyed pirates, remember?" Pickles reminded her. Annie smiled as she remembered Moby Dick and his eye patch.

"That's a design flaw," Sister chimed in as she stopped stirring her coffee. "One-eyed whales, platypus, giraffes—ya gotta wonder, dude, what was God's thinking? So when are we going to do this whale gig Annie?"

Annie took a deep breath and exhaled. She looked at Pickles. "When?"

"Tomorrow!"

"Tomorrow!"

Pickles lifted his arms in triumph and accidentally stomped on the long tail of Twigs who was passing under the table on crumb patrol.

Twigs yelped, the chair went sideways, and Pickles crumpled to the floor as Twigs turned and gave Pickles a dirty look and slithered under the safety of the wood stove.

"That's a good omen," Annie said, tracing the rim of her coffee mug, her fingers lingering on a chip shaped like the state of Texas.

"What we really need is some new coffee mugs," she mumbled into her cup as she took a long drink.

That night, Annie was startled awake, gasping and in a cold sweat. Throwing off the covers, she lay spread-eagled on the bed and struggled to control her breathing as she reached up and curled her fingers around her two familiar touch points on the headboard of the bed.

Panic attack, Annie thought to herself as she continued deep breathing.

"I need to stay rational." *Was this about riding the whale? Or was it because the twins' future was still not settled? The county officials that were still trying to get the island for a park? Taxes?* "I'm not afraid of death," Annie reminded herself aloud, and Pickles had her will containing her contingency plan in case her sisters somehow couldn't make good on their promise to give her the seven extra years; still there was a fear. *What was it?*

For an hour Annie wrestled with the problem, until shivering, she had to retreat back to her flannel sheets and her quilt. Closing her eyes, she realized that her fear was that grandmothers were supposed to be conservative and wise and here she was about to pioneer whale-surfing! Was this the legacy she wanted to leave behind? And as she drifted away, she knew in her heart that no matter what happened, the twins would always know they came from stock that was not afraid to take on a challenge.

"We're risk-takers, risk-takers," Annie mumbled into the mute darkness.

But even as she slept, Annie did not loosen her grip on the headboard.

Chapter
TWENTY-ONE

Pickles brought the Volkswagen van to Port Gamble and was surprised when half the island showed up. Ziggy and Matty took the overflow after Annie buckled Annie and Zack into their car seats and sat next to Colby who decided he wanted to do the video. Talish and Alisha sat next to the toddlers. Pickles slammed the old van into gear and they were headed to the coast.

"They sure grow fast," Alisha remarked as she tickled Zack under his ribs and he gurgled and laughed a good belly laugh. Zack scrunched up his face, determined not to hiccup, but Alisha continued to play their game while Little Annie watched.

Finally, Zack burped up a little breakfast and began to hiccup. Alisha grabbed the burp rag and cleaned him up and gave a satisfied smirk as she settled back in her seat.

When the bus rumbled through Port Townsend, the acrid fumes from the smoke stacks of the paper mill stung their noses.

"Ummm, smells like money to me," Pickles snorted as he tried in vain to drive the smell from his nose. In Port Angeles, everyone was ready for a potty break—for the old timers and diapers for the twins.

An hour and a half later they motored into Forks down a long narrow road that glided across an old narrow steel and rivet bridge and onto the single street of commerce. The sign near the chamber of commerce read "Forks…population 3331….150 plus inches of rain a year. Rainiest town in America." Someone had handwritten a sign on a piece of cardboard and tacked it to the bottom of the sign that read Beware of Vampires.

"Vampires," Pickles grumbled. "Only if they wear snorkels when they sleep in their coffins."

Another half hour down the road, the party had reached the reservation. The ragtag town of single-story weathered and curly cedar-shingled buildings that followed the arch of the gravel beach and the last building, called The End of the World Laundromat. Beyond stretched the Pacific Ocean, with no landfall for three thousand miles.

Pickles parked next to two cars, one with two flat tires and the other missing its hood, that signified the only signs of life in front of the Chinook Café.

Spotted Elk, a tribal elder, ushered them into the café and barked orders at the staff who charged out with mugs of hot chocolate, coffee, and plates of blueberry pancakes and giant bowls of homemade blackberry jelly and wild heather honey from the tribes' hundreds of hibernating hives that were stacked head high behind the café, waiting to be hoisted on the back of flatbed trucks and, when the snow melted, hauled up into the lush mountain meadows of the Olympic Mountains.

Spotted Elk dressed Old School in black wool pants and a thick dogwood-gray and white wool sweater with Haida symbols of whales and ravens. He moved with the grace of a man used to living in nature. His heavily tanned hands had worked the salmon runs for seventy-plus seasons and the lines on his face had been etched deep by the ocean winds. There was a sadness in his soft brown eyes that were watery, not from perpetual windburn, but from seeing his culture slowly edged toward extinction.

The tribal young had left for Seattle long ago and Spotted Elk was left with old men and women. Proud of their culture, the tribe was poor and had been defeated in so many ways, from the remoteness of the tribal lands to the poor runs of salmon. Spotted Elk closed his eyes and refused to look out the window at the bleak coastline, the rusting cars and the rotting wooden boats that stood on their stick cradles waiting for the salmon runs to begin to trickle back. He took a deep breath, closed the curtains, dimmed the lights, and began his video.

First there was the sound of drums in the darkness and then the large screen flashed too bright like coming over the hill into high beams.

Makah Production Company. There was a pie chart showing how the federal grant money was to be spent and a graph of possible revenue generated from the whale-riding, as well as footage of the fledgling attempt to train bottle-nosed dolphins for Homeland Security surveillance.

The next segment was the use of jerky hand-held cameras that had documented trainers cultivating what the tribe hoped was a friendship with the gray whales that lived in the lagoon. Homers, the tribe called them, for although they migrated down to the inner waters of the Baja to calf, these gray whales always came back the thousands of miles to flourish near the Neah Bay reservation. Because the whales could not be trained with fish, there was only one way to cultivate their friendship: to call forth on the great whales' spiritual union with the tribe over the thousands of years they had both shared these waters.

The film turned more graphic. A commentator explained:

Mistakes had been made. A decade ago, two whales were killed in a solidarity movement to assert the tribal rights over their waters and its fisheries. Unfortunately, the use of outboard motors to hunt down the whales, the shotgun blasts to the great mammals' head to finish the kill, and the anguish of the dying whales, were all recorded on television cameras, so the hunt came off as nothing more than brutality, and not the noble return of a struggle between man and nature the tribe had hoped for.

That downside paled in comparison to the fact that no one in the tribe wanted to eat the great hunks of meat and blubber that still sat in the tribal freezer.

The next phase was a document of a time of healing between friends. Tribal drums and singing had been electronically sent into the ocean, for thousands of hours and studies of the gray whale language of grunts, whistles and clicks had attempted to be translated with the help of the local tribe elders and other tribes associated with whales from Florida, Tierra del Fuego, and New Zealand. And then there was a breakthrough.

Spotted Elk stopped the video. "As you may know," he related, "the incidence of autism in Native Americans is unusually low, but there was a mildly autistic young man in the tribe who heard the recording of gray whale language and he is able to replicate the sounds and, we believe, communicate with the whales here in the ocean. Not perfectly, but we think there has been a breakthrough. The State Department has made this classified information and the young man is now working with the Department of Defense and Homeland Security. The boy is called Charlie Talks with Whales.

"Our riders have made hundreds of safe trips on the backs of the whales for up to two hundred yards. I will show footage of the actual whale-riding."

The lights dimmed and there were twenty minutes of successful rides. A jet-powered boat would go up next to the surfaced whale and the diver would step on the back and surf on the back of the barnacle-encrusted whale until it slowly slipped beneath the surface and the diver would be swiftly hoisted aboard the trail boat. The video ended and in the darkness Sister Mary Catherine's voice called out loud and clear. "Hook me up, Bro."

Within the hour, the island folk were speeding along out in the ocean in two twenty-five-foot aluminum launches powered by a two-hundred horsepower jet engine. John and a camera crew from KING 5 TV were on a lead boat to catch the action and another boat of Native divers was trailing to ensure Annie and Sister Mary Catherine's safety.

The two women were dressed in orange hooded dry suits with studded boots to help secure the footing on the back of the whale.

"Not really my color," Mary Catherine complained good-naturedly. "I'm just a basic black with pearls kinda gal." She expertly shielded the flame with her off hand and lit her Camel straight with the boat speeding along at forty knots.

Annie had just finished tucking her hair into the hood when they came upon the two forty-five-foot mammals. The backs of the whales, as broad as a Cadillac, were a mottled black and gray and riddled with barnacles.

"What are their names just in case?" Annie yelled over the roar of the motor.

"This is Skookum and Kalakala is over there on the right. I can tell by the barnacle formation and the slots in their flukes," Spotted Elk yelled.

"Skookum means strong."

"And what does Kalakala mean?" Mary Catherine leaned over to hear the answer.

"Flying Bird is the closest translation," Spotted Elk yelled over the drone of the engines as he helped Annie out onto a gangplank with a stainless steel rail that would swing over the back of the whale.

"Go for it!" he yelled as Annie stepped from the plank onto the back of Kalakala and took a surfer's stance, one foot in front of the other. Annie looked back at the boat and gave a thumbs-up as the boat deposited Sister Mary Catherine on the back of Skookum. With the ash flying off her cigarette like a blow torch, she couldn't help but cackle for joy as she bent low on her whale and looked over at Annie.

Mary Catherine completed a spin move and Annie nosed forward until the surf was just breaking over her toes and not more than twenty seconds later the whales both silently submerged without a flip of their tail, leaving the two women bobbing in the ocean waves.

The spotters pulled the women out of the water and John was pumping his fist and hooting in the film boat while the two women looked at each other and just smiled.

"Hallelujah! Praise the Lord and, pass the biscuits," Mary Catherine kept repeating.

While Annie kept babbling about the power of the animal and how she could feel it breathing and the salt spray hitting her in the face. It was just the beauty and nobility of the creature. Just the nobility, she kept repeating.

Still shivering a half hour later, Annie and Sister Mary Catherine were stripped and tucked into down sleeping bags in front of a roaring fire in the lodge.

"Dèja vu," Pickles beamed, "you're gonna be famous again, Annie."

As Pickles predicted, the television news played the whale surfing over and over until the reservation line for whale-surfing at the Makah reservation was booked through the summer and Annie's political stock went up twenty-two points in the polls.

"Your YouTube and our Facebook page are getting a bunch of hits," Pickles kept telling Annie, but she never knew what he was talking about until one day Sister Mary Catherine took her to an internet café in Port Townsend and there was the footage for all the world to see.

Chapter
TWENTY-TWO

I t was the end of March and the island was poised for spring, but it seemed that winter was going to last forever. Sure there were signs. The native sumac was leafing out, brave frogs were croaking, dogwood trees were beginning to blossom, the Brandt geese stopped by on their way north, Ziggy's marijuana starts had turned the corner, and the days were getting longer—but it was not enough for Professor Spud.

He came into Annie's kitchen, slammed his soggy sou'wester on the table, and set his ice cooler on the floor. "I've had enough winter to last me a lifetime. I need a change," he declared.

Spud was grateful that the house was toasty warm as Annie set a steaming mug of black coffee on the table that would have scorched the palate of an ordinary man, but not Spud, who washed the fiery fluid down absentmindedly and drummed his fingers on the table. "You know, Annie, I just have hit a threshold where I can't…"

There was a gentle knock on the door and Twigs, somewhat of a perfume *aficionado*, lifted his head up from under the stove and then slumped. He'd accessed the threat level with his nose and decided that anyone that could afford to wear the Prada fragrance couldn't be much of a threat. There was a time he had ambitions of a more executive level, but his training as a service dog, microbrew malt snorter, and drug sniffer at Sea-Tac International, had proved fruitless. He had the nose but he was diagnosed early on as being dyslexic and ADHD and was washed out of the programs early on. *Just as well,* Twigs smirked, as he nodded off to sleep. *Being an island dog was a real job and he had made it his own.*

Spud opened the door and stared at eye level into the biggest pair of breasts he'd seen north of Vegas in a long time. Strategically placed across the pink sweatshirt was Double DD Construction and topping the breasts was a strawberry blonde woman in her mid-forties. Spud peeked around the door jamb and spotted three carbon copies lining the porch. He couldn't help but give a little squeal of delight.

"Carol Ann sent me out to insulate your cabins," the woman explained to a still-transfixed Spud, holding open the door. "Your island qualified as low-income housing and Carol Ann found a government grant."

"Come on in," Annie called from the kitchen. "Coffee?"

"Sure," the women all chimed in and brushed their way past a grateful Spud and settled into the kitchen chairs.

In his early seventies, the Spud was the youngest of three children and his mother held onto Spud as long as she could. She breast-fed her baby boy until he was four and could stand up and take nourishment while playing paddle ball.

The women pulled off their sweatshirts to unveil skin-tight t-shirts with the same Double DD logo. Big boobs, hard nipples, and sweet-smelling women. Spud knew he was in over his head and needed support. He hustled his arthritic knees down the trail to find every man jack available. John, Ziggy, Owl, White Bear, and the entire contingent of canoe carvers all trooped up to the house and sat across from the table where Double D forces had fanned out a number of their calling cards.

Spud passed the electric pink cards around and pulled his glasses from his top pocket. The card read: DD construction/ dykes on bikes/ drill team Zeke's 3216 ½ 14th Ave South, Beacon Hill, Seattle.

"Do you mean there are more of you?" John asked with a sly smile.

"Fifteen of us in this chapter," the strawberry blonde answered directly. My name is Marilyn and these are my associates: Jackie, Ginger and Vicki C."

The company shook hands all around. While many men prefer other body parts of a woman, The Spud had been clearly a breast man early on and had never wavered. The three former Spud spouses were chosen because all carried a definite physical proclivity that Spud fully acknowledged was shallow and demeaning, but carried a great deal of weight in his mating decisions. While a man of science and a high I.Q., Spud made no excuses. He often used the Woody Allen muse…the heart wants what the heart wants. He just wished his buddy Steve Hawking was here to appreciate these beauties.

While the men were trying to wrap their minds around the theatrics of the Double D's, Annie piped up, "So, you're here to insulate the shacks? How is that going to happen?"

Vicki C pulled out a prospectus. "We're planning on putting draft protection on all the shacks or houses with a product called Tyvek and then putting two inches of rigid foam insulation on the inside walls and ceilings and a finish of select grade tongue-and-groove pine one-by-eights on the inside. The cabins will look just as rustic from the outside as they do now, but the heating efficiency will go up five-fold."

"What about my place?" Owl looked puzzled. "I've got windows and doors from a '57 Buick Special. How is that going to work?"

Ginger fielded the question. "We will do our best to accommodate the existing structure. We always aim to please."

"So you do more than insulation work?" John asked.

"A lot more," Ginger added. "We all ride Harleys and our drill team has kicked off the Gay Pride parade in Frisco for the last five years, the Seattle chapter of Dykes on Bikes."

"So all of you gals look the same." Ziggy tried to wrap himself around the visual.

"We're all double D's whether naturally or artificially, we all drive the same turquoise Harley speedsters, dye our hair blonde, and of course we go topless with leather thongs in the parades. We always get a standing O."

"Don't you get, uh, cold?" John said pointedly. "San Francisco can get windy."

"Well, some of us…" Ginger began.

"We need to focus on the business at hand," Marilyn took over the conversation. "We'd like to start tomorrow and work from the farthest cabin out on the spit to the closest. We can move out any furniture and personal gear and put it out under a blue tarp."

Annie was tickled. "You know, it's getting harder to find driftwood to fuel the stoves to heat the cabins. Would you ladies like to stay here in the house while you work?" Annie reasoned. "It would make it easier and I'd be glad to cook."

"That would be great," Marilyn nodded. "We can bring our personal gear and insulating equipment over on the morning tide."

"Just one more question," Ziggy wondered aloud as he pulled a pen from behind his ear and prepared to write on his hand. "Are you girls going to work topless here on the island and when is the San Francisco Gay Pride parade?"

Marilyn gave Ziggy a withered look, but he was enjoying himself too much to notice.

The Double D's worked on the island a little longer than expected. The men set up lawn chairs in front of each cabin and watched the women work their magic day after day and they ponied up extra money so Annie could put on gourmet meals every evening. And for the two weeks, every night Spud plied the women in his cabin with expensive wine, great mounds of imported Swiss chocolate from his standing order of a ten-pound block every two weeks from the Port Gamble market, and tantalized them with his show-and-tell collection. For both sides, it was great performance art.

When the Double D's reluctantly left, they had each gained a few pounds and Spud had serendipitously worked his way through his spring crisis into warmer days and softer nights.

The warmer spring winds that piped up in the evening made for interesting casket sailboat races. The spring challenge series consisted of five races on the inside of the spit around three buoys where the water was relatively calm.

The simple Spartan glossy black casket with the pointed prow of Sister Mary Catherine slipped through the water as if ordained to win and had taken the first two races handily, while Owl's chunky blue beauty was like the Spanish armada in comparison with its heavy bronze cleats and blunt nose. Rather than change the design for the third race, Owl had slyly installed a small battery-operated propeller on the bottom of the boat, near the middle and unseen.

Sister Mary was baffled how the awkward craft seemed to all of a sudden be able to sail in light air while her sails were slack. At the end of four races, the score was Sister two wins, Owl two wins, and John and Ziggy had retired their caskets to the dock.

Owl had been doing a lot of trash talking in the days before the last race and had made a side bet with Sister that the loser would have to reward the winner with three geoduck clams. Sister Mary knew the clams were difficult to dig as they burrowed down three feet in the sand, but she had prayed hard over the results and she did have an ace up her long sleeve.

Her disciple, Joe, had slithered out of his bunker the night before the last race and did a quick reconnaissance of Owl's boat and discovered the motor. He bent Owl's shaft and installed a slightly larger propeller in Sister Mary Catherine's—barely larger than a fifty-cent piece. Sister took an early lead to Owl's befuddlement. He thought she was using more sail, but then he was confident she had caught him out. He tried to ram sister's coffin but never quite caught up to her and she sailed cleanly to the finish line, setting off her air horn amidst the whoops and hollers of the crowd on the beach.

Sheepishly, Owl brought his boat in and pointed out the tiny propeller to Sister. Sister never confessed. Some things were best left to communion was her usual motto. "Let that be a lesson to you, my son," she admonished him. "The Lord works in strange and mysterious ways."

Several days later, a minus tide of 2.4 happened in the early morning. A perfect time to pry the giant clam from his lair. Owl grumbled over having to fulfill his wager as he waited until the tide reached slack and the clams' necks tentatively reached up through the sand with their clean bivalve snorkel. He drew a circle around the necks with his shovel and marked the spots with small sticks and waited. He knew the clam neck was extended up through the sand a good three feet from the body which never moved. Owl knew the clams lived to be a good sixty years old or more if undisturbed and had no predators.

The geoduck, with the well-endowed neck, sometimes brought well over a hundred dollars a pound in Japan and could weigh up to twelve pounds in the shell. It was this trophy that Owl knew would test his mettle as the residual water in the sand would keep collapsing the hole as he dug. There were techniques that included driving a ten-inch pipe down over the clam and then slowly dipping the sand out till the digger could pry the beast loose, but that was for lesser men. Owl preferred the *mano a mano* technique that required digging like a madman down the side of the neck and then thrusting his arm deep into the hole, his head disappearing into the hole and digging the last foot with his fingers till he felt the thick opening of the mantle from which the neck extended. It was time-sensitive to wiggle the shell enough to extract the giant clam before the sand closed in around his arm and the tide came in and buried them both.

Black clouds closed in on the island and the air was electric as the sound of thunder echoed down the waters of Hood Canal as if a cannonade in the battle of Shiloh in the American Civil War. The thunder grew closer and lightning crackled as the island shuddered. Still Owl dug on, throwing away his shovel and putting both hands deep into the hole, resting his forehead on the wet sand. It was an epic struggle as Owl clawed his way deeper into the pit. He had always likened the battle to Hemingway's *Old Man and the Sea*, a clean contest between equals that Hemingway would have found a nobility in its purity. The thunder rolled in ever closer and the lightning was on top of the island when the giant clam relinquished its grip in the sand and was brought to the surface.

Owl's chest was heaving as he lay on the sand clutching the clam to his chest and then he rolled to his feet, raised his shovel with one hand and the giant clam in the other, and began a victory dance.

Sister Mary had watched the epic struggle and was yelling to him to get off the beach when she heard the crack of lightning and saw the bolt strike the upraised shovel. There was a puff of smoke and the smell of ozone. Owl disappeared from her sight as she was knocked senseless by the explosion.

Dazed and temporarily deaf, Sister struggled to her feet and ran to the spot where Owl had begun his dance. She smelled the burnt rubber, but there was nothing on the beach except his footprints. No shovel, no geoduck, no clothing—nothing where a man had stood moments before.

The entire island searched most of the day and it wasn't until evening that the three-legged bloodhound, Trooper, finally left his post guarding Trish's girls and brought Owl's charred right rubber boot to Ziggy.

Ziggy gave a war hoop and everyone came running. Annie shook the boot and something rattled inside. She tipped it over and Owl's charred big toe, the nail a smoky copper color, dropped onto the beach rocks. Everyone was stunned and then Spud began to chortle and then he rolled into a belly laugh.

"Spud, stop this spectacle. A man has died," Annie admonished Spud.

Spud could barely stop laughing long enough to point to the toe. "It's the toe," he gasped. "It's the toe. It's the left toe in the right boot. How the hell did that old merry prankster ever pull that off?" He paused just long enough and then convulsed onto the sand in uncontrollable laughter.

They all looked and, sure enough, it was true. The left toe was in the right boot. The swell started in a small way with guffaws and some minor chortling, but soon the entire island was laughing hysterically until they could barely breathe and then they would collectively bring themselves under control. And then someone would point to the toe and begin to chuckle and it would start again and they would have another fit until they all had cried themselves out with relief. Owl was still playing with them.

Owl hadn't left them after all and damn, wasn't that a classy way to go out—"no fuss, no muss, no lingering, and what a sense of humor," White Bear observed.

That night the toe stood in state in the sky blue blunt-nosed casket on the beach with a huge crackling fire in Owl's honor and the Wild Turkey wake lasted until early morning.

When Ziggy and John were roused from their hangover late that morning, they went to the Port Gamble store and alerted Pickles who came with the Jerry Garcia van to take the entourage over to Seattle to find Owl's daughter, Julia Latham, partner in the law firm of Latham & Associates.

Annie had let the men handle the arrangements and Ziggy, in his typical understated way, had phoned from the dock and explained that her father had died and they were bringing the remains over to her office near Westlake Mall. She was appalled, but agreed to meet them on the street.

When she came down from her office, she was carrying an umbrella in the light spring drizzle. John gave her the notarized will that Owl had kept in the casket. The document stated that Owl wanted his body placed in the casket and taken out into the Puget Sound and sunk to the bottom. All his possessions would go directly to his grandchildren, including a sizable trust fund.

Then Ziggy and Pickles placed the casket on the sidewalk and opened the lid. They tipped the toe out of the boot onto the denim casket lining at which Owl's barrister daughter began screaming. She folded up her umbrella and began beating the men over their heads, forcing them back into the van, and even then she kept pounding the side of the van until Pickles pulled his way into traffic to escape. The three men were rattled.

"Whew, I didn't see that coming," Ziggy wheezed as he lit off a joint and passed it through the cab.

"I don't think that went as well as it could've," Pickles agreed.

The three drove around through Tacoma and stopped at the 13 Coins and toasted their compatriot. The men ruminated about Owl and they were saddened to know that the man with the photographic memory of the entire Bremerton sewer system, the spirit of a warrior, and with a healthy respect for Wild Turkey whiskey, would not pass their way again.

There had been the hope that Owl's wishes would be honored, but when Carol Ann phoned the daughter, there was a sharp rebuke about the "savages" on the island and the phone went dead. Word came down that the body was laid to rest in a new family plot in a cemetery near the Snoqualmie River near Issaquah and there had been no invitation to the island.

The island was frozen in a funk again. The wound was fresh in their minds: woodworking tools left scattered in the workshop, empty cases of Wild Turkey still stacked behind the cabin, and they kept remembering the way Owl, who could never abide his hearing aids, could never quite hear what you were talking about, and there was his never-say-quit spirit. "There just ain't no closure," Ziggy complained.

Annie suggested a potluck, but no one was in the mood.

A few days later, a Mango Express storm from Indonesia rampaged in from the Pacific battering the Cascade Mountains with ten inches of rain, followed by warm Chinook trade winds that caused a quick thaw in the mountain slopes, flooding the Issaquah valley. The Snoqualmie River crested twenty feet over flood stage, jumped the sand bag river bank, and tore through the cemetery where the evening news traffic copter caught pictures of dozens of caskets unearthed and floating down the Snoqualmie River to Puget Sound.

Knowing the odds were ridiculous, *The Ark* nevertheless headed out to find one of its own and on the third day, with the help of a Coast Guard helicopter pilot that Joe had cajoled, they discovered two caskets floating near Bainbridge Island by Port Madison. The second casket contained Owl's toe in the blue casket and the other casket was towed to a nearby boat ramp to be discovered.

There was a great bonfire that night again and many toasts to the prodigal son, but there was no insight into how the left toe found its way into the right boot, but as Sister said, "The Lord works in mysterious ways." And no one could doubt that. The casket and toe were taken with great ceremony to the cold storage plant in Tacoma for burial later in the summer. Owl was the first of the island giants to fall that year, but there would be others.

The next day, a man dressed in a Bremerton City Sewer jumpsuit feathered his boat just off shore. "Does anyone here know where Famous Al lives around here?" the man shouted.

"Who wants to know?" Ziggy asked suspiciously.

"Well, we have a leak in a sewer main and we can't locate the lateral. I brought a map and I was hoping he could help me."

"You know the usual price, right?" Ziggy yelled across the water.

"Yeah, I've got the case of Wild Turkey right here," the man said, holding up the box.

Ziggy waded out and retrieved the box, returned to shore, and set the box down.

"So where is he?" the sewer man asked, hoping to complete his business.

"He died a few weeks ago, sonny," Ziggy grunted, as he picked up the case of Wild Turkey.

"In that case, I want my booze back," the man threatened.

"Shit happens, sonny," Ziggy said, walking away from the beach. "Shit Happens."

Ziggy knew that Owl would be proud that he used his favorite phrase for a very good cause.

Chapter
TWENTY-THREE

The morning was already warm and when the sun broke through the new maple leaves it dappled the apple orchard with patches of Impressionist light. A Pileated Woodpecker drummed his mating song on Annie's metal chimney top and then with his high-pitched call he diphthonged his way across the pasture with his unique flap and glide style.

The Trumpet vine tendrils were wending through the crumbling wall of the boat house searching for summer and the wild strawberry plants with the petite white blossoms that stubbornly grew along the path to Annie's house were sending out their runners.

This glorious morning there was an important meeting to finalize preparations for the potlatch that would launch White Bear on his way north to finish his vision quest. Annie began, "There will be sixty or more tribes coming from all over the world, primarily from the Northwest, but also from New Zealand, New York, and maybe Africa. We will be hosting the potlatch for the three days. That's the basics and now John will get into the specifics."

John read from his laptop. "The Makah tribe will be providing the king salmon, clams, oysters, shrimp and halibut. Dorie and Pinky, the Honeybuckets. Side dishes by Mom's Diner and Pickles. The tribes will stage themselves in Port Gamble and protocol is that they will be greeted here at Seven Sisters one by one.

"Camps will be set up on the beaches. We are expecting two to four thousand people on the first day and fewer the next two days. John Colby and Ziggy will be in charge of fire control. We expect that White Bear's voyage will get international attention and that the focus will shift away from the island as the journey begins and the island will return to normal. Any questions?"

"What is normal?" Ziggy looked perplexed.

Talisha raised her hand. "What about Starbuck?"

"John and Max are repairing the pen so he will be safe from boats."

"If no one has any objections, I'd like to serve barbecued possum." Pickles looked hopeful.

"White Bear, any discussion on that?" John deferred.

White Bear shrugged. "Sure, I don't have any problem with that as long as we have lots of sauce."

"Okay then, any more questions you can bring them to me. This is going to be a world-class event," John ended.

The island swung into full potlatch mode. Pickles had closed his shop and Wiggins, at the store, was on high alert with everything from cheap beer to sunscreen. The Makah had staged their salmon fillets and shellfish in a freezer trailer next to the store and the island cave was stacked high with blocks of ice and filled with vegetables and beverages.

Pinky and Dorie barged in fifty of their finest blue Sani-cans and lined them up in the orchard. Even the weather seemed to be in a cooperative mood with a sunny day and white wispy clouds.

The anticipation was so powerful that it seemed to White Bear that the wind and the waves were suspended in time as he strained his eyes to the south to catch a glimpse of the first canoe bearing his tribesmen.

He had aged considerably over the last six months. His eyes were weepy and his back bowed as if he carried a great weight, but as the first canoe came around the end of the island and past the Seven Sisters rocks, he straightened his back and lifted his chin to the north to catch the fresh salt wind that sprang from the deep waters of Hood Canal. White Bear was going to finish his vision quest on his terms. A life fully completed. A vision quest complete—Old School.

The videographers from the University of Washington, who had spent the last six months chronicling the building of the canoe, let the cameras roll. They too could feel the end of a life journey that had begun long before they were born. There was a sense of spiritual timelessness and their senses were heightened as they too smelled the salt air for the first time and listened to the waves gently wash the beach stones of fifteen thousand years of history. They would be documenting something extraordinary.

As the canoes nosed into the sandy beach, White Bear greeted them with a song of thanksgiving. The paddlers sat stoically resting their paddle grips on their hips and raising the pointed blade skyward until all canoes could be welcomed as one. The tribes would only disembark when the convoy was all accounted for. It was the centuries-old protocol of the Pacific Northwest Native potlatch.

The island was already crowded with families of the paddlers as the canoes came from Bella Bella, British Columbia, La Push, Quinault, Lummi, Muckelshoot, Cowichan, Tulalip, and another fifty tribes of "the water people." Canoes came from Hawaii and the Maori of New Zealand and a birch bark canoe sponsored by the original twelve tribes of New York, the paddlers a bevy of tall, leggy Native American tribal models sponsored by Saks Fifth Avenue and wearing designer clothes and Jimmy Choo heels.

The models thought they would create a buzz, but they were soon assimilated into an atmosphere of First Nation pride and belonging. The canoes lined the beach for a hundred yards when the Suquamish chief gave the welcome speech and the paddlers gave a tremendous shout and came ashore to revive old friendships and greet their families. There were dogs and children, young and old creating a mighty confluence of Native culture that flowed down into the pasture to see White Bear's canoe and to watch the continuing video in the church that explained the canoe-building process—from cutting the mammoth tree, sculpting the shape with the adz, and putting boiling stones to boil the water inside the canoe to flare the gunwales.

As the day wore on, there were sixty-foot-long pits dug in the gravel and mounds of firewood churned to a bright glow as the sun set over the Olympic Mountains and disappeared between the cleavage of the twin mountains called The Brothers. It was then that great slabs of salmon were racked onto green alder branches and stabbed upright next to the coals until the meat sizzled and the juices dripped down the support poles, sending up bursts of flames as the spirit of the salmon met the coals.

Jones Soda, based in Seattle, had offered to memorialize the event with special concoctions they invented for the occasion. A flavor called Salmon and another, a salute to seaweed and ginger, got mixed reviews; the salmon color drew raves and the deep-green, bile-like color of seaweed not so much. Pickles' B.Q. Possum never quite found its audience.

Finally, the revelers gathered for the feast and the dancing that throbbed far into the night. The sound of five hundred rawhide drums filled the darkness and echoed across the lagoon. White Bear lay in his cabin and dreamed of a young warrior long ago and the white bear who became his spiritual guide.

The next morning, Annie looked out onto the beach where hundreds of tents lay shimmering in the morning dew. She warmed her hands around the hot mug of coffee and looked over where Zack and Little Annie were flopped on the couch after staying up too late to drink in the atmosphere. Bedtime was usually a strict eight o'clock, but these were not normal times. There was an ancient magic that had enveloped the island.

The second day brought the games. Footraces, wrestling, canoe races—and more feasting. The mood was warm and embracing. The Bella Bella tribe, who were great carvers from British Columbia, erected a forty-foot totem pole next to the great cedar stump to honor White Bear's spiritual journey. On the top was a carving of the great white bear. Almost instantly, the totem became an icon of spiritual journeys that would appear in books ranging from psychology and religion to, inexplicably, *Rolling Stone* magazine.

The evening brought speeches explaining some of the lost art of the first peoples. Medicine, well-being, and inspirational success stories of tribesmen that had gone into the world and succeeded far beyond the dreams of their reservations. There were plays that reënacted Pacific Northwest folklore. Stories of the Raven stealing the sun from the gods for the Pacific Northwest tribes; how the loon got its necklace; and a film of the whale hunt on the Makah reservation several years before.

There was an anger at the loss of culture and a solidarity to work together to improve the future of the next generation. The first stirrings of a mentoring program were talked about in circles around the campfires. There was an optimism that the culture—full of mysticism and with a deep connection to nature—could still be relevant in the computer age, and this primal vision quest would be the beginning.

Later, there would be more dancing and the teenagers danced to contemporary music that angered some of the older tribesmen, but it had been decided not to embrace both the past *and* the future would be a mistake. Too much had been lost over the centuries and they could not afford to lose any of their youth.

At midnight, in front of a huge bonfire with sparks that rained upward towards the heavens, White Bear told of his vision quest as a young man and how the white bear had guided him successfully through life, and why now he was undertaking the long journey to Kermode Island to complete the circle of life.

Sunday morning, hundreds of youth, girls as well as boys, lifted the heavy, forty-foot boat over their heads and carried it down the sand spit in front of the new totem pole. The canoe was placed down reverently and a prayer was said for the journey by a Suquamish tribal minister.

The sail had not arrived from Bellingham in time so Annie had sewn together two of her sisters' quilts for the maiden voyage—one with a pattern of sunflowers and one called wedding ring. White Bear protested as he slowly lowered himself into the boat, but Annie said he could use the quilts to keep warm during the voyage after the sail caught up with him.

The paddlers waded out to the canoe and climbed aboard. The composition had changed. There were still eight in all: Three men who were filming the documentary, a woman from the Double D construction crew, two college students from the Suquamish tribe, a woman who was from the Western Washington University female crew, and a young African male exchange student from Zimbabwe.

White Bear had offered a bonus of another two thousand dollars on top of the ten thousand dollars to those who finished the voyage, plus a trip home to Seattle on the Alaskan ferry that plied the Inland Passage along the British Columbia coast from Seattle to Alaska.

Paddles poised, a team of boys shoved the canoe out into the water and with a mighty cheer the paddlers began searching for their rhythm as White Bear struggled to raise the quilted sail. A flotilla of forty-some canoes escorted White Bear to the edge of the island and then floated quietly on the outgoing tide until his canoe became a small dot on the eastern horizon.

Annie looked up into the branches of an old Douglas fir near the top of the island, looking for the Raven who had taken up residence during the canoe-building, but the bird was gone.

That evening, the island was returned to Seven Sisters. The footprints of the celebration had been washed away by the evening tide, and the only remnant was a new totem pole.

Chapter
TWENTY-FOUR

A red sunrise drifted in from the east over Mount Rainier. A lone kayaker floated off the point of the spit about a mile and a half away. Imperceptible to the eye, the kayak was painted a light blue-black to match the mirrored surface of the water and the profile of the lone paddler barely rose above the cockpit as he surveyed the island spit with binoculars.

Snodgrass reached down into his crotch and clawed at an itch he had picked up on the remote peninsula of Kamchatka in Eastern Russia. Joe had just gone to sleep in his bunker when his gps system radar went off.

"Aw shit," he grumbled, as he put on his glasses and looked at the radar screen. He twisted the silencer on his 50 caliber Browning magnum sniper rifle and poked it through an open port, spotting the intruder in the early morning light.

Joe debated on a kill shot as he was growing weary of his adversaries' feeble attempts at espionage. He took a deep breath, fired two rapid shots, and blew off the entire back end of the kayak. Then, with three more shots, the front end shattered and the intruder was left flailing in the water, trying to put on his life preserver. The only sound was a *phht phht* of the bullets punctuating the stillness of the morning air. Joe put the rifle back in its case and fell asleep.

That evening, when kayak pieces washed ashore, Sister was worried some kayaker had been run over by the propeller of a tugboat. She shared her concern to Joe.

"Naw," said Joe. He stopped rubbing Sister's feet and smiled. "I had to do a little vermin eradication this morning." Sister immediately knew who he meant.

"How did you even know he was here?" she asked.

"Computer chip in his neck, like a dog tag ID," Joe answered absentmindedly.

"You mean?" Sister began.

"Yep," Joe nodded.

The next week brought mild bluebird weather to the island. Max and the two girls, Talisha and Alisha, had brought the pumpkin seedlings that they had started from seeds and planted them lovingly behind Max's cabin.

Starbuck had been fed earlier and had left for his constitutional into the strait beyond the island. Lately, he had completely lost his fear of strangers and had gone "Hollywood," rushing to greet passing boats and spy-hopping for their cameras.

"He's become a regular publicity hound," Alisha complained as she dug down into the composted dirt, tapped the side of the plastic cup, and spilled the tiny pumpkin root ball into her hand.

"There." Talisha stood up and looked on their handiwork. "We're almost done." She took a plastic squirt bottle of slug sauce and made a small circle around each plant.

Max had decided on a medley of Jerry Lee Lewis' "Great Balls of Fire," Dolly Parton's "Here You Come Again," and the Stones' "Jumpin'

Jack Flash," to be played continuously on the battery-powered radio for the next week to inspire the seeds to the greatness that lay inside their genetic code.

"I wonder what form my father will come back to me this year." Max pursed her lips trying to imagine how the other seeds she sold to Moby fans would measure up to the island garden. "This could easily get out of hand," she prophesied.

The girls had just finished putting the Baptist-inspired great wall of waters, plastic cylinders that surrounded the seedling and would absorb the sun's heat and disperse the radiant warmth during the colder nights to protect the tender shoots, when Annie ran up to them.

"Starbuck's been hurt," she blurted out and pointed to the lagoon.

They ran to the edge of the boat dock and tried to lure Starbuck closer with a salmon and then they saw the wide-open gash on his side, the blood trailing in the water. Starbuck seemed to be in shock and sculled just beyond their reach, listing slightly toward his injury. "I've got to call John over on Whidbey," Max called out as she ran toward *The Ark*. "You girls keep an eye on him and see if you can lure him back into the pen."

She fired up the diesel inboard, slammed the throttle into high, and headed towards Port Gamble. Max ran into the mercantile. "Wiggins," she called out. "Starbuck's been hurt. I need to use the phone."

"Why don't you dinosaurs use cell phones?" Wiggins complained.

"I know, I know." Max gave a deep sigh. "Annie's island is Old School."

While she waited for the phone to ring, she noticed that Wiggins had put out his Moby Pumpkin starts in the south-facing window next to the porch where they could absorb the sunlight. A sign in the window read:

"$ 15.00 Moby Dick pumpkin starts."

The phone kept ringing. Max thought to herself, *Pick up the phone. Isn't anyone in the office? Does it take everyone to go out in the patrol boat to protect the orcas from the constant stream of tourist boats? Answer the phone!*

Finally, a female voiced answered. "Orca Watch."

"I need to get ahold of John Colby, quick," Max shouted. "We have a wounded orca over on Seven Sisters island."

"Starbuck?" the woman asked. "Is it Starbuck?"

"Yes," Max confirmed. "He has an open wound on his right side."

"I'll call John right away and he will probably come over in the patrol boat," the woman replied anxiously. "Good luck."

By the time Max got back to the island, everyone was on the dock craning to catch a glimpse of Starbuck, who still was not coming towards them. They could hear the roar of the three-hundred-horse outboard long before the patrol boat came into view. John vaulted out of the boat and onto the dock before the boat had settled in against the pilings.

"What happened? Did anyone see what happened?" he asked as he squinted out to where Starbuck's dorsal fin lay sticking out of the surf. John leaned out from the dock and waved his hand in a circular motion for Starbuck to come, but he didn't move.

"He must be in shock," John surmised. "I need to get a good look at the wound. I'm going to go out in the raft." He popped into the raft, lay over the front, and stroked out to Starbuck, who looked at him with doleful eyes as John put his hand on the great mammal's forehead and peered at the injury.

The wound was recent—about two feet long and four inches deep and then a shorter gouge trailing toward the tail. "It looks like you tangled with an outboard, my friend." John stroked the orca near his nose to soothe him.

"We're gonna have to get you back home, big guy," John informed the orphan. "You're gonna go home." John lured the orca into the netted pen, closed the wire gate, and paddled into the dock.

"He just needs a little R and R. Starbuck looks like he got too close to someone's outboard prop. The wound will heal itself, but he needs a little quiet time and we need to get him back up to his pod. We can't wait for the pod to come down here. I'm guessing we're going to have to find a way to get him back up near Nanaimo, up in British Columbia. Getting across international waters may not be easy though."

Starbuck took a week off from his duties although he didn't get much rest and neither did anyone else. The word had spread fast. The Sweet Adelines came up from Silverdale and serenaded Starbuck with peppy songs that were even older than Annie's recollection. "Has Anybody Seen My Gal," "Over There," from World War I, and "Mockingbird Hill," which at least Sister recognized.

The Seattle Philharmonic Orchestra insisted on sending over four harpists, who lulled most of the island into an early nap and John had to poke Starbuck, who seemed to be dozing off.

Washington Fish and Wildlife came by boat to the island, surveyed the scene, and threatened to arrest anyone who dared molest or move Starbuck. They demanded that he not be restrained at any time, but they left no one in charge when they departed.

The Canadian government sent an inspector down to examine Starbuck and to explain to everyone that they had some jurisdiction because L pod, Starbuck's family group, spent most of its time near the Fraser River eating their personal favorite, Chinook salmon.

A tribal shaman from the Apache tribe flew in, smoked some of Ziggy's personal weed, dropped some mescaline, and determined that Starbuck was the reincarnation of a recently deceased Apache chief who had died in a tragic highway accident caused when the cross-dressing chief was channeling Thelma and Louise on a dirt road on the rim of the grand canyon when his brakes failed on his pink Cadillac, sending him hurtling to the bottom of a fifteen-hundred-foot cliff.

Howard Schultz, CEO of Starbucks, heard about the ruckus and personally came over with a court order to cease and desist using the name Starbuck, but changed his mind after feeding Starbuck and instead went home to his Seattle villa above Lake Washington and created a new Orcachino latte, using dark chocolate from Madagascar and pure vanilla from Borneo, infused into heavy cream marbled by a light swirling motion using a sterling silver spoon—all served in a black and white souvenir mug.

Lila came over at the end of the week for a Starbuck reading and found him morose and depressed. She did drop some mango colonic tonic down his blow hole and he seemed to perk up for a short time, but quickly settled back into floating around the open pen and doing little else. "This dear animal has got to go home," she would tell anyone who would listen.

Fortunately, despite the intrusions, the propeller cut was healing nicely by the end of the week, and John Colby called a meeting to discuss Starbuck's future.

Joe had built a roaring fire that illuminated the bra that still joined the two bunkers. Ziggy looked longingly at the cleavage, but decided to stay for the meeting anyway. There would be time later.

Colby showed pictures of Starbuck's mother, Big Mamma. "That's the orca I first saw when I was on the *Green Cucumber* with Pickles," Max exclaimed. "Wow, I had no idea."

"And here is the picture of Starbuck's aunt that Lila said he got into a snit with and essentially ran away from home. Her name is Typhoon."

"She looks like trouble to me," South piped up to defend Starbuck.

"Right now," continued Colby, "the pod is operating somewhere between the Fraser River up the British Columbia coast and Pedder Bay near Victoria on Vancouver Island. They could be anywhere in between or they may vanish out into the ocean overnight, but it's a chance we have to take. We've been threatened by every state, federal, and Canadian authority not to interfere with Starbuck."

There was a great deal of sympathy for Starbuck's plight and in the end the vote was unanimous to try and take him home, no matter what the risk. "Damn straight," Sister mumbled to no one in particular.

Several days later, a plan was in place. Joe had drawn a map of the route through Puget Sound, past Point Roberts where immigration between Canada and the US ordinarily would take place. Then, sliding up between the San Juan Islands, across the Strait of Juan de Fuca, and up the east coast of Vancouver Island.

John pointed to the map of the coast of Vancouver Island. "Off the eastern shore is where they were spotted yesterday, but they could be a hundred miles away in the next couple of days. It's just going to be dumb pig luck if we can get this family together. I think we have to get Starbuck at least within a two-hundred-yard radius of the family before he might react."

Joe took over. "I have put surveillance in place on the Coast Guard, Immigration Service, Fish and Wildlife, and the feds. I think we have the capability of nullifying any of their counteraction."

"How about the Canucks?" Colby asked.

"Got that covered," Joe affirmed, giving his palm a judo chop.

Annie stood up. "We have sent out coded messages to every women's group up and down the Puget Sound and Canada and the response has been overwhelming. Several local tribes are on our side and I think once we get going we are sure to get a lot of positive publicity from television, and the University of Washington is doing another documentary," she added.

"John and his crew are putting together a floating net cage about sixty feet by thirty to keep Starbuck safe. Reuniting an orca has never been tried before, but it is our best hope because we have to move swiftly before the authorities close in on us. Joe is picking up some buzz to that effect. We move two days from now. Ye haw!" Annie yelped and got air as she high-fived Sister Mary Catherine.

On the rising tide, just past midnight, two retired tugboats slid into the lagoon and loaded the precious cargo. The *Pissant* and her sister ship *Little Loo Loo* suspended the net cage between them on cleats while Max lured a suddenly animated Starbuck into the open-topped chamber with a salmon.

"I think he knows he's going home," Lila beamed. "I don't think we'll have any problem." She adjusted her navy blue skull cap and wiped her hands on her freshly minted hoddy that had Starbuck's Bustin' Out across the chest.

As the two tugs slowly steamed out into the channel in unison, their perfectly matched 1930's diesel engines with eighteen-inch pistons gently churned a powerful wake in the murky waters of Hood Canal. Starbuck had no trouble in matching the speed and had plenty of time to do some minor spy-hopping where he could see Talisha and Alisha on deck of the *Pissant*. Trish was adamant that the girls become advocates for social change.

"I don't want my girls sitting on the sidelines," she had managed to slur as the ALS had almost taken her speech, but not her heart. That her heart would go on beating in her girls forever, that was her only legacy and her only reason for continuing the fight against the insidious disease. Trish did not live with hope, only with courage.

At Port Gamble, two fiberglass yachts joined alongside the tugboats and as the boats broke into open water there were over two hundred boats that were floating just off Foulweather Bluff. There were open launches of twelve to sixteen feet, proud, classic wooden boats—their gleaming bronze fittings that hadn't left the marinas in decades but somehow whispered into their owners' ears that this was the chance of a lifetime—kayaks, rowboats, rafts, two Hawaiian catamarans, an imported gondola from Venice that struggled to keep up, and the obnoxious jet skis who fell in behind to protect the rear.

At Port Townsend—the bastion of nonconformity and always looking for a good scrap—the marina belched forth another hundred-plus boats that collegially clustered in around the two tugs like worker bees around the queen.

Now there was a great floating sea of red and green lights that pierced the darkness as the flotilla skirted the western coast of Whidbey Island and past Fort Ebey, built during World War II to protect the narrow channel. The batteries silenced long ago and only the harbor seals on the rock barked at the passing parade. The lights of the Victorian seacoast town of Victoria, British Columbia, dazzled the night sky in the early morning as the loons called between themselves to begin a new day.

The day dawned with quiet seas as the boats moved past the roiling waters of Deception Pass and ducked into obscurity between Lopez and San Juan islands. Mysteriously, the computer and phone communication between the Coast Guard, immigration authorities, and the Washington State Fish and Wildlife Service had been offline since the middle of the night. Joe and Pickles had tucked themselves into the yellow submarine and had left just before Starbuck was loaded and were plying themselves north to wreak havoc as only Joe knew how.

The fleet chugged through the straits between the islands and cut left on the west side of Shaw Island, past Deer Harbor, and up the west coast of Orcas Island and past Waldron Island as the afternoon wore on. Boats would head in to the marinas along the way to re-fuel, re-gather, and by the time the armada was steaming towards the open water past Bellingham, news helicopters were hovering overhead.

A hundred and twenty boats joined from Bellingham and ten of the tribes, including the Lummi, had launched their canoes in full support. There was buzz that in the waters just across the invisible border that cut across the Straits of Georgia, another two hundred-plus Canadian boats waited to greet Starbuck, the prodigal son.

Starbuck was buoyed by the continual activity of the journey and he could sense the change in salinity where the ocean met the Salish Sea.

Annie's twins were pointing to the sky and they loved it when Annie and Max held onto them and let them lean over the side of the tug to watch Starbuck. The documentary team caught it all and decades later the twins would annually host the opening of the Port Townsend Film Festival with the classic documentary film *Hands across the Water*.

At Point Roberts, both the American and Canadian interceptor boats found that someone had welded their propellers to the rudder and were frantically trying to contact the nearest underwater welding shops, but as the hundred of support boats and Starbuck neared the water border, two American Coast Guard cutters had gone into containment mode and stretched a twelve-inch hawser between them to stop the crossing dead in their wake.

The boats stalled a scant fifty yards from the rope as if it were a herd of stampeding elephants stopped by a mouse. The *Pissant* gave a startling blast from her air horn and from around the stern of the boat, habit flying in the wind, came Sister Mary Catherine on a jet ski slamming hell bent through the chop while brandishing a curved scimitar with a ruby encrusted handle and screaming like a banshee. She stopped at the rope and, with one swift chop, severed the barrier and waved the boats through.

The Coast Guard cutters had no backup plan, and when they asked for guidance they found that bureaucrats everywhere were nowhere to be found that day. The flotilla, now five hundred boats-strong, steamed up the coast, finally stopping at the confluence of the Fraser River and the Straits of Georgia that led to the Inland Passage all the way to Alaska.

Now it was up to the gods to return Starbuck to his family—the gods and the orcas' insatiable appetite for salmon. The great Fraser River was known worldwide for its legendary salmon runs of between fifteen to fifty million fish whose brains were hard-wired to return instinctively to the waters of their birth. The snow-driven headwaters began twelve hundred miles to the east in the snowfields and glaciers of the Rocky Mountains. The Great Rockies, volcanic mountains up to thirteen thousand feet, the bedrock laid seventy million years ago by volcanoes and pushed by Tetonic plates to form the spine of the North American continent that stretches from Alaska to Mexico.

For millennia, five distinct salmon runs had returned to the Fraser: Pink salmon in odd-numbered years; June through July, the largest of all salmon, the King or Chinook salmon; the Sockeye in August; and in October, the Chum and Coho salmon.

"Orcas are all about the Chinook," John remarked, standing on the deck of the *Pissant* and looking through his binoculars for any sign of the pod. Suddenly, just before sunset, the CB crackled that the L pod was heading east from Nanaimo to the mouth of the Fraser. The only question was, would they get there soon enough to thwart the authorities and, more importantly, would they accept Starbuck back into the pod. At dusk, the pod could be heard coming from a mile away. Their rhythmic whoosh from the blowhole as they traveled gave John Colby goosebumps.

"Now we'll see if this can be done," he mumbled to himself.

He ordered the net lowered and Starbuck swam free among the free-floating boats and the collective holding of breath as everyone waited to see what would happen. Starbuck sensed the presence of the pod and spy-hopped higher than John thought possible. The orca slowly sank into the murky water.

Big Mamma was in the lead and she stopped abruptly and spy-hopped in rapid succession and then dove deep into the water. John could hear distinctive squeaks and grunts from the underwater audio detector that was connected to the *Pissant* speakers. *Two separate orcas*, he nodded to himself. And then one of the sounds became more faint, while Starbuck's squeals grew more frantic. John looked where the pod sat poised and identified Typhoon from her dorsal fin. He watched as she spy-hopped once and then began swimming away with the rest of the pod.

"That's Typhoon," John said quietly.

"Bitch," South yelled across the water.

The reunion looked doomed as John shook his head and he let the tears run freely. "It's not going to work," John shook his head. "It's not going to work. There's nothing we can do now." John turned from the rail.

Starbuck appeared at the bow of the tug. He looked lost and then he sank beneath the waves.

"I've got it covered!" Lila screamed from the bow of the *Pissant* and John turned to see her in her Camo fatigues, with pink scarves tied to her wrists, dive over the ship's rail and into the sea where he had last seen Starbuck. And then just as quickly as the pod appeared, all the orcas were gone, including Starbuck.

Lila never returned to the surface. The flotilla was stunned as word was passed from boat to boat. Where was Lila? Who was Lila? And where were Starbuck and the pod?

Darkness quickly closed and the boats huddled together for support. What had started to be a noble undertaking suddenly had no closure. One of the tugs suddenly tooted their horn and passed the word they had found Lila, alive, but unconscious, floating in the water. The *Pissant* coasted over and they found Lila lying in the captain's berth; her breathing was shallow and she was still unconscious.

"What happened?" Annie demanded too loud.

"I don't really know," the tugboat crewman shook his head. "We found her floating face up in the water with a good-size orca pushing her toward the boat and when we scooped her up, the orca disappeared."

"Was it Starbuck?" John looked confused.

"I don't know," the crewman answered. "It wasn't a real big orca. Medium-size, I would guess."

By morning most of the boats were gone and the *Pissant* and her sister ship limped home to Seven Sisters Island, but Lila had yet to recover. She just lay in Pinky and Dorie's bed staring at the ceiling. "Is she in a coma?" Dorie wondered to Annie.

"I think she's just dazed. She's definitely in shock. I'm just glad she's still alive."

The unknown fate of Starbuck and Lila's health put a heavy fog at Annie's breakfast table the next morning as Lila lay in the downstairs bedroom still not talking.

"I just don't get it," Pickles said as he sat looking into his coffee mug. "Everything went so smoothly with Starbuck, and we had all that positive energy and then Lila." Pickles fell silent.

"What was Lila doing?" Max wondered aloud as Little Annie squirmed in her lap. "It doesn't make sense." Max adjusted her weight on the organ bench, and stared at fingers poised over the ivory keys, but she had no music in her heart.

Chapter
TWENTY-FIVE

Annie stared down at the pan of over-easy eggs, the edges fliver-
ing in the bacon grease as if they were the wings of manta rays.
Annie was someone who almost always knew what she was
going to say before she began speaking, but she began to ruminate.
"Lila wasn't like the rest of us. She worked from pure feral emotion.
She had an empathy that ranged from elephants to aardvarks, from
orcas to ostriches. You remember that time she charmed that mama
eagle into raising those orphan osprey chicks? I thought that eagle
was going to have a stroke when those osprey fleged out and dove
into the water going fifty miles an hour. She was fit to be tied," Annie
chuckled. "Or that time she got that mother pig to raise those baby
white tigers. Lila is a pistol all right."

"She is one of a kind," Max smiled. "She is an artist. So energetic
and full of herself."

"The best thing we can do," Annie began as she expertly flipped
over the eggs and brought them to the table. "The best thing we
can do is embrace Lila's spirit, make it our own, and take it into the

world. I think that's what she would have wanted. I'm sure she had an inspired plan when she dove into the water after Starbuck and, knowing Lila, Starbuck didn't have much of a choice in the matter. Like they say in poker, when she pushed her chips into the middle of the table, she was all in."

"Who's all in?" Lila stood in the doorway and she was back—bigger than life.

"My God, you're back," Dorie screamed and ran to Lila's side.

"I'm hungry," Lila announced. "What's for breakfast?"

"Whatever you want, Mama," Annie sang out from the stove.

Max cut up the cantaloupe into bite-size pieces for Zack and Little Annie and put on their high chair trays so they could continue grazing. Little Annie picked up a cantaloupe chunk and hurled it across the table and into Trooper's waiting mouth.

"I think you've got it, I think you've got it," laughed Christine at the piano and she began to play the soundtrack from *My Fair Lady* starting with "The Rain in Spain," vocal soundtrack compliments of Pickles and Pinky.

The island sang and danced the morning away. Lila had come back. Maybe not as good as new, but she was back.

Hawking had been pestering Spud to be involved in crop circles for months, but it was Sister Mary Catherine's purview and when she finally agreed, everybody and their uncle wanted in—the admiral's mother, Trish, South (when she was still talking to Spud after the Double D lecher adventure), Ziggy, John, Muffy, Pinky, and Pickles.

"A troop of geriatric misfits if ever I saw one," Sister complained. "Working conditions require a full moon," she added, "and then I need a good field near the airport."

Pickles allowed as how he knew of just the place and coded invitations were sent. The logistics of moving Hawking and Trish would require Christine's father's dump truck with the crane attachment and the use of several other lower profile rigs to handle the overflow. And because Hawking was in, somehow Bill Gates wrangled an invite too. Sister was fit to be tied.

"I will not take everybody and their brother; this is serious business." she fumed, until Joe said he would be in charge of Hawking and Gates. Hawking had flown in several days in advance to discuss his worm hole theory, the super collider in Switzerland, and, of course, he had gathered a lot of new dirty jokes he'd heard from his handlers. Roars of synthetic laughter had radiated out of Spud's cabin in one continuous party since Hawking had arrived by helicopter.

The admiral's mother was staying with Annie when the harvest moon pushed its way up over the Cascade Mountains. Most of the principals were staged on the dock at Port Gamble, but they were missing Spud, Hawking and Gates.

Sister jumped into the *Ark* and rousted more rpms than the old boat had produced in years. She burst into Spud's shack.

"What in the Bells of St. Mary are you bozos up to in there? Judas priest, we have crop circles to build."

The men froze. They all wore little skull caps made out of tin foil that Spud had made for the occasion and Bill Gates was holding a funnel connected to Hawking's feeding tube to his stomach. In the other hand, he held the remains of a communal bottle of peppermint schnapps.

"Hawking, I would have thought better of you," Sister chastised. "And Gates, what are you thinking? I want your asses in that helicopter pronto and on the Port Gamble dock in the next ten minutes."

Hawking gave a wry grin and Gates took a swig of the schnapps and defiantly poured the rest into the funnel.

"You men!" Sister spat. "Grow up!" she hurled as she slammed the door.

Ten minutes later, the entire crew was huddled in the dump truck.

"Why does everything smell like peppermint?" Trish grimaced. Hawking gagged and burped.

The truck rocked and hurtled through the darkened pastures, past the Egg and I road, and down near a fresh hay field. The troops assembled under darkness and Sister shook her finger at each conspirator and laid down the rules.

"No unnecessary talking, no tracks, and there is enough moonlight so don't use your flashlight. Hawking, wipe that smirk off your face. You're going to have one of the ropes tied to your wheelchair and I don't want any more of your monkey business, understand?"

Hawking's rubber lips smirked even wider.

They broke up into three groups, carrying their planks, rope, and the diagram with instructions of where each crop circle footprint would be placed in the field.

"Damn rookies," Sister mumbled as she ushered her group down the side of the field of waist-high grass and put them in place. Three grueling hours later, the moon had disappeared behind a furrow of clouds and Sister's troops were assembled back at the truck. Everyone was spattered with mud and Hawking's wheelchair developed a short going through a mud puddle and he had to be hooked up to a small Honda generator for a short time, which put Sister on the short track to Purgatory.

"We have to maintain integrity," she hissed. "Thousands of years of crop circle cults have kept the secret. I don't know why I let you bunch of misfits in on this gig.

"You wait here," she instructed. "I need to check to make sure we didn't leave any evidence. No wheel marks, no clothes, no ropes."

With hands on hips, Sister stood on a stump surveying the field covered with fresh concentric circles. "Not bad," she murmured, gathering up the soggy hem of her habit and trudging back to the truck.

"All right, let's load up, and Gates, why do you keep fiddling with your glasses? Why don't you get laser surgery like everybody else? Can't afford it? Heh, heh."

At daybreak, the ensemble was fast asleep on the island and by that evening *The Seattle Times* had a picture of the crop circles with the usual bewildered statement wondering what caused this phenomenon—aliens, the wind, or cosmic events.

Three weeks later, there was a report from Gold River, on the western banks of Vancouver Island, that a young adolescent orca was seen trailing a few hundred yards behind L pod.

Lila couldn't remember what happened after she jumped into the water after Starbuck, but John felt sure that somehow Starbuck was re-bonding with the pod and that Lila was responsible for that miracle.

The word spread rapidly through the boating community and there were private toasts at marinas up and down the Sound. The result had not been what everyone had hoped for, but Annie kept saying, "Whether it's orcas or people, this is about family and you know it's going to be difficult and it's going to take time."

Pickles had other fish to fry. As Annie's campaign manager, he had done the requisite work. He had his client constantly in the newspapers. Annie was either pictured raising the twins, or returning orphaned orcas to their mother, spearheading the Seahawk Grannies cheerleading squad, or riding whales in the Pacific Ocean.

Annie would have seemed like a dream candidate except for one problem—her opponent was attacking her strengths. Too old, out of touch, didn't own a car, possible lesbian connections, absentee mom, and an antisocial proponent of civil disobedience—these were being floated out in the public by her opponent Lee Harley Oswalt. Annie stormed into Pickles' store with a flier she had found stapled to a telephone post.

"Pickles," she shouted over the overhead music.

Pickles just waved his hand. He was just beginning to play his collection of great Broadway musicals gone Hollywood. He had run the hose on the old pine boards in his store, started an overhead sprinkler, plugged in two lamp posts from Home Depot, and was waiting for the first strains from the Whistling Oyster flat screen he had bought from Sister Mary.

"I'll be with you in a minute," he whispered. "I've got to get my cardio in, you know. He turned up the volume and began to dance karaoke-style with Gene Kelly in his famous *Singin' in the Rain* scene. With a pink umbrella, sporting a pink tutu, black London fog raincoat, and *on pointe* with his pink tap shoes, Pickles looked downright regal as he shimmied, pranced, sashayed, pirouetted, and slid his way through the puddles on the floor. Smoke began to curl out of his electronic cash register as the overhead sprinkler shorted the power strip and still Pickles danced on.

Finally, with chest heaving and his jumping barely noticeable, Pickles ended the classic scene. "Whew, don't you just love those old tunes? I'm working on Fred Astaire's, 'Puttin' on the Ritz' for next week and then *Dr. Zhivago*."

"*Zhivago* isn't a musical," protested Annie.

"I know," panted Pickles. "I love a challenge. I expect my cardio to go off the chart on that one. I'm going to do the part where he marches across the snow after he escapes from the train. It's gonna be brutal, but I found some Russian peasant songs from the Gulag and I've been reading some Solzhenitsyn to get in the mood. I just hope the snow and ice machine I rented will work inside the store."

"So, what do ya think about these fliers?" Annie shook the paper in Pickles' face.

"Not to worry." Pickles wanted to laugh but it hurt too much. "The guy hasn't got a chance. Didn't you see his name? Lee Harley Oswalt! His mother must have still been under anesthesia when she signed the birth certificate to stick a kid with that name." Pickles managed a grin.

"The election is in the bag, baby." Pickles untied his tap shoes and massaged his feet. "My feet are killing me," he complained to Annie as he thrust his black-and-white zebra-striped toenails toward her.

"What's with the toes?" Annie asked.

"Oh, that's just left over from a little parody I did of Dr. Doolittle last week."

"Just what part were *you* playing?" Annie asked coyly.

Sister Mary Catherine was having her own problems. The situation with the man who had been abusing his father had somewhat improved, but there was still mental abuse that the old man had documented with a tape recorder.

"We have to go back in," she exhorted her troops. "There is simply no way around it."

"Aw, Sister, do we have to?" whined Ziggy. "Besides, we're missing the Owl, God rest his soul. And I still think those chicken costumes have fleas," Ziggy complained as he scratched under his armpit at the mere suggestion.

"Yes," Sister insisted. "We have to go one last time before we are forced to take legal action."

Resigned to their fate, Ziggy, Sister and Joe drove up the long driveway to the secluded home and slipped on their chicken suits.

"I'm itching already," Ziggy complained out loud.

Sister slapped Ziggy on the back of his chicken head. "You've got the head on backwards again. Turn it around."

Joe joined the other two just before they knocked on the door.

"Oh, sweet Jesus?" the man said, opening the door as he closed his eyes and shook his head in defeat. "What do you want?" He had resigned himself to some kind of penance.

Joe's eyes wandered across the lawn and rested on the turbo-charged diesel crew cab pickup in the driveway.

"Oh no," the man pleaded. "Not my truck. I promised I'd leave the old man alone; just leave my truck alone. It took me six months to get all the options on it. You don't know how hard it was. It took fifty grand of the old man's…"

Joe blew the truck a beaky kiss and the truck jumped a good forty feet in the air and landed on the garage roof. When the three islanders turned and walked down the sidewalk, all they could hear was the man saying, "No, no, no, no, no! I'll get you bastards."

Joe turned and pointed his battery-powered laser trigger, training it on the man's aluminum fishing boat.

Gone.

Joe then turned and pointed at the man's tool shed.

The man shrieked as he fell face down on his lawn and looked up at Joe with tears in his eyes. "Not my new riding mower. Stop, I know when I've been beat. The old man will be put in a rest home tomorrow. The finest rest home. I'll spare no expense, just let me be. Just let me *be*."

The troupe chugged down to the Whistling Oyster where Sister won a twenty-two cubic foot stainless refrigerator and a set of juice glasses in the karaoke contest.

With all the hoopla, Annie kept putting off her spring trip to the Pike Place Farmers Market in Seattle, but it was time. She caught the morning sun peeking over the Cascade Mountains and trafficked her way past the shrimp pots to the channel. The wind was slapping the kingfisher teal awning and the water lay before her like a pond stretching into forever. The *pocket-a–pocket-a* of the diesel engine created a harmonic alternative universe that triggered Annie's soul. Her eyes began to water and she felt a deep sob claw its way out from her chest as she leaned on the tiller for support. She screeched out a primal scream and then the dam broke over the spillway.

Annie sat dead in the water halfway between home and Seattle and broke into smaller and smaller pieces until she lay slumped on the boat's deck with the powerful diesel stuck in neutral still ready to comply with Annie's needs, but Annie's burden had grown too heavy.

On her back and unable to move, she stared blankly at the brass grommets that attached the awning to the cold, rust-defying stainless steel roof rail circling the boat as her mind spun into a vertigo.

"This is like a bad Hitchcock movie," Annie moaned as she closed her eyes and dreamt of her childhood and the *Virginia V.*

At the turn of the twentieth century, Puget Sound transportation belonged to the Mosquito Fleet with hundreds of wooden boats built by shipwrights on the salt water shores before the advent of power tools. The thick, fir planks were steam bent over stout ribs clinker-style forming the body of the vessel. These less-than-nimble crafts were the life blood of all commerce. Laden with live chickens, farm produce, lumber and passengers, the boats were seldom on time and more often sworn *at* than sworn *by.*

The power plants were huge, fire-breathing dragon steam engines powered by wood and coal that constantly belched a wad of cinders and burning ash, forcing the boats' crews to carry wet towels to quench the fires' appetite for roasting their hosts.

One mariner summed up the boats as "thin floors and partitions, light framing and siding, soft resinous woods dried by the sun, impregnated with oil and turpentine...little more than an orderly pile of kindling wood."

The boats had names like *Alaskan, Olympian, Alice Gertrude, George E. Starr, Rosalie,* and some were known mostly for their shortcomings. There was the paddle wheeler from the city of Shelton lacking a spray guard over the paddle wheel and thus nicknamed *Old Wet-Butt.*

The once-sleek craft named *Bailey Gatzert,* having lost her figure to middle age, was commonly called *Barely–gets–there.*

Many boats went aground in the dense fog and the only way a captain could reckon where the shore started was to blow the steamboat whistle and count the time it took to hear the echo. Science told them that sound travels a thousand eighty feet a second, so if the echo bounced off the shoreline after one second, the shore was five hundred feet away. Only one problem: Sometimes the sound bounced off a log boom, a buoy, or even a solid fog bank. Then it was fight for the life jackets.

Some boats even inspired songs.

> *Paddle paddle George E. Starr*
> *How we wonder where you are*
> > *Leaves for Seattle at half past ten....*
> *Gets to Seattle who knows when!*

It was these ships of her youth and the *Virginia V* in particular that stole their way into Annie's dream. Annie's sister, Adeline, Addy for short, was with her father delivering oysters, chickens and apples to the Seattle market when *The Ark I* caught fire from her small steam engine and burned the boat to the water line.

The captain of the *Virginia V*, queen of the Seattle fleet, came by the hapless pair treading water and surrounded by bobbing apples and irate, floundering, wet-feathered chickens.

He looked down from his helm and all he could see of Addy was her waist-length red hair fanned out atop the water and her more than ample chest holding her afloat. Annie and her sisters were always envious of their sister's boobs and so too was the captain. Promptly smitten, he married Addy not six months later.

Captain Fulton called his wife Addy "Bounty," after the mermaid who saved the sailor in the epic Greek poem. But Addy was childless, as were all seven sisters except for Annie's only foray into motherhood. And it was this fate that tore into Annie's soul. A soul that had lost her daughter, her granddaughter, and that was fast running out of time to raise the next generation, Zack and Little Annie. It was a soul that had pined to retire to the warm weather and waters of the Caribbean. It was a soul that had never taken the time to mourn her lost destiny.

Addy called out from her small Silver Slipper rowboat, climbed over the transom, and sat next to Annie. Dense fog shrouded the boat and Annie could hear the fog horns in the distance calling out her name in a slow metronome ....*Annnnnnnnnie* ......*Annnnnnnie*............ *Annnnnnnnnnie.*

Addy put her arms around her sister and pulled her shawl around both of them. Annie could smell the lilac in Addy's hair, and rested her head on her sister's shoulder. She began to weep and sob haltingly as she blurted out the responsibility, fear and injustice of leaving the two toddlers alone in the world.

Addy cradled Annie's head. "You will be given the time allowed, but when that time is over, you must choose wisely, Sister. There are those to whom the island will mean a great deal. They will show themselves in time, and always remember, we will be with you always."

Annie had promised herself that she would question her sisters the next time they came to her. "How do I know you are here?" she challenged.

"You will know we are all around you when you hear the cry of gulls and the sound of the waves lapping on the shore. When you hear the wind coming off the…"

"Yatta, yatta…" Annie interrupted. "I'm working my…"

Addy put her hand over Annie's mouth. "Don't say it," she threatened.

Annie pried Addy's finger off and continued, "The wind and gulls are *always* making noise."

"You're wrong, little sister," Addy shook her head as only a big sister could. "Little sister, we're always here."

"But, I'd like an unmistakable, special kind of sign that you're around," Annie insisted.

Addy sighed. She knew from experience how Annie could be once she got her teeth into something. Like that quilt design she insisted on making that depicted the whole island. When Annie's high school graduation deadline approached, all of the sisters had to pitch in to get it done. Annie was always biting off too much.

With an exasperated tone she began, "I don't think it's allowed, but I will ask around and see what can be done. In the meantime…"

A ship's horn blasted Annie into the present and the *Willapa*, a ferry from Bremerton, slid by on Annie's starboard side and plowed its way across Elliott Bay to the Seattle ferry depot.

Annie took the sleeve from her Carhartt jacket and wiped away her tears and rubbed her nose

Well, she thought to herself, *I held my own pretty well that time.*

"Addy might think she is in charge, but *I'm* in control now," Annie said quietly under the noise of the engine. You never know when an older sister like Addy might come back with a vengeance. Annie had seen her older sisters clear a room with just a sideways look, a snide remark or, if necessary, the threat of the back of their hand.

It would be wise not to cross Addy, Annie decided. While nothing was settled with the twins, Annie knew deep in her heart that the family wouldn't leave them unprotected. And, knowing that, she took a deep breath and began to rebuild her mojo as she steered *The Ark* into a slip at the public dock.

John Hunt hailed her from the street. He had brought two truck gardeners from the public market to help load his station wagon. The men carefully loaded the apple-faced dolls that Annie had dried over the stove during the long gray days of winter and grunted as they lifted the great soggy sacks of oysters.

Annie looked back as John bumped up the steep cobblestone streets; the confused bobble heads still couldn't make up their mind. Annie laughed. "Reminds me of somebody I know."

John entered the one-way cobblestone street from the wrong end. Annie tuned out the hustle and bustle, closed her eyes, and took a deep breath. She smelled fresh clams in the huge stainless cauldrons; just-baked brioche from the French bakery; and the distinctive aroma of spring Copper River king salmon out of British Columbia.

A policeman on a horse wheeled around to upbraid John for going the wrong way, but when he saw Annie in the passenger seat he tipped his hat. Annie was a Pacific Northwest icon; she could do no wrong in his town.

John stopped the wagon in front of the bronze pig named Rachel, the flash point of Pike Market blind dates, stationed at the Market's entrance, and the two men hopped out and loaded Annie's wares onto large carts with bicycle wheels and wheeled them into the stall opposite Uli's sausage.

Annie looked down over the row of flower peddlers with their bouquets of purple peonies, blue and pink lupine, daisies, red and orange poppies, and the blue bearded iris with their yellow faces. *So beautiful and this isn't even peak season*, Annie thought.

Annie looked wistfully across the aisle where her old friend Madeline, of the pouty crimson lips and provocative outfits, used to serve up her sexual fantasy lotions.

"Madeline and Pickles hit the mother lode with that one," Annie mumbled to herself. She still pined for the old days and Madeline's funky costumes, but she knew the market was always in flux, although Annie's booth and some of the fishmongers had been in place for a hundred-plus years. She was looking up at the Seven Sisters apple and oyster sign on top of the building when she spotted a Raven sitting on the sign. She cocked her head and wondered if it was the same Raven that had been looking over White Bear, and if the Raven was back, then...

"Look out, Annie, here he comes," John warned as he had just finished putting the last of the Apple Annie and Sea Grannies bobble heads on the shelf. He quickly excused himself when he saw the piroshki man, Ivan, dodging between produce trucks as he wove his way across the narrow alley way, leaving in his wake a trail of flour dust in the air. As he scooted out of sight, John noted that Ivan was pretty light on his feet for a stout Russian immigrant. He reminded John of that kid in the *Peanuts* cartoon. What was his name? Pigpen. Yeah, Pigpen. John congratulated himself on escaping the inevitable floured handprints on the back of his sports jacket, but not before Ivan spotted him hiding behind a pillar and yelled out, "John Boy, is that you? Goodnight John Boy."

John retreated deeper into the labyrinth of subterranean shops that made up the century-old market. Past the incense booth, the Bhutanese Restaurant, and the magic shop with the old five-cent fortune teller glass booth featuring the scarf-wrapped head of a swami who dispensed corny cards that said, "Seven days without eating fish, makes one weak. Eat at Ivar's fish bar on Pier 54."

Or T-Shirts that read: "It must be Summer. The rain is warmer."

Annie had nowhere to run so she braced herself. Ivan swooped in, lifted Annie into the air, and twirled around Russian-style. Ivan had learned English from watching American movies in Russia and since he jumped ship in the Seattle harbor, nothing had changed as he prattled his lines: "Hello gorgeous! You complete me." Or, "You had me at good-bye. I've got tone Goose."

Pressed against Ivan and holding on to her hat, Annie's bladder began to rebel. "Put me down, you crazy Russian," she crowed. "You're going to embarrass me." Ivan put her down and Annie excused herself as she scuttled down the walkway to the vendors' bathrooms.

When she came back, Ivan was just crossing back across the street. When he saw Annie, he stopped and thrust his fist into the air. "Attica, Attica, Attica," he shouted and then disappeared inside his shop. Annie peered into the white sack that Ivan had left. Two apple cinnamon piroshki stared up at her. Annie sat in her rocking chair and munched on the delicious gift, brushing the powdered sugar that had rained down on her green cable knit sweater and her gray wool slacks. Annie looked over her booth. No apples, but the oysters and dolls would keep her busy enough.

Pickles had turned Annie into a cottage industry—there were wines, barbecue rubs, dried fruit leather, breads, and a hundred items that Pickles had sold with the Apple Annie/Seven Sisters Island logo. She had a hard time keeping up with Pickles. Everyone did. *And lord knows what else is coming down the pike*, Annie thought to herself as she licked her fingers.

Like the incoming tide on a long Puget Sound tide flat, the crowds filled in quickly between the stalls, and at flood stage the throng, shoulder to shoulder, moved in a slow sculling motion, back and forth as if stuck in a tide pool. The long rows between the booths were hundreds of feet long and the flow of patrons moved in opposing directions. Always the nurse, Annie was reminded of her student days looking through a microscope, the two channels like arteries and veins moving in a rhythmic pace until someone stopped to buy or ogle in the middle of the channel. A clot would slowly build, and after a purchase would be slowly absorbed once more into the flow of humanity.

Annie sold her apple dolls, bobble heads, posed for pictures, and signed autographs. The loose bills in the five-gallon crock pot for tips was held down with a cobblestone Annie found in the street. By late afternoon, she was left with ten soggy and smelly oyster gunny bags and one headless bobble head Sea Granny. She was contemplating her next move when she heard the familiar, "Hello, Gorgeous" once again.

Ivan had returned with another offering for his mentor. The two of them sat on a display bench, their legs dangling in the soft spring air, eating a cabbage and beef piroshki. Annie had kicked her shoes and socks off and Ivan was admiring her blue toenails, courtesy of the island's G.I. Joe, who had discovered a latent joy in painting women's nails.

They looked out to the west over the bustle of the Seattle port. The car and passenger ferries left their long sweeping wakes as they nursed themselves into the docks to load and unload, and the scary red cargo cranes to the south looked like praying mantis as they slowly sucked the containerized cargo from inside the six-hundred-foot ships from Korea and Japan. To the south soared Mt. Rainier, which dominated the lowlands from its fourteen thousand-foot summit, sheathed in snowy white, the top looking as though someone had taken a bite from a Dairy Queen ice cream cone. The ensemble Olympic Mountains to the west were dark blue with a delicate white pleated skirt in the foothills from a late spring dusting.

"Greed is good," Ivan suddenly blurted.

"Where do you get this stuff and how do you know when to use that crazy movie lingo?" Annie shook her head.

"Gecko," Ivan replied between bites. "Gecko said, 'Greed is good for lack of a better word.'"

"Frankly, my dear. I don't give a damn," Annie countered.

"Make my day," Ivan retorted.

"Badges," Annie echoed a scene from *The Treasure of the Sierra Madre*. "We don't need no stinking badges."

"Bond. James Bond. A martini, shaken not stirred," Ivan batted back.

"I have always depended on the kindness of strangers," Annie smirked in her sweetest southern drawl.

Ivan jumped down from his perch and bowed ever so slightly. "*Hasta la vista,* baby," and he was gone.

John stopped by and took her to dinner at Etta's, just down the road from the market. Chef Tom Douglas, looking disheveled as always, whipped up an Italian sausage frittata with a cinnamon chutney scallion sauce that the three of them washed down with a pitcher of Ridgetop Red ale. Exhausted by the long day, the warmth of the bistro, and the chattering of people and dishware, Annie had to be herded into the station wagon and helped onto *The Ark* by the two men.

The trip back, long after sunset, was cold. Annie zippered her jacket and tucked her chin under the collar. Moving out to the tip of the tiller, she sidled up next to the warm engine in the middle of the boat and felt its strong throbbing vibration against her thighs. She closed her eyes and became one with the boat, drifting off into a dream when she shook herself and pulled off her watch cap to let the cold breeze sift through her hair.

"You're not going there again, old girl," Annie chided herself and began to loudly recite a Robert Frost poem that ended with the words, *and miles to go before I sleep.*

Practically sleepwalking, Annie docked the boat, emptied the day's cash into an empty oyster sack, and dragged it up the hill. She stopped at the stove to see if the coffee was still hot. It wasn't. Checking in on the twins, she found them sleeping between Spud and South on the sleigh bed downstairs. Annie put her shoulder to the wall and slid up the stairs, kicked off her boots, pulled her quilt over her head, and slept like the dead.

"Annie, Annie, wake up. Wake up." Annie groaned and turned over. "This better be important," she threatened, not opening her eyes.

"It's Spud. Are you awake?"

Annie yawned and opened her eyes. "Spud, what is it?" She squinted and tried to frame him in the backlight of the kerosene lamp he had carried up and set on the table next to the bed.

"Annie, I have to leave something very important with you." Spud turned serious as he pulled a flat wooden box from under his jacket.

He opened the elaborate brass latch and extracted a ten-inch black-and-white disc and placed it on the table. It was on a small wooden stand with the light shining behind it.

"What is it?" Annie asked, not moving her head off the mattress.

"It's a pre-Columbian obsidian mirror from the Incas. It's volcanic glass polished on two convex sides and it has these strange, dark occlusions that are both translucent and reflective. We think it was seen as the threshold between the earthly world and beyond. But that's not the important part." Spud caressed the round mirror.

"So?" Annie was not impressed.

Spud didn't pick up on Annie's ambivalence. "There's only three of these in the world. The Incas had one, the Aztecs had one, and the Maya had one. And if you put them together in a triangle with light behind them, they are supposed to create a holograph of the Milky Way. That's what was inscribed on the side of the temple of the moon in Tikal in Guatemala."

"So?" Annie closed her eyes.

"So! So!" Spud was gaining speed. "These are ancient artifacts and if they do create a holograph of the Milky Way then it's evidence that aliens were here, in South and Central America. There is no way these ancient civilizations could have figured out the Milky Way. You know, there's a lot of other proof of aliens from sightings, pictures, and historical records from every civilization.

"This is one of the things that Professor Hawking and I have been putting together," Spud explained patiently. "One mirror is in the Vatican, one is in a private collection in New York, and I have the other one. We're right on the edge of putting these mirrors together, but there are other forces out there trying to stop the information from getting out. I need to leave the mirror with you for awhile. Do you have a safe place?"

Annie stretched and made a loud yawn as she swung her legs over the side of the bed. She got up and painstakingly put on her two ripped and torn flannel robes that had pilled up beyond expectation. She walked over to the edge of the room and stomped on the end of a floorboard that lifted up to reveal a space between the floor joist and the ceiling in the dining room. "Put it in there," Annie poked her finger at the floor, "and let me get back to sleep."

Spud placed the mirror back in the wooden box and slipped it into a velvet bag with drawstrings and reverently placed it in the hole.

"Ok," Annie pursed her lips, "la dee da, la dee da." And she let the floorboard drop back into place.

"May the force be with you, Annie," Spud mumbled as he walked towards the stairway.

In the morning, Annie woke to hear the twins chattering with South and Ziggy downstairs. She threw on her robes and charged up to the outhouse. She opened the door and paused to look up into the corner where last year's spider egg sac was still welded to the wall.

"Good. No baby spiders yet. I sure hope their mother told them that there is a truce in effect between us," Annie cackled as she wiped the dew from the toilet seat and peered into the gaping hole below.

"Now there's a black hole for you, Spudster," she said aloud to see if there was an echo. No luck. Annie did her business and, closing the outhouse door with the crescent moon window, wondered if she should give up the old outhouse for one of the space age contraptions with the solar power that White Bear had provided.

No rush, she thought. *It's still a good reality check.* She wondered how her sisters might react if she replaced the old outhouse. *No reason to push any hot buttons on those old fussbudgets*, Annie sighed. On the way down to the house, Annie felt heartened that White Bear's Raven was back and had taken up his post on the totem pole at the end of the orchard.

The twins were busy with breakfast. Zack had herded his cantaloupe pieces, half-grapes and Cheerios into one large pile and was scooping handfuls into his mouth. Meanwhile, Little Annie had gone to extreme measures to keep everything separated and was trying—unsuccessfully—to manipulate spoon to mouth.

Annie rubbed her hands over the top of the wood stove, ladled out five steaming bowls of oatmeal apple crisp, and poured mugs of coffee for the Max/ John Colby wedding planning party as she heard Pickles, Sister Mary Catherine, and Dorie chattering on the porch.

"Where's the bride-to-be?" Annie asked as the party settled in around the open oven door and grabbed for their coffee and crisp.

"She said to start without her and she'll be along in a little while. She said to just start brainstorming," Dorie confirmed, unlacing her shoes.

They all pulled off their shoes and stuck their feet on the warm oven door and silently slurped their breakfast. Before long, all four had slumped against the back of their chairs with their mouths open and were snoring away in front of the fire.

A few minutes later, Max burst inside the kitchen door. "How's the planning going?" she chirped as she took off her long wool coat. The snoring was still echoing upward near the coved ceiling when Annie woke with a start. "Going good," she croaked with a dry mouth.

Annie licked her lips and elbowed Sister, who snorted and looked owlish and then jostled the other two.

"Yeah, going good," Sister looked up at Max. "Going real good." She settled back in her chair trying to remember what they had discussed.

"So." Max brought a chair over to the stove. "When do you think is the best month?" Simultaneously they all answered. "June, September, July."

"August," Annie joined in last. "The flowers are at their peak and you can usually trust the weather."

"Yeah, August," the rest agreed, wanting Max to think they had made some progress.

"All right," Max sat down. "Now we're cooking. Where do you think it should be then?" Max looked around at the planners. "In Port Townsend, Seattle, on the *Pissant*, where?"

"At the church here on the island because I would have wanted my wedding here," Annie said firmly.

"Yeah, on the island," they all agreed.

"Ok," South announced, getting up from her chair. "I think we've done a lot here and I have to go to the little girls' room." And she was gone.

"I'd like to discuss the flowers at the florist shop in Port Townsend," Pickles announced. "That way we can see what we're talking about."

"I was going to get them on the Internet," said Max.

"It's up to you, dear," Pickles rubbed his head. "But I think we should buy local and did I tell you I have a master's degree from Tokyo in Ikebana and Kabuki theatre?

Beauty is most appreciated

When it is least expected," Pickles quoted.

"I was also honored with the highest rank in Ikebana arrangement for my composition Twisted Willow by the Light of the August Moon, which won me the highest honor possible from the Sogetsu School of Ikebana in London—the honorary title of Riji. The equivalent of eighth degree black belt in karate, if there is any equivalent," Pickles explained with humility.

"And," he declared, "they are *both* disciplines. I would be honored to create the arrangements," he droned on.

Max put her hand on his shoulder. "Enough already, Pickles, you're hired." Pickles looked smug.

"How about the wedding dress?" Max brought up next. "I was thinking of going to David's bridal. They have a lot of choices."

"Agggash!" Pickles choked. "I have a major collection of wedding dresses at my shop you might consider and I can alter them myself, of course. That is, if you care to take a look," Pickles said snippily.

"Like what, for instance?" Annie challenged him.

"Like…" Pickles sat down in his chair. "I have the wedding dresses from the movie *Father of the Bride*, part one and two, the wedding dress worn by Katharine Ross in *The Graduate*, and Grace Kelly's wedding dress when she married Prince Rainier III that took three dozen seamstresses six weeks to build. They don't even know it's missing from their archives, yet. You have the body of a young Princess Grace, you know," Pickles observed, looking at Max. "Although your bosom is a bit larger, I could see you in the Grace Kelly number. Hmm-m," he further scrutinized Max's body.

"Although…" he began.

Sister Mary Catherine lit her cigarette, sucked deeply, and then leaned back in her chair and exhaled. "Jesus H Christ, Pickles, the woman needs her own dress—not some cast-off princess rag," Sister railed. "She needs something original, she needs to make her own statement, you ragamuffin."

"Who are you calling a ragamuffin?" Pickles took offense.

"I said ragamuffin and I *mean* ragamuffin," Sister repeated.

"Whoa, whoa," Annie jumped in the middle of the bristled pair. "This is Max and John's wedding and they need to make their own decisions."

"Well, I want to do the flowers," Pickles said petulantly.

"Pickles can do the flowers," Max committed. "And maybe the dress, too. We'll just have to see."

Sister blew a quick puff of smoke into Pickles' face, but he merely scrunched his nose in a gotcha way and radiated a beatific smile of contentment.

"I think we've done very good for our first and maybe last meeting," Max threatened with a 'I'm in charge' look. The group looked sheepish, except for Sister who looked defiant.

"We want everything to be beautiful," Annie confessed. "We don't want this to turn messy."

"You are all family to me," Max said, smiling. "And, remember, Alisha and Talisha are going to be in the wedding."

"I have a little something from Shirley Temple…" Pickles began, but Max was already out the door and running down the path to greet Colby who had just arrived in his boat.

Pickles was relieved he would be an integral part of the wedding, but he had other possums to fry. He had come up with an idea to unload the extra thousand pounds of prime New Zealand possum loins that had been sitting in a freezer locker in Ballard for the last six months.

He scurried over to the Fremont district in Seattle where his franchise flagship store, Boots Whips Brews and Oil Change, continued to do a landslide business. He met his partner Madeline, who was sucking down her third pint of one of their top-selling microbrews, Sister Sludge, a heavy, dark roast malt with the full body of crankcase oil and the finish of turpentine. With an alcohol content of 11.5 percent, SS was especially good with a cone of sweet potato fries.

Madeline slid off the stool, straightened her red leather mini-skirt, and sashayed all six-foot-two in spiky boots over to survey Pickles' sign: FREE PLATE POSSUM SLIDER WITH EVERY OIL CHANGE. She crossed her arms over her riveted red ostrich leather bustier and cocked her head as she dug the knife blade heel into the straight grained Doug fir floorboards. She leaned back and gave a small shudder as one of her pit bulls strained on his leash and licked her leg.

"What's it gonna cost me?" She raised her eyebrows.

"Us. Cost us," Pickles emphasized. "Not much at all. I need to unload the inventory because I'm cooking up a new product line."

"How much?" Madeline insisted.

"About two or three bucks an oil change, but with the fourth of July coming up I figure we can easily get the money back in volume. The meat is a little greasy, but I figure maybe we market a little BBQ sauce on the side and we break even. I even came up with a name. What do you think of 'Madeline's BBQ seduction sauce.' Huh?"

Not surprisingly, Madeline was always on the lookout for horizontal expansion. She kicked the pit bull away and leaned against the bar. "I'm liking it," she said decidedly. "It appeals to my nasty girl rep."

"Do you mean mojo sauce?" Pickles seemed confused.

"Maybe." Madeline licked her crimson lips and ran her tongue across her upper teeth. "What else you got on your mind, partner?" She beckoned Pickles to belly up to the Oil Change bar.

Pickles pulled up a stool and whispered into Madeline's heavily pierced ear. "Camel's milk."

"Camel's milk?" Madeline mouthed the words. "What the…?"

"Yep," Pickles spoke loud. "We can make milk, yogurt, cheese, ice cream and in Switzerland some guy used it to make five thousand pounds of high grade chocolate. It's low in lactose, non-allergenic, and it's considered an aphrodisiac in Ethiopia.

"We can market it as one hump or two. You know the Bactrian camel has the two humps and the one hump camel is called an Arabian dromedary."

Madeline sighed dreamily. "Aphrodisiac?"

"It has three times the vitamin c of cows' milk," Pickles went on, "low fat, maybe gluten free, has properties that help the autoimmune system, and is said to really help people with MS and autism."

"Aphrodisiac?" Madeline mumbled.

Pickles ignored her. "I already have a recipe for a garlic cheese dip and the cheese is commonly aged in wine or olive oil. And it is illegal to import—like that's a problem with our connections—but some guy in Arizona is building up a herd of camels. The one hump milk is supposed to be better," Pickles concluded quietly.

"So what do we do?" Madeline asked. "Buy a bunch of DQ stores or what?"

"I'm working…on it. It's going to take some…time." Pickles melodically drew out the words.

"Well, I've got to be pushing on." Pickles got up from his stool. "I'll e-mail you some more info."

Chapter
TWENTY-SIX

From inside his bunker, Joe had been hearing scuttlebutt for months that the Department of Defense was planning on closing ten percent of their Veterans' hospitals in an effort to save money. He'd never had much respect for politics since he coptered out frantic Americans off the embassy roof in Viet Nam at the end of the war. He always adhered to the tenet of SunTzu's Art of War and the American corollary: a patriot must always be ready to defend his country against the government.

It was nearly sunrise and Joe was taking a tour around his compound. He had stopped to rearrange the plastic flamingo flock he had acquired when Sister Mary Catherine insisted he needed yard art in front of his bunker. Joe had bristled in those days, but complied, and now he was considering a small gnome for balance—feng shui, Sister kept calling it.

Joe was also keeping an eye out for a blip on his radar unit that showed an approaching boat. He tilted his night binoculars up and spotted a rowboat in a direct line with the island; the rower was wearing fatigues and a World War II flak helmet.

The small wooden launch landed and a pretzel-shaped man about Joe's age pried himself over the edge of the boat, his long, gray hair creeping out from under the helmet. The man marched stiff-legged up to Joe. He saluted and handed Joe a large orange envelope. "Headquarters," was all he said as he stood at ease.

Joe leafed through a sheaf of classified reports that confirmed that the Spokane Veterans' Hospital was scheduled to be shut down within two weeks. Included was a handwritten note from a man he remembered he had pulled out of a burning troop carrier in Somalia some years back. The man had lost both legs and had then gone on to law school at Gonzaga University and had become an advocate for veterans back in D.C.

"Do you know the contents of this envelope, soldier?" Joe asked.

"Yes sir, most of it. I've served as the legal secretary for Mr. Grant for the last twenty years on the Hill. If he says it's going down, it's going down, sir. Will you come, sir? Will you help us?"

"I need to have a little more confirmation, soldier," Joe answered, folding the envelope and tucking it inside his shirt. Joe beckoned to the fire he had built for Sister Mary. "Rest over there. What's wrong with your leg, soldier?"

"Lost it in Nam, sir, along with a few other body parts," he answered, and began to limp over to the fire.

"Be right back," Joe called out as he rifled through his hip pocket, found a half pint of Bacardi Gold, and tossed it over to the man. Then he walked over the sand bar, shifted a piece of driftwood, and entered the twenty-foot tunnel to his bunker.

Twenty minutes later, Joe emerged, carrying his canvas backpack and a small duffel bag. Out to the east, a helicopter from Whidbey Island, outlined against the sunrise, was nearing the island. It landed on the spit, throwing sand and gravel against the weather-beaten gray shingles on the side of Sister Mary's cabin. A minute later, the two men were gone.

Sister Mary put on her glasses and peered out her open door just in time to see the helicopter vanishing against the reddened clouds. "That man just doesn't know when to quit!" she mumbled to herself. Noticing the red clouds over the Cascades, she prophesied, "Looks like trouble brewing out there." Sister closed the door and went back to bed.

As the helicopter banked toward the crimson sky, Joe leaned over to help the soldier strap on his harness. "You know," Joe yelled over the sound of the whirling blades overhead, "I told Igor Sikorsky—the guy who perfected the helicopter—I said, if a man needs to be rescued, an airplane can drop flowers on him, but a helicopter can come in and save his ass. I love these birds," Joe shouted as he patted the aluminum rib of the craft.

The brick five-story Spokane VA hospital stood near the freeway as the helicopter buzzed over the top of the building and landed four blocks away near the covert headquarters, an abandoned fire station. The two men stepped out into the early morning sunshine and waved to the pilot as the unauthorized copter strained at the bond of gravity, gained altitude, and paddled for home. They knew the flight would disappear in the flight book—everyone in command owed Joe either their life or a favor. The word No was something that G.I. Joe O'Riley never accepted or heard from the military, but now he was taking on the "big boys," the Department of Defense.

The command post was down a dark stairway that led to a well-lit daylight basement. On the wall was a strategic map of the hospital the size of a large dining room table. Sitting around the heavily varnished brown plywood bingo tables was a ragtag grassroots group of veterans—wounded, mutilated, and forgotten by an America that was always looking toward the future and had little time for stragglers.

The stories and myths of Joe and his rescues from Korea to Iraq and the hundreds of unauthorized and secret missions were legend, but very few of them had ever seen the man.

The small, unassuming man that walked in the room in fatigues, a ball cap, a small WWII canvas backpack, and a single survivor knife hanging at his hip, was a warrior from another time. Joe didn't need a rank. He needed a mission. He walked to the front of the room and set his pack on the table.

"Military protocol demands that we do not leave any soldiers behind in the battlefield," Joe announced as he pounded the table.

"We will call this operation Rolling Thunder, and by god, starting on Memorial Day, they will wish they'd never started this war. We're going to occupy the hospital."

Day One: Memorial Day

Operation Rolling Thunder was begun with the raising of the revolutionary flag on the flagpole at the entrance to the hospital. It read: Don't Tread on Me, with a coiled rattlesnake on a field of cobalt blue. Eighty honey buckets had been delivered by a company run by two Viet Nam veterans. Sixty-two buses of veterans, including two that were full of retired army and navy doctors, were unloaded under the hospital's portico, and then the buses were chained to the surrounding fence.

World War II vintage pup tents were set up by college ROTC groups. Sympathetic Civil War enactment groups rolled in their cannon and set up camps in the rose garden of the hospital. The VFW set up their command post on the banks of the Spokane River behind the hospital, and the Veterans of Pearl Harbor manned the front gates with tents and several vintage tanks borrowed from the nearby National Guard Armory. Hospital personnel were allowed to come and go as they wished.

In three hours the hospital was under siege in command of Captain Joe O'Riley, veteran and decorated war hero.

The blitzkrieg had taken the town and the hospital by surprise. The Spokane police and the sheriff's department immediately sent their SWAT team to the site, but they were immediately stymied when they realized the enemy was everything from veterans in wheelchairs to Boy Scouts. Force was not an option at this point.

The hospital employees, to a man, decided to save their jobs and joined the coalition of the more than willing.

Day Two: A Standoff

The police took up a command post in an abandoned Godfather's Pizza building four blocks from the hospital after first clearing away hundreds of pizza takeout boxes and cases of Bud Light. Photos taped to the pizza covers showed pictures of air surveillance—an occupying force of well over a thousand-strong with no estimates of personnel in the hospital, and the entire four acres of grounds covered with troops and gear.

A contingent of POWs moved in and set up camp on the banks of the Spokane River to augment the position of the VFW.

Day Three: City and State Respond

Spokane Mayor Scotty Bogbottom declared in the headlines of the *Spokane Sentinel* that "This un-American activity will not stand in this city and he is appealing to the National Guard to run roughshod over the entire debacle."

Washington Governor Gary Lockhead took a more reasoned and dithering approach and decided not to call out the Guard, but to set up a blue ribbon panel of veterans to work out an equitable solution.

There were plans to cut the power and water to the hospital, but with veterans on life support and the resourcefulness of the occupiers, it was not an option.

Day Four: Money Game
The Spokane merchants came in force to the office of Mayor Bogbottom and showed him glowing retail receipts of landslide sales with optimism in every sector from pizzas to beer. With the sudden unexpected wealth rolling into his fair city, Bogbottom quickly raised the B&O tax and started to have new hopes for his pet project, the python petting zoo championed by his pole dancing gal pal at the Serpents Lounge and Launderia. And if things kept turning his way, there was also a chance for the renovation of the old civic auditorium as well as another term in office. The Mayor began to preach tolerance and planned a photo op at the VA Hospital once they learned of his change of heart.

The Governor saw a no-win situation for himself and immediately disbanded the panel before it had a chance to meet, and turned the whole situation over to the feds. It's their property anyway, he reasoned.

Addressing the press through the bars of the front gate, Joe took the opportunity to educate them about the plight of veterans from Civil War days to the present. That opened up the newspaper editor's eyes—if they could just keep this siege going long enough to run a series of exposés, he could smell a Pulitzer.

Day Five: Show Time
Gridlock clogged the city streets of Spokane as tourists, local sympathizers, and news media poured in from all over the world. Motels and hotels were packed and the campgrounds had no vacancies.

The National Guard found that most of their vehicles had been sabotaged and parts were being flown in from neighboring guard units.

Joe had decided to allow the Civil War enactment group to stage mock battles, complete with cannon salvos and thundering horses to entertain the spectators who lined the hospital's perimeter fences, reasoning that the explosions would play to the chaos factor and confuse the bureaucrats.

The press reported that several of the militia were carrying guns, including a gaunt elderly soldier dressed in garb that identified him as formerly part of the Third Mountain division that trained on Mount Rainier before World War II. The old soldier insisted on carrying ancient wooden skis with leather bindings strapped to his pack and an M-1 carbine with a bayonet attached.

Joe assured the media he had given the order that all guns must be deactivated and bayonets left in the tents. And yes, the old man with the skis was in the early throes of senility, but he had been highly decorated from his service in the Italian Alps.

Day Six: The Feds

The F.B.I. screeched up to the front gate in black SUVs with mirrored windows. They wore wraparound sunglasses, black suits, and earphones. They scouted the premises and left without comment.

An entertainment schedule was hung on the front gate with the times of the Civil War battles and what battle they were fighting. There was a can for donations.

Mayor Bogbottom, or "Bogsy" as he was known within the hospital arena, raised the B&O tax again, for the third time.

Day Seven: Acceptance and the Flying Nuns

The mayor moved freely within the compound and the Boy Scouts vowed to come back on the weekend after school was out. Joe instituted a recycling program and the green horse dung was mixed with sawdust and sold out the side gate as Freedom Do Regard.

Sister Mary Catherine had been chomping at the bit to join the fray, so right after she inaugurated the opening of the side-winder kamikaze roller coaster in Chattanooga, she gathered up her fellow-flyers.

The fifteen nuns skydived from eight thousand feet, forming first a star and then a crucifix on the way down, then floating gently into the compound accompanied by a roar from the crowd. Sally Field, stung by former criticism and in between taking Boniva and her latest Lifetime made-for-TV movie, showed up in a nun costume and did several photo ops.

"Joe," Sister asked as they sat in a tent beside the hospital porch, "how are you going to pay for all this?"

Joe gave a sly smile and went to the back of the tent. A few moments later, he brought back a suitcase. He opened it up and there were stacks of U.S. currency—hundred-dollar bills bound by paper wrappers that said Bank of Baghdad. "You know those billions of dollars that Saddam Hussein had stashed away that no one ever found? *I* found 'em."

Day Eight: Other Celebs
John Travolta filled his 707 Boeing with movie luminaries. Robert Redford, Kevin Bacon, Madonna, Britney Spears, and a cast of fifty or more, streamed into the hospital grounds in a show of solidarity. They put on a theatrical production of song, dance and drama for the strikers.

Day Nine: Jay Leno
Leno, hooking into a sure thing, taped his late night show at the hospital with guests Liza Minnelli, Harrison Ford, and Pee Wee Herman, but the showstoppers were Sister Mary Catherine and her Toe Tapping Nuns who did their Rockette rendition of show tunes from *Oklahoma, South Pacific,* and *West Side Story.*

Day Ten: Enough Was Too Much
Sensing a situation that was spinning out of control—getting bigger by the minute—and hearing rumors that the Russian President and the Cuban Dictator were scheduled to appear, the Defense Department parlayed with the president and sent their best man to negotiate.

Mayor "Bogsy" instituted his fourth B&O tax hike.

Day Eleven: Four-Star General Lincoln MacArthur (or "Mac") comes to town
Lincoln MacArthur was a soldier's soldier. Starting at the bottom of the military food chain and chosen for officers' candidate school on his own merit, Mac had climbed the ladder to command based on his ability to follow the chain of command and to be politically correct at all times.

A large black man standing a good six-foot-four, Mac was deeply religious and had shilled for the president, based on the constitutional authority that the military was the mighty arm of the executive branch and did their bidding as such. Many times Mac had put his reputation on the line as he fed false information that caused the United States to engage in several wars and skirmishes that could have been avoided. He knew what they called him—the president's stooge, the lawn jockey—but Lincoln was nothing if not loyal to his oath to serve his country.

Mac landed at Fairchild Air Force Base and in full dress uniform with his three attachés made his way to the compound. He shook hands with the Pearl Harbor survivors and was authentically gracious to everyone he met as he toured the facility. He began to worry that there was no *one* agency to negotiate with until he was escorted to the top floor of the hospital to a command unit overlooking the front gate. Dressed in fatigues, the ball cap from the POWS, and wearing dark sunglasses, Joe greeted the general with a warm handshake.

Mac was surprised to see Joe in charge. There was an abundance of senior officers on deck. He had heard the legend of GI Joe of course, but he didn't realize the man still existed. Joe offered a tour of the facility and Mac accepted. Joe showed the general the leaky ceilings, the outdated plumbing, the rat holes in the walls, and the outmoded equipment. Mac also met the patients—mutilated veterans with bed sores. The dirty linen, the overcrowded rooms filled with beds, the smell of urine and the stench of diseased veterans, caused Mac's nose to run and he fought nausea.

"Did you know that eight veterans committed suicide in the out-patient section here just last year?" Joe showed Mac the reports. The two soldiers continued touring and eventually meandered back to the command post to parlay.

"Why would you want to keep a hell hole like this alive?" Mac sat back in the office chair and put his hands behind his head.

"They are *all* like this," Joe shrugged. "From Walter Reed to Pensacola. They are all substandard and veterans are not getting the kind of care they were promised."

"I've been to Bethesda," Mac countered. "It was bright and spot-less and state-of-the-art."

"You only saw what they wanted you to see, sir." Joe rubbed his scratchy ten-day-old beard he hadn't had time to shave off.

Mac wasn't much for bargaining so he put his cards on the table.

"You can only stay here so long," he began. "Pretty soon the glow will wear off and everyone will have to go home and your cause will wither and die and blow away in the wind." *Wither and die… blow in the wind.* Mac nodded to himself. *Eloquent,* he thought, for a man who usually couldn't turn a phrase.

Mac leaned forward. He had noticed there were a dozen or more open cases on the desk that he knew had contained service medals. He counted the empty cases of seven Purple Hearts.

"What happened to those medals?" Mac rubbed his chin.

"I gave them to the heroes here at the hospital," Joe answered nonchalantly.

"I heard they offered you the Congressional Medal three times," Mac pried. It was a rumor he had heard any number of times.

"That medal is for those men who paid the ultimate price," Joe replied, sweeping the boxes into a drawer.

Mac stood up. "I'd like to find my own way out, if you don't mind. I need to make a full report to the Cabinet and to the president."

"Be my guest." Joe rose and shook Mac's hand. "Good luck, General."

As Mac went down in the elevator, he was relieved that the smell had grown faint and he stopped to wash his hands in the men's room on the first floor. It was late and all the administrators had gone home; Mac was confused as to which way he had entered. As he stood in the darkened hall, a hand reached out and tugged on his gold embroidered sleeve. Mac smelled the urine even before he looked down and saw the bony fingers with long yellow nails of a black man in a wheelchair. The man wore a disheveled ball cap that said "Tuskegee airmen 50th anniversary" and one side of his face was slack.

"Excuse me, sir." The man in the wheelchair dropped his hand on the blanket covering his lap.

"Do you smell gunpowder, sir? I've been smelling it for a couple of days now and I know they need me at the front. I'm having the darnedest time getting this chair to work since my stroke. I've only got the one good arm."

Mac saw that the entire left side of the man was slumped and there was a Red Ryder bb gun hanging on a sling on the handle of the wheelchair.

"Where'd you get the gun, soldier?" Mac asked.

"The nurses got it for me. I've been practicing some on the back lawn."

"Are you sure you won't shoot your eye out?" Mac smiled.

"Don't worry about me, sonny. You just wheel me up to the front lines. I was an expert marksman and a pilot in the Army Air Corps."

"World War Two?" Mac guessed.

"Yep, the big one," the man replied. "We made sure everyone got home carrying their shield or on it. That was our motto. We lost a mess of boys over there. One of my best friends…." and the old soldier went silent.

Mac wheeled the man out onto the porch and set the brake so the chair would stay safe on the porch overlooking the front gate.

"This must be a pretty big fracas," the man said, shading his eyes from the setting sun. "I can take it from here, sir. Thanks for the help." He offered his hand and, reluctantly, Mac took his freshly laundered hand and shook the soldier's.

"Whoa, you've got a pretty good grip there, soldier," Mac recoiled slightly.

"I can take care of myself. You don't have to worry about me," the old soldier said.

Mac was halfway across the yard when the south wind freshened and the smell of gunpowder from the Civil War cannons whipped past his nose. He walked past a quartet of bagpipers who were piping down the flag when he heard a single shot that came from the porch.

Mac rushed back and saw an elderly nun had knelt down and was holding Joe's head as he lay on the concrete porch. There was blood bubbling from an entry wound on his right side just below the ribs.

The old soldier with the skis laced to his backpack was sitting against the hospital wall sobbing, "I didn't know there was a round in the chamber. I forgot. I took out the magazine. I just forgot."

Mac had never seen a man die in front of him. His father had passed away two years ago while Mac was an envoy to Egypt. Mac knew his father only had a short time, but his duty had always been to his country. He still felt like he should have been there. Mac looked at the old nun and she shook her head. Joe twitched and struggled to open his eyes. He looked up at Sister Mary and whispered, "on the field of battle…it's always been my dream." Then Joe slumped into Sister's arms and he was gone.

The entire compound had heard the shot and when they learned of Joe's death they wept openly—for the man, the soldier, the cause, and for themselves. Mac helped lay Joe's body on an old green army blanket to absorb the blood and grabbed a corner as they struggled up the stairs and into an office where they lay Joe to rest on an office desk with a pillow under his head. The nun put Joe's dark blue Special Forces hat on his head and put his arms down to his side. Outside, the bagpipers, who had just finished performing before the shooting, played a dirge and then continued on playing "Danny Boy."

Mac was used to soldiering on as he swallowed his emotion and asked if there was anything he could do. There wasn't, so he left. As he walked across the parade field again, he looked on the bright side. It looked like the siege of the hospital was probably over and he could get back to Washington.

He was halfway across the grounds again, past the bagpipers and the smell of gunpowder from the cannons, when the general broke down.

He gave a great wrenching cry and collapsed near an old oak tree on the parade grounds that had been planted by Marcus Whitman before the turn of the last century. Lincoln MacArthur sobbed and cried out as the Pearl Harbor survivors lifted him up and put him in a wheelchair, wrapped a blanket around his shoulders, and held him in their arms. They had all been where the four-star general was now and there were no answers—only the comfort one warrior can give to another on the battlefield.

Hours later, Mac would make the call to Washington.

"Mac, you old son of a gun," the defense cabinet chairman sang out. "Sounds like you got the job done out there. I happen to be with the president and the Secretary of State right now. I'll put you on speaker phone."

Mac had rehearsed what he would say. "I'm not coming back, sir. One of America's great warriors has gone down on the field of battle and I will be part of the honor guard as he lies in state. Then I will be taking his place, sir. I will be in command here until this matter is resolved in favor of the American veterans who have given their last full measure of devotion to their country. These are patriots out here, sir, and I am proud to stand up for them."

"Mac," the cabinet official sputtered. "We need you back here, now."

"I'm sorry, sir. I'm staying with my men," Mac said firmly.

"This is mutiny, Lincoln. This is treason. This is Benedict Arnold. This is unpatriotic. Do you know that, Lincoln?" threatened the official.

"No, sir. This is patriotism. What you're doing to these men is political. I'm staying with my men, sir. No one is going to be left behind on the field of battle." Mac hung up.

Two days later, Congress passed a bill to clean up the veterans' hospitals. The president put four-star general Lincoln MacArthur in charge. The Congress said they might deliberate about the Congressional Medal of Honor for Joe when they came back from recess.

Sister Mary Catherine went right to work. She had been praying for months over the spirit of Joe and there was no time to waste. She ushered everyone out of the room, locked the door, closed all of the windows, and drew the drapes.

Sister had seen death many times, but she had only been able to capture a spirit twice before in her long life. An exorcism was to cast the evil spirit out of the body, but the spirit—far more delicate— would have to be coaxed out carefully.

The soul she knew would return to god and more than likely, if her prayers were heard, Joe would go into purgatory. Sister could live with that, knowing the threshold for direct ascent to heaven was not even in her future. She knew she'd have to do some fast talking when she got to the great beyond, but she was looking forward to the challenge. There were no sure things in dealing with the soul. But the spirit of a human being was something altogether different. It was a physical manifestation that could be captured and redirected into another.

Working by candlelight, Sister reached into her traveling bag and retrieved a small mahogany chest with a rounded top and a brass clasp. The box was made of aromatic cedar, and the joints were mortised and tenoned for strength. Like the crucifix, the box must be made of wood.

Sister prepared the body in a ritual she had learned as a young novitiate when she had assisted in an exorcism in Paris. She took out Joe's shaving mug, lathered up his face, and with a straight-edged razor shaved him smooth. She had heard the beard would continue to grow even after death and wondered if that were true. She combed his hair and removed his shirt. She gasped at Joe's chest and trunk. The core of the body was missing great hunks of flesh. The scars cut deep tracks across the ribs and torso and where muscles had been removed; deep puckered pockets had been drawn together with stitches. Sister found it hard to imagine that one body could sustain the kind of brutality Joe must have experienced.

"He must have been eligible for fifty Purple Hearts," Sister mumbled to herself as she cleaned around the puncture wound where the blood was still oozing and trailing onto the blanket.

Sister cleansed the upper body with alcohol and then she sat down on a wooden bench to meditate. She knew she wasn't qualified to capture a spirit; ordinarily it would fall within the purview of a bishop—probably a cardinal—but she learned the prayer deep in the catacombs of a castle on the coast of Normandy just after World War II and she had kept the secret close to her heart.

When she was finally composed, she took a stone knife of black obsidian and cut a deep two-inch exit point between the fourth and fifth ribs on the right side of Joe's chest. Then Sister Mary began to rock forward and then back and when she felt the power welling inside her she began her prayer chant.

Almost a half hour later, when she finished the recitation, she pushed on Joe's chest and a small, winged gossamer apparition, the size of a moth, unfolded itself and emerged from Joe's ribs. The spirit circled the body twice, then flew directly into a corner of the ceiling and sat on the wall. Sister could see the gray wedge-shaped wings that she had seen twice before. She slowly opened the box, placed it on Joe's chest, and sat back against the wall. There was a long interval and then the spirit flew around the perimeter of the room, hovered over Joe's body and disappeared. Sister leaned forward and looked inside the box. She saw the wings fluttering in the bottom. She quickly closed the lid and locked the clasp.

Sister Mary Catherine felt dizzy with relief. She tucked the box into her night bag and opened the door to the room. She turned and gave the sign of the benediction. God could have his soul, but Joe's spirit would remain here on earth where it belonged, to be shared wherever men sought freedom from oppression.

"Someday," Sister Mary prayed. "Someday, Joe's spirit will rejoin his soul."

History could have the legend. Sister Mary was hightailing for the island.

Because Joe had no family, the military took responsibility for his body and flew him under full military escort directly to Washington, D.C.

It was one of those balmy East coast late spring days. The pink cherry blossoms had long since dropped into the Reflecting Pool and the oak trees were fully leafed. Grey squirrels were resting their bellies on the cool tops of the white marble headstones.

At the base of the hill at Arlington National Cemetery, the flag-draped casket was loaded onto a caisson and a trail of three hundred sixty men of the official eight hundred eighty-three men that Joe had personally rescued over the years walked slowly behind it up the winding hill to a spot the military had been reserving for Joe and his boys.

Just below the mansion where Robert E. Lee had his residence, the hill sloped to the north. One hundred and seventy men Joe had rescued had already been laid to rest awaiting their hero, and in the next twenty years they would all be reunited.

The small circle of men with the Medal of Honor were incensed that Joe might be overlooked and six of them sent their medals to the Pentagon to be buried with Joe, but after General Lincoln MacArthur caused "holy hell" in the halls of the Pentagon, Congress had hastily come up with Joe's own Medal of Honor, which Joe himself had helped set the bar high. *A soldier that had paid the ultimate price for his country.*

There were bugles, rifle fire, bagpipes and flags, but Joe's spirit was safely resting on Seven Sisters Island in Puget Sound, waiting for a time when the country might need such a man again.

It was several weeks before Sister Mary found the strength to dive into the tunnel and investigate Joe's bunkers. Before entering, she straightened up the five fiberglass flamingos that were looking a little tipsy from the prevailing south wind. She rolled up the remains of the wind-tattered bra that had tied the two bunkers together.

"Lord," Sister squinted at the two bunkers. *They do look a little on the suggestive side of giant boobs,* she had to admit. *I hope there is no more trouble.* She looked out into the gray water and lit a Camel straight. Then another and another until the pack was empty.

With a resigned sigh, she pushed the burnt log from the tunnel opening and made her way down a short tunnel that opened into a half-dome room the size of a good-size dining room. The room was rimmed with electronic computer screens and towers that even now buzzed and snapped, powered by a bank of batteries along the side of one curved wall. A wooden framed cot stood against the wall with neatly folded blankets nestled near a pillow and freshly laundered and pressed fatigues sat on a shelf just over the bed. A wooden box was filled with shiny aluminum packages of freeze-dried food. Sister shuddered as she picked up an unopened flat package labeled 'meat loaf.'

In the middle of the room was a small table, the top stacked with topographical maps with intersecting vectors drawn into towns and places that Sister had never heard of, and an empty bottle of Evian water.

On another table in front of a computer flat screen, sitting next to a mouse pad, was a half-eaten box of Lucky Charms. *So that's what kept him going,* smiled Sister.

She was drawn to a small spray of sunlight that reflected from one wall about eye level. She looked out through an eye-piece connected to a lens that gave her a fish-eye view of the entire spit. Next to the lens was a grenade rocket launcher loaded and ready to fire.

She dropped down into a small hole and crawled along a wood-lined tunnel to the second bunker. In the middle of a similar-size room as the first bunker was a wooden pallet with a camouflage tarp covering a squarish object as wide as Sister's arms and about shoulder high. She slipped off the tarp to find the entire mound was thousands of stacks of United States hundred-dollar bills bundled with paper stickers that said National Bank of Iraq. "Oh my…" Sister blinked.

She wished she hadn't smoked her last Camel and dug around her pockets until she found a stub. She squatted near the pile and smoked the butt down to the nib.

Sister Mary Catherine made a shaky exit and looked out onto the shoreline where a pink flamingo had just landed next to the fiberglass herd. Sister was not surprised at all.

"It's about time you got here," she said as the bird sidled up to his compatriots.

The sunset that began as golden turned to coral and then crimson. "God, I wish Joe was here to share this," Sister called out to the Olympic Mountains, now disappearing into darkness. Later that night, Sister heard on the radio that a flamingo called Pink Floyd had escaped from the Woodland Park Zoo.

"I suppose Lila will be here in the morning," Sister mumbled as she tried unsuccessfully to massage her own feet in front of the fire.

Chapter
TWENTY-SEVEN

The twins were all about walking and sippy cups these days. Despite everyone's attempt to keep things positive, their favorite word was No. Zack had shown signs of being a charming child from day one with his smirky smile, but his sister, with her wispy red hair that she liked to have tufted into two Pebble Flintstone knots with green ribbons, was a throwback to another time.

"She's willful, I'll tell you that." Annie took a sip of coffee and watched Little Annie wrestle the cushions off the couch for the tenth time that morning, trying unsuccessfully to build a tunnel against the couch framework.

Zack was drinking from his cup and rubbing his ear with his two fingers.

"I sure hope he doesn't have another ear infection," Dorie said, adjusting her whistling hearing aid. "That kid has already taken a barrelful of amoxicillin."

"Maybe he needs tubes in his ears," suggested Ziggy, still buzzing from his morning joint.

Max took a deep breath. "I think we need to think about doing something for Trish. Maybe she needs full-time care. She's can't raise her hands anymore, barely moves her fingers, and all her food has to be liquefied. She's pretty much living on broth and liquid vitamins, and she is having a tough time breathing, especially at night."

"She can't be separated from her girls," Annie said, shaking her head. "There's no good solution. We'll just have to play it day by day. If the ex-husband finds those girls, they're gone forever."

"I still think they're safer on the island," Dorie joined in.

"Day by day. It's all we can do," Annie said decidedly.

The documentary team from the University of Washington, teaming with the Suquamish tribe's Clearwater Casino, was having a community salmon buffet to debut the screening of White Bear's canoe voyage to the Great Bear Rainforest on Princess Royal Island.

The gaming tables were closed in honor of the ancient tribal tradition of vision quest, which the tribe hoped to revive for a nation stuck in spiritual neutral but economic overdrive. The islanders had arrived in full force and were celebrities in their own right, but the day belonged to White Bear.

Before the movie began, there was a play from the Longhouse native players from Blake Island, who told the story of Raven stealing the sun from the gods and giving it to the coastal tribes. The shadowy figures moved about the stage as the fog swirled and slowly lifted as the dancers—in shredded cedar clothing, colorful blankets, and masks—told the story.

The sound of wooden flutes and drums created an eerie backdrop until the stage went completely black and the film rolled without credits.

The story began with White Bear sitting on a log at the edge of a gravel beach telling of his vision quest long ago on the shores of

Hood Canal, and how his life was linked to the great white bear who became his mentor.

"I was twelve years old and had been surviving alone on the saltwater shores, only eating what I could catch with my hands and drinking from a glacial mountain stream that came from high in the Olympic Mountains. I was not yet a man as I waited for my animal spiritual guide to appear. On the seventh day, hungry and dizzy from lack of food, I fell asleep along the shoreline. When I awoke, I saw the white bear appear on the edge of the stream, scoop up a salmon, and begin to eat. I was not afraid and I approached the bear and sat down on a rock to watch. When the bear finished eating, it caught another salmon and placed it on the rocky stream bed before me and looked directly into my eyes—and our spirits became as one. I was happy because I knew from tribal legends that the figure of the bear was quick and resourceful, as well as cunning and powerful.

"When I told the story to the tribal shaman, he confirmed that this sighting of a white ghost bear had never been documented in our tribe before, and that from then on, I would be known as White Bear and I would always be pure of heart. For a gambler like me, it was a great tragedy, but over the years the spirit of the ghost bear and I learned to work things out for both our interests."

The film continued with narration: The camera caught the grumbling sound of the chainsaw and the image of the twelve hundred-year-old cedar falling out of the sky and stubbornly refusing to leave the shore of Seven Sisters. The film captured the artists from Blake Island, who sculpted the canoe using only the traditional tools of the adze, the draw knife, and fire as they talked around the campfire at night drinking their whiskey and relating how they could feel the spirit of the tree talking through the tools.

The potlatch scene depicted the fifty plus tribes from around the Pacific Northwest and the world, dancing and singing songs of their ancestors that launched the canoe, with Annie's borrowed quilt flapping in the wind. It was preceded by a 1920 film clip from the Ansel Adams archives of a man wearing an eagle costume, flapping his wings in the bow of a large wooden canoe.

The documentary continued with hand-held footage of the voyage, the rocking images, the lens covered with overspray from the waves as the canoe plied its way north. At the villages of the Tulalip and Lummi island, there were extended lavish ceremonial landings as the tribes would wade out to greet the boat and then celebrate the voyage with food and a good night's sleep before the journey would continue. More than once, the landing caught other tribal elders along the journey by surprise. Once there was even a coupon-driven dinner at Applebee's and drinks at a local microbrew pub, which met with approval by the paddlers, but every tribe along the route was proud to extend hospitality and were touched by White Bear's journey.

The camera caught the backs of the paddlers straining to propel the wooden canoe, while the lone figure of White Bear—wrapped in the quilt, nose to the wind, his gray pigtail swinging beneath his ball cap—was chanting and playing his box drum, rising up and down with the rhythm of the waves.

At Point Roberts, the tipping point where the customs and immigration offices for Canada and the United States were stationed on a dock, the forgetful paddlers were reminded they needed passports. The officials from the two nations parlayed and decided anyone crazy enough to paddle six hundred miles didn't pose much of a threat to national security.

For their records, they asked which tribe each paddler was affiliated with. The native paddlers answered—"Suquamish," "Muckleshoot," "Udub Huskies," "Rainbow," and the tall black foreign soccer-playing exchange student shouted out proudly "Masai."

The officials only grinned as they waved the canoe onto the open waters between Vancouver Island and Vancouver, British Columbia.

The canoe bounced along the eastern coast of Vancouver Island past Nanaimo, Qualicum Beach, Courtenay, Campbell River, and finally Port Hardy at the end of the island, just over halfway to the home of the Ghost Bear.

There had been defections, mutinies, and some paddlers disappeared overnight, but until now the path to the Great Bear Rainforest had always been buffered by islands. From now on, the open seas of the Pacific would come crashing against the wooden craft. White Bear spent more time huddled in his quilt behind the bow, but when strength permitted, he chanted a primal song to his Ghost Spirit that he was coming home.

At Port Hardy, two paddlers from the Double D joined for the final leg of the journey. It was going to be a long pull across Queen Charlotte Strait, but by paying attention to the tides and a good stiff southwest breeze, the canoe surfed across the channel to Penrose Island and into the beach at the marine provincial park.

The rest of the trip took two weeks as the paddlers slalomed between the island crags, finally nestling into the safety of Douglas Channel that spiked into the heart of the island. Camping by a stream that flowed among smooth, humping, granite slabs that looked like surfacing bowfin whales, the spent team lay exhausted, but was buoyed by the fact that they were at journey's end and White Bear's promise that the spirit bear would now come to him.

On the third day, a Ghost bear appeared as it had eighty years ago. Fishing in the shallows and chasing a run of Chinook salmon was a magnificent snow white sow with two blonde yearlings. White Bear wasted no time.

While the camera rolled, White Bear shook the hands of all the paddlers, zipped up his plumbing Carhartt jacket, strapped on his hunting knife, and slowly approached the white bear. He began to talk to her in a language he had never heard before. She stood up on her haunches and cocked her head to hear and then walked over to

White Bear. She let him stroke her ears and then she turned and man and bear walked into the forest—two spirits joined together at last. At the edge of the woods, White Bear turned and raised his hand to salute his friends, and then he was gone.

"Cluster shit," the Masai warrior attempted to channel his best American slang. "I don't believe what I saw, but we got it on tape, right?"

"Oh yeah, we got it," his companion from the university confirmed as he skimmed a guidebook for the Great Bear Rainforest. "It says here that the bears have been isolated for thousands of years and that they have no instinctive fear of people."

"Unbelievable!" The Masai shook his head. "It was as if those two knew each other in another life."

"Maybe they did," his companion agreed.

The paddlers spent two more days resting and waiting to see if White Bear would return, and when he didn't, they knew their journey was ended and they consulted the ferry schedule, paddled out into the Hecate Strait, and drifted for three hours until the Alaskan Ferry—on its return from Juneau to Seattle—steamed by and plucked the paddlers and the canoe out of the cold waters.

The casino put on a fireworks display and everyone had warm feelings about the evening and the Tribal Vision Quest revival committee raised twenty-three thousand dollars.

Chapter
TWENTY-EIGHT

Many times Annie had walked by the old Apple tree where she used to hide her treasures, but this morning she vowed to fish her hand into the muck to see if anything from her childhood was still buried in the opening where a branch socket had rotted away before she was born.

Annie took Little Annie by the hand and together they toddled down to the pasture. When they reached the tall wet grass, Annie tried to pick up her great-granddaughter but Little Annie announced with determination, "I do it myself."

Little Annie took a single step into the grass that towered over her head and immediately retreated. "Annie need help," she said, reaching her hands up to her namesake.

Annie grunted as she swung the child to her hip and they waded to the middle of the orchard, her pants sticking to her knees as she silently grumbled why she thought this was a good day for this particular adventure, but Little Annie was gabbing up a storm and pointing to a robin. "Cheep, cheep," she said proudly. "Cheep, cheep."

"And what does the doggy say?" Annie prodded as Twigs made a late entry with only the tall grass moving to indicate his presence. Little Annie leaned over and stared intently where the grass was moving. Just then, Twigs poked his head up and she laughed. "Arf, arf," she said with conviction.

"Good girl," Annie puffed as she leaned against the tree for a breather and then tried to peek into the hole, but it was just over her head. Annie remembered her tomboy days, when she would have easily swung up into the crotch of the tree with one move and stuffed her hand in the hollow.

"Here goes nothing," she warned Little Annie.

Annie's hand went tentatively toward the opening and just before she entered, she was startled by a frog croaking inside the socket. Annie pulled her hand back and soon a small brown red-legged frog peeked over the edge at the intruder and then jumped onto the grass.

Annie took a stick and rapped on the tree trunk where woodpeckers had mined a thousand small holes, making the trunk look like a crooked cribbage board. She remembered someone saying the holes were to encourage insects to use the holes for refuge, providing a nice fast food snack for the woodpecker; while other ornithologists claimed the woodpecker was searching for insects in the tree trunk. Either way it didn't look like the tree was the worse for wear. Annie shrugged and voted for door number two.

No animal life appeared, so Annie plunged her hand into the old limb socket. She felt the cold slime of ten thousand rains and her childhood slip between her fingers. She pulled out some of the gunk and dropped it on the ground. Little Annie was straining over Annie to see what was happening.

Annie was almost up to her elbow when she hit pay dirt. She felt round flat objects and two round spheres the size of a quarter. Her hand closed over the objects as the goods slipped into her palm.

Sluck, the sound of her hand clearing the muck, made Little Annie shudder and she sat back abruptly, causing the two spelunkers to tumble backward into the grass.

Lying there like a turtle, Annie began to laugh, but Little Annie was not amused, until Twigs began to lick her face and made her giggle. Annie sat up and looked at her muddy fist and began to smile. She remembered exactly what she had left in the hole. She struggled to her knees as the shine broke from behind a cotton ball cloud. She dropped her treasures into a nearby mud puddle and when the clouds wafted away, there were five silver dollars her grandfather gave her for her fifth birthday. The face of Lady Liberty stared up at Annie, along with her two childhood favorite marbles, an amber peerie and a clear blue pupiled cat's eye.

Annie remembered how her six sisters had schemed to get her to part with her silver, till after dark she had snuck down into the orchard, shinnied up the trunk, and entrusted them to the old tree. She had forgotten about the money. The old tree had stood sentry duty all these years.

She could hardly wait for the twins' fifth birthday so she could duplicate her grandfather's gift. And maybe, just maybe, Annie said in a silent prayer, they too, having heard the story, would hide their birthday gift on the island and someday when they were very old, and their lives were full of memories, they would come back to the island and find their birthday gift waiting for them. "That," Annie said aloud to her great-granddaughter, "would be my wish for you, little one."

The two soul mates had a great adventure and Annie began to whistle the theme song from the movie *The Bridge on the River Kwai* as she high-stepped through the tall grass on their way back to the house. They stopped to examine all the bumblebees on the blue lupine at the edge of the orchard. Then, closer to the island cemetery, were the purple and blue bells of the foxgloves, their stems tall and majestic as if they were the towers on a Gaudi cathedral in Barcelona.

Soaked to the skin, great-grandmother and great-granddaughter both stripped in front of the heat of the stove, dressed again, and proceeded to take a nap.

Annie's sleep was restless and troubled. The island was in deep peril. She dreamed she ran down the spit from shack to shack and found them all empty. Everyone had disappeared in the island's hour of need. She thrashed under her quilt in helplessness as she ran to the boathouse and raised the red signal flag in hope that someone from the mainland in Port Gamble would come to the island's aid. She could hear the voices of GI Joe, Moby Dick and the Owl warning her of doom. And then she heard a gunshot.

Her clothes soaked in sweat and her hair sticking to her face, Annie was groggy as she tried to rally herself into the present. Another volley of automatic gunfire.

Annie bounced off the bed and stared out the window onto the spit. There was a long needle-nosed, mustard-colored fiberglass speedboat beached near the cabins and two men in black leather jackets waving pistols were running out to the end of the spit near Joe's bunkers. As Annie raced down the stairs, her first thought was the safety of the twins. She quickly roused South who was dozing with the twins.

"Wake up," Annie shouted as she gathered up the twins and carried them up to the cave with South trailing behind. Locking them in, Annie peered down the spit. The two men hadn't found the opening to the bunker and had begun to rummage the beach shacks. It wouldn't be long before the two gunmen would be kicking open Trisha's door. Annie didn't know if the two girls were there or had gone with Max and Matty to the mainland.

Annie crept past the boatshed. She could hear grunting and swearing as the men strained to get traction in the gravel. She found a groggy Ziggy propped up against his door, his face bloodied from a jagged pistol-whipped cut on the side of his face. Annie helped him into his shack and onto the bed.

"Who are they?" She lifted Ziggy's feet up onto the bed.

Ziggy put his hand to his forehead. "I need a joint," he said as he fumbled into his jacket pocket and shakily struck a match and inhaled, exhaled. Only then could he answer. "I don't know who they are. They look like drug guys. Dreadlocks and rotten teeth, bad breath. That's all I remember."

Rotten teeth and meth use confirmed Annie's fears. "They're probably hooked up with Trish's husband," she said.

"Well, they have guns," Ziggy exhaled.

"All right." Annie patted Ziggy's shoulder. "I'm going to go out and see what I can do."

Ziggy nodded. "Want a toke?" he offered. "You want me to go with you?"

"No, I'll have a better chance alone." Annie shut the door and heard Ziggy lock the deadbolt.

She could see the two men still scrambling two shacks away from Trish's when from around the corner came a three-legged terror who launched in full stride at the first gunman and took him to the ground. The man screamed for help and his buddy took a shot. Trooper slumped over, but his teeth still remained clamped on the man's leg.

"Shit! Where did this devil come from?" complained the man with the olive complexion and dreadlocks as he leaned over his partner.

"Damn, dude. This critter's teeth are locked in. He grabbed a kindling stick from outside Max's shack and pried open Trooper's mouth.

"Damn! That hurts." The wounded man rubbed his bloodied leg and gave Trooper a kick to the ribs. All of the air seemed to go out of the prone dog.

Annie stepped from behind Ziggy's shack, not more than twenty feet away from the two gunmen who whirled, guns drawn. "Don't shoot the bitch," the injured man shouted. "The boss won't like it."

As the men trained their pistols on Annie, she walked towards them.

The guns worried her, but she'd had guns pulled on her before with men far more desperate than these two. Bad skin, rotten teeth, and scraggly beards. *These guys are a walking disaster*, she thought. "What's wrong with you scruffies and where did you get those butt-ugly leather coats?"

"What?" The man rubbing his leg looked defensively down at the sleeve of his jacket.

"Men's Wearhouse, so what's your problem?" He sneered as he waved his gun barrel at Annie.

"We come to get the boss's kids," the other man vigorously scratched the top of his head, jiggling his dreadlocks. *Head lice or bed bugs*, Annie kept her guess to herself.

"Leave the kids alone." Annie wished Joe was in the bunker right now.

"We got orders, lady." The taller man walked toward Trish's cabin.

"I wouldn't open that if I were you," Annie threatened.

"Yeah?" the man sneered. "If I wuz you I'd keep my big mouth shut."

He opened the door toward him and a black-and-white whirling dervish cartwheeled out of the darkness and delivered a judo roundhouse kick that hit the man squarely on the chin, and while he tottered in a daze, Sister kicked him in the solar plexus and he began fluttering to the ground like a deflated balloon. Sister was mid-flight to delivering another blow when the last man standing fired a shot into the air.

"Yo, Karate Kid. Don't be pulling none of that flying grasshopper shit with me!"

"I ain't gonna shoot no nun unless you force me to, Sister." He pointed the gun at her. Sister stopped abruptly and crouched, looking for a second opportunity. The man helped his bloodied and wheezing accomplice up and they stared inside the door into the blackened interior.

"Any more surprises?" the doubled-up man gasped.

"I dunno, but I've had enough of this frigging Bruce Lee movie to last me a lifetime." His partner edged towards the door opening and tried to adjust his eyes to the darkness.

Tied to her wheelchair, Trish, her eyes darting, gave out a silent scream of terror, her vocal chords paralyzed the week before from the insidious disease. Behind Trish stood her two girls, staring out defiantly.

"All right, come out ladies," the man motioned with his pistol. "Your daddy is waiting for you back in town." The girls struggled and kicked at the men while Trish, helpless to defend her daughters, grunted obscenities. Even after their hands were tied together with zip ties, the girls still spit and swore as they were loaded aboard the yellow speedster and were whisked away to the eastern horizon toward Seattle. Annie tried to comfort Trish, but it was useless. Tears rolled down her cheeks as her worst fears had been realized and she was helpless to protect her children.

Sister Mary Catherine leaned over Trooper and found him still breathing. The bullet had just missed his spine and made a clean exit out the top of his back. Still revved with adrenaline, it wasn't long before he was up pacing on his three arthritic legs and snarling at the far shore. Resigned, Annie let Trish cry herself out while she and Sister cleaned Trooper's wound and plotted to get the girls back.

"I sure wish Joe had been here," Annie shook her head. "They wouldn't have been able to get off the boat."

"That's a fact," Sister agreed as she squeezed out a dollop of Neosporin and put it on Trooper's exit wound. "We're on our own. We've got to get the word out to the county sheriff and the Seattle police." Sister stared at the ground. "We're going to need some help," she said as she unconsciously lit a second Camel straight and stuffed it between her lips next to the first one from the moment before.

She looked at Annie with the two dangling from her lips and realized what she was doing. "What? Am I stressed, dude?" she said angrily as she stomped the first one out on the gravel.

Annie fired up *The Ark* and scooted into Port Gamble to alert John to get the police to put surveillance on the girls' father at the strip club, while Sister tried to calm Trish. With no leads in three days, the Seattle police booked the father, who gave his name as Noxxus "Nipper" Nixon III. They held Nipper for forty-eight hours in solitary, and then, with no evidence, had to let him go.

Trish was on a heavy dose of sedatives to prevent serial panic attacks and Annie bided her time, trying to keep Trish sleeping as much as possible, hoping for a break in the case. Max, on the other hand, was doing enough crying for them all. She wailed all day and night as she stayed with Trish.

The next day, Bunny Slattery came over from the mainland. Having only just received the news of the kidnapping, she was sputtering mad. "I'll castrate that son-of-a-bitch," she threatened. She wanted to immediately go over to the remaining car dealership that Nipper hadn't snorted up his nose. "I want to ambush that slime bucket," she fumed.

"We're just going to have to find the girls. John has two private detectives working on it and Pickles and Madeline have turned their oil change business over to a manager and are canvassing Seattle, looking for leads from the car dealership in the Fremont District. Madeline has lots of slimy contacts from her sex juice business," Annie explained to Bunny.

Lila came over by boat the next day to pick up some of the girls' clothes to do a "fact-finding séance." Spud, always interested in the occult, aliens and a self-described sucker for any conspiracy theory, wanted to sit in.

"No problem," Lila announced as she trundled up the path to Annie's with some of the girls' clothes, "but you have to be quiet," she threatened. "And Spud, you're in charge of bringing the watermelon. Make it seedless."

That evening, after sundown, Lila lit candles and placed them around the living room on shelves, tables and the piano. Then she placed red, green and clear crystals the size of small traffic cones in a triangle around the girls' clothes. Spud was directed to split a watermelon into two equal halves and place the halves on either side of the piles of clothes.

Annie had brought in extra chairs and there was comforting coffee and cobbler before the séance. When everyone was seated, Lila flowed into the room from offstage on tiptoe wearing only a see-through gown that caught her dowager figure in the moonlight. She offered up her hands to the moon and sat down cross-legged in front of the clothes in the center of the crystal vortex. The candles caught the crystal facets and the colored lights splashed across Lila's forehead. She mumbled and then her head bowed down and her rhythmic breathing was the only sound in the room. Within a few minutes, she began a free association of words that made no sense.

Dungeness crab…wind straw…salt water…personal pan pizza… chamber of horror…and then she slumped over onto the floor in slow motion.

"Not sure of the protocol," said Spud. He waited a deferential thirty seconds before he went over to assist Lila. She woke up from her trance in stages. Finally she lifted up her head and asked Spud to repeat her words as she wrote them down.

"I think we're on our way," she announced. "I do so love watermelon, so let's everyone have a slice."

"I thought the watermelon was part of the séance props," Spud said, biting into a crescent slice. "No silly," Lila laughed. "I just need to rehydrate after a reading."

As they ate, Lila explained that this was the first of three séances. "It takes a while for the crystals to pick up the vibrations of the past and I have other feelers out there," she said cryptically. "Tomorrow we will do it again. I need a day's rest. Since that escapade with Starbuck, my powers are terribly diluted."

The second day, Lila brought out a single crystal ball and had Spud bring a bowl of strawberries with stems. Under the moonlight she put a single piece of paper with Noxxus Nixon's name under the globe and a single candle on the window sill.

Again she slumped over and conjured these words from the spirit world: King Tut…Lexus…spit in the ocean…Gravel Gertie…Johnny Walker Black…

Spud revived Lila and began to eat the strawberries. When they were halfway to his mouth, Lila screamed out. "Don't eat the berries. You have to cast them out into the incoming tide and I will read them in the morning on the beach."

"You mean like tea leaves," Spud said quizzically.

"Exactly," Lila confirmed.

In the morning, Madeline was putting together a carafe medley of her seduce juice of the week when she heard over the police scanner that Nixon was thought to be on the Olympic peninsula near Port Angeles, near the Strait of Juan de Fuca. She immediately got ahold of Pickles and the island entourage headed north in the dump truck and several cars.

"He's driving a silver Lexus," Madeline confided.

A Lexus, Pickles thought. Maybe the séance will do some good after all.

All afternoon the islanders combed the roads for signs of the car, to no avail. That evening they all stopped for dinner at the Ajax Café in Hadlock. The Café had gotten mixed reviews over the years, but with its bevy of oddball hats available to the diners as well as an eclectic Pacific seafood / Home on the Range menu, Pickles thought it might pick up the defeated clan. A garlic cloud wrapped around the diners as they opened the door. The Café was packed and noisy as a trio featuring three-fingered Jack with two prosthetic fingers attempted to play a medley of Willie Nelson tunes.

Spud had the ribs coated with a Jack Daniels BBQ sauce. Annie had the blackened salmon with gazpacho and cilantro, one of her favorites. Spud and South shared the seafood plate and everyone else had the crab cakes, but although the food was delicious, there was a cloud of garlic doom over the table.

South was having one of her spells and kept eating the shells and throwing the meat back into the soup, which didn't hurt Spud's feelings as he sopped up the remaining clam-laden pesto nectar with a sourdough roll.

They returned to the island in defeat late at night, too tired to help Lila. Spud found three errant strawberries floating on the tide as he walked back to the cabin with South and ate them—stem and all—hoping it wouldn't affect the reading, but not willing to give up a floating treat.

In the morning, they all met at Annie's for a briefing. Bunny had written the latest séance words on a chalkboard: Light house… Boogie Woogie Bugle Boy…oxygen…hourglass…subterranean… Pepto Bismol. And below that list, the words from the days before.

"I don't see any correlation," Christine said, shaking her head.

"Well, I see a few words about crypts or the underground," Spud observed, holding his Styrofoam ice chest on his lap.

Lila was exasperated. "I know the answer's in there somewhere." She tried to connect King Tut, subterranean and chamber of horror together. "But, I'm not feeling it right now," she admitted.

"It's been over a week now," Max pleaded. "We have to come up with something. The girls are out there scared to death."

"Let's hit the road," Ziggy suggested. "Let's meet down at the boat in half an hour and keep looking."

Lila took her own car up to Sequim to make a house call on a bipolar llama that lived on a lavender farm. Since the Starbuck affair, she was especially tuned into mammals, but had lost all touch with Australian marsupials.

Halfway up to Sequim, the local radio station came on with a report that Nixon and a female companion had skidded off the road, were thrown out of a van, and both had died on impact when they hit a Burma Shave sign. The news spread rapidly and the islanders met at the field close to Lila's and asked the police if they could examine the back of the van.

"You can look, but don't touch," barked Sergeant Matthew O'Brien, a graduate of St. Francis the Divine parochial school, who automatically recoiled his fingers and then put his hands behind his back when he saw Sister get out of the car.

The forensic team was taking pictures of the trunk, removing soil and fiber samples, a diagram of an underground crypt, and depositing the evidence in plastic bags. In the back of the van were two shovels and a length of two-inch plastic pipe ten feet long. Nothing else.

The defeated island team was at a loss as they walked across the parking lot at the Oak Table Restaurant in Sequim for lunch. Spud looked up at the cloudy sky. "Think it's gonna rain?" he asked no one in particular.

"Not bloody likely," Pickles rejoined. "This place is in a rain shadow."

"Oh, yeah. I forgot," Spud nodded. No sooner had they taken a table when Lila breezed in.

"Ok. I think I have a breakthrough," she said excitedly, tipping over a glass of water. Sopping up the water with the tablecloth, Annie said, "Spill it."

"I went by the Sequim game farm and there was Rick the rhino grazing by the fence. So I stopped to check in with him," Lila continued.

"Rick has been getting cell phone calls on his horn. Kind of like people who can listen to radio signals that come through their fillings."

"Is there some info here?" Pickles was peeved because some of the spilled water had dripped onto his Capezio suede pumps and he knew they would be stained forever. He knew he should have scotch-guarded them when he brought them home from the Bainbridge Rotary auction and salvage sale.

"Rick said he eavesdropped on a call," Lila began, ignoring the attitude, "and a guy said he buried the kids on the Dungeness spit in a hole about four feet down. He said they have a breathing tube and water. Rick said that was two days ago and he had no way to get ahold of me. It was blind pig luck I ran into him."

"Who else knows about this?" Annie asked excitedly. "Have the police been notified?"

"I don't have a lot of credibility with them, so I made an anonymous call into the police and I think they'll act on it. I doubt they have any other leads."

Annie could already hear choppers in the air and there were volunteer groups organizing in the parking lot when they skidded into the gravel lot.

A Jefferson county sheriff came over to admonish them and was surprised when Annie told him that the children had been kidnapped from the island.

"Right in front of me," Annie proclaimed loudly.

"I was there too, officer," Sister chimed in, searching her soft pack for the last of her filter-tipped Camels. She found one, twisted off the filter, lit the rest with her Zippo lighter, tipped her head back and exhaled into the sea breeze.

"You can go out on the spit if you follow behind the search team," the officer informed the group. "But that dog can't go out there. He might compromise the scent for the K-9 units. He looks like he's stoved up anyway."

"He has to go. He's my service dog," Sister lied. "I'm allergic to peanuts."

"Whatever," the officer rolled his eyes. "Just stay back from the main group. There will be a hundred volunteers combing the spit towards the lighthouse.

"And look out that the tide doesn't come in on you," the sheriff repeated and then turned to a mountain rescue team that had just pulled up.

The island team walked down where the spit met the mainland and a weathered gray cedar sign provided a crude map and site statistics.

"Five and a half miles," Ziggy gasped. "I don't know if I can walk that far."

"Let's go," Annie waved the troupe forward down the trail.

Trooper's rear end collapsed twice and he moaned in pain as Ziggy and his wife Matty boosted the old dog onto his feet. "He'll be all right once he gets the scent and he's warmed up a little," Ziggy predicted, hoping he wouldn't have to carry the old bloodhound back up the trail.

"He's pretty strong for a critter with three legs." Matty patted Trooper on the head and scratched his rump.

The driftwood-littered gravel spit arched south with the lighthouse on the tip, a mere dot on the horizon. Lila stopped abruptly and raised her hands to the wind. "I'm getting a vibe," she announced.

Ziggy was glad for the respite and propped up his shovel against a driftwood log. He took the opportunity to pry open his lunch sack and dig into his liverwurst sandwich. Lila closed her eyes and turned her head toward the south wind. "I'm smelling…liverwurst?" She opened her eyes. "Ziggy, will you please get downwind?" Ziggy grumbled as he complied.

Lila went back to her rapture stance, legs spread, hands in the wind, and waited for a sign. "I'm getting shit," she admitted after five minutes. "We're on our own. Look for some kind of snorkel pipe sticking out of the ground. Be meticulous, the pipes are probably camouflaged," she warned.

The TV helicopters had caught wind of the search and were buzzing the spit that averaged less than a hundred yards wide at high tide. The beach on the sides of the spit broke sharply into the water and the driftwood was bunched into the center as if it were a five-mile-long game of pick-up sticks.

The island team trailed the rest of the searchers and the K-9 units by a good two hundred yards and were falling back rapidly. Poking and prodding the gravel and looking under logs for telltale signs of activity was slow work even as the whirring sound of the choppers disappeared down the beach.

"This is like walking on ball bearings," Spud complained as he plodded through the pea gravel. He looked back and saw that Trooper was game, but he was already falling behind.

"It doesn't make sense," Sister added. "I wonder why he didn't just dig them in alongside the road? It would have been easier."

"I suppose it's easier to cover your tracks out here on the beach 'cause the tide washes away your footprints and nobody can see the spit from the mainland with the park here." Matty tried to reason why anyone would go to all that trouble. "And why don't the other teams have K-9 dogs or something?"

The other teams were distant specks when Annie called a rest. She could see Trooper was having trouble breaching a two-foot-high log near the center of the spit. And then he disappeared. The old hound began to bugle, the call slicing into the hollow of a south wind.

"Let's go," Annie shouted. She started running and as she neared the site, she spotted a Raven sitting on a snag just above Trooper. The hound was howling and pawing at an old fishing net filled with seaweed that had washed ashore and snagged under a root ball near the middle of the spit.

Ziggy and Spud strained to pull away the heavy black nylon net to expose four white pvc pipes that would be a scant three inches above flood stage at high tide.

"Judas priest," Sister swore. "If the tide were any higher they would have drowned. We've got to get them out of there." She cleared the debris and gravel away from the pipe. "Hello," she called into the darkness of the pipe. She gagged as the smell of chloroform wafted from the tube. No answer.

Sister and Bunny began digging with their hands. Annie looked down the beach for help, but there was no one in sight. All the boats, helicopters and searchers were halfway down the spit and the cell phone the sheriff had given her had no service. "We're on our own as usual," she said, grabbing a shovel. "Let's go for it."

They began to dig frantically with shovels, horse clam shells and boards, following the pipes. The gravel kept creeping back in, but finally they unearthed the top of a flat black plastic box about four feet long. Ziggy wrestled one of the pipes off and called for quiet.

"I hear breathing," he said as he listened again. "They're still alive."

Ziggy took his pocket knife and slowly cut through the stiff plastic until he could curl up a corner and look in.

"It's Talisha," he said. "I didn't see her move. I think she's unconscious or in shock. There is no room down there. Her head and feet are touching the ends and the top is six inches away from her nose."

Spud, Lila and South had worked their way down to the top of the other chamber and pulled off the pipe. There was no sound of life and their fingernails were ripped and bleeding. Lila waited while Spud cut the top away.

Finally, the tops were pried off the two crypts and the girls lay as if they were two African princesses. Spud and Ziggy threw their coats over the girls to keep them warm while Sister shakily lit a cigarette, straddled a log, and stared out across the incoming tide.

Max got into the crypt and put her ear against Alisha's chest. "She's breathing. She's alive," Max cried out.

Finally, the rescue units came back. First the Boston Whaler convoy, then the helicopters, and finally the ground search units trudged back up the spit. The EMTs snapped facemasks on the girls and filled them with oxygen. The girls never regained consciousness as they were transported to Port Townsend General.

The island folk were being interviewed by the local TV news crews while big dual-axle trucks with satellite equipment were jockeying for position in the parking lot.

The years had taken their toll and Trooper had been getting by on his lip-reading skills so he probably didn't hear the beep, beep, beep warning sounds of the truck; tuckered out from the day's adventures, he was deep in puppy dreams when the dual-axel tires backed toward the curb. Annie heard one ear-splitting yelp and then silence.

She ran behind one of the trucks where Trooper had been sleeping. Hearing the bark, the truck driver had pulled forward, but Trooper's ribs were crushed and blood dripped from his mouth. Annie picked up his head and he licked her face once, then laid his head on her arm, closed his eyes, and died. The hero of the day—and one of the last links to Moby Dick that brought Seven Sisters island back from life support—was gone for all time. Trooper's once-powerful body had failed to warn him of danger.

Annie sobbed, burying her head into the mahogany neck of the great hound who never gave up and had endured his handicap with the grace of his species.

The newscasters that night showed photos of the arthritic raw-boned hound from earlier in the day. They said he was a hero, but they could never do justice to his heart. Dog owners, with memorials of flowers, chew toys, bones and bags of dog food poured into the parking lot where a picture of the hound graced the side of an old red fire hydrant. There was a Three Dog Night tribute band who played far into the night near the hydrant for a week and the local library sponsored a Heroic Dog series, reading books about famous dogs to preschoolers on a blanket under a dogwood tree.

For the locals, Trooper would be forever coupled with dog greats like Old Yeller, Good dog Carl, Lassie, Hemingway's Alaskan Buck, and a host of luminaries. Afterwards, his picture was hung near the library checkout desk with a bronze name tag and the newspaper article behind Plexiglas chronicling his exploits in saving the girls.

The local animal control office that cleared the lot each morning said that Trooper was the hound that kept on giving as she continued to pick up the dog food to take to the animal control center. "She's right about that," Annie agreed when Ziggy told her.

What little was left of Trish's withered body convulsed into spasms as she became dehydrated from all the stress and crying, so she had been on an IV drip most of the week. Atrophied muscles that had been betraying her for the last six months decided to have one last revenge and the pain was excruciating.

In a morphine haze, she couldn't even communicate by blinking her eyes and she had to be tied in a sitting position with an oxygen mask over her face. The girls were still dazed by their ordeal and their mother's latest setback in the long, slow slide to her death.

No one knew where normal was anymore, and so Max continued to come up with missions and take the girls into Port Townsend for lunch and to see a movie. Today they added Pickles' Second-hand Emporium to their travels. The good news was that, for a long time now, Pickles had had no clue where normal was anymore.

The small copper bell announced their entry as Max pushed open the shop door. The entire store was darkened except for the two projection screens on either side of the twenty-foot-wide shop. So loud, "your eyeballs wanted to bleed," Max told Annie later. One screen was showing *The Birth of a Nation* with roaring cannonades and rifle fire from the American Civil War sequence; the other screen was showing *The Sound of Music* with a ten-foot-tall Julie Andrews singing in a meadow.

As the girls plugged their ears with their hands and tried to adjust their eyes to the darkness to take in the flickering movies, Pickles exploded upward like a jack-in-the-box from the middle of a pyramid pile of Cheerio cereal boxes emblazoned with pictures of gymnast Mary Lou Retton.

Twirling an electrified baton and resplendent in a booty tight red, white and blue leotard, sporting a Dorothy Hamill wig and wearing pink marching boots with gold tassels, Pickles began to prance around the shop in a drum major strut while singing… "Do, a deer, a female deer…Re, a drop of golden sun, Mi, a name I call myself, Fa, a long long way to run…So, a needle pulling thread…" careening between the piles of salvaged gas masks, mismatched paratrooper boots, and the rest of his collective wares.

When Maria and Pickles finally finished the song, beads of sweat poured from under his wig and a wheezing Pickles supported himself against one of the burnished ten-inch-square structural posts that had held up the building's beams since the turn of the last century.

Pickles turned off his baton and invited them in for a "bit of tea." Pushing the kitchen door open with his baton, Pickles threw the wig on the seat of the Fifties chrome and cherry red vinyl dining chair, and began rifling through the fridge.

"A-ha," he cackled, "Virgin Mojitos." He muddled two quarts of lime juice, six sprigs of mint, two teaspoons of sugar, filled a pitcher with ice and then club soda, gave a quick stir, and presented a box of Costco mini cream puffs.

"Breakfast of Champions," Pickles crooned as he plunked brunch on the table, snagged a modesty-saving pink grass hula skirt from atop a plant stand, and shuffled off to put on water for tea.

Max served the mojitos while the girls listened to the movie soundtrack that trickled under the canvas separating the thin wall between retail sales and Pickles' personalized living space. They stared up at the turn-of-the-century tin ceiling, across which was strung in a spider web of translucent deep sea nylon fishing line, a portion of his collection of thousands of stiletto high heels that seemed to literally float in air.

Talisha had begun to count just the green shoes, and was up to five hundred sixty-two when Pickles marched back into the room holding a silver tea service high above his head, the pink hula skirt swishing against his knees.

"There," he announced as he poured the Earl Grey tea and passed out the mojitos, eased back on the legs on his chair, put his hands behind his head, and smugly surveyed his shoe collection.

He pointed at the shoes. "Mercer Island, Mercer Island, Aberdeen, Bellingham, Tukwila," as he named the places where he had found the shoes in garage sales and lately on craigslist.

"Do you know where all those shoes come from?" Alisha asked admiringly.

"Of course I do," he replied. Pickles pointed to a pair of seven-inch heel leopard pumps near the center of the room.

"Those right there are one of your mom's," he announced. "Frankly, I don't know how she walked in those babies." Pickles shook his head. "It seems like you could break your neck if you fell over. You've got some big shoes to fill when you follow in your mother's footsteps," Pickles mused through half-closed eyes as he thoughtfully licked the filling from the cream puff halves. "Uh-huh," Talisha said glumly.

Pickles sensed his mistake and shifted gears. "So how is the pregnancy coming, Max?"

"What makes you think I'm pregnant?" Max said defensively.

"Lila predicted it a long time ago and since when do you wear aprons all the time?"

The girls set down their teacups and directed their gaze at Max, waiting for her reply.

"All right then. I give. I'm preggers," Max admitted, as her hands reached for the tiny round pot belly, barely protruding between the apron pockets.

"Wow," Talisha and Alisha said in unison as they leaned over to examine the bulge. "I guess the cat's out of the bag now," Max said with resignation. "I kinda wanted to keep it a secret until after the adoption proceedings, Pickles," Max said with a grimace.

"Oops!" Pickles rolled his eyes in apology. "Nobody told me it was on the QT. How many months?"

"Six months plus a little," Max admitted. "Turns out I'm a fertile Myrtle. After all these years, who knew?"

"So, what is it gonna be?" Talisha took ownership. "A boy or a girl?"

"Don't even want to know," Max said, taking a sip of tea.

"So when is it going to be born?" Alisha asked, patting Max's stomach.

"September sometime. I just hope I hatch before the pumpkin weigh-in in Portland. I'm supposed to be the Great Pumpkin Goddess this year," Max said. "I just thought with all the drama on the island everyone just needed to take a breather," she continued.

Pickles poured himself another cup of tea. "Remember, the Pickles sees all and knows all." He smugly gave in to his OCD and counted out four sugar cubes, dropping them exactly six inches above the cup like miniature depth charges.

"Girls, drink up," Max said. "We need to get home to your mother. She'll be worried and we need to water the pumpkins and feed them their liquid growth hormones."

Annie saw Max and the girls glide *The Ark* into the boatshed that evening and hailed them to come up for dessert. She scooped out steaming mounds of apple cobbler topped with roasted oats and brown sugar topping into thick-lipped bowls that Colby had thrown on his foot-powered potters' wheel in a back room of the orca watch station on Whidbey Island. As the girls and Max finished their cobbler, they peered inside to see a replica of Starbuck molded into the bottom as a surprise. Annie cackled as she waited for the girls' discovery. "So, what's Pickles up to these days?"

"Oh, the usual," Max replied as she sucked her spoon clean.

"He was dressed up like a drum major in drag," snorted Talisha.

"Yeah, but his baton was cool, especially in the dark, It was like it was on fire." Alisha stuck her tongue out at her sister.

Talisha took a roundhouse swing at her sister, but she ducked and came up with her tongue wagging in defiance.

"I'm not surprised." Annie countered the sisterly feud by hugging Talisha around her shoulders to prevent any more retaliation.

Chapter
TWENTY-NINE

nnie pulled her pillowed Morris chair over to the stove, pulled
down the oven door, kicked off her shoes, and put her stocking feet in the stove. She yawned, stretched her arms above her head, leaned back luxuriously, and let down her guard. Too early, the dust bunnies of remorse snuck out of the pockets of her apron and the suppressed mourning surrounded Annie like fog on a lighthouse.

She had never fully grieved over the death of her daughter Calypso, her granddaughter and her husband in that fluke airplane crash that left the twins behind, robbing them and the island of an enduring legacy. Like a soft Northwest spring rain, the tears cascaded down her cheeks until Twigs rolled out from under the stove, shifted his arthritic bones into motion, shuffled over to Annie, and pressed his sympathetic nose onto her leg. Eventually, even the rain clouds in the Evergreen State that feed the spring rains have to stop and Annie drifted into a restless slumber.

The last thing she remembered thinking was, "Oh, great! All I need now is a visit from my sisters." And then she fell into a deep sleep.

"Annie, wake up!" a voice called into Annie's REM. "Wake up!"

In her haze, Annie called out, "I don't want to deal with family right now. I'm all worn out."

The voice persisted and shook Annie by the shoulder.

Spud danced back as Annie took a swing at the voice in the darkness.

Taking no offense, Spud stirred the stove fire with kindling, fed in a smooth-barked madrona log, then closed the fire door with a clank.

Annie reluctantly opened one eye. "What?" she demanded.

"Annie, it's Spud. I want you to know that South and I may be leaving the island abruptly."

"Abruptly?" Annie looked puzzled.

"Abruptly," Spud repeated. "Things are getting too hot. Conspiracy groups are after the leaked evidence I've gathered on politicians and dictators. Information that could change the course of nations and then there are the aliens, of course."

"Aliens." Annie grimaced.

"Sure." Spud looked incredulous that Annie would question alien existence. "What do you think Hawking and I have been talking about? We have the coordinates of the radial power thrusts from the earth's core, the most recent alien transmissions from space, and our experiments on cold fusion as a cheap, inexhaustible power source. I want you to know if we suddenly disappear, it's for the best," Spud concluded.

"Uh-huh, will do," Annie nodded as Spud slipped out the door and Annie went back to sleep with the new warmth radiating on her feet from the stove and mumbling about aliens.

Days later, Annie's morning was filled with the twins' breakfast and Zack's projectile vomit episode. It wasn't until Annie wrestled

Zack into his new overalls and found the only dress that Little Annie would wear without crying that Annie thought about Professor Spud's diatribe.

"Professor Spud with the candelabra in the loony bin," Annie mumbled to herself. She was still grumbling when Ziggy and Matty came up the path with a basket of fresh-baked bran muffins.

"What's in there?" Annie pressed her lips suspiciously.

"Just bran and a little of the magic weed," Ziggy said proudly.

Annie hesitated. *Whatever,* she thought. *With the morning I've had I deserve a break today.* She washed down three muffins with coffee and set out in search of Spud and South. Annie stopped at their cabin and flung wide the half-open door. Everything was scattered around the room, drawers were pulled out and pancake flour dusted the top of the heaps of clothing like an early fall snow in the Olympic Mountains.

Annie was scared. She searched the rest of the cabins down the spit. She found Trish sitting in the dark, sleeping, and episodic snoring at Sister's cabin where a half-empty bottle of Wild Turkey was used to prop open the door.

Annie walked towards the end of the spit where the sandy beach disappeared into the water. She found two sets of footprints walking down the beach. Twenty feet from the incoming tide, Annie found two sets of shoes and the clothes South and Spud usually wore in two neat, crumpled piles as if the two souls had been sucked up into the heavens. Ten feet away, floating in a tide pool was the Styrofoam ice chest that Spud never allowed to leave his hands. The top was missing and the chest empty.

Annie looked for other footprints, but the beach was clean. No one had been close to them when they disappeared and they wouldn't have walked out into the surf without leaving prints.

Annie bolted for the house and breathlessly collapsed on the bedroom floor. The wooden fir planks looked just as she had left them; a sprinkling of dust glowed in the late summer sun. She pried up the boards with a butter knife she kept in the bureau and peered inside the cavity. Completely empty except for an envelope. She lay back on her bed, gave a deep sigh, and put her pillow over her head. Then she opened the envelope.

> *Annie,*
> *Just to let you know, South and I have had to be relocated for safety reasons. Don't worry about us. We'll be fine. It would be best to say we had a suicide pact and just disappeared. Sorry to turn into such drama queens, but it's for the best. Thanks for the hospitality.*
> *Spud and South*

What bothered Annie was that she had no way of knowing if the couple had left of their own accord. What if they were hijacked? She thought about it all afternoon until it came to mind that if South had time to take her candlesticks then she would know they were all right. South would never leave without her birthday gift. Not after opening them hundreds of times.

Annie opened the door to their cabin. *What a mess! I gotta clean this up,* she thought. She walked over to the table next to the window. She could have written her name in the dust, but there were two clean spots where the crystal candle holders always sat. Annie let out a sigh. Now she was sure they were probably safe. She just had to convince the rest of the island.

She had an emergency number that Spud had given her to get ahold of Stephen Hawking. That would be her first move when she got to Port Gamble. Maybe he knew what was going on.

Garnet, at Mom's Diner, was going in for her final radiation treatment this weekend, so she asked John Hunt to stop by for a consult.

"It don't look good for me," she confided to John, adjusting her bandana. "Do you want to give it another try with a guest chef at the diner?"

John's face turned red. He had failed with Tex-Mex and the Hicky Chick, but he didn't want to even think about *that* experience!

"Oh, my god, you're blushing," Garnet declared. "I haven't seen a man your age blush for fifty years at least."

John shook his head. "I, I...don't know what to say. I haven't found a cuisine or a chef that the locals didn't want to ride out on a rail. But," he brightened, "I'd like to try again. Let's go Italiano."

"Works for me," Mom said, twirling her hands above her head in whirlwind gestures as they let the diner screen door slam behind them.

"John, you know where the key is," Garnet continued, and then her voice faded as she pulled shut the driver's door on her ancient Plymouth Savoy with the gigantic fins, and spun out of the parking lot.

John knew he had gotten bad reviews when he turned the diner over to the battling Soldano brothers and their Tex-Mex offering, and the Hicky Chick fiasco. This time he was going to go with a cutting edge, three-star Italian restaurant, Salute, run by the two Ferrari sisters named after the cities where they were conceived. Roma and Sicily. John wondered if put into a battle royale, which group would triumph. He guessed the Ferrari sisters.

Roma cooked in the style of central Calabria, a hot arid land on the vamp of the Italian boot filled with rugged coastlines and sandy beaches, while Sicily was all about Tuscany, sculpted rolling hills, vineyards of green grape rows marching up the hills, moss-covered castles and villas parked on the eastern shore of central Italy.

The two women used a mantra of "Go Big or Go Home" and their signature dishes were always hot and spicy.

The takeover would feature Roma on Saturday, with her freshly ground forty-pound loaf of nduja, a closely guarded family secret, described as flaming liquid salami sprung from the loins of the Roman gladiators, the love child of fiery pepperoni and French rillettes. A blend of fat, pork brains, lungs and tripe coupled with hot chilies, run through a grinder three times, and then aging the paste in a natural casing for several weeks.

The beauty of the spreadable, dragon breath, ruddy paste, sometimes called "spicy pork butter and chili, was its versatility. It could be spread on eggs, pasta, bread, pizza or cardboard, and had a visceral Italian following from San Francisco to Vancouver, British Columbia.

Sunday would feature Sicily and a two-hundred-pound wild boar she had personally tracked and killed on a Texas free range game ranch. It had been a huge male boar with testicles the size of grapefruits. Sicily had packed the entire carcass hair, guts and balls in ice and had it express shipped to Seattle just for the weekend event.

John had been priming the event for weeks in his Seattle column and had hired a Tony Bennett tribute band to provide nonstop music, and two local wineries from Sequim were primed to tap their new casks.

For twenty miles in either direction, the sides of the roads were festooned with horizontally striped orange, white and green Italian flags hanging from barbed wire fences and overpasses that led down the winding coastal country lanes leading to Mom's.

Saturday dawned with a March frost that nipped, but did no harm to the daffodils and primroses that had dared to greet the Northwest spring as John shivered from his perch on a road overpass. He heard the sounds long before he saw the cars round the corner that skirted the Egg and I road and turned into the Chimacum valley.

A Crayola box of toy colors marked the passage of Fiats, Lancia, Alfa Romeo, and car clubs of Ferraris and Lamborghini, the cacophony of their distinctive sharp chirping horns announcing their arrival, disrupting the morning quiet and overwhelming the placid black and white Holstein cows that stampeded into the maple forest lining the foothills. They hid behind the tree trunks and peered out behind the leaves with their caramel brown eyes.

The gravel parking lot was full and the diner was like an overstuffed manicotti as the wine flowed and the band played on. Only then did Roma, with a flourish worthy of the shroud of Turin, lift a towel and unveil the forty-pound loaf of nduja and its mega chili power.

There was a unified gasp as the scent saturated the air and stung the senses. Old men and women wept at the sight and the anticipation of the impending eating orgy, their eyes instantly red and stinging as the pleasure/pain of the Italian emotions conjured up sensory feelings and aromas of the Old Country. Of immigrants leaving their homeland and patiently standing in lines beneath the Statue of Liberty on Ellis Island with their past in their suitcases and their hearts beating to a future of a new country, a new beginning.

The nduja loaf signaled a rite of passage that had been passed down from generations of immigrants and the mood intensified as the tribute band swung into the Italian national anthem. The diner crowd swayed and sang with one voice and at the end someone yelled, "Concrete's here!" and the diner rocked with laughter at the old Italian joke when immigrants were all connected to the plaster and masonry industry.

"Mamma mia," Roma spouted as she stabbed a wooden spoon into the nduja loaf and slathered the paste on pizzas, egg dishes, soups and slabs of fresh-baked whole grain bread for lunch. Later would come the pastas.

"How do you pronounce it anyway?" John patted the loaf with his hand as if it was an old friend.

"En-doo-ya," Roma mouthed the word slowly. "It will maka-you-sweata—lika the-swine"; she crossed her Catholic heart with a spatula.

John had only read about the legend of nduja, making the best food from the poorest ingredients, and as he bit into the toast, he closed his eyes and savored the bite.

"It's rather like Spam," he observed, opening his eyes only a little, and then it hit him. It felt like the top of his head was coming off. The internal heat sent powerful convulsions through his system and puckered his sphincters. He opened his mouth to scream, but no sound came out. The vocal chords had spasmed shut.

John swooned, and there was a single moment of clarity, a primitive enlightenment connecting to other-worldly hallucinations found only in the deep in the Amazonian rain forest.

And then it was a transcending force from the Old World, the marching of the Roman Empire and further back into the Middle Ages when wooden ships and courageous sailors set out to explore the New World. It was Freud, Einstein and Lady GaGa in a forty-pound loaf.

John grasped a partially drained pint of beer and chugged the liquid in a single gulp and lowered his head to rest on the Formica counter.

"Oo la la, oo la la, oo la la. O bloody obloodah life goes on…" he slipped into the old Beatles tune that he kept chanting for the next twenty minutes as his fluids drained uncontrollably. It was a pleasure–pain epiphany. This was a food it would take a lifetime for his body to adjust to the heat and he had taken a man-sized bite of the forbidden fruit from the tree of knowledge and nothing would ever be the same.

He slid his head off the counter, swiped a cloth napkin across his beaded forehead, and wiped his reddened eyes. He thought sure he must be bleeding somewhere. "Probably internally," he mumbled to himself.

The Italian party rambled on into the night. They began a pickup game of soccer in the nearby cow pasture, close to a hundred revelers to a side, and using the headlights of two Ferraris and two Lamborghinis as goal posts. No local could find a seat in Mom's Diner that Saturday, but one of the high school cross country runners, Cisco Morris, happened by and scored ten goals. Blessed virgin, by four in the morning the game was over. Ferrari 324, Lamborghini 285.

Before the soccer game started, Sicily was already preparing the boar, but not before she set up the DVD of her Texas boar hunt on the 72-inch flat screen television that would play the loop continually for the next twenty-four hours. Like a drive-in movie, the light from the screen bounced off the branches of the just-awakened maple trees that bowed over the fire pit and flickered on the bloody boar head with its enormous tusks that had been jammed on a stake near the screen.

The documentary video loop began.

Sicily boarding a Boeing 737 at SeaTac airport, but not before she had wedged herself into her brand-new Cabela's skin-tight camouflaged overalls and—with help—slithered into a new pair of snakeproof 18-inch leather boots with Vibram soles.

The camera followed her as she clomped down the aisle of the plane and wiggled into the middle seat between a black hip hop artist on the aisle and a geeky Harry Potter kid at the window. She promptly pulled her camo sleeping mask over her eyes and began to snore.

Sicily snored all four hours to Dallas. She woke up alone with her two arms straddling the empty seats. She was met at the airport by a rawboned cowboy—dusty boots, spurs, a cheroot dangling from his mouth, and wearing a low-slung black hat and a frayed manure-brown serape with blue fringe. By name, Tex. No surprise there. He had obviously seen way too many Clint Eastwood movies. He did a lot of squinting and grunting, but he managed to find his Ford pickup truck and ushered Sicily and her cameraman to the El Rancho game preserve whose motto was: "We guarantee the critter of your choice 150% of the time."

The first day, Sicily and her guide spotted two herds of hogs, but they both spooked and the day's footage ended with Sicily sticking her tongue out at the camera lens.

The second day, stalking down an arroyo, Sicily spotted a huge boar rooting deep in the underbrush under a cottonwood tree. A good three hundred pounds of cranky, it had descended from the first hogs that had escaped from the early Spanish explorers and had prospered over the years with no real enemies on the Texas plains except farmers protecting their crops. They grew big and they grew mean.

Steadying her rifle against a scrub gum tree, Sicily fired a single shot and the hog dropped over on his side as pretty as a picture—as if Jimmy Dean himself had become a hog whisperer. The remaining herd squealed and scattered down the dry graveled gulch.

Tex drew his revolver from under his serape and carefully stalked his way around the cottonwood trees where the hog lay with his beady red eyes open to the blue Texan sky. The yellow tusks were four inches long and still had dirt clinging to the gums.

Tex grunted three times and grimaced twice—no matter how many times Sicily had watched the video, this seemed to be the harbinger of disaster. He rubbed a mesquite branch across the hog's eyes and there was no reaction.

Tex curled his lip and then pulled out a camera and motioned for Sicily to come sit astride the beast.

No sooner had she sat on the boar than the hog jumped up and made straight for Tex, who jumped aside and began running bowlegged down the dry creek bed with the huge animal in pursuit. As he scrambled into the fork of a tree, Tex screamed as the boar gored him in the leg. He looked down at the enemy, bloody foam dripping from its mouth and looking to resume the battle.

The boar, now satisfied he had controlled Tex, pivoted and decided to take vengeance on Sicily. The dust trailed the boar's stubby legs as he galloped across the dry creek bed. Sicily dropped to her knee and fired three shots into the charging beast, and still he came. She closed her eyes and took one more prayer shot and the boar skidded to a dead stop and lay his nose on her new leather snakeproof boots, breathing a final gasp that ruffled the bow on her leather shoelace.

There were trails of blood up and down the creek bed and Sicily was spattered everywhere as she started to go into shock. She sang a chorus of "O Canada" and two verses of "Dixie." Songs she had never sung before as Tex, who had made his way down from his tree perch, poured water from his canteen onto his bandana and cleaned the blood from Sicily's face and hair while she sang. He grunted at least twenty times and snarled repeatedly during the process.

All of this the videographer captured for the big pig roast.

At the time, Sicily didn't understand, but after she had been back in Seattle with the hog for a week, Tex sent a bouquet of the Texas state flower, the bluebonnet, and an original Tex love sonnet. Apparently he was in love.

Not so for Sicily. Twice married before to Mr. Wrong and Mr. More Wrong, she shuddered, grunted, and kept her vow to follow her cooking muse and her allegiance to her twelve-amp, industrial, hand-held kitchen pulsating appliance—the lifetime-guaranteed chopper, mincer, grinder, beater with the thirty-two quick change tools. One for her every mood and desire.

The boar had been scraped and cleaned and sliced chin to brisket and a thick split pole skewered the carcass. For three days it had marinated in a Toys 'R' Us wading pool filled with six cases of Trader Joe's Four Buck Chuck and six racks of Bud Light and now it was show time as the briquettes glowed and the alder logs smoked.

With the guest of honor's legs pointing toward hog heaven, Sicily began to lob her ingredients into the cavity of the dressed two hundred-pounder. She carefully distributed ten pounds of diced Walla Walla sweet onions; eight pounds of sliced Honey Crisp apples; five pounds of wild rice; two gallons of cheap port wine; a gallon of Hurricane Ridge heather honey; two fistfuls each of tarragon, marjoram, salt and pepper; five pounds of brown sugar; four pounds of pitted prunes; sixteen ounces of cinnamon; a half rack of Rainier beer; and then sewed the long gaping opening with the skill of a surgeon, using nylon cord and a six-inch curved needle. Under the tail of the hog, she screwed in her signature meat thermometer, a wooden bung that would explode against the hanging garbage can lid. When the gong sounded, the feast would begin.

Two loggers meanwhile had become entranced by the video credits showing Sicily stripped naked to the waist, singing "O Canada" while Tex finger-painted her breasts with hog blood in a ritualistic celebration of killing her first boar.

"Hey, you two. Yeah, you with the suspenders," Sicily bellowed. "Grab this pole and hang this hog over the fire for me. I still have a half rack of Rainier in pay."

The men obliged, then snapped the tab on their beers and continued to watch the pig hunt credits, continually, until near midnight.

The pig snapped, stewed and sizzled through the darkness and into the early morning as the crowd of locals gathered for breakfast, but Mom's Diner remained closed. There would only be one feast this day. Grumbling to each other, the locals shuffled over to the mini mart and gorged on pink Hostess Sno Balls and Ho Ho's, washed down with convivial good-natured bitching about how the diner was ignoring their culinary needs and local politics.

By afternoon, the boar had developed a nicely blackened crust and Sicily continued to thrust her two-foot-long meat thermometer into its rump with the precision of a matador. Evaluating the results with a shake of her head, she stretched out on her brown La-Z-Boy, but not before she ladled a mug of the marinade into a cup and ruminated near the fire, occasionally reaching over the side of the chair and stirring a forty-gallon cauldron of beans and fixins' with a wooden canoe paddle.

"How's it going in there?" Sicily yelled into the kitchen where Roma was slaving over the last giant tub of coleslaw that sat between the trays of cornbread ready to be baked.

Roma brushed back a flailing hank of her Mediterranean black hair that had fallen over her face and snarled back, "Just busting my chops in here, sweetie. And you?"

The older sibling by two years, Sicily—fifty years later still enjoying the entitlement of the first child—was nonplussed. "Oh, working hard too," she smiled at the kitchen door opening. "Let me know if you need help in there."

"Like that's going to happen," Roma grunted just out of Sicily's hearing.

By late afternoon, the expensive Italian sports cars flotilla had begun showing up and two scenic tour buses had trooped in and were paying homage by the fire.

Money was collected by the honor system in a barrel near the video and occasionally Sicily would take the paddle, still dripping with beans, and tamp the bills flat. The marinade level in the wading pool was dropping fast by the time the wooden bung was launched with a resounding gong that dented the steel garbage can lid, while steam rolled out of the orifice like a steam engine.

Time to feast.

Four men wrestled the boar onto a wooden picnic table, and with little ceremony Sicily began to slice giant steaming slabs off the beast with her cordless Sawzall and nestled the offerings onto large stainless platters.

Mounds of creamy coleslaw, artisan loaves of olive bread, and the savory chili-laden beans, soothed the appreciative crowd that sat around the rekindled fire in a village picnic style as a gypsy band began to play.

The locals, missing their signature blueberry pancakes and intimidated by the strong ethnic flavor of the weekend extravaganza, watched from the roadside and then wandered home as the sun began to set over the Olympic Mountains.

The wine flowed and the rib bones of the wild boar began to appear as the great mounds of flesh began to disappear and the music became wilder with the heavy harmonic throb of the mandolins. From out of nowhere a raven-haired gypsy princess with a gossamer trail of scarves tied to her bare arms danced around the fire as if driven mad by the flames. She danced ever nearer until sometimes the scarves caught fire and trailed her into the thick black night, but she whirled too fast and the flames became a smoke trail.

The crowd cheered and chanted and a roar erupted as two other women emerged from the audience, overcome by the music. Raffia-wrapped casks of sambuca were swigged by the crowd as the fire grew ever higher and the air smelled of anise. Hundreds of white linen sheets were thrown in piles on the ground and someone yelled out "toga party" and soon clothes were shucked and the crowd began to surround the fire in circles as if driven by a primordial force, while the gypsy band began to play a Tarantella. The circles moved slowly and then ever faster in opposite directions around the fire, driven by the scantily clad gypsy princesses.

It was at this moment that Tex made his move, dashing from just outside the reach of the flickering firelight.

"Ye-haw!"...he gave his mating call as he rushed over to claim his prize.

All Sicily saw when she turned around was a blur of leather chaps, ten gallon hat, jingling spurs, satin shirt, and cowboy boots. As he drew closer on a dead run, she picked up the bean paddle and gave him a well-aimed smack to the forehead as he put out his outstretched arms. She hit him three more times in succession as the blood spurted from his forehead, but it seemed to only encourage him as he circled his prize.

The torrid music, the heat from the fire, and the blood spurting from Tex's forehead somehow aroused Sicily and she allowed Tex to throw her over his shoulder and sprint into the darkness where the two rolled around the brush in a Confederate mating ritual that ended with Sicily mounted Texas-style, tethered by leather thongs and a riding bit between her teeth.

When Tex finished and lay his head back in an Alamo war cry of victory, Sicily laid him out for the last time with a smart smack to the head with the bean paddle. Tex keeled over like a sack of Yukon gold potatoes and lay comatose on the ground as Sicily cut herself loose with one of his spurs. Then she tied him spread-eagled between four trees and had him twice herself before she brushed the leaves from her hair and went back to the party.

By the time Sicily had pushed her way back through the woods and crossed the field-littered bottles and stray clothing, the Clallam County sheriff's posse had put an end to the toga party. The buses were gone and a rutted field of tire tracks was the only evidence of the expensive imported Italian sports cars. The paddy wagon was filled with loud and boisterous revelers bound in tattered sheets and still in party mode.

Roma had been cuffed and was cursing a blue streak through her gag as Sicily entered the field. The posse had helped themselves to large platters of boar brisket and beans and had moved out of spitting distance from Roma, who had been chained to a tree stump.

"Good grits, mama," a tall, anorexic sheriff, with a ripped pocket on his shirt and scratches on his face, warbled as he shoveled in another forkful of beans. "This your shindig?"

"My sister and I are the guest chefs, but the party got a little out of hand," Sicily admitted... "It's kinda like that. Things just got a little crazy, I guess."

"Well, we will just make a little report and haul these good people in the wagon off to the hoosegow."

"I don't suppose Mom is going to be anything less than pissed with all this mess," a bulky sergeant, with bite marks on his arms, barked as he rested his hand on his pistol for emphasis.

"My sister and I will clean everything up if you release her and then we'll be back on the road to Seattle. I promise," Sicily said contritely.

"If it's all the same to you, mama, I think I'll leave the key for the cuffs with you and you can release your sister. We don't want any trouble. It took five of us just to cuff her."

Sicily nodded as he handed her the keys.

The five men turned, two limping badly, and started towards their prowl cars when the sergeant turned to Sicily. "Do you gals hear someone singing 'The Yellow Rose of Texas' out there in the woods?"

Sicily listened to Tex, singing at the top of his lungs, swing into the second verse. "No, I don't hear anything," she confessed. "It's probably just freeway noise or something."

"Probably," the sheriff decided. "You take care now, mama."

Sicily took several hours to clean up the field, loaded all the pots and pans into the trunk of her Buick, and then unchained her sister.

Sicily tossed the keys to Roma's Alfa Romeo into some tall grass, and ran for her car. She figured by the time Roma found her car keys, she would be halfway back to Seattle. Not back to her apartment—she would have to lay low for a week or so.

Sicily stopped where Tex had parked his Cadillac Escalade. She listened. Tex had morphed into the Willie Nelson tune, "Of All the Girls I've Loved Before." She flattened each Escalade tire with a ten-inch chef's knife. She hoped Tex would get the message.

John received a call from the sheriff and had sworn all the way to the diner. He'd failed again to find a good match to keep Mom's legacy alive. When he reached the diner the parking lot was empty and the pasture grass was ruffled. The barbecue pit was still smoldering. He kicked at the fire and swore he heard singing. He stepped towards the edge of the woods and he distinctly heard … "a tall shanghai rooster and a one-spotted hog." He pushed his way to a clearing and found Tex, happily strung between four trees and naked as a jaybird. With Tex still singing, John cut him loose with his pocket knife, and Tex gathered up his clothes and wandered deeper into the forest singing "I been workin' on the railroad all the live long day."

John shook his head and tickled a piece of pork from the bony hog carcass on the picnic table. "Pretty good," he decided, reaching for a toothpick.

Chapter
THIRTY

Today the message would be different.

Max and Annie sat on a bench near the wall. Trish sat in the shadows of the cabin out of the direct light that hurt her eyes. The wheelchair arms supported her limbs and a Velcro strap held her torso erect. Her chin was propped up on a chrome saddle attached to an arm rest and the whishing sound of the solar-powered air pump led to a c pap in her nose.

Tears continually rolled down her fashion-model mahogany cheekbones and even as her limbs had atrophied and bedsores flared overnight, anyone looking closely could see she once had been beautiful and that the snap in her caramel-colored eyes led to a brain that was still alive and determined to control this last communion with her children. Trish had determined that this reprieve—this gift, this small window—would be her last chance to go out with dignity. She would not be muted.

The two girls sat in chairs in front of her and each held their mother's hands as Annie read the testament that Trish had dictated months before when she could still speak.

I want my girls to grow to be strong, independent and courageous women. It is your responsibility to be adventurers and to embrace the future. The worst remorse in life is having challenges that were ignored. There are no limitations in your life except those you put on yourself. Love with all your heart and grasp each moment of each day, for time is promised to no one. I loved you every day of my life and that will not change in my death.

Love transcends all things. It is your strength. Do you remember the story of the Velveteen Rabbit? *"You're only real when a child really loves you for a long time."*

You girls and your love have made me real. And I will live for all time as long as your love is passed along.

Trooper found you girls for a reason. He overcame great physical pain to bring you back to me. You have a destiny.

Remember that the door between mother and daughter will always be open and I will be checking in with you from time to time. You'll know when I'm around. I'll always be watching over you.

Atticus Finch in To Kill a Mockingbird *said that courage is "when you know you're licked before you begin but you begin anyway and see it through no matter what."*

And now I will have to leave you while my mind is clear and my heart is strong. Be sad, but continue your life journey and never forget.

I have shown you courage and now I will show you grace and dignity. I chose to go out on my own terms. Look into my eyes and remember I will always love you.

Annie cried softly as she detached the breathing pump and watched as Trish smiled at her children and took one last deep breath. Annie watched as her eyes turned from sparkle to dull. Trish closed her eyes and she was gone.

There was a long collective wail from the cabin as the women sat by the fire next to Trish until morning light. Max tucked the girls into bed at Annie's while Pickles and John wrapped Trish in Annie's sister's quilt and drove to Tacoma to the cold storage plant where she was flash frozen, waiting the communal burial for the island warriors.

Chapter
THIRTY-ONE

At first, Sister Mary Catherine had prayed incessantly over the gold and piles of hundred dollar bills that Joe had left on the pallets in the second bunker, but as yet there was no word from her usual source. She began to get night sweats, lost weight and finally decided to take matters into her own hands. She'd done some rough calculations and figured there was between forty to fifty million dollars, depending on the price of gold.

Sister had no use for money, but she knew the money could be a game changer in the right hands. She had taken Annie into her confidence and they decided to put the money behind Annie's house in caves that had been used as cold storage. The two women had wrestled the bars of gold shaped like Hershey Bars and stamped with the seal of the Bank of Iraq along with the stacks of Benjamin bills into Ziploc storage bags which they tucked into backpacks.

For a solid month they made the trek—sometimes twice a day—and to make the tedious job less stressful, Sister unconsciously began to hum "Whistle While You Work" incessantly, even in her dreams, until she thought she was going to go mad, but finally the deed was done.

Pulling a brown tarp over the stash, Annie shook her head. "I don't know what you're going to do with this stuff, but there's no reason to give the money to the government. They'd just waste it again."

"And what do you mean *me*? I'm not taking responsibility for all this loot. You're in this just as much as I am, sister," Sister Mary said pointing her finger at Annie.

Annie laughed. "My grandmother always said the gold was in the apples. She'd be surprised to find the gold in the cave."

Sister Mary crossed herself, "Amen to that, sister!"

Annie put a note in her bank deposit box explaining where the money came from, and then she went back to the house where she and Sister nursed a fifth of Wild Turkey for two days and slept until they were their old selves again. The Snow White Disney tune never entered their heads again.

Chapter
THIRTY-TWO

The island had been going in so many directions through the summer that Annie decided to call an island potluck and get everyone together. With a week's notice, she hoped that everyone could attend. She knew that this fall there were going to be funerals and a wedding and felt more planning was in order.

On the day of the meeting, Christine came over early to cultivate her dad's pumpkins. True to their breeding, the still-growing pumpkins were all well-hung, although none reached the mammoth size of the granddaddy of the year before. Christine constantly received pictures over the Internet of pumpkin groupies that were having much greater success. Pumpkins up to seven hundred pounds with the distinctive shape were common and she was vying with two seed companies that wanted exclusive rights to the new "Moby Pumpkin."

Playboy was also in the early stages of running a photo shoot on "Anatomic vegetables in America," and the early edits were disturbing on many levels.

Christine gave a deep sigh as she looked over the garden and turned up the volume on the tape player so the Supertramp could work its magic on the ample vines and fruit.

"I hope you're happy, dad," she smiled, thinking of her father, the Hollywood B list porno star, and knowing the old attention hound would be tickled.

Because of the short summer, the potluck table was steaming with fall comfort food. Lila had brought a huge casserole dish of five-cheese macaroni and cheese with a beautiful brown crust. Sister Mary Catherine had made fresh hot cross buns. Max and Colby brought a soft-smoked salmon. Christine had spent the afternoon preparing acorn squash with brown sugar and butter, fresh from between the pumpkin vines. John Hunt had done a fresh green salad with butter lettuce, avocado, tomatoes, and mandarin oranges. Pickles brought pot roast and carrots and swore the meat was not possum, although there was reason for suspicion. Ziggy and Matty brought a strange offering of rum-soaked fruit cake. Annie had made coffee and apple crisp and set the table with her family's best mismatched china, survivors of the last hundred and fifty years on the island.

The crackling warmth of the fireplace radiated through the ancient Victorian farmhouse and the yellow glow of the kerosene lamps that hung from the ceiling created a timeless scene as if from an Ansel Adams lithograph of long ago. Outside, a light mist fell from the heavens, blanketing the island as if adding a layer of insulation from the unsure world outside.

"We'll never eat all this food," Annie prophesied as the island guardians lined up by the table to survey the offerings. Little Annie, naked for the third time since lunch, had climbed behind the sun-bleached overstuffed red mohair sofa and peered out from behind the fort she had built out of the cushions.

"Thank goodness she's finally potty-trained," Pickles said as he dug the sterling silver serving spoon in through the crust of the macaroni and cheese and sucked out a hot steaming portion of the elbow macaroni swimming in cheese sauce.

There was far more food than could be eaten in one sitting, and soon after the meal most of the patrons settled into a nice nap on the sofas or lying on pillows next to the fire. Max and Christine did the dishes in red-rimmed white steel colored dish tubs on the stove while Talisha and Alisha dried and put the dishes on the buffet table and the pots in the drawer in the old oak kitchen queen.

Annie roused herself from her pillow by the fire and walked stiff-legged to the stove. She shoveled two madrona logs into the firebox, then added heaping measures of ground coffee into the basket of the old stainless percolator and set it on the stove. As the brown liquid gushed up through the stem and splashed against the clear glass knob on the lid, the smell waffled through the room, stirring the island faithful to the table for dessert.

Prominently placed on the table were slabs of Pickles' fruit cake filled with large chunks of pineapple, candied cherries and bits of walnuts, exuding a strong smell of rum mingling with the creamy elegance of slices of provolone cheese, an enticing companion.

Annie's apple crisp seemed pedestrian by comparison, but with large mugs of freshly brewed coffee, soon all the dessert dishes had been finger-licked clean.

Annie put a white board on an easel and laid out the agenda. Funerals and the Max and John Colby wedding. She outlined the memorial services of the fallen island champions and how their funerals would be handled.

Professor Spud would be represented by the head of the department of Anthropology and Sociology at Boise State University with an explanation of Spud's academic works of anthropology, his treatise on worm hole theory, aliens, and his seminal book, *Beyond Survival*, the future of mankind, not to mention his Big Foot Diaries with an introductory message written by Stephen Hawking.

South would be eulogized by her family and a presentation of pictures going back through the Storm family history as wreckers on the coast of South Carolina.

Trish would be memorialized by the Women's Studies department head at the University of Washington and a tasteful pole dancing routine to Louis Armstrong's, "It's a Wonderful World."

"Owl" Al—whose daughter forbade any memorial, but whose handmade coffin had been washed downstream during a flood of the Snoqualmie River to Puget Sound (also against her wishes)—would be represented by his geoduck shovel with the large divot made where the lightning had struck him and would be eulogized by the Bremerton Waste Water and Sewer Department with a performance by their internationally renowned and perennial Macy Parade award-winning forty-man synchronized shovel and garbage can team, the Pooper Scoopers.

White Bear would be represented by the Suquamish Tribe who would arrive by canoe, put on a skit using authentic Tlingit masks showing how the Raven stole the sun from the gods and brought it to the First Peoples, perform a short eulogy, and retreat by canoe to the sound of drums.

"Again with the Raven thing already," Ziggy harrumphed. "How many times is that? About fifty?" Annie gave him her "look."

GI Joe would be eulogized by Sister Mary Catherine, a team of Japanese taiko drummers, and a comingled Navy and Army color guard ceremony with a taps bugler and flag presentation. "Any questions?" Annie asked.

"What about Trooper?" Alisha demanded with folded arms.

"Oh yes, PAWS will be doing a salute to Trooper."

"When should we go over to the cold storage?" Pickles asked earnestly.

"The day before," Annie answered. "It will be an open casket like Trish requested. And, we will be putting up tents in case it rains."

"The Good News...the wedding is still on." The crowd clapped and cheered as Max and John Colby took the stage.

"John is still all in," Max smiled. "And as you may know, I'm seven and a half months pregnant." John looked sheepish, but happy.

"Duh," Pickles puffed out his cheeks, and the crowd clapped again.

"I know you're all dying to see my wedding dress." Max gave a hapless smile. "Here it is and I want Pickles to explain it to you."

Pickles' nose was running and he dabbed his eyes with a lace handkerchief as he began. "The gown was inspired by orcas and, of course, most notably, Starbuck." Pickles traced the drawing as he explained. "Most of the material comes from my vintage collection. The gown is antique white from fabric used by Princess Grace at her wedding to Prince Rainier; and then we have embroidery from Princess Di's gown; the pearls down the front come from *Father of the Bride* Part One.

"The gown is a fitted A-frame with a pleated flare at the bottom and a sweetheart neck. The veil is Arabian lace with ivory frame and the train, as you can see, is black and white.

"Flowing, flowing, flowing," Pickles rhapsodized as he orchestrated the air with his hands. "Movement, movement, movement. And here will be black piping to be determined later," Pickles continued, "and the shoes..."

There was a murmuring from the room. Someone clacked their teeth.

"The shoes," Pickles said, defiantly picking up the inference, "will be brand-new out of the box. Jimmy Choo is a personal friend and we have collaborated on several styles over the years and he is creating what he is calling a Cinderella look for us and I expect the shoes sometime in the next two weeks."

"Make sure they Fed Ex 'em straight to you, Max," someone called out.

"I resent that," Pickles glared, putting his hand on his hips.

"No, you resemble that," the same voice called out, and ducked behind the couch. Everyone laughed and Max gave Pickles a kiss on the cheek and a promising Hollywood kiss for John.

With the fruit cake still in research mode, John decided to prime the food chain. "I'm hungry. Anybody else got the munchies? We have plenty left."

The crowd murmured approval and surged toward the table, fed their munchies, and laughed and giggled till nearly midnight when they were exhausted, but content.

Later that evening, Annie wrapped her jacket around her and strolled to the tip of the spit where the sand melded into the sea. Her attention was drawn to the sound of the drone of powerful engines; squinting into the fog she could barely make out the green and red lights of a tugboat. The west wind whipped at her ears and Annie closed her eyes and felt the mist build droplets on her eyelashes. She bowed her head to the memorials that had become a trademark of island life.

Orphans, she thought. The island was the refuge of orphans. The twins, Starbuck, Talisha and Alisha, South, Spud, Moby, Joe, Sister Mary Catherine, Christine. The cast of characters was always changing. And yet it was a tighter-knit community than anything she'd ever known.

Annie wiped the water that tickled her lip with the back of her sleeve and looked where she had last seen the outline of the tug, but it was gone. She closed her eyes and listened as the ripping force of the waves rhythmically washed the graveled shoreline. It was a sound she had heard a thousand times before, the collective sound of each rounded rock tumbling to escape the sea and then, as the foaming water receded with a hiss, each rock captured and thrown helplessly against its brothers over and over again. Annie felt a calmness as the rocks washing against each other on Seven Sisters created a symphony that had been playing the same chorus for thousands of years.

She also knew that soon her sisters would come again to try and take her away and that she would resist. She was not yet ready to become part of the wash. *I still have work to do.* "And, dammit, that's all there is to it!" she said out loud.

Chapter
THIRTY-THREE

S ister Mary was awakened in the night by a soft bumping sound coming from the rosewood box that housed Joe's spirit. She realized it was time to let it go. Joe's spirit was needed somewhere else.

She felt a great sadness at losing the last part of Joe. She had no doubt that his foot rubs alone had broken all of her vows. Releasing his spirit would create a great joy somewhere else in the world. She knew the rarity of the warrior spirit and hoped the energy would stay earthbound, but she also knew there were no promises. She had been selfish to keep him for herself for so long.

Sister said a prayer, took a deep breath, and loosened the leather strap, opened the lid and set the box on a flat rock near the fire. The spirit sat fluttering on the edge of the box as if testing its wings, then flew to the edge of the firelight and hovered for an instant, circled Sister Mary once, and was gone.

She sat by the fire and smiled. Joe was on the move again.

John Hunt and Pickles had come over early in the morning to perfect the fruit cake recipe with Ziggy and had seen Sister sitting on the ground. They assumed she was praying as they made their way up to Annie's.

Annie had put on a fresh batch of coffee and had warmed up the oven in anticipation. "So, I suppose you boys are up to no good as usual," Annie greeted them.

"What do you mean?" Pickles grew defensive. *Did Annie know something?*

"Up to no good as usual," John chirped back as he laid a sack of flour on the table.

John and Pickles whipped up five variations of their fruit cake and waited for Ziggy to bring up the Magic ingredient. Annie busied herself sorting apples for her fall run to the Pike Place Market. She had given Zack and Little Annie an apple and, after taking a bite and examining the front toothmark, Zack began kicking the apple across the floor barefoot while Little Annie, always a chowhound, sat up in a rocking chair and ate her apple down to the stem while she watched the proceedings.

"Are kids supposed to eat the core?" Pickles directed the question at Annie.

"It's the European way," Annie shot back. "I don't think it will hurt her."

"Oh, just wondering." Pickles nodded his head as Ziggy finally showed up and dumped a cup of Magic in each bowl.

John greased five bread loaf pans and spooned in the batter.

"Geez, that's hot!" Pickles dropped the stove door with a thump.

"Use the potholders," Annie suggested without looking up.

John slid the loaves in carefully on the middle shelf and the trio sat down to mugs of coffee and sly grins.

"Is that a new pair of shoes, Annie?" Pickles craned his neck around the edge of the table as Annie faced the stove.

"Not really," Annie answered, tapping a soup spoon against the rim of a copper kettle of clam chowder to get rid of a stubborn potato.

"Doc Martin's?" Pickles pulled his glasses down his nose for a better look.

"Yes," Annie answered and turned around. "Remember, I got them from you?"

"Oh, yeah, now I remember." Pickles turned back to his coffee when he saw his toothmarks on the steel toes.

"After you boys get your fruit cake out, if you want to help me pick chanterelles for market tomorrow I'll feed you guys cornbread and clam chowder for dinner."

"We're in," Pickles answered for all of them.

Matty came up to babysit the children as the late afternoon sun momentarily streamed in through the window, the south wind piped up, and the gray rain clouds rolled in from the Pacific. Annie slalomed her mushroom party through the twisted trunks of the apple orchard and soon the party was wheezing up the mossy trail to the Douglas fir forest that formed the spine of the island. Annie stopped near the top and let the men sit to catch their breath. She threw a Mountain Candy Bar at their feet as they hung their heads between their knees.

Ziggy tore off the wrapper and looked at the egg-sized nutty chocolate mountain-shaped mound and bit into the snowy powdered sugar, egg white and vanilla center. Always on the lookout for a snack, Ziggy popped the morsel into his mouth. "Yum. What is this?"

"It's a local candy bar inspired by Mt. Rainier," Annie answered, "with a cherry-flavored center."

"I'm liking this," John agreed.

"How come I never see these in the stores?" Pickles asked, savoring his bite.

"Well, like everything else, they used to be bigger when I was a kid and I think they export most of them to the Orient where they revere their mountains and the cherry ones are really popular in Japan. Has something to do with pink as a happy color and Mt. Fuji I guess," Annie answered absently, getting to her feet.

John grimaced as he raised himself up. "The last time I was up here getting mushrooms, my wife Betsy was with us," he reminisced. "She loved the island. Her last words to me were 'take care of the silver fish.' That's why I have that big sailfish in my cabin that she got in Mexico. It sure takes up a lot of room, but it's the least I can do in her memory."

"I always wondered about that. Are you sure she said *fish*?" Pickles grunted as he started to move up the trail after Annie. "It's never made sense to me. Maybe she said kiss, dish or wish. You know. I've almost poked my eye out a few times with that monster spear hanging out from the side of your cabin."

As they completed the switchback journey to the mushroom patch, a steady coastal mist bore into the island and tendrils of fog snaked between the pencil-straight Douglas fir tree trunks backlit by the setting sun over the Olympic Mountains. Soon the fog smothered the forest and the air was heavy with dew.

"Uh-oh, we're in for it now," predicted John. The mist turned to rain and now the chanterelle hunt was on as the air was filled with the steady drumbeat of water droplets splashing against Salal and the huckleberry leaves.

Chanterelles were a distinctive pumpkin-yellow color, ribbed stem mushrooms difficult to spot in the open. "These damn yellow maple leaves sure do a good job of camouflaging those critters," Annie complained, already soaked to the skin. "Make sure you cut them off with a knife and leave the mycelium under the ground to propagate another day," she called out to her fellow-pickers.

"I love when you talk dirty," Pickles sang out.

An hour later, the team had filled three gunny bags.

"All right, let's go home," Annie ordered as she tipped the water from her sou'wester.

On the way back, John kept thinking about what Pickles had said.

"Maybe she did say 'dish,'" John said out loud. "That might make more sense. I know we have an expensive silver dish engraved with our family tree that she researched a good twenty years. She traced the family genealogy back to the 1500s.

"Hey, anybody want a sailfish for their cabin?" John sang out as he labored down the trail with the wet sack of mushrooms on his back.

Back at Annie's, the men shed their clothes and wrapped blankets around themselves, huddling near the fireplace in the living room while Annie hung the clothes behind the stove to dry.

"Ugh," Annie grunted as she hoisted the first mushroom bag up on the ten-foot-long dining table.

"Oh, sorry. Let me get the rest, Annie," Pickles said, guiltily wrapping his blanket toga-like over his shoulder.

The mushrooms were spread on newspapers to dry out and the men cleared enough elbow room to set down their coffee as they picked at the fir needles, leaves and organic compost that had found their way into the crevices.

"Man, those shrooms sure give off a woody, pumpkin, earthy smell," John mused as he buried his nose in a pile and filled his nose with the aroma.

"Smells like money to me," Annie said economically speaking as she gathered her robe and poked a log into the cook stove. "They'll bring about sixteen to twenty dollars a pound over in the market."

"Wow, that's about eighty pounds at twenty bucks, um-mm," Ziggy contemplated, although his mind was on the fruit cake.

"Sixteen hundred," John piped up.

"Yeah, sixteen hundred," Ziggy agreed as he got up to check on the fruit cake with a toothpick. "Yep, we're done all right."

Annie started a batch of cornbread and checked to make sure the chowder didn't boil or scorch.

"This is award-winning chowder right here," Annie announced, stirring the kettle. "There's only one magic ingredient I'm holding out."

"What's that?" Pickles asked nervously, hoping that Annie wasn't on to them.

"Can't tell ya or I'd have to kill ya," she said cheerily.

"Oh."

Annie slipped two muffin tins of cornbread into the oven and the four islanders sipped coffee and swapped lies until it was time for dinner.

When the cornbread came out of the oven, the mushrooms were shoved to one end of the table to make room, and John poured the two wines that he had uncorked earlier.

"A well-oaked Chardonnay," John explained as he poured four generous servings into the long-stemmed wine glasses. "And then you might try this new pear wine from the Hoodsport winery. It's really very good." He gave a knowing smile and passed out large earthen bowls and soup spoons.

Annie slipped in the apple crisp after sprinkling the top with brown sugar and then brought over the kettle of clam chowder, a basket of cornbread, butter, and fireweed honey.

After she ladled out the soup, John brought the spoon to his mouth and blew on the hot soup. He let the chowder roll over his tongue and swallowed.

"What the hell is this?" he challenged. "What kind of clams are these, Annie?"

Annie smirked. "This is the clam I canned that Owl was holding when the lightning hit him."

"Are you sure you didn't can a little Owl meat instead?" John said, chuckling. "But really, this chowder is sweet and pithy. This is the best chowder I've ever eaten and I know chowder, Jack. Remember, I wrote the food column for the *Boston Globe* for five years before I came out here and they know their clams back there. What is this stuff, Annie?"

"Geoduck." Annie took a bite of cornbread.

"This is a whole new taste for chowder," John exclaimed. "Why haven't I had this before?"

"Most of the geoducks are shipped to Asia for premium prices." Annie nodded, as she devoured a spoonful of soup. She continued, "Ivar Haglund, the old-time guy that started Ivar's restaurants, told me that the reason he didn't make geoduck chowder was that he was afraid that after tasting the chowder, people would quit building planes and logging the forests and spend all of their time digging for geoducks. He was a character."

"I think he was right. I could open a restaurant and just serve this chowder," John said, slurping down another mouthful.

Pickles crumbled a corn muffin into the soup while Annie winced. This was against chowder etiquette in the Northwest. Ziggy never looked up until he saw the bottom of his bowl and then filled it again. The fellas finished all of the soup, the two bottles of wine, never bothered with the dessert, loaded up their fruit cake, and happily went home.

Annie was up early to pack the boat and Christine had come over to check on her pumpkins and decided to ride back on *The Ark* with Annie. The sun sparkled on the water like a thousand suns as an extra insult to the short summer, frustrating children looking out schoolhouse windows. The water was as smooth as the finest silk ring shawl. Working boats—freighters, ferries, tugs with barges, and Navy ships—filled the shipping lanes. All boats are she's, but *The Ark* was in a different league with her snappy fringed teal canvas awning, bright white hull, and a likeness to the *African Queen*. *The Ark* was well-hailed and Annie gave them all a deep-throated blast on her air horn in return, which had a *HMS Queen Mary* effect. True to his word, John had made the trek back to Seattle and was there waiting for them at the public dock with a dolly.

John and Christine unloaded the Gravenstein apples, jars of applesauce, dried apple dolls, oysters, and the chanterelles onto a cart and pushed it up the gangway to the sidewalk.

Out of breath, John looked up and down Alaskan Way, the street next to the Seattle port named for the great migration created by the Alaskan Gold Rush. The gold rush was over, and all John could see was a huge horse-and-carriage charging down the street toward him with a man in a cowboy hat futilely pulling back on the reins. The horse was coal black with wild yellow eyes and nostrils flaring as John cowered and screamed as the carriage skidded to a stop.

"Whoa, Pegasus." A diminutive leather-faced man, wearing a too-loud cowboy shirt and an enormous cowboy hat that screamed 'all hat and no ranch,' gripped the reins as if he actually had control over the huge draft horse.

The man's practiced front foot caromed off the front wheel of the carriage and he landed in a crouch on the sidewalk and with a sweep of his immaculate white Stetson, said, "Pecos Butler at your service, madam."

"Pecos." Annie stood with her hands on her hips. "We were almost killed by that menace."

Pecos pursed his lips. "Now ma'am, don't take no offense to Pegasus here. He is an apple slut pure and simple and there ain't no way a controllin' the critter iffen he smells an apple."

Over her fear, Annie smiled. "And just how big is Pegasus?"

"Nineteen hands, ma'am, seventy-six inches at the shoulder, and nigh onto twenty-three hundred pounds of Black Sabbath Percheron fury. As near a record this side of the Mississippi as I've heard about. He's a big boy."

"He *is* a big boy," Annie agreed.

"Do you think you and Pegasus could take my produce to the Pike Market if we pay you and bribe him with an apple?"

"It'd be a pleasure, ma'am." Pecos dipped his head and gathered up the two dripping sacks of oysters, depositing them on the shelf at the back of the carriage.

"Get away from there," John barked, taking a swipe at Pegasus who jerked back his head, curled his lips, and stared back defiantly.

"Annie, he just ate two of your dried apple dolls, including the denim dress."

"Oh, lordy, looks like this will be a free trip," Pecos shook his head and grabbed the halter strap. "But don't worry none. That denim won't bind him up none. He likes to eat t-shirts too. I think he likes the salt in 'em."

Annie laughed. "Just get us all up to the market and Pegasus can have a few Gravenstein apples."

"That's his favorite, ma'am, and that's a fact." Pecos finished loading and swung up into the driver's seat. The market street was bustling as Pegasus pulled up next to Rachel, the bronze photo op pig that served as the resident perch for kid photos and a place to meet and ditch blind dates, should the need arise.

"One thing about Rachel," Annie tickled the swine behind the ears, "she gets shinier as the day wears on from all those kids climbing all over her. You know, I might just ask the produce committee to bronze my ass and stack me right next to Rachel. Seems like a good way to pass time."

"That'll do, pig," a gruff voice startled Annie as she turned around.
"Auhnnie, you make my heart go pit-a-pat, when are you coming back?" Ivan the piroshki man sang as he patted Rachel on her rump, leaving a floured handprint.

Annie dragged Ivan down through the maze of truck farmers with their flowers and perfectly placed fruits and ducked as the Flying Fish Market fish butcher pried a King salmon from the freshly shoveled ice chips and launched it over their heads, its tail wiggling as if working its way upstream through the shallows and coming to rest, cradled in newspaper behind the counter, and slapped on the scale. "Whew!" Ivan complained. "We almost left with salmon eggs on our face."

Past the pottery whistles, the tie-dyed t-shirts, the Frankfurter shop—and then they both stalled for a moment, transfixed by the miniature doughnut machine with its awe-inspiring Rube Goldberg stainless steel gears, chains and knobs that automatically dropped perfectly formed doughnut batter circles into the hot grease, and then as the doughnut floated merrily along, automatically flipped them over with tiny paddles to bake the other side, then sending the finished product up a ramp to drain the excess grease, and into a hopper. The Donut King machine—from dough to doughnut in less than a minute and a mere three feet long—was akin to putting a man on the moon.

"America," Ivan shook his head. "What a country!"

Finally, they arrived at Annie's booth. Annie opened up a gunny sack full of chanterelles. "Put your nose in the sack," Annie motioned to Ivan.

Ivan held the bag up to his nose, closed his eyes, and took a deep breath. "A-hhh." A big smile came over his face. "It smells like fall in the Urals in Mother Russia." He took a deeper whiff. "I am smelling pine cones."

Ivan took a large bite of the mushroom crown and chewed slowly with his mouth open. "A hint of licorice and nutmeg and…" Ivan inhaled again. "I am tasting peppery with blacked oak notes, apricots, chocolate, buttery with a WD-40 finish?" Ivan opened his eyes. "Oh, I think there was some WD-40 on the outside of the sack that got on my hand."

Ivan held another good-sized golden mushroom up to the light. "What is it? I must know."

"Chanterelle mushrooms," Annie announced triumphantly. "Remember, I was telling you about them?"

"You are pulling the leg off Ivan. I was thinking mushroom like in movie. *Wonderland of Alice's.* Sometimes make you small and some make you big. JFK, LBJ and LSD."

"No, nothing like that," Annie said, scooping up three double handfuls into a brown paper bag. "Clean the dirt and fir needles off the mushrooms and then sauté them in a frying pan with butter till they cook down and then add them to one of your piroshkis. The ones with the seasoned hamburger or ground pork. Put out a sign Chanterelle Piroshkis and stand back. Mark my words," Annie said smugly, handing the bag to Ivan. He listened intently, then took the paper sack of mushrooms and scampered off through the crowd back to his shop.

Annie and Christine stocked the stall with the produce and the Sea Grannie bobble head dolls. Annie noticed the market was selling chanterelles for sixteen dollars a pound so she sold hers for twenty.

"Chanterelles from Seven Sisters are always good for a twenty-five percent mark-up," she grinned.

Business was brisk all morning with the bobble heads flying off the shelves. At noon, Annie pulled on Christine's sleeve and they went over to see how Ivan was faring. His shop was no more than ten feet wide and sixteen feet deep, but Ivan had put a handwritten sign in the window:

CHANTERELLE PIROSHKIS FROM SEVEN SISTERS, and the line was out the door.

Annie pressed her nose against the storefront window where Ivan rolled out his dough in performance art mode not more than three feet away. His white shirtsleeves were rolled up above the elbow and his large hairy arms expertly kneaded the dough on the wooden counter, then rolled it out and cut the squares with a scimitar knife before he would add the dollop of filling, fold and then brush the top with a mixture of egg before popping the tray into the oven. From time to time, Ivan reached inside an open sack of flour and sprinkled the counter to stop the dough from sticking.

Annie tapped on the glass and Ivan looked up. He threw his head back and gave the happy scream of a man totally engrossed in the moment and then he gave Annie a flour-covered thumbs-up.

Annie and Christine laughed and then went down to the Three Sisters Bakery for a rounded loaf of fresh rye bread and bought two bowls of clam chowder next door at Salty's. They sat bowlegged on the sidewalk over a concrete retaining wall above the street, dunking the rye in the chowder and looking out over the panoramic waters of the Seattle port that was filled with ferry traffic, cargo ships and seagulls that cartwheeled down right next to them, squawking for tidbits.

At the end of the day, *The Ark* had cleared the Seattle breakwater when the white-capped chop slammed against the hull and sprayed over the top of the canvas.

"It's going to be a roller coaster going home," Annie shouted into the wind. She turned *The Ark* north to catch the waves diagonally to more easily cut through the rolling breakers that were breaking over the bow. Annie pushed the diesel throttle up three notches and goosed the engine in the wave troughs to catch each wave under power. She was grateful for the soft, rounded, chine-like hull that allowed the water to slip under the wooden planked boat with less resistance, and the sharp flare at the top of the hull deflected most of the water away.

Still, it was white-knuckle boating, and occasionally, no matter how vigilant Annie was, a rogue wave would break over the bow and drench the two sailors. The boat shuddered as each wave struck the hull and sent vibrations through the rudder and into the wooden tiller. Soon it took both women leaning on the tiller to counteract one of the most powerful forces of nature. But even with the salt water stinging their eyes and dripping off their noses, and the wind howling and whistling through the hoods of their rain gear, making it impossible to hear, the two women were laughing. They were standing strong against nature and bending it to their will.

The waves were slapping against the Seven Sisters rocks as *The Ark* finally put the wind to her stern and Annie throttled the engine back to a soft purr as the boat swung wide to go into the boathouse.

"Wow, that was like rough sex," Christine said as she pulled her hood off and shook the water from her long blonde hair. "Truly exhilarating."

Annie smiled, "Not exactly what I was thinking, but come to think of it…"

Chapter
THIRTY-FOUR

The weeks before the Max and John Colby wedding were hectic with the stress affecting everyone, especially Pickles, who felt the self-induced extra pressure of putting on an event for Max's east coast elite parents and socialites. He felt like he was representing the entire west coast and had been anxiously scanning the back sections of *The New York Times'* Style and Society section for months, reading two years' worth of back issues of *Bride Magazine*, and hanging out at bridal fairs from Vancouver, British Columbia to Portland, Oregon.

Pickles was never seen these days without a pair of virgin pumps attached to his belt buckle; the enamel on his crowned incisors was a rainbow of fuchsia, blues and yellow; the circles around his eyes looked like a miniature racetrack of burnt rubber; and he had gained ten pounds from eating mood-altering, rejected fruit cake recipes.

"I'm a fruit cake junkie," Pickles screeched as he stopped hemming Max's wedding dress, popped a piece of fruit cake layered with a thick slice of pepper jack into this mouth and looked toward the heavens for solace. Pickles then contemplated his hands as he chewed at the Band-Aids® that covered his raw fingertips.

"I can't make these deadlines. It's humanly impossible," Pickles cried plaintively to Max as she brought in a teapot of Darjeeling and more slices of fruit cake.

Pickles slapped his thighs. "If I keep eating this crap I won't be able to slip into my gown—your gown," Pickles caught himself. "See, what am I talking about? I can't even remember who I am anymore.

"Well, I am Pickles, hear me roar," he protested and greedily snatched up the orange Jimmy Choo single-strap ankle biter from his belt and chewed on the strap like it was a dried pepperoni stick. Max set down the tray. She put her hand on Pickles' shoulder. "Maybe this is too much. I can go into Seattle and get a wedding planner. I hear there are some good ones and I could stop at David's Bridal. You can still be in charge. My parents can afford it. Remember, they sent a blank signed check and said spend whatever we need to."

"Blasphemy," Pickles roared. "Those bitches are not getting any-where near my turf! Surely you're not even thinking like that, are you?" Pickles wailed and stuffed another piece of fruit cake in his mouth and drank the tea in one long gulp, leaving un-Pickles-like crumbs in the bottom of the cup.

"There," he said to himself. "Pickles is feeling much better now."

The store side delivery doorbell rang. "Uh-oh, Pickles hears the door bell," Pickles said. "Poor Pickles," Pickles mumbled to himself, "always a bridesmaid, never a bride."

Max rolled her eyes and went to the door. It was another back-ordered bolt of tulle left by UPS.

The next morning, Ziggy and Christine gathered the Moby Pumpkins they had harvested and loaded the phallic vegetables into

Jerry Garcia, the VW van that had formed the basis for Pickles, Ziggy and Matty's business partnership.

The large, orgasmic van experience—or LOVE, as Pickles had named the company—was having startup problems due to the tough economy and the difficulty coming up with parts.

Several times in the past they had taken promising prospective clients on rides, but Ziggy was tired of men taking a swing at him after his successful demonstration with their wives. Sensing a need to remove themselves from the actual "hands-on" marketing, the business trio had made a video to substantiate the van's ability to satisfy women, but still no real money men had stepped forward.

Pickles thought the next move might be to use the van as a trail vehicle in the annual Seattle/Portland bike ride. The good news was a Pentacostal retreat committee had rented the van for two weeks and it received rave reviews.

Knowing the prowess of the "Jerry" van, Christine said to Ziggy, "I'll drive and you can sit in the passenger seat."

The trip to Portland was smooth sailing and at lunchtime the van pulled into a giant parking lot that was once a Super Safeway and now was the domain of the Voo Doo Doughnut Palace that sponsored the "Great Northwest Pumpkin Challenge."

Once strictly an underground movement, giant pumpkins had gone mainstream the decade before and there were booths filled with supplemental fertilizers, seed companies, garden tool manufacturers, and champion growers with books filled with tips.

There had been no real breakthrough in giant pumpkin growing. They just kept getting bigger and less pumpkin-looking all the time and that's why the pumpkin world was set on its ear by the Moby Pumpkins the year before.

"Glad you're here. I was beginning to worry a bit," explained the man with the orange visor that said Pumpkin Judge on the brim.

"The Moby Pumpkins are a revelation," he said, motioning the van down the rows of exhibits toward the main stage.

The crowd surrounded the van and the judge cheerfully threw open the side door and peered inside. "Great balls of fire!" The judge shook his head. "They just keep getting better."

As the pumpkins were handed fire bucket-style from one person to another, there was a quiet reverence in their voices as the pumpkins made their way to the stage. When the van was finally empty, there was an even dozen pumpkins sitting chest-high on a roll of black crushed velvet.

"Splendid," the judge marveled and Christine blushed as they pushed her forward for pictures and a KING television interview that was heavily edited, but nevertheless did show a fleeting glimpse of the X-rated pumpkins on the five o'clock Northwest news.

Jean Enersen, the lead anchor, still had her hand covering her mouth when the footage stopped panning over the phallic pumpkins and turned to the newscaster. "Oh my, they're big aren't they?" was all she said. And that wasn't even footage of the grand champion Moby Dick pumpkin that weighed in at nine hundred and forty-eight pounds.

Pickles had wrestled with the wedding dress and Max's eight-month pregnancy all along, but a few days after he scuttled the form-fitting dress with the sweetheart neckline and the bottom flare, everything fell into place. He and Max decided to go with a swooping neckline that accented her ever-burgeoning "twins," as Max began to call them, with looping strands of pearls on the shell bodice. For the equally burgeoning belly, they decided on an apron with sprays of pearls flaring out from the center.

"It's kind of a maternal Madonna look," Pickles cackled with the yellow tape around his neck, hunched over to fluff up the skirt.

"I think it works, too," Max agreed. "I love the ruffles. It's kind of a Vera Wang meets Little House on the Prairie. I'm thirty-six years old, I'm going to be married, and I'm going to be a mother. These are all wonderful events and I'm going to celebrate life, not hide it."

"Pickles is happy," Pickles said wistfully, sticking stray pins in his wrist pin cushion.

"It's all going to happen in a week. Aren't you glad it will finally be over?" Max twirled in front of the mirror as Pickles took a picture to send to Max's parents in New York.

"U-huh. Pickles will be happy when he finishes the wedding cake," Pickles nodded.

"Pickles, you don't have to do the cake. You and I designed it. We can get someone else to bake it and decorate it. Haven't you done enough?" Max said firmly.

"Pickles…is…doing…the…cake, end of story," Pickles said emphatically with his hands on his hips.

With Max's parents' unlimited budget, John sent a limo out to the Seattle/Tacoma airport for Max's mother, "Bitsy," the slave of New York society, and her father, known as "Three Max," the third in a long line of investment bankers. Three Max, at first, pined for a son, but that was a long time ago and his daughter Maxine had wrapped her father around her finger early on in the relationship and theirs was one of mutual admiration.

"That girl has more guts than any man I ever met," Three Max would say and had defended his daughter's adventures since she was four years old when she made a parachute of her *101 Dalmatians* silk bedsheet and jumped from the third story of the family's vacation "bungalow" in Provincetown on Cape Cod, and broke her leg in two places.

"She's every bit an O'Hara," he would say with a Cuban cigar clenched and jutting out the side of his mouth as the smoke curled upward over his unibrow below his furrowed bald head. Max always said her father looked like the monopoly game banker with the mustache.

As soon as Bitsy and her "baker's dozen" of society friends were installed in the Four Seasons Hotel, Pickles lured them into the Northwest culture. He hired a luxury bus and guide to take them on excursions.

The September weather that had soured the locals' psyche toyed with them one last time before the blanket of fog, overcast and rain would settle in for the next eight months. The weather was bluebird perfect as the bus hit the high spots of the great Northwest: Paradise at Mt. Rainier, Hurricane Ridge in the Olympic Mountains, Pike Place Market, Mount St. Helens and the blast zone, the Pacific Ocean near Astoria. And as they rolled through the Eastern Washington countryside, the visitors could avail themselves of all kinds of Northwest fare since the front of the bus was filled with a free bar full of Starbucks coffee, apples, Aplets, Cotlets, and plenty of Pickles' "special" fruit cake. The last stop on the fourth day was historic Port Townsend where Pickles met the bus himself. "Welcome, welcome, Pickles welcomes you to Port Townsend, the only Victorian seaport town on the West Coast." Pickles showed them through town and had a special showing of *An Officer and a Gentleman* at the refurbished Victorian movie house in the center of town and gave them real buttered popcorn pumped in three layers.

"I had no idea this part of the country was so charmin'," Bitsy's friends kept saying. "You know, I don't even like fruit cake, but out west here, it just seems right. It puts a smile on my face and I haven't laughed this much in years. I just can't stop eating just one more slice."

The bus made one last stop at Port Gamble where the party and luggage were picked up by one of the Seattle amphibious ducks and ferried to Seven Sisters. The more adventurous were put in the shacks on the spit and the rest filled Annie's house.

That night, out on the spit between two great bonfires, Pickles arranged for the Blake Island native actors to put on a play, complete with drums, reed flutes, and wooden masks, that told the story of how the Raven stole the Sun and brought it to the tribes in the Pacific Northwest. Again. And again there was a collective groan from the island folk.

The New Yorkers were entranced as they were herded up to Annie's for apple pan dowdy and coffee. They all went to bed exhausted but satisfied. Tomorrow would be the wedding day.

The weather held, but wise to the fickle Northwest weather gods, Pickles had set up a huge, three-poled canvas tent in the apple orchard for the reception. All day long the guests arrived on the duck from Port Gamble and at six in the evening, with the sun going down over the Olympics, they gathered at the edge of the high tide and waited near the light of the bonfires. Ivan, Madeline, Lila and what remained of the island's champions were in attendance.

They could hear the chanting of the S'Klallam paddlers long before the canoe emerged from the dusk and passed by the Seven Sisters rocks that were washed by a gentle rising tide. Max was standing in the back, her veil trailing in the wind just like Pickles had imagined it as he achingly captured every detail in his mind.

As White Bear's long black canoe neared the shore, the paddlers struck a pose with their paddle grips against their hips and the paddles pointing straight up into the starry night.

The *Pissant*, under the helm of Pinky and Dorie, stole in behind the canoe and silently anchored as John Colby, dressed in a black Armani tuxedo and wearing Helly Hansen knee boots, waded out to the canoe, gathered Max into his arms, and carried her up the beach to the island church.

Don't you just love it when everything goes as planned? Pickles thought to himself.

Max was carried up the trail littered with a carpet of clam shells. The *crunch, crunch, crunch* of the shells sent chills down Pickles' back as the crowd trooped in after the couple.

The entire church floor was ankle-deep in dry maple leaves and the sanctuary was backlit with hundreds of candles that eerily warmed the walls of the old church with an ancient glow. At Annie's request, four men stood ready with fire extinguishers. It was a risky move, but Max, Pickles and Annie were all about the sensual drama in this first wedding on the island in a century.

As the crowd filed into their seats, a choir of monks in the balcony began an ecclesiastic chant that echoed down the church aisle and across the bay, and Sister Mary Catherine smiled as the organ in the *Pissant* chimed in perfect concert.

The families were seated and there was a short silence and a prayer by Sister Mary Catherine lifted from the text by Chief Seattle. Then, with John waiting at the altar, Dorie swung into an exaggerated—holding on to every note—traditional wedding march on the organ built deep within the oak ribs of the tugboat. Little Annie and Zack walked down the aisle with baskets of sand dollars, followed by Max, walking barefoot and carrying a bouquet of sword ferns and Stargazer lilies, with Alisha and Talisha holding the train up to keep it from dragging on the maple leaves. Pickles was relieved when the music ended a dramatic thirty seconds after John and Max turned to each other and held hands. They recited their own vows to each other, kissed after a long embrace, and then faced the audience, who burst into applause.

Max looked beautiful, and more than that, she looked happy as she tossed her bouquet to Christine and the newlyweds walked down the aisle while Alisha and Talisha rang the church bell a good five minutes longer than Pickles had told them. *Never work with animals or children,* Pickles mused.

Pickles had mowed a short, clipped path into the apple orchard whose trunks and bare branches were flickered by two gigantic bonfires on either side of the orchard. A hundred mirrored Styrofoam balls that he had painstakingly glued each night hung from the branches from translucent fish line. Apple disco, he called it. The effect was other-worldly as the spinning balls threw darts of reflected light into the black forest night, in response to the flickering flames.

Long before the ceremony, the S'Klallam tribe had built a long trench fire with wire racks waist-high above the coals where huge three-foot-long slabs of King Salmon simmered and bubbled in the radiant heat, slathered with a recipe for candied salmon. It was a recipe invented by John's best friend, Mike Okoniewski—the "Magnificent Polack"—whose time-tested brown sugar, butter, olive oil, and few more secret ingredients, made for unforgettable salmon.

When the guests were seated and the girls finally stopped ringing the church bell, John and Max welcomed the guests to the party. Instantly, lines formed as the tribe sectioned out generous cuts of salmon and ushered them onto the next table filled with salads, beans and fixin's, cornbread, rolls, and barbecued chicken. There were tubs of wine and beer and Sister Mary Catherine was making mojitos and lemon drops as fast as she could crank them out.

At the end of the table stood the four-foot-tall, five-tiered wedding cake with a white butter cream base and festooned with green, orange, yellow and blue paisley designs with large daisies, inspired by the large quantities of the magic rum-soaked fruit cake that Pickles consumed as he worked through the night before.

Too large to be transported, the cake had to be decorated onsite, and Pickles—under the influences of joy and drugs—had kept the same level of intensity by decorating part of the table, a loose flap of the tent, and the trunk of a Gravenstein apple tree until he ran out of frosting.

Some people thought the cake gauche, overdone and inappropriate, but because it was from Pickles' heart—as was everything Pickles touched—John and Max loved it all the more. Later, Pickles would say, "Pickles doesn't remember what happened. Pickles was in the zone."

There was a half hour where Max kept looking out from the head table and thought that time was standing still. There was no wind and the surreal light from the bonfires, the mirrors hanging on the bare apple tree limbs, the revelers—everything seemed to be moving in slow motion and the waves were gently lapping the beach. It was as though everything was in suspended animation.

Max didn't know that there were powerful unseen forces at work. A stalled front had broken through off the Pacific Coast and a wind that came to be known as the Domino Express was fast bearing down on the island and her life was about to change forever.

The feasting was nearing the end when John rang an old school bell from the church for quiet, but at the first sound, the Domino Express blew up over the top of the island, caromed down the other side, and the entire tent bloated up like a jelly fish, broke the hemp rope mooring lines, and in one motion swam into the night sky. Thunderstruck, the entire party was silent in the darkness and then came a lone voice. "My water just broke."

Bitsy was the first to break rank "It's coming," she screamed at the top of her voice and raised her hands so fast that twenty thousand dollars of tennis bracelets flew into the air and wouldn't be found until spring.

As Max was ushered up to the house, Bitsy took over. "Relax, people," she said, massaging her naked wrist as she pulled her windblown hair from around her face. "It took me over ten hours when I had Maxine. We have plenty of time. Finish your meal and you will be updated as soon as we get Maxine to the mainland. We're going to have a baby," she calmly explained and then bolted for Annie's house, tossing aside three party members off the trail as she raced to catch up with her daughter.

There was only the single gust and then quiet.

Pickles suggested the cake be carried up to Annie's so it was carefully loaded onto an oak pallet and trundled up to the house. The meal continued for another half hour and then the heavens opened up and the wind howled back. Sheets of diagonal rain forced the patrons to pluck the remaining bottles of champagne from the wooden barrel coolers and sprint for the house.

Over a hundred people filled the house while a half dozen brave souls put on rain gear and rescued most of the food and luckily discovered four cases of magnum champagne that were unopened.

The party was stranded. There was too much wind and rain to safely cross the channel to Port Gamble, so they hunkered in from attic to outhouse. They partied on. Drinking, eating and waiting.

Bitsy was beside herself with worry. "O'Hara women don't have babies in houses. We have babies in hospitals like civilized people. This is just wrong. So wrong!" she fretted.

But Pickles had taken her under his maternal wing. He wrapped Bitsy in one of Annie's sisters' quilts when she began to shake from the cold and wet and assured her that Annie knew what she was doing, and how about another drink of champagne to toast the wedding while she sat in the chair watching Max have the baby.

Bitsy watched as Alisha and Talisha sprang into action, trained from all those months taking care of their mother. They mopped Max's forehead, held her hand, and wrung their hands in empathy as Max strained and moaned.

Annie had done midwifery duty for over fifty years and Max was no different than her other patients. Scared, anxious and determined, Max was into her third hour when the baby arrived with one final push.

The baby wailed at being plucked from its cozy nest and the whole house became suddenly quiet and then animated again. Life on the island was beginning anew.

Talisha, who had overseen the whole process, peered over the blanket as Annie cleaned the screaming infant.

"It's a man," Sister Mary yelled as she tumbled down the stairs to make the announcement that would ripple through the house.

Annie put the baby on a scale her mother had used for canning and the weight was six pounds four ounces and was twenty-two inches long.

"Well, that's all there is to it," Annie announced, swaddling the baby and giving him to Max.

John moved aside the discarded wedding dress from the wingback chair and sat looking at his new life. "This is going to be so great," he beamed. "I guess we're committed now. We have an instant family with a boy and two girls in the first couple of hours."

Christine put in four solid hours at the piano. Sister Mary had done her entire karaoke repertoire twice, and by a little after midnight everyone was exhausted. Still the rain was spilling over the gutters and the breakers were thrashing against the dock pilings and so the party hunkered down under whatever blankets were available and waited till morning.

The top of the wood stove was belching steam as Annie and Sister Mary Catherine brewed coffee from eight old percolator coffee pots scrounged from the cellar and shacks and had just slipped in their umpteenth batch of biscuits and fourteenth loaf of fruit cake, when the rain let up.

The island was soaked with drips and puddles everywhere and groggy, disheveled partygoers were scampering out into the woods to do their business while Alisha doled out tissues on the back porch.

It had been a night to remember and Bitsy was pleased. She trusted her daughter, but she wasn't really sure these "West Coast ragamuffins" would know how to throw a party.

"And, my Gawd! Adopting those two black girls!" Bitsy screeched to her friends. Sure they were cute and needed a mother but surely not her Max. But Bitsy had to admit those two girls were troopers. They obviously loved Max and the wedding and the whole event, culminating with her first grandchild, couldn't have been more entertaining.

After Bitsy had helped place the last of the guests on the duck back to the mainland—all clucking about how this was a wedding for the ages—Bitsy decided she didn't want to leave for a while. She was becoming comfortable and she suddenly realized she had more family on the west coast than she ever had back in New York. Her society friends would all have to get along without her for a while, Bitsy decided. And there was still the missing tennis bracelets.

"Can this be the same Bitsy that proclaimed when she landed on the island that she could 'hold her water' till she could reach a proper toilet on the mainland?" her husband reminded her.

Bitsy slapped him on the shoulder. "I said no such thing," and then she laughed until there were tears in her eyes.

Chapter
THIRTY-FIVE

ickles disappeared for three weeks. There were rumors about some kind of breakdown and rehab, but when Annie saw Pickles' yacht, the *Green Cucumber*, slide into the harbor, she knew his laser-like focus was about to be honed in on her.

Pickles hailed Annie as she stood on the porch. A short time later, he gave her a wry smile as he sat at the kitchen table while Annie poured him a cup of coffee.

"How are you?" Annie pried.

"Pickles is good," Pickles answered, but he kept his lip down over his two front teeth.

Annie reached across the table and pulled up Pickles lip. His two front teeth had been worn down to nubs.

"Damn it, Pickles," Annie started in.

"I know. I know." Pickles put his hand out in protest. "Pickles is going to the dentist this week. The teeth are guaranteed and he's feeling a lot better now. I just needed a little *me* time and I'm back now and ready to work on your campaign. The primaries are next week."

"I thought those teeth were made out of some kind of armor plating," Annie remembered.

"Yeah, well," Pickles began. "Pickles burned through almost his entire shoe collection. It wasn't till I found myself nibbling on a pair of Danner boots I found in a dumpster that I knew I had hit bottom. Anyway, Pickles has gone cold turkey and haven't had any shoes for about a week, and he's gone back to his support group on the Internet."

Annie took a deep breath and held her tongue. "When you go to get your teeth fixed will you take Sister Mary along with you? I think her braces might be ready to be taken off. It's been a while and I noticed some strands of spaghetti squash were still hanging on a few days after the party."

"Will do," Pickles conceded. "Now about the election. There's a clam chowder cook-off at the Jefferson County Fair and a political forum afterward I'd like you to speak at. John Hunt says your chowder is second to none and a first-place prize would get you some publicity and we could use some press. It's been a while."

"All right," Annie said with resignation. "It's not like I'm not getting my quota of drama around here," she said candidly as she swung a passing Zack up onto her lap, wiped his nose, and set him down again as his feet never stopped churning.

"Exactly what I was thinking," Pickles brightened. "See you later in the week. Don't forget about the chowder."

Annie procrastinated for a few days and then, knowing that the chowder would be better if it seasoned for two days, she got out a jar of Owl's canned geoduck and some of her Yukon gold potatoes from the storage cave. She peeked around the corner and the gold and cash were still under the tarps. She carefully closed the door to the cave and clicked the padlock shut.

Annie began cutting the Walla Walla sweets into quarter-inch cubes on the counter next to the wood stove. The counter, a three-inch-thick cut of straight-grained Douglas fir, had mellowed to a rich honey-brown color with blackened bruises and cuts that had accrued from over a hundred years of meals. One spot on the counter had been carved into a deep bowl where Annie and her ancestors did most of their vegetable preparation. Annie scooped out a double handful of onions corralled in the wooden valley and tossed them into the iron skillet primed with olive oil.

The Walla Walla sweets sizzled and snapped as Annie used another pan to fry the bacon and then added the other ingredients to the milk. She went upstairs to visit Max who had just come over for the day from the mainland.

Little Annie and Zack looked wistfully at Max breast-feeding while sitting in a wicker rocker. Max greeted Annie with a wave of her hand, not wanting to interrupt the feeding. Annie waited until the baby was fed and then Max squeezed out some milk in a cup for Annie.

Annie smiled and left to go back to the stove. It was important never to bring the chowder to a boil, her mother always said, so Annie moved the chowder away from the firebox where the ingredients could work their magic. Annie didn't really know why the milk couldn't boil, but then what was there to question? The chowder was an old family recipe.

The day of the Jefferson County Fair Chowder Cook-Off came and, as Pickles predicted, Annie won the Golden Clam award. Upon burping, then excusing himself, one of the judges said the chowder was as smooth as mother's milk. Another called it the nectar of the gods.

Annie gave her political speech about how America had always been guided by inspired inventors and entrepreneurs and how governmental regulations were strangling individual freedoms, and how the older generation should be considered national treasures—if not from their sacrifices, because of their experience. It was from the heart and the crowd clapped long and hard.

Pickles, Ziggy and John's fruit cake had won first place and the People's Choice Award in the bread division and there were several latte businesses around Port Townsend that wanted to sell their product. Even Starbuck's coffee had expressed a passing interest.

Now, when the wind would blow, the yellow-brown maple leaves spiraled from the trees and the twirling helicopter seed pods perched in the orchard grass waiting for the promise of spring.

Annie knew she was running out of time to honor the champions who had brought the island to life. She kept thinking of the ashes in the attic of her daughter Calypso and her granddaughter—and Calypso's husband—and that someday, when she was stronger, she would scatter their ashes. But, she kept telling herself it was too soon and she was waiting for Little Annie and Zack to be old enough to understand, but Annie herself did not understand. The concept of untimely death was too unfair and final to be grasped.

The living just had to keep sucking it up and moving on, second-by-second, minute-by-minute, day-by-day till the end of their days, and if they were lucky, they too would be missed and would inspire those left behind.

The good news was that the tent that was rented for the wedding was found in a cow pasture up in Chimacum and the better news was that the rental company had already been paid by the insurance policy that Pickles had signed. They didn't want the tent back, so Annie hauled it back to the island and set it up to house the memorial services.

Pickles was just starting to enjoy his new teeth again and was pretending to work at the twelve-step program set up by his shoe fetish support group and was in too fragile a state to take on the burden, so Annie and Sister Mary Catherine made all the arrangements and contacts. Mary Catherine flashed a too-white smile as she showed Annie how straight her teeth had become.

"They threw in a free teeth whitening," Sister explained, giving Annie a toothy grin.

"Really." Annie looked away as the glare was too bright.

The services were to be held in two weeks and Sister found her book indexing patron saints and began to pray for good weather, using Saint Medard, the patron saint against bad weather, as her conduit. Later in the afternoon she stopped by.

"The weather's covered, Annie," she said, poking her head in the screen door.

Annie waved a skeptical hand. "Good luck with that," she answered.

Remembering what happened last time they had a hard time defrosting the body, Pickles and Ziggy started out two days before the funeral and took the VW van over to pick up Trish, Owl and Trooper at the Cold Storage plant on the Tacoma tideflats.

The foreman led them to a remote corner of the cold storage where he neatly slid the forks under the wooden boxes and nestled them into the back of the van. The foreman reached up and closed the overhead hatch door.

"Be careful," he warned. "Whatever is in there is frozen solid. If you drop the box, it could shatter. It's super-brittle. It'll take a few days to thaw out."

"No problem." Pickles shook the man's hand. "We've done this before." Congratulating themselves, the men decided to stop at Quick Pick Burgers just outside the industrial area and indulged in the classic double cheeseburger, hand-cut fries, and chocolate shakes.

"We're living large," Ziggy boasted as they pulled out of the parking lot.

As they hit a speed bump, there was a sickening clunk from the back of the van and Ziggy turned back in time to see one of the wooden crates slide out the back and hit the pavement.

"Sweet Jesus," Ziggy swore. "We forgot to slam the back hatch."

Pickles and Ziggy slowly got out of the van and went to the back. The box was fully intact.

"Let's get this baby back in," Ziggy said, grabbing the frosty box.

Pickles grabbed the other side and lifted, but there was something rattling inside.

"Aw shit. We broke her," Pickles said as they shoved the box into the van and carefully slammed the hatch door shut. He leaned on the steering wheel.

"We need to find out what's wrong in there before she thaws out. There's a Home Depot up the road. Let's stop there and get a crow bar and pry the damn box open. But let's make sure no one sees us."

Pickles parked in a remote area of the store, pried open the box and looked in. The short-sleeved flimsy dress was frozen stiff, but on one side of the box they could see where her arm had fallen off above the elbow and there were two other conical mounds above her head in the corner of the box. The severed arm was obvious, but the other two pieces were mysteries until Ziggy flipped one over with a stick from the nearby dumpster.

"Nipple," they both said in unison. They stared at each other.

"Silicone," Pickles finally said. "Silicone implants, that's why her boobs never shrank with the rest of her."

Stressed, Ziggy lit off a joint, inhaled deeply, and sat on the curb. "This is just a bit ghoulish. What are we gonna do?" he squeaked, holding his breath. He finally expelled the smoke.

"We're gonna have to put her back together," Pickles said slowly as he scanned the nearly empty parking lot. "I'm going into the store and see what I can find and you close up the box and keep an eye out."

It wasn't long before Pickles came out carrying a plastic bag. He removed a white tube. "I've sealed gutters with this stuff before," he said, reading the side of the tube. "Dries clear. Good for metal, glass and wood and underwater applications," he read aloud.

Pickles pulled out a pair of insulated rubber gloves, took out a knife and cut the front of the dress. There were jagged spots where the breasts had broken off the body.

"This should go all right," he said, trying to sound encouraging. "Piece o' cake. The broken boob part has to match up with the jagged edges."

Ziggy inserted the tube of silicone into the metal glue gun and squirted it onto the rough edges of the chest. Pickles tried to pick up one of the loose pieces with one hand but it was too big and took both hands. Luckily the fit seemed good. They did the remaining piece and looked down at their work. They stood back and looked again.

"Hmm-m, it seems like one boob is facing up and the other down," Ziggy offered. "What'cha think?"

Pickles, who prided himself on mastery of the female form, was perplexed. They fit so well it felt right but it looked wrong. "Ok," he said as he knelt down and rotated one boob so they both faced up. "I don't know for sure, but I'm going to settle for perky boobs. I think Trish would agree with that. They may be upside down and on the wrong sides, but we have to make a field decision."

Ziggy scraped off the excess material with a stick and they glued the dress back together. The arm was easier and after they made a splint out of more wood scraps they tied it all together with thin nylon rope. The men stood back and looked at their handiwork.

"She looks good," Ziggy offered. "Except..." He leaned down and picked up an ear lobe lying on the bottom of the box.

"Squirt some of that sticky stuff on there," Pickles said. Then he reattached the lobe.

"That was a lot easier. No guesswork," Ziggy said.

The men closed the lid and hammered in the nails with a rock and were back to the island with the caskets by dusk.

"How'd it go?" Annie asked as she met *The Ark* at the boatshed.

"Ok," mumbled Ziggy. "We should probably leave them down here in the boatshed for awhile."

Later that night, the men stole down with a flashlight and took off the arm splint. Everything was thawing out. Pickles gently tugged on the arm and pushed against the boobs.

"I think it's going to work," he grinned. "And we still have some left to fix gutters."

The Port Townsend Leader, The Kitsap Sun, The Seattle Times and surrounding community newspapers had picked up the obituaries that Annie had sent out, but Annie never knew how many people would show up at these memorials. She and Sister Mary had taken a few thousand out of Joe's stash to pay for a small foot ferry from Port Gamble and a salmon cookout catered by the S'Klallam tribal casino.

As promised by Sister Mary Catherine, Saint Medard furnished a crisp but bright blue day with only a few wispy clouds ranging over the Olympics.

"The Gods are smiling on us," Annie shouted out to Sister, who gave the thumbs-up and continued down to the orchard to the circus tent where she was meeting with the Japanese Takei drummers.

The eulogizers were scheduled for the nine o'clock run from Port Gamble to allow time for organization and the services would run together starting at eleven, last about two-and-a-half, maybe three hours, Annie explained to the casino caterers, who were already setting up their fires and food tables. Annie had been coerced into making geoduck chowder again so she explained the huge pot of chowder needed to be stirred often and never brought to a boil.

Max and the baby came down to oversee the chowder. "You tapped me out," Max called out to Annie, who shrugged and rolled her eyes.

"It's all about timing, Sweetie.

"Most of the people will be sitting on blankets in the orchard," Annie explained to the caterers. "The tent is for shade or if the weather gets ugly. When we see how may people we have, you can get ahold of the casino kitchen and we'll make a special trip over on the boat with the food. They have my credit card."

There were poster-size pictures on easels of the champions to be honored and Annie looked forward to educating the diverse crowd on how each one of these men and women contributed to the world they had inherited and maybe to inspire each listener to follow their dreams, no matter how eccentric.

By the time Talisha and Alisha rang the church bell, there were seven hundred people sitting on blankets in the orchard and several reporters from Seattle newspapers waiting for Sister Mary Catherine to begin with the prayer.

As the Suquamish tribal members beat softly on their drums, Sister read the entire Chief Seattle prayer and then turned the microphone over to the head of the Anthropology Department, Dr. Jack Crosier. For five minutes, Crosier explained how Professor Nickolas Spudich—or Professor Spud as he was known on campus—had taught at the college for forty years and had inspired thousands of students to question their world. Then he played a recording sent over by the world-renowned physicist Stephen Hawking who, using a synthesized voice machine, told the audience that Spud was an adventurer and a man of science who was not afraid to speculate on the origins of black holes, worm theories, or the possibility of Big Foot.

"The man was a giant in his field and those fields were vast and complex but," Hawking finished, "Professor Spudich could enjoy a good joke, he loved single malt whiskey, he told wonderful stories, and most important of all, he was my friend and I loved him."

South Carolina Storm was next and her entire family took turns at the podium. Her son began with the family history when, in the eighteen hundreds, the family lived on the Carolina coast and made their living as wreckers who lured boats into reefs and shallows with fake fires and flares and then salvaged the boats and their cargo.

"But," he went on, "there were two sisters named South Carolina Storm and North Carolina Storm who came west and they were as opposite as you could imagine and they battled over everything.

"Our birth mother was North Carolina Storm, but she was a hellion and she wasn't around much, so I was raised most of the time by South Carolina Storm and her husband. South was not a woman who lived a high profile life or needed a lot of attention to go about her life. Like many of us, she was a woman who enjoyed a simple life and she was a rock upon which you could build a good, solid life. She lived vicariously, as you might expect from a librarian, and I can say that while many women can have a child, there are some women who are born to be mothers and South Carolina Storm was one of those. She was our mother."

Talisha and Alisha brought out their mother's glamour photo of her dressed in her favorite leopard dress and five-inch heels, while Ziggy and Pickles carried the leopard-painted open casket onto the stage. Annie had fitted Trish's favorite leopard dress on Trish and wondered why there were dark marks around the breasts.

"Freezer burn most likely," Pickles improvised.

After Annie had made her up, Trish looked like she could still turn heads, pole dance, *and* run a graduate course in Women's Studies.

While Trish's two girls cried next to the casket, the Associate Dean of Sociology and Women's Studies at the University of Washington told the story of how Trish had pioneered studies of prostitution in Europe and the Americas and helped unionize the prostitutes in Germany and Brazil, as well as organized the first medical plan and a gay STD eradication program in San Francisco. The Dean pointed at the picture of Trish. "Trish was stunningly beautiful and proud to be a black woman who thrived in academia."

Then four women from "The Studio" did an interpretive pole dance to "It's a Wonderful Life." And Talisha and Alisha haltingly read a poem they dedicated to their mother.

Al (Owl) was next, and while his daughter had refused to be involved, there was a big group of Bremerton Sewer and Wastewater former coworkers who had come to pay their respects.

Annie explained what a kind and gentle man Al was and showed the shovel that had conducted the lightning bolt that had vaporized him. She pointed to the large kettle of chowder that was made from geoducks.

Then the " Pooper Scoopers" from Bremerton, a forty-strong synchronized marching team who had won numerous awards at parades including "best of show" at last year's New Year's Tournament of Roses Parade in Pasadena, did their garbage can and shovel dance routine, while whistling "Puttin' on the Ritz."

White Bear was introduced by a tribal spokesman as the vision quest canoe was paddled into the shore, accompanied by the tribal drum corps. The spokesman from the film crew told the audience of the vision quest and the trials of paddling the canoe up to British Columbia, and showed a poster of the last time they saw White Bear, walking into the forest with the daughter of the "Great White Bear," thereby completing the vision quest.

The memorial was concluded by the Blake Island Dancers, who came back for an encore performance of "How the loon got its necklace."

G.I. Joe's death had sent ripples all the way to the Pentagon. He was the last of his generation and the most decorated rogue warrior since MacArthur. They knew Joe had dirt on everyone from four-star generals to admirals to privates from his fifty years, and there was a rumor that he had left a pile of money to do his bidding after he was gone.

Veterans' groups had put pressure on the Blue Angels, who happened to be in transit at Fort Lewis before going to Hawaii for a performance. They were scheduled to leave that Saturday and meet "Fat Albert" halfway across the Pacific for refueling. The word had come down from the top. *Absolutely No Flyover*, for any reason; budget concerns.

That bothered Commander Brace Walker. There wasn't a man in the military that hadn't heard of GI Joe, the helicopter pilot from hell who had officially pulled at least a thousand men off the field of battle. An equal opportunity hero, he saved Marines, Navy and Army in actions that sometimes were never officially recognized, and almost always under hostile fire. There was a flyer's prayer that had been passed from cockpit to gunner. "I'm down Joe, come and get me."

There were still hundreds of survivors that were alive because of Joe and they would wreak havoc if the Angels were this close and didn't pay honor to a patriot of Joe's caliber. The funeral time had been sent to Commander Walker and he knew every pilot on the Angels squad had gotten the same email. But, there were written orders that couldn't be countermanded.

Walker assembled his flyers and explained, "I know you want to honor the man, but that can't happen. You are officers and you have orders to fly directly to the rendezvous point with Fat Albert and continue to MCAS Kaneohe Bay in Hawaii. Failure to follow orders will kill your career path and you will no longer be flying anything except a desk—if you're lucky. Am I clear?"

The fliers answered to a man, "Affirmative, sir."

Joe never wanted a grand send-off, but he had once mentioned to Sister Mary that he had been impressed by the Takei drummers with their six-foot drums. "It's a warrior's song," Joe said at the time.

Seems that the Takei drummers could be had for money and Joe had left plenty of that, Sister reasoned, so there they were, drumming for Joe.

As the last echo of the drums rolled across the lagoon, a color guard came forward and an officer listed Joe's many medals. It was then that Sister Mary Catherine knew why generals and admirals fled the room when Joe was forced to wear his colors.

The list of Joe's achievements and battles had been announced and the bugler was about to play taps when there was a roaring sound from the east.

When the six F/A-18-Hornets took off from McChord Air Force Base, Walker watched them rise in formation and then veer sharply to the east, the opposite direction to which they'd been ordered.

"Damn it!" Walker looked at the ground and looked up again hopefully. Still the formation was clearly headed in the wrong direction. They were going to do the flyover.

It had always been a dilemma of orders and honor. They all knew orders were paramount in the military world. Commander Walker also knew he wouldn't have given a shit for any of his flyers that wouldn't have disobeyed such a ridiculous order, but it was his ass on the line and he knew what he had to do.

Walker nodded his head. He'd take the heat. He would tell command that he had ordered the flyover. He walked to the command center to log in the flight.

The bugler on the island looked confused as he pivoted to the east and everyone stood up on their blankets when the jets, which had swooped down within a hundred yards of the water, screamed by so close the crowd felt the heated turbulence. Then one jet broke formation and flew straight up in the missing man formation. No one could see the grins on the pilots' faces as they flew over, nor did they know they had defied orders, but everyone knew the pilots were duty-bound to an honor code that went back to the dawn of time. *Leave no one behind and honor fallen warriors.*

After the jets disappeared over the Olympic Mountains, the bugler played taps and an American flag that had flown over the U.S. Capitol was folded and given to Sister Mary.

A large poster of the three-legged, raw-boned hound Trooper, formerly known as Tripod, stood next to the podium near a large earthen bowl that would be set in the meadow graveyard to water passing birds and island creatures.

The funerals were over and Annie called the families to dinner.

An hour after the flyover, orders came in that Commander Walker could make a discretionary command decision about the flyover.

A few days later, Annie received a cryptic note in the mail from Carol Ann at the hospice agency in Seattle.

> *Annie,*
>
> *Hope you are fine…It would seem you're down a few eccentrics…am sending three replacements…You will know them when you see them.*
>
> > *Regards,*
> > *Carol Ann*

Annie was just pulling away from the Port Gamble dock when she heard a voice.

"May I come aboard, captain?"

Annie looked up and down the dock, but there was no one in sight.

"Captain, permission to come aboard?"

Annie looked out into the water. There were no other boats, but when she turned back she noticed a pair of small knuckles holding onto the side of the boat. She peered over the side and there was the smallest man she'd ever seen. The man took off his ball cap and waved it at Annie.

"Are you Annie? Can the two of us get a ride out to the island? Carol Ann sent us." The man cocked his head.

"Yes, I'm Annie," she confirmed. "Where's your friend?"

The small man put his fingers in his mouth and gave a shrill whistle and from the end of the dock a man appeared at the top of the gangway and haltingly made his way down the walkway to the boat.

The small man put one hand on his hip, looked at Annie, and, jerking his thumb toward his partner, announced, "We're the famous professional wrestling team of David and Goliath, most recently we're the Thunder of the Land Down Under."

Annie couldn't help staring at the two men. A dwarf that didn't top three feet and another man that had to be over seven-and-a-half-feet tall.

"So, can we get in?" David was getting impatient.

Annie just nodded.

She slid to the other side of the seat to counterbalance, but she knew that the chances of sinking next to the dock were good.

"Wait a minute while I maneuver the stern against the dock. That's our best bet." Annie hit the starter that kicked the diesel to life. "If I was a betting woman I'd have to bet we won't make it to the island alive," she mumbled.

The shorter man vaulted into the boat before Annie could turn the boat around.

"Okay, big fella," David coaxed his six-hundred-pound friend over the stern and onto the seat.

"Goliath is the name, mate." The big man offered his hand and Annie shook his finger and smiled.

The bow was sticking three feet in the air and there was less than a foot of freeboard on the stern.

"Carol Ann," Annie mumbled as she shook her head. "Somehow I'm going to get even."

Several days later, at twilight, Annie fired off the eight-foot memorial rocket filled with the ashes of G.I. Joe and Moby Dick. Spitting fire and smoke, the rocket soared toward Elliott Bay near the ferry terminal and exploded at two thousand feet with a thunderous blast that reverberated over the Puget Sound basin from Bellingham to Olympia.

Startled residents jammed the 911 lines and the Internet was flooded with pictures and speculation that ranged from a meteorite, sheet lightning, to those damned Blue Angels breaking the sound barrier again. Windows in the Seattle area, from Magnolia to Beacon Hill, suddenly cracked and two hundred-plus flying crows heading to their nightly perches fell stone dead into Lake Washington. Three jets were scrambled from Whidbey Island, but no one found any substantial evidence.

"An unusual geothermal occurrence, similar to an event last year," the news anchor reported on Channel 5 during the evening news.

"Now that's what I call a send-off," Annie chirped, dusting off her hands and toasting the echo of the fallen warriors with a swig of Wild Turkey.

Chapter
THIRTY-SIX

John Hunt had heard that Garnet was not expected to make it to Christmas, but true to her word to keep Mom's Diner open, she had found a new cook and this was the grand re-opening.

When John pulled into the rutted gravel parking lot that morning, he dodged two wheel-eating mud puddles and wedged his car close to the entrance. His breath condensed in the freezing air as he noticed the red neon diner sign had been repaired since his last failed attempt at a new chef.

With the first frost of the season, the restaurant windows were sweating and rivulets of water streaked down the inside beams and puddled on the wood window sill.

The screen door spring screeched in protest as John squeezed by and pushed the café door open. Every bar stool had a fanny parked on it and Susan, the waitress, was laughing as she slapped the dice in the leather cup on the weathered Formica counter to try and double or nothing the price of a patron's meal.

There was one seat open as John slid down the bench across from a grayed and broken lumberjack still dressed in red Stihl suspenders, caulk boots, striped black-and-white shirt, and black dungarees; it seemed as if the forest giants hadn't all been cut down decades ago.

John nodded to the man.

Susan had won her bet and had turned to lip off to one of her oldest customers as she poured John's coffee without looking down and slapped a menu on the table. John was enjoying the breakfast buzz and the good-natured banter when suddenly the lumberjack slammed his fist on the table, his coffee sloshing out of the cup, and onto the floor.

"Smitty" Smith was still living on his family's dairy farm just south of Chimacum near the Egg and I road on the rolling verdant acreage of Smitty's Happy Cow Ranch.

Smitty had cut his teeth on Garnet's chicken fried steak Saturday mornings starting as a kindergartner when he would clamber up on the running boards, shinny across the smooth black vinyl seat, and stand behind his father's shoulder where he could look out onto his world through the split windshield of the new shiny green '53 GMC pickup.

Father and son would drive to the feed store for bales of bedding straw or a salt lick for the impatient Holsteins who expected a fresh bed every night to keep them happy, and then father and son always stopped for breakfast at Mom's Diner.

Smitty had been thrown off his feed since Garnet had become sick and now he knew she wasn't coming back. He also knew his biscuits and gravy.

"I been eatin' here for forty-five years," he roared. "When I order shit on a shingle, I want my biscuits swimmin' in gravy. You call this piddly ass mud puddle gravy? This is a disgrace. I want Garnet back in the kitchen and I want her *now*."

Susan sighed. She had over a dozen locals whose comfort level was at risk. She came over and put her hand on Smitty's shoulder.

"Smitty, we all want Garnet back, but she can't come to work anymore. You know she's dying. We're all upset. You know that."

The man pulled his stubbled face up from his plate and John could see his eyes were full of tears.

"I want more gravy! I want Garnet!," he roared one more time, looking up at Susan.

"What the hell is all the ruckus out there?" a voice called out from the kitchen.

The swinging café doors opened and a rush of steam rolled down the aisle toward the logger as a short, stout woman with a green Michael Jordan sweatband below a shock of dictatorial red hair, beady blue eyes, and large red mole on her chin—charitably called by some a beauty mark—stood holding a frying pan. Hand on hip, the woman squinted past the stools and focused on Smitty.

John blinked. *My god*, he thought. *It was the reincarnation of Garnet, right down to the mole.* The woman marched down the aisle and stopped in front of the logger with a frying pan full of steaming milk gravy.

"It's Garnet's sister Opal from Chicago and she's on the warpath. Everyone take cover," Susan yelled as she scooted behind the counter.

"You want more gravy?" the woman challenged the logger, who nodded blankly. The cook poured all the gravy in the pan onto the plate of biscuits and the volcanic mass flowed off the dish, onto the table, and onto the logger's crotch.

Smitty didn't move. The thick Carhartt overalls shed the molten liquid, but the heat was frying his crotch and still Smitty looked up at the cook with a big smile, threw his head back, and roared with laughter.

John smiled. He had been obsessed with keeping the legacy of Mom's Diner alive. "Johnny, don't be a worry wart," his mother had gently scolded him when, as an eight-year-old, he sat on the kitchen counter listening to the radio and watching his mother make an apple pie. "Just relax, Johnny."

As his mother was distracted rolling out the top crust, John would thieve fat slices of apple dripping with granulated sugar and cinnamon from the unfinished pie and sometimes they would sing along with the radio. He remembered the times they would sing at the top of their voice as Doris Day sang with soft sweetness, "Qué Sera, Sera….."

When I was just a little girl
I asked my mother, what will I be
Will I be pretty, will I be rich
Here's what she said to me
Qué Sera, Sera
Whatever will be, will be
The futures's not ours to see
Qué Sera, Sera
What will be, will be

And then John remembered the wisdom from Professor Spud. He drained the last of his coffee and put the mug up to his ear and listened. At first all he could hear was the constant ringing in his ears. But as he listened harder, behind the ringing he could hear the harmonic roar of what Spud had called the echo of the Big Bang moment when the universe was created.

He recalled Stephen Hawking's goofy, all-knowing, perpetual smile and Spud's slurred words of wisdom as Steve, Ziggy and John had donned aluminum foil hats, sat around the campfire, and downed a fifth of Peppermint Schnapps between them.

Spud had put a comforting arm on John's shoulder and rested his head against Stephen's forehead.

"Johnny, don't worry so much. Einstein, Steve, Walt Whitman and I all agree. The universe is too big to fail."

John looked over at Smitty groveling in his biscuits and gravy and, after sixty-three years, he finally got it.

Opal was still holding the dripping frying pan when John leaned over and gave her a big wet kiss.

THE END

Seven Sisters Chocolate
Floating Island

Cream together: ¾ cup white sugar
                            1 Tbsp. butter
Sift together: 1 cup flour
                            1 tsp. baking powder
                            ¼ tsp. salt
                            1 ½ Tbsp. cocoa

Stir dry mixture into first mixture along with ½ cup milk. Put into buttered 9-inch cake pan. Sprinkle with walnuts.

In another bowl, mix   ½ cup brown sugar
                            ½ cup white sugar
                            3 Tbsp. cocoa

Spread this evenly over mix in pan. Pour 1 ¼ cups boiling water over top and bake 30 minutes at 350 degrees.

Alternative: You could splash a dollop of whipped cream, drizzle with huckleberry sauce, and garnish with a mint leaf, but why would you bother?